SILVER'S

ODYSSEY

A NOVEL OF SURVIVAL IN 17th CENTURY SPANISH
COLONIAL FLORIDA FROM THE SHIPWRECKED
ATOCHA GALLEON.

Henry C. Duggan, III

Published 2012

ISBN : 9781721978939

Library of Congress Control Number:

To Pat.............

and for Cole, Elizabeth, Drew,

Carson, Caleb, and Trevor.

CONTENTS

I am rich Potosí,
Treasure of the world.
The king of all mountains.
And the envy of all kings.
Coat of arms legend
Silvermine capital
17th century Potosí, Perú
1546

If Spain had spent less on war
and more on Peace, it would
have achieved world domination.
Diego Saavedra Fajardo
1640

The main goal of divine Providence
In the discovery of these tribes is the
Conversion and well-being of souls and to
This goal everything temporal must
Necessarily be subordinated and directed.
Fray Bartolomé de Las Casas
1563

Preface

It's 1622 in the Golden Age of Spain and silver from Perú is the king's lifeblood to fight European religious wars. Young Alférez (Lieutenant) Luis Armador is assigned to the military that guards the annual silver fleet to and from the Indies. Bidding goodby to his betrothed Isabela in Seville, he plans to return in six months for their wedding. It turns intoa four-year trek, as his returning treasure-laden galleon, Nuestra Señora de Atocha, wrecks off the Florida Keys in the hurricane of September 6,1622.

260 go to a watery grave, but not before Luis is washed overboard and comes ashore in colonial Florida amongst the fierce Calusa Indians. Wilderness challenges of storms, captivity, subsistence, animal attacks, swordfights, an underground river, the farflung St. Augustine outpost and the Barbary pirates off Spain's coast all confront him.

Dugout canoeing is one of his major means of travel on the coast, as well as on Florida's Withlacoochee, Suwannee, and Alapaha Rivers. He is aided by the Portuguese ex-slaver Pedro Martins, the Congolese mulatto Lunga, the half-breed Tocobaga Indian Owahee, the Arapaha Indian Chukka, wilderness friars, and the fighting Christian Knight Groz Guotman. Armador is plotted against by a mad priest and falsely imprisoned and unwillfully conscripted by Florida Governor Luis de Rojas y Borgia. Through sheer determination and natural instincts, he is dauntless in his quest to return home. The image of Isabela both haunts and inspires him.

Map of Florida, 1597

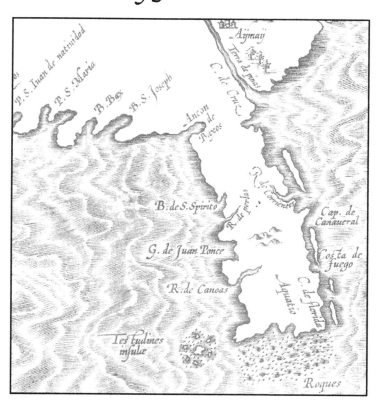

Map courtesy of University of South Florida Tampa Library Special and Digital Collections.

MAJOR CHARACTERS

Luis Armador--protagonist, Spanish Alférez (Lieutenant)

Isabela--Luis' bethrothed in Seville

Captain Nodal--captain of Atocha galleon

Pilot Ximenéz--pilot of Atocha

Surgeon Ribera--Atocha physician

Jacove de Vreder--Atocha silver overseer

Boatswain Martín--Senior Mate on Atocha

Father Val--chaplain of Atocha

Alferéz Sologuren--Atocha young Lieutenant

Most of the above characters introduced in the early chapters of the novel came from the actual Atocha galleon 1622 manifest copy. This was graciously supplied by the Mel Fisher Maritime Museum in Key West.

The following list of characters introduced in the novel's subsequent chapters are fictional, with the exception of the Governor in St. Augustine, Florida, below. Two others there, though not listed below, were produced from historical record.

Lunga--escaped mulatto slave

Pedro Martins--Portuguese ex-slaver

Friar Mobilla--Franciscan friar at San Juan de Guacara Mission

Chukka--Arapaha Indian

Friar Díaz--friar at Arapaja Mission

Governor Borgia--Florida Governor at St. Augustine

Groz Guotman--Christian Knight

Author's Note: _Except for Luis and Isabela, all 7 above-mentioned initial characters aboard the Atocha sink with the ship. No need to remember the names._

Initial chapters slowly "set the stage", then active survival action begins.

Author's email address on last page.

PROLOGUE

Help! Help!

Eight year-old Luis Armador heard the cries and turned to see his friend José go under the waters of Seville's Guadalquivir River. Luis was about a stone's throw away when he began to swim as fast as he could in that direction. A head bobbed up and once more yelled– *Help! Help!* This time it sounded with increasing alarm. Luis watched him go under a second time, and he did not resurface.

Luis' father, grandfather, and José's father were all nearby on the riverside strand, the Arénal. They were shipwrights observing a galleon being built by their firm. The boys had been allowed to take a cooling swim on a bright summer day, as both were good swimmers. Alarmed by the call of help, both fathers immediately plunged into the deep waters and swam toward the lad's supposed last sighting. Luis dove under and anxiously felt around for his friend.

Where did he go?

All work along the quay stopped, as onlookers gathered, apprehension filling the air. Cries as well as prayers went up at once. The fathers surfaced and dove time and again, but with no success. Luis continued searching, but his youthful body began to tire, his mind distraught. From out of nowhere, he felt a strong arm grab him, as Grandfather Juan eased him back to shore.

"Abuelito, Abuelito, where is José?" Luis sobbed. "He was here only a few moments ago, and now he's gone."

The search continued for some time. Many men and servants set out in longboats with grappling hooks, but no luck. The next day the youth's frail body washed up downriver. Everyone was heartsick, especially Luis, for the loss of his boyhood amigo. That night his grandfather came to his room and observed the boy's red eyes, as was his own. He held Luis in his arms for a time.

"I'm so sorry about your friend, but we must take comfort that he is now in Heaven, where no more harm will come to him. He might have had a cramp and was unable to swim. He may have panicked. He was just a lad, as are you, and no one, including you, is to blame."

He then forced a smile. "Remember, it's always important to control emotions. In troubling times, if possible, it's best to first relax, think. Then one takes action."

*All the waves crashed together on shore,
and a new life was in the offing.*

1
HURRICANE
September, 1622

*Truly I was born to be an
example of misfortune and a target at
which the arrows of adversity are aimed.*
<u>Don Quixote</u>
Cervantes

GULF OF MEXICO, NORTH OF CUBA

A howling wind and blinding rain blew in gale force. Luis trudged across the slippery planks, holding on to anything to keep from washing overboard. His mind flashed back to José's drowning 14 years earlier. The violent sea rose high, waves towering above the ship. As water hissed across the deck, the wind tore at him like a savage beast. He prodded his body towards the mizzen mast where five seamen, lashed high on a tiny platform, were trying to ride out the storm. He couldn't fathom it but proceeded to climb up the rigging and lash onto the mast also.

For some reason they have done this to survive here instead of staying below.

"Make it tight, Alférez," yelled a seaman.

Handling an unwieldy wet rope, he tried to avert salt spray stinging his eyes. When the vessel rolled, he held tightly to the mast to avoid going overboard. With much effort, he wrapped the hemp around his body, fastened it, and prayed it would hold.

"Will this save me?!" he bellowed.

A seaman screamed back.

"If we hit a reef! If the ship goes straight down, and the bottom's not over 50-60 feet, we remain at the highest point! Everyone below could be trapped! Should we capsize, look to your own!"

Luis found comfort in the answer. He wanted to stay on the perch and hoped the storm would abate by morning. He reasoned it far better than facing the human drama taking place below. Emotions and anguish roiled there, though nature's full wrath surged on deck.

But perchance, up here I have an advantage if we sink.

All evening the storm raged, churning the seas, sending rain sideways, drenching Luis and the five others. As minutes turned to hours, he felt terror, then numbness, as though his mind and body became inured to the storm.

Have I done the right thing? The Captain and officers remain below with the others. Did I follow yet another fabled superstition of a few distraught mariners?

Sometime during the night, the wind shifted and began blowing from the south. It pushed the Atocha north, toward the dreaded reefs of the Mártires, the south Florida islands whose west end sat not far away. Wave after wave continued to crash over the bow deck, sluicing tons of salty water on the helpless men. The roar of wind, rain, and waves continued to heighten.

Luis deemed returning below impossible even if he wanted to do so. Amidst the tumult, he sought distraction by letting his mind drift. Eyes closed against the spray. Thinking of the last few weeks.

***

Back in August the 28-ship Terre Firme fleet set sail for Habana. With the galleons' silver loaded at Porto Bello plus a stop back in Cartegena, only one port remained. Then they would set sail to Spain. The Atocha, being a large fortified galleon, brought up the rear guard as Almiranta. Three thousand travelers were all hungry for home, but apprehensive as the hurricane season approached. News came that a recent slave revolt transpired on a merchant ship out of Porto Bello, headed also to Habana. It was reported that several escaped, which could portend trouble on the Spanish Main. It made Luis think of the tall mulatto with the nosebone that he'd seen at the slave auction in Porto Bello.

He leaned against a rail on deck and mused thoughts of home and his betrothed Isabela. A voice brought him from his reverie.

"How is my young Alférez friend?" asked Jacove de Vreder, the Atocha's Silvermaster.

Smiling, Luis replied. "Good. You, more than anyone, remind me of our mission and of the vast quantity and value of our cargo."

"I see," he responded, eyes lighting up. "Would you like a peek at the Cargo Manifest?"

"Of course, Silvermaster, but I didn't think you could share it."

"Alférez, my observation is that you are noble and trustworthy. But you must swear an oath of secrecy. Come to my cabin and you can see it. The silver alone will have traveled 7,000 miles from the mines in the mountains at Potosí, Peru, once we make Seville."

"I vow, no word will be spoken," he said, barely contained his excitement.

Nuestra Señora de Atocha

Treasure Manifest – Summary

24 tons–901 silver bars

133 King Felipe IV's silver
bars

161 pieces of gold

250,827 silver reales de a ocho

1200 pounds of silverware

Jacove de Vreder, Mastre de Plata

Luis gasped when de Vreder unrolled the documents, the Summary list on top. He stared in awe, unable to speak, his mind overwhelmed.

A king's ransom…a pirate's dream…an irreplaceable fortune should it face shipwreck…all on my galleon…the Atocha…

***

LA HABANA
August, 1622

The Terra Firme fleet had sailed into the bay at Habana, the most favored port in the Indies. Luis stood on deck and watched along with the Assistant Pilot and Chaplain Fernandez Val.

"Ah, Habana. What a joy to see," said the Assistant Pilot. "A narrow entrance, with no bar or rock problems. Only a protective chain across the waterway, let down for us near Fort El Morro. Pilot's delight. We sail into this cloverleaf bay right up to the quay. See the houses on the right? Over a thousand now. We love Habana, for its closeness to the ocean river and for the most ideal weather possible."

"When will we join with the New Spain fleet from Vera Cruz?" asked Luis.

"Their ships should be here now. Safety in numbers, you know, for the sail back to Seville," said Chaplain Val.

"What is the forthcoming route to Spain?" Luis asked.

"If we sail in a few weeks, we go north in the Gulf of Mexico to a reading between latitudes 23-24°. Then east into the ocean river. Along the Mártires, up La Florida's east coast, then cross the Atlantic to the Azores. The mission takes on a different perspective then. The ships sit more laden, corsairs lurk, and the crews tire of life on board. To say nothing of the oft-dangerous autumn weather," the Assistant Pilot voiced.

"What do you mean – *if we sail?"* said Luis.

"The biggest factor in deciding?" came the response, "the upcoming weather. Pilot Ximenéz will devote much time in port to studying and then give his recommendations to our Captain."

"You mean his best estimates," said Chaplain Val, with a grin and glint in his eyes.

"Now, Chaplain, if you don't neglect your duty to bless the fleet, I'm certain of success."

The Chaplain stiffened his lean and erect frame. Gazing toward the bay, he responded.

"Yes, of course, we plan to do that. Even so, many passengers speak to me of fear. They don't want to winter in Habana, but neither do they want to sail into a hurricane. They too have asked for prayer. A Mass will be celebrated for safe passage before the final departure."

Sensing a discomfiting topic, Luis decided not to pursue it.

They discovered the New Spain fleet from Vera Cruz had arrived in Habana before their own Terre Firme fleet. It brought more gold and silver, plus cargo from the Manila galleons. The New Spain fleet did not stay in Habana, instead, sailing on to Spain. Orders required them to unload their treasure and goods for the coming Terre Firme galleons, including the Atocha. Several weeks then dragged on as the already burdened ships transferred more to their holds. The Atocha alone took on 582 Cuban copper slabs, 350 bales of indigo, and 525 bales of tobacco. Added to the precious metals and containers of cochineal and spices, the vessel sat overloaded. Luis wondered at the enormous weight and also why nautical tardiness reigned as a Spanish tradition.

***

He awoke one morning in the port of Habana to odd noises, patting feet and clicking teeth. Looking over the side of his cot, he saw to his horror two large rats gnawing on his satchel in search of food. Without hesitation, he dispatched both with his sword. He questioned why, with all the places on the Atocha, they picked his quarters. Even on an empty stomach, he grappled with a hint of nausea. After dressing, he lifted the lifeless creatures and ascended up top.

The unbelievable sight of others tossing dead rodents overboard greeted him.

"They've gnawed through jars of provisions and barrels of meat. Some caught in the chicken coops," said the Steward. Wringing his hands, he moaned that his storeroom would need to be re-provisioned. "I must have killed ten of the little monsters this morning, all chewing into the wine casks. So many have fallen into the water barrels, the apprentices have emptied and scoured at least twenty of them."

"They say that one of the merchant vessels has killed 1000. They'll go after anything, with stored meat their favorite target," added the Boatswain's Mate. "Faced with a plague of rodents, our men use every weapon they possess."

The Boatswain had placed him in charge of the rat purge. With wooden rods, swords, and anything available, his crew went over every inch of the ship's five decks. There were some bloody, gruesome, and screeching scenes, but all necessary. Passengers either left the vessel or waited on the top deck.

"Our men killed two hundred of the fury beasts," said the Steward. "This is one time I'll be happy to leave Habana. It's as if we fostered a welcome to them on the quay, and the rascals used all their skills to take our provisions. Argggg!"

***

Luis enjoyed a cup of coffee early. Its aroma and taste reminded him of his favorite Seville tavern. He thought of how he would spend the winter, should they have to stay over in Habana because of hurricane season. At the same time, he watched seamen high in the riggings and was amazed at their agility and surefootedness, even while barefooted. Soon he would convene his troops for morning roll call.

Iiiiiii!

The scream preceded a bone-crushing clump on deck. The sailor fell 75 feet and now lay crumpled and writhing in pain. The blood-spattered scene revealed his left leg cut and contorted. An immediate call went out for Surgeon Ribera.

Hands gathered round as the sailor's face cringed in pain.

Iiiiiii, it hurts! Please help me," he pleaded.

After cutting up a pants legging and examining the limb, Ribera turned and spoke in hushed tones to Luis.

"No surgeon relishes using the bone saw, but the man's leg is crushed and fractured beyond repair."

He then turned to the despairing sailor.

"I am sorry, my good man, but this leg must come off." He spoke in a confident and decisive manner, as he had done many times before.

"Noooooo! Don't take my leg!" wailed the seaman.

Not just scared of blood loss or sepsis, but of losing his livelihood.

Several men pressed cloths to slow the bleeding. Boatswain Martín knelt down, placed a cushion under his head and sought to relieve his anguish.

"Mate, you must relax and let our Surgeon work. Your fellows look to your welfare, and a man with one leg bests no legs. Pegs are used by many. Help us by calming. Chaplain Val will be praying for you and the Surgeon. He also plans to administer last rites, in case of need."

The 21 year-old seaman of Sanlúcar lay with protruded lips, now quivering, and deep-set eyes glazed over. They placed him on a makeshift platform, for the Surgeon, and pressed a stick between his teeth. After he received a sedative dose of rum, the amigos holding him down asked for drafts also. A tourniquet was set six inches above his knee and a stick twisted. Tightened, Surgeon Ribera tied it in place. The mate soon became groggy. Ribera checked his scalpel and amputating saw and requested tar be heated in the kettle for cauterizing. Luis had never witnessed an upclose scene as this, though he'd seen a plaza execution from a distance. Dizziness made him climb atop the sterncastle to rest.

"You look pale, Alférez," said the nearby Sailing Master. "I've witnessed this more times than I care to remember. The rum is here in reserve. Take a draft."

Without speaking, Luis took a drink and expressed his appreciation. They both sat and allowed the breeze from the bay to soothe their brows. Soothing was short-lived.

"*Owwwww!*"

With little strength left in his voice, the young seaman reacted to the initial knife cuts above his knee. Held down by four seamen, he screamed while the Surgeon sliced flesh, tendons and muscle. He fainted, to his advantage, but continued to jerk and writhe. Ribera's next step was to tie off major blood vessels to prevent flow when he loosened the tourniquet. Arteries clamped with forceps and their ends tied with silk ligatures evidenced the Surgeon's skill. Next came the amputating saw, and its serrated edges went to work.

"Hold'em down, boys," shouted the Boatswain.

The sound of metal on bone recalled the shipyards for Luis. Grating and crunching made awful noises, and the crudeness magnified the sound. Luis began to shudder and perspire. At length the leg separated, then was tossed overboard. Ribera overlapped and stitched the ragged skin edges. He called next for tar, now steaming in the pot. The kettle sat above a grate, with a sandbox fire underneath. At his instructions, two handlers painted on the hot gooey substance, covering the stump. The excess spilled along the deck, mixing with lost blood. Appprentices swabbed it all up. As the smell of seared flesh permeated, only whimpering could be heard from Seaman Gomez. Taken below, they strapped him to a cot to prevent further injury. On awakening, he would need rum. One of the merchant's wives, in the form of an angel, offered to nurse him when he opened his eyes. Recovery awaited in Habana, as sailing with the fleet would be doubtful.

Luis felt relief as the episode ended. He fancied this as not the last time he could view such an incident. He also knew the man could still contract gangrene, with his stump becoming putrid. Deciding to go below and compose himself, he stopped first at Surgeon Ribera's quarters to compliment his work. He knocked, then opened the door.

"Cicilio, your surgery…," his words trailed off.

Astounded, he found Ribera puffing his pipe, from which emitted an odd aroma.

"What is it?"

"Alférez, now you know my secret."

Luis realized it was opium, judging by the open medical box. A small can of ingredients lay scattered on his cot, along with tobacco.

"I have performed that sort of surgery many times, and skill-wise, it gets easier. Still, the emotions hang heavy, as a slab of stone placed on one's back. Removing a man's limb often saves his life, but the possibility continues that we could lose him if it becomes septic. Sometimes, I feel powerless." His forlorn gaze focused on the wall.

Luis became aware that here sat a dedicated man of medicine. But just as a soldier must face the bloody discomfits of battle, the surgeon deals with his own inner battles.

"Does it…possess you?"

"Noo, it's a post-surgery relaxant. It's under control."

"So, it functions as your nepenthe?"

"Yes, I fain take it to erase gruesome memories."

Luis wanted to believe him, but he knew of the stranglehold that opiates could bring upon a man. Ribera maintained a supply for patients.

Is it possible he's maintaining it mostly for himself?

"Nonetheless, Cicilio, I leave you to your time alone. Please make certain to safecare your humors."

As did most, Luis believed that four liquids, or humors, within the body, controlled one's health. An imbalanced humor was supposed to cause illness.

***

Five knots and lively speed! Luis reminisced in port of the endless top deck reports he heard while sailing. Chip log-wielding apprentices shouted to either the Pilot or Assistant at every turn of the hourglass and impressed all.

Piloting fascinated Luis, so he inquired often of Pilot Ximenéz, who displayed his array of maps, limited in scope, but still enlightening.

They stood and observed a map of La Florida.

"More than just the protruding peninsular on the south, it extends west to the Mississippi and north to the big bay," said the Pilot.

"Ximenéz, are the maps your only guides?"

"I like to use the rutters, the written directions of earlier pilots that cite landmarks. We can determine north-south latitude using the astrolabe and the sun. Not so for east-west longitude. So it's difficult to know distance covered sailing across the Atlantic. Old records approximate the days it takes to sail east to west. Tossing the chip log with rope and knots into the water provides some sense of speed. We relate that to the old distance records to determine position. Celestial navigation also aids, which requires I sleep during the day."

He continued. "Shoreline and harbor loom as my most critical time. If we proceed safely through shoals, I am praised. Should we run aground, I barely escape the lash. We have to remain alert as to speed and depth. I have learned much that they did not teach me at school in the Canaries."

Luis pored over the cartographers' works. They gave an overview of La Florida's peninsula, and he strived to absorb as much as possible. He observed that the southern tip of a Florida map noted islands known as *Los Mártires. On the southwest coast it cited a tribe known as the Maneaters. He determined not to go there. Above that was Ponce de León's Bay, explored and named a hundred years earlier. North of that, about half-way up the peninsula's west coast lay a large bay. It was termed **Bay Espíritu Santo, named by de Soto.

The east coast marked Cabo Cañaveral and above it San Agustín, Florida's only settlement.

Luis heard it existed as a primitive town with poor military quarters. He did not want to volunteer to serve there. In fact, he cared little to even set foot in Florida. A jungle where hostile savages rule, he knew it kept no treasures.

A vast cistern that holds no water, he figured.

He contemplated that should they sail to Spain soon, the fleet would stay in Habana only a few weeks for loadings. But he agonized over the possibity of wintering there to avoid the storm season at sea. If that happened, he would be gone a year from Isabela. He decided to write to her and to find a ship of delivery.

*Keys   **Tampa Bay

La Habana
August 27, 1622
My dearest love,

Today I know not if I will be home to you this fall or next spring. Everyone is in fear of sailing during the hurricane season. Soon our Marquis will decide, and he knows of the kings' immediate need of our silver aboard.

Each evening I ascend to the weather deck to observe the moon. I think of you under the same light, with its beams reflecting your beautiful features. Though it has been a long five months, you have been with me each waking hour. The memory of your smiling face, the red of your lips, the dark allure of your eyes, and the tenderness of your touch all sustain me.

I long for the moment when we are reunited. Please know that I am yours and only yours. Regardless of the port or the season, I remain faithful to you and to our future.

The port of La Habana is refreshing and the merchants are happy for us to spend our pesos, but I do little. However, I have made purchases for gifts to bring to you and my family. Please give my love to Mamaceita.

Until we meet, I remain affectionately your ardent and loving admirer,

Luis

It was written in the typical florid style expected of a gallant. Afterwards, he inquired in the harbor of any imminent departures to Europe. Told of a lone Portuguese slaver in port that just completed its task, he rushed to make contact. It would sail on the morrow, so he paid its Boatswain and asked that the letter be dispatched to Seville after arrival in Lisbon. He knew if his fleet sailed soon it was possible he would reach home before the letter. On returning, he walked the wide plank from the quay to the Atocha's railing where cargo and crew could move on and off shore. Crossing behind him came a short, sprightly man, who, intense and direct, addressed Luis.

"Buenos dias, Alférez. I need to see your Boatswain."

"May I inquire for what purpose?" asked Luis.

"Sir, I am the Marquis' Scribe, gatherer of the port's manifests for all our vessels. I have no need to explain this to you!"

"Certainly," said Luis. "I shall seek him for you."

After the Boatswain came on deck, Luis observed from afar. The Scribe did most of the talking, the Boatswain nodding. Soon he tendered a manifest of crew and passengers to the Scribe, who left. Seeing Luis, Boatswain Martín walked over.

"I would guess he was discourteous to you, Luis."

Luis nodded.

"Short in height but heavy in temperament. Unable to obtain a commission, for various reasons, so he likes to rankle officers, especially an Alférez. He hides behind the Marquis' shadow."

Luis nodded again.

He next greeted Surgeon Ribera returning and walking across the plank.

"Cicilio, what business in Habana?"

"To the apothecary to retrieve powders and aloe, both in short supply. I'm on my way to bleed a Don, who has the fever and desires aid. Do you want to come and assist?"

"No, but thank you. I'll stay up top."

Luis knew of cup bleedings, an ancient art that sometimes cured, sometimes not. He wondered what caused humors to be out of balance and how bleeding helped. Excessive blood loss in battle can cause death, so the procedure existed as a delicate practice that he did not understand.

With time to spare, he decided to wait in Ribera's quarters. He felt uncertain if his goal was medical inquisitiveness or a desire to caution the Surgeon of opium use. When Ribera returned, Luis noticed he did not reach for his pipe.

"Cicilio, would you show me the procedure for sewing up a wound?"

Glad to accommodate, he prepared his needle and thread much like a tailor. Splitting a cloth, he proceeded to reattach it just as he did skin.

"It must be done not long after a cut, or the wound is irreparable and more difficult to heal. Afterwards, I rub on aloe and then tie on a cloth, which must be changed often, as the wound may seep."

"Luis, have you heard of the Doctrine of Signatures?"

As Luis responded in the negative, Ribera pulled a book from his large satchel. It contained drawings of well-known plants and beside each a drawing of part of the human body.

"Plants disclose secret signs based on their resemblance to man's parts. For instance, see the comparison of the walnut and the human brain? Some believe, in this case, that consuming the walnut aids the mind."

"Do you practice this?"

"Sometimes, though I'm not certain how effective it is. Many things are being questioned nowadays. Some even believe that blood courses through vessels to and from the heart, that it may not ebb and flow like the tide. I know that I want to learn more."

"And you will, Cicilio."

As he thanked the Surgeon and excused himself, he thought of the tension on board between the common soldiers and seamen. Little existed between the officers, as long as no one tried to usurp another's duties. As an officer, he appreciated this, as his time with the Pilot and Surgeon had taught him much. Perhaps someday it would be useful. *Knowledge is power,* he had been told.

***

Word began to spread that several captains, masters, and pilots also feared sailing home in the midst of hurricane season. Pleasant weather with sunshine, light breezes and sapphire blue water did not allay their anxiety. In addition, superstition, ever present below the surface, reared its head. Murmurings could be heard from the Atocha seamen, who now wore fig amulets, considered good luck. Many wanted cannon salvos on the day of departure, if it came soon, to honor Our Lady of Atocha, from a shrine to Mary and the source of the galleon's name.

Agreeable conditions existed, but Pilot Martin Ximenéz of the Atocha worried as he conferred with the Captain, the Sailing Master and Vice-Admiral.

"Not only do we reside in hurricane season, my calculations tell me that the moon, sun, and earth approach an ominous planetary *conjunction*. It could cause terrible circumstances with the coming new moon."

The Master admired the Pilot, as did all aboard, so he nodded in respect. After pausing, he gave an opposite view.

"I'm aware of the conjunction theory, but September arrives in a few days, and we have no inclement weather. Look outside, all bright and calm."

"It may look accommodating on the weather deck, but therein lies the guise at this time of year. The calm. I would caution against sailing into the storm season. It would be like entering the bullring not knowing if you faced one or fifteen bulls," said the Pilot.

Captain Nodal spoke. "We will all be meeting with the Marquis and Admiral soon, and much discussion can be expected. Due to Dutch in the area, some captains want to sail forthwith. Plus the Marquis feels pressure from the Crown, who needs the treasure for its near-bankrupt treasury. Caution accompanies me also, but I'm prepared to follow orders. Silver, you know, is our *invisible lead vessel.*"

Pilot Ximenéz, excused, went to his quarters to sleep, his custom during daylight hours. That night for certain would find him on deck taking readings and watching the weather, as he knew sailing could come soon. As he left, shivers of doubt raced through him.

Did I speak as a man too cautious? Too bold? Did it matter?

A gamut of emotions gripped him, and he gave over to a sense of foreboding. Tossing in his hammock, a dream of torment descended on him.

Alone on the deck at night, he discovered a gaping hole in the ship's side. Water poured in like a split cask losing wine. He ran about the galleon sounding alarm, but no one heard him or would awaken.

As a panic seized him, he awoke, sat up, startled and sweating. His head spun round and round.

Holy Lord, I pray it remains only a dream.

***

"We sail!" Captain Nodal sounded upon returning aboard after receiving his orders.

After conferring with the ships' senior officers and hearing mixed recommendations a week earlier, the Marquis had waited until September 4 to decide. Morning, and he arose to a clear dawn and smooth breeze, taken as good signs. He gave orders to embark, and the entire fleet made ready. It was the day before the *conjunction*.

Upon hearing the news, a rich caballero from Jaén, Spain, petitioned Captain Nodal. He requested and received permission to transfer to a lesser vessel, the Santa Cruz. He reasoned that he enjoyed smaller vessels with spartan quarters, as they reminded him of his youth, plus his now-aching joints would be relieved. His personal silver bars remained packed away on the Atocha.

With provisions well-packed and the crew aboard, the last to board would be the wealthy passengers. A messenger hurried into town, and they responded. Silk dresses and parasols adorned the ladies, as if they prepared for a carriage ride. The men came suited with waistcoats, ruffled shirts and starched pants. To the stunned military men and seamen, a fashion parade seemed to materialized on ship.

Luis stood on deck, while the Atocha awaited its turn to cast away, and mulled his beleaguered Pilot's concern. Pilot Ximenéz had acquiesced to sail, as did the other pilots, even the doubtful Pilot Major. Alférez Sologuren joined him to witness the ongoing spectacle as the boats departed Habana one by one. Locals thronged narrow cobblestone streets and stone quays at harbor's edge to wave goodbye. Thankful merchants cheered, Fort El Morro's drums rolled and cannons boomed salutes. It took about two hours for all 28 ships to clear the harbor, led by the Marquis' Capitana vessel, the Candelaria.

"Look at those colored flags flying," said Sologuren. "Are they glad to see us leave, or saddened?"

"Judging by your colorful and energetic behavior at the tavern last night, I'd say there is one señorita who may feel both ways," said Luis, with a big smile.

"Well, nevertheless, I'll feel much better when we move into the ocean river and set course for Seville. My heart beats for our Old World maidens. Chaplain Val's blessings this morning made me feel as if I were home."

"I trust you noticed, Cristóbal, that we are sailing on a Sunday, the best day, so our voyage should be fortuitous. I must say that the sight of 28 vessels, all leaving, is impressive. I feel a part of history, of something big unfolding. We should be toasting!"

"I agree. I also noticed a well-dressed passenger changing today to a smaller ship before cast-off. I heard him respond to another, something like, ... 'but I also value my life'... Why is that?"

"Well, he's wise and observant. I think he's concerned about sailing on the Atocha should we encounter a hurricane. We sit well down in the water now and would wallow in a storm."

"Are you afraid, Luis?" Sologuren asked, his face drawn and questioning.

"Somewhat, but what can we do? As soldiers, following orders is our only path, so there you have it."

***

During the week prior to sailing, the port had conducted a fiesta for their esteemed visitors. Cannons blasted and evening rockets lit up the harbor. Mass followed August 28, the feast of San Agustín, which included a long procession to the church. But now, leaving proceeded. The Atocha went forth with a value of one million pesos of treasure and cargo. It included 82 soldiers, 54 seamen, 48 passengers, 42 apprentices, 15 pages and 24 servants, 265 total. Many stood on deck and waved goodbye, as the Atocha cleared the harbor last.

The first day of sail passed pleasant. A blue azure sea and an adequate breeze carried all N by NW. After the evening meal, Luis strode the deck and admired the deep red sunset behind them.

"Looks beautiful, doesn't it?" said Pilot Ximénez, just arising from his late afternoon nap, a contemplative look covering his face.

"What a grand sight to bid us farewell to the North Sea," said Luis.

"That is what distresses me. That and the bank of clouds in the SE. It portends trouble for tomorrow, the time of conjunction."

Luis was puzzled as to how a sunset that left him transfixed and at peace could foretell a hurricane. As many now settled in to sleep at dusk, the slap of the waves could be heard against the ship. Soon it became punctuated by groans from the massive beams. The boat rocking increased, but Luis only smiled, relaxed, and thought of Isabela.

Just a few weeks longer.

Pilot Ximenéz, as well as the Sailing Master, took notice of the rocking with an amount of concern. Wind changes were normal, but knowing the morrow, their senses heightened. Stronger gusts now became apparent to anyone on deck. That included the helmsman, guard watch, and the Pilot. The helmsman spouted out about seeing St. Elmo's fire around a soldier's head, but Ximenéz dismissed it, not wanting to alarm anyone.

Another ominous sailing superstition, he thought, *and I don't know if it has validity or not.*

An uneasy sleep came to Alférez Armador that first night out, as if deep inside he sensed the next few days could bring misfortune. He rolled around in his bunk to a dream unlike any other he'd experienced.

Soaring through the air like a bird, frightened at first, then exhilarated. After a time, I came to rest atop a large rain cloud, which poured volumes of water onto a furious sea.

Vessels began sinking, with all aboard crying, desperate for help. I knew a great sorrow for them. In an instant the cloud dissipated, and I fell into the sea, now emerald green and smooth as silk. I swam as a fish, devouring smaller fish around me.

Pitch dark and the Sailing Master walked the deck shouting orders as the choppy sea produced frothy waves from increasing winds. The sea did roll. He hoped for a storm approaching that would be gone by morning, but he agonized.

He, like the Pilot, had read the signs at sunset, and now strong winds and waves continued plus a rain began to fall. Many below tossed in their bunks that night. As gray dawn streaked across the horizon, the seamen received orders to secure all deck cargo and batten down all the hatchways. Soon the ship turned east and entered the flowing ocean river. It increased their speed two knots.

"What do you make of it, Pilot Ximenéz?"

The Captain strained to maintain a sense of control over his building emotions. They had gathered mid-morning with the Sailing Master and Vice-Admiral in the Captain's cabin, all grasping onto something firm to counter the ship's jostling.

"It's most likely a hurricane blowing from the area around Puerto Rico. The Atocha is well-built, but she is overloaded, and we don't know the strength of the storm," he replied, lines creasing his face.

The Vice-Admiral asked, "can we sail northwest to deeper water, away from the treacherous reefs of the Mártires?"

"Sir, it's difficult to hold a course with the winds, now ferocious and of gale force," said the Pilot. "And the now northeast wind is at cross-currents with the ocean river, which increases the turbulence. Plus, the vessel is tossing so much from front to back that the tiller is useless. The waves are ten feet high."

"What of the passengers?" inquired the Vice-Admiral. "They become fearful."

"They must stay below just as we stay in the sterncastle. Pray for the storm's passing," said Captain Nodal. "We now seek mercy."

"Sharks, sharks, following the boat!" yelled a seaman above. "A bad omen!"

"Nonsense," cautioned the Boatswain's Mate. "It's a pure coincidence"

Panic spread on the galleon, but little could be done. Fear gripped all, even the Captain. The sky blackened, but a lantern lit on the poop deck provided some measure of light. First the topsails were taken down and later the mainsail reefed to try to stabilize the craft. Other ships of the fleet could barely be seen now, as the waves towered higher and higher. As further reminders, the pumps below issued forth their repetitive creakings.

The sea boiled, the decks blew awash, and the sails' yardarms dipped into the water as the Atocha rolled. Wind-driven onto a wave, it would be lifted on a crest and thrown into a cavernous trough with its bow plunging into the sea. No one had to proclaim that this was a tropical hurricane. Dark clouds, dark rain and dark water continued all day and into the evening. The constant lurching prevented eating. The storm's fury led even to the Captain's quarters, where furniture and glassware now crashed back and forth.

The few mariners on deck witnessed the horrifying sight of its sister ship, the Santa Margarita, crashing into a reef and sinking. The Master asked that they delay telling those below. When day turned to night, it went unnoticed. The storm now bared all its teeth. Waves broke over in avalanches on the weather deck. The screeching wind blew thick white foam across the ocean's surface. Rain came sideways in torrents. The galleon pitched, rolled, and listed at such angles that all dreaded a capsizing. But, it held fast.

Sometime during the night, the rain and wind abated, and the stars came out. An eerieness prevailed as the eye passed over. Afterwards, the storm returned with a vengeance.

With it came an increased height of alarm that gave over to more superstitions and showings of faith. Some crept back up top to throw food and jewels overboard, somehow trying to assure their ascent to Heaven. A few could be seen on their knees praying for the storm to cease, while flagellating themselves and making vows to God. Seamen resorted to odd traditions. One could be seen slicing his finger and using his blood to create a sign on the floor. Some considered throwing women overboard, believing possible witches aboard made the sea angry.

Passengers realized the storm must be truly terrifying, as hardened sailors around them stopped cursing and started praying. Many in the passengers' deck area huddled in fright amidst dimly-lit oil lamps. Children squalled as the vessel was pounded on both sides. Mothers attempted to soothe but needed comfort of their own. No one could sleep, and walking was a challenge. The ship rolled sideways back and forth as if a mammoth boulder careened inside from one wall to the other. Seasickness, now rampant, resulted in a growing stench from vomiting. Passengers wailed and cried.

Some disposed to acceptance of their perceived fate. Couples conversed in hushed tones what they believed to be last loving words to one another.

In the sailors' area, rogue seamen whimpered in anguish. Some in deep despair moved to a darkened corner, as an animal when it expects to die. A handful of composed officers made deck rounds throughout the ship, trying to instill peace. Chaplain Val heard confessions and the Augustinian friars held a prayer session. Throughout the ship could be heard the Lord's Prayer, the Ave María, and the 23rd Psalm. All this in the midst of a reeling ship.

Silver and treasure made no consequence now in the travelers' minds, except for the fact that the heavy cargo made the vessel wallow and founder more-so. Excep for the fear of punishment, should the galleon survive, each aboard would have gladly tossed all extra weight overboard, including precious metals. In life or death, the King's treasure superseded everything. One passenger, perhaps due to his vain attachment to silver, proceeded down to the cargo hold.

"All my work, all my trials, all my planning, all my life. Must it come to this?"

Lorrenzo de Arriola lay on the floor with his arms wrapped around the padded boxes holding his 60 silver bars. With trembling voice, he lamented, though none could hear.

"Owed to another, but I alone earned it, and now it will not arrive in Seville."

He sobbed into the night.

Restless, Luis moved from the soldiers' area to the seamen's. Feeling swallowed by a whale like Jonah, with no way out, thoughts of family flashed through his mind. Entering the middle deck, he noticed three seamen jostling Steward Medina in a corner.

"You go with us now!" said one.

"I can't help you!" replied the Steward.

"We must have rum! We're going to die!" yelled another.

"I don't hold the storeroom key anymore," he said.

"We don't believe you! You're coming with us!" yelled the third seaman, holding a lantern.

Wild-eyed and desperate, they hustled him across the room and toward the stairs leading down. He offered little resistance. Luis followed. Descending the stairs, along the dim corridor, he came upon them at the locked storeroom door.

"Open it! Open it!" they yelled, slamming the Steward against it over and over.

Feeling the effects of a mob where hysteria reigned, he fell to the floor and covered his head with his arms.

"Hold there! Move away or be run through. All of you!" Luis was standing tall in the combat position, pointing his sword at each man in turn.

"Let him go! The Captain has the key. Anyway, rum cannot save your soul. I order you to step away!"

Luis viewed them irrational and in a frenzy, but he counted on his composure, rank and sword as deterrents. One-by-one, they backed off and headed down the corridor to the stairs. Luis helped the poor man to his feet.

"Be wary, my friend, as many have clouded thinking. Like animals gone mad and not aware of their actions."

"Thank you, Alférez. God be with you."

Together they went back to the gun deck, where the scene remained unsettling. Luis continued troubled by the moaning and wailing. He thought of an unusual weather deck action he witnessed when heading below, that of three seamen and two slaves lashing themselves to the mizzen mast.

How could they hope to survive, with the waves crashing on deck and the winds battering everything? They had mettle. Or else acted as lunatics.

Something, an unknown urging, perhaps Providential encouragement, made him move toward the stairs leading to that top deck. Just as he stepped up, a firm hand grabbed his arm.

"Take it, young man, you may need it."

Turning around, he met the grim face of Silvermaster Jacove de Vreder, who shoved a leather satchel against him. Without questioning, he took it, as though tendered some type of lifesaving contrivance.

With tears in his eyes, de Vreder whispered, "Vaya con Dios, my young amigo." He then turned and disappeared into the shadowy room. Luis attached the satchel to his waist. As he again started up, a familiar voice yelled out – his friend Alférez Sologuren.

"Don't go up top, Luis! You will die!"

Luis said nothing. He checked his sword and scabbard, moved up the stairs, grappled with the top hatch and crawled onto the sloshing outside deck. He faced an astounding scene.

2
OVERBOARD

September, 1622

*To all this line of islands and rock islets they
gave the name of Los Mártires because as seen
from a distance, the rocks as they rose to view
appeared like men who were suffering,
and the name remained fitting because of the
many who have been lost there since.*
                    Antonio de Herrara
                    1513

GULF OF MEXICO
OFF FLORIDA PENINSULAR SW COAST

Luis' recallings of the previous weeks suddenly evaporated when a large wave washed over the men lashed to the mizzen mast. Though tied, his body flailed about.

This is the Nuestra Señora de Atocha, the Almiranta, the grandest galleon in the fleet. 550 tons. 112 feet long. Posh. 20 bronze cannons.
Built in Habana for the king. Not old. It must survive......

It happened in an instant.

Another giant wave crashed over the ship. His entire body trembled, wrenched free, and catapulted off the ship into the turbulent sea. His rope had loosened, and the breakers claimed him. He plunged into the massive, frothy swells and submerged, with no sense of up or down. His focus in complete disarray. All forces engulfed him into a nightmarish state, immersed and helpless. Feeling suspended between life and death, swallowed by the ocean at the edge of the world, he accepted an imminent end to life.

But, he buoyed to the surface like a ball fired from a musket. The noise on reemerging overwhelmed him. As he took breath, thankful of life, the vast sea reminded him of its presence, with a torrent of water pouring down. The raging ocean tossed him about like a cork with no attendant line. First wallowing in troughs, then covered with the thunderous waves, he pitched end-over-end.

Constant pounding on his body made him feel like a waterborne Flagellant, as the penitent souls that beat themselves, seeking absolution and penance during the Plague. Salt water engulfed his nostrils and infused its way into every pore. Like being in a large wooden milk churn, or on the constable's dunking stool. From out of nowhere, a crunching blow to the head jolted him into a higher level of awareness. The broken plank of a ship's hull had come crushing down with a giant wave. Reeling, he reached out to grasp it, but watched it float away. Swimming to it, he grabbed and held on with of all his strength.

It just might save my life.

Over and over he rolled in the current of sea and foam as the tempest surged. With each successive breaker spilling onto him, a terrible weakness pervaded his body. He shook, nausea set in, and he began retching and purging. The only benefit became the ridding of salt water in his belly. No point of reference could be seen, no sun, no horizon, only gray and white and a dark sky. Luis held on, as a coldness set upon him. His teeth began to chatter, and his leg muscles cramped. He sought to move his limbs as much as possible so to dissipate the agony.

Slowly, he developed an inner resolve and focused on his survival possibilities. Stupefied, he held on, and from somewhere in the deep recesses of his mind, Isabela came to him. With bright shining eyes and smiling face, she blew kiss after kiss. It helped to sustain and to remind of the reward of life and love that could be his. He fantasized of food. Thus, Mamaceita's last evening meal glowed in his mind.

Each piece of bread, dabbed with oil, each green vegetable, each bite of beefsteak could be seen and almost tasted… the sight…the smell…

He reached out to take it…..and another wave enveloped him.

It's fitful, unending.

He wanted to cry, but no tears issued forth. He wanted to let go and sink, end it all. But he held on in a death grip.

I will not effect it. It will have to take me. I still live.

Once again, scenes of the past formed, and he clung to them as if to an imaginary lifeline. Memories of departing Spain now filled his mind………

Atlantic Crossing and Indies

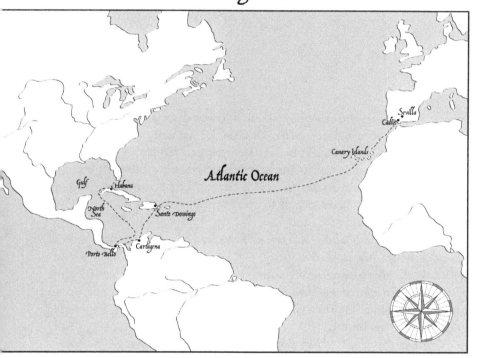

3

Launch To The Indies

March, 1622

*In this world there are three kinds of human beings,
the living, the dead, and those who sail the sea.*

Anacharis
600 B.C.

SEVILLE
March, 1622

Luis descended to the Atocha galleon's lower deck and down the narrow corridor to settle into his tiny officer's cubicle. Its only furnishings, a worn cot and a washbowl, greeted him. As he dropped his leather satchel onto the floor, his mind returned to the warmth of Isabela's farewell kiss. He imagined it still present on his lips. Her rosewater perfume lingered, almost intoxicating him. His head began to spin, so he lay upon the cot. The feelings overtook him.

I still have time to slip topside and flee, or I can pretend a severe malady and request permission to be left behind.

He knew the anxiousness of coming separation from her vexed him. Luis strained like a man *keelhauled,* one rope pulling from the galleon and one from her home. As the condemned seaman underwater, he gasped, unable to catch his breath.

So this is how it's to be? What about honor, glory, and eagerness for the New World?

Among the jumble of thoughts, he knew that certain as the sun would rise on the morrow, he would be aboard. *Madre always said that to overcome apprehension, you must replace it with joy for the task at hand.* He thought of Cervantes relating Don Quixote's desire to leave home and become a knight—*spurred on by the conviction that the world needed his immediate presence.* Luis identified with the Don, however fabled he may be.

***

His thoughts were of the day's goodbyes.

"Luis, come down and take your breakfast, your day of travel beckons!"

Daylight and madre's voice called with a hint of sadness. Her 22 year-old, tall, dark-haired, athletic son was leaving. After two years at the

Universidad and a year in the shipyards, he joined the military. Family influence and purity of blood succeeded in his commission as an alférez. Now he would sail as a guardian soldier on the Atocha to the Indies. Luis' emotions mingled as family members doted on his every move and comment. After lengthy goodbyes, he grabbed his satchel of goods and headed down the street to the tavern to bid farewell to good friends Lope and Andrés. At least a half-year would pass before he'd see them again. Crossing the tavern threshold, familiar sounds and aromas greeted him.

"Hola, señor soldier," said Lope. "Are you ready to re-conquer Castilla del Oro or New Spain?"

Andrés smiled and asked, "Is your beautiful Isabela going to be locked in her room while you sail away this year, or do you trust we amigos to see to her?"

Luis smiled, waved them away and then clasped their hands. They sat at their favorite table, pipes and coffee in hand. Carlos, the tavern keeper, ambled over with the same for Luis.

"Today my young friend, these come to you on the house. Just beware of the fevers in the New World because we want to see you again. And chew these mint leaves and dab on this oil when you leave so you can smell good for your señorita."

"What about the cannibals?" said Lope.

"What about the Dutch corsairs?" asked Andrés.

"Nonsense, nonsense," said Luis. "That is the difference between you and me. I seek the world, and you are but content with it. Nonetheless I favor you. I look forward to my return, unless I am entrapped by a beautiful Indio princess. In that case I will send word to you of my status." With that, he produced a wide smile and took a puff from his pipe.

The good-natured banter lasted for about forty-five minutes, after which they embraced, and Luis took his leave to walk several blocks to Isabela's home to say his farewell. A bright smile and dazzling eyes greeted his knock on the door. Soon the sweethearts strolled arm in arm through the house into the garden, followed at a distance by her madre.

"Luis, I am sad and fearful," Isabela spoke, tears welling up in her eyes. "My heart is heavy, as I do not know if you will survive to return to me."

"My love, nothing, not Indios, cannibals, pirates or dragons shall keep me from returning. You know I have a restlessness that must be answered, both for my destiny and my family's honor."

"Do I not also have a destiny with you? I feel that your love for me follows second to your desire for adventure, and it wounds me."

"Sweet one, I shall think of you every hour of the day and long to return. Our wedding and our life together remain of great importance to me. This trip serves to enhance our future and that of our children to come. You must trust me."

What if something forestalls me, he pondered, *causing the trip to be extended beyond all that I planned?*

"We should be in the Indies by late May, be through and leaving Habana by mid-August. Six months hence, and I stand at your front door." He smiled and made his best effort to portray confidence.

"But what shall become of me should you not return?"

Luis took a few moments before answering.

"If fate flies against me, and one year passes and you do not see me, I could not expect you to wait forever. Another may claim your hand."

His heart sunk as the words passed his lips. Taking her hand in his, Luis led Isabela behind the hedges and took her into his arms for a lingering kiss. He felt a strong stirring inside and wondered what possessed him to embark on a voyage to the middle of nowhere and leave this fascinating creature. Soon, they heard madre's call, announcing the mid-day meal. The two trudged to the house, recounting picnics, sailings and parties. As longings tugged their hearts, they vowed to resume these precious activities upon his return.

Later, Luis could not recall the conversation with Isabela's family during the repast. A vague remembrance of small talk came to mind, yet overshadowed by the memory of her eyes, misty and threatening to flow at any moment. They seldom left his, as her fork pushed food from one end of her plate to the other. Neither savored the fare served for the departure feast. The betrothed parted within the hour following. Isabella used her handkerchief both to wave goodbye and to wipe away tears that no longer stayed within their boundaries.

Sunlight warmed his face while walking the streets, as he soaked it all in, knowing it would be months before he would see it again. Residing in the major port in the Golden Age of Spain, he realized he would be leaving behind politics, commerce, fiestas, the Holy Mass and monthly parades. He hoped all would be intact on his returning.

Walking past the Alcázar grounds, he became lightheaded as he thought of legendary years past when kings met in the castle with the likes of Narváez, Balboa, and Magellan to solidify their dreams for America. He felt a strong kinship with all the past explorers as he set out upon his own quest. Those thoughts vanished as the Arénal scene unfolded. This sandy beach area between city walls and docked vessels on the river overflowed with merchants, sailors, captains, galley slaves, soldiers, notaries, and all sorts of humanity. A gathering place of street women, indigent adventurers, criminals needing to escape, and poor pilgrims needing a new start. The strand that launched the careers of Vespucci and Mendoza, who sailed far away and returned. The anointed ships stretched along the shore for a good arrow's flight, most within sight of the shining gold dome of the Toro del Oro. The special building where arriving precious metals sought storage. As Luis boarded the Atocha, he heard a booming voice.

"Hola, amigo!" Alférez Cristóbal de Sologuren, a fellow young officer to be stationed on the Atocha, beamed. "Are you ready to be a protector for the fleet?"

"Yes, and thankful not to be headed to *Flanders. Bloodshed there could go on for years."

They clasped hands and congratulated each other on the venture of a lifetime. Soon another officer arrived.

"Hola, amigos," he exclaimed. "Have you taken your malaria powders? Not only must we guard against Indios and corsairs, but also the diseases."

As Boatswain Mateo Martín approached, the twinkle in his eyes belied his comments. Only a few years older, to Luis he bore the marks of experience and confidence. Like many seamen, he lacked a few teeth, but he wore no scars, and his bearing instilled respect.

"We should be there and back before the hurricane season this fall," he said, trying to alleviate any apprehension of the young men.

"You're presuming no sequestering or butchering at Porto Bello," said Sologuren.

"Doubtful, my friend," said Luis, "with our swordfighting skills, we're invincible. If Cortés and Pizzaro could go and return, so can we."

"Of course," said Martín. "Plus good fortune shines with me aboard." He smiled.

Luis gazed in awe at the Terre Firme fleet's ships. Eight in all, spectacular, with three masts each, sails furled, new riggings, and outstanding wooden trim carvings. His ship bore a large painting on the sterncastle's back, noting its name source, Our Lady of Atocha shrine. Many believed it would bring good fortune.

The bustle of activity in preparation for sailing dazzled Luis. His nostrils filled with the smells of fish, hemp, and sweat, while the multitude of foreign languages swelled his ears. Sailors and soldiers arrived and settled

* Flanders- with whom Spain was at war; ultimately part of Belgium.

in on the Atocha and the other vessels. Seamen loaded large jars with nuts,meats, and vegetables, all preserved in olive oil, along with large casks of salt-laden fish. Suppliers expected immediate payment, so the fleet Marquis' treasurer disbursed from his duly-appointed space.

That evening Luis and Alférez Sologuren shared an invitation to sup in Captain Bartolemé García Nodal's quarters, along with a roomful of senior officers. They pursued the utmost in gentility and in paying proper homage. The Captain addressed the group following the meal, and his commanding demeanor impressed the young officers.

"Gentlemen, it is now time to review our route and answer any questions you may have. Some have sailed before, but a few haven't. Come morning, the Bishop will be here to bless the fleet, and many will gather to wish us safe voyage. We will go downriver to the Gulf, which will take about a week, slow for the Pilot because of shifting shallows. The ships will cross the bar at high tide at Sanlúcar, then spend time there and at Cádiz, taking on passengers and the rest of our supplies. Our eight vessels will sail first to the Canary Islands and then to the Indies. Merchant goods will be deposited and silver loaded, and we should be enroute home mid-August."

His eyes scanned the room. "Any questions?"

"Captain, any reports on Dutch corsairs?" asked the Pilot.

The captain shrugged, drew in a deep breath and faced him directly.

"Nothing new, but the Dutch would like nothing better than to take an entire Spanish fleet. In fact, the French would like to capture us, sever our noses, ears, and tongues. Then hang us in trees and spread honey on the wounds so vermin could have their way. Of course, we know the English are not too fond of us."

This brought laughter by all present. The Captain continued.

"Everybody wants a piece of Spain. At least they want to participate in the Indies trade and acquire our silver. This will not happen, as they would face our Armada de la Guardia of our own Terre Firme Fleet. With eighty-two soldiers and twenty cannons aboard the Atocha alone, plus the might of our other guard galleons, we will succeed in defending as needed."

Luis noticed the Captain enjoyed exhorting his answers, and that his brow glistened with perspiration.

"Other questions?"

"Captain." Alférez Armador did his best to convey a sense of seriousness and militarism.

"What about sea monsters?"

As soon as the words left his mouth, he wanted so much to retrieve them. *What am I, a nine year-old whose imagination is amuck?*

Sologuren peered at him with mouth agape.

The Captain remained composed as he answered.

"No monsters, no dragons, no devils, and we don't sail on Fridays. We do avoid the albatross, the sharks, the petrias, and of course the mermaids."

Following that, the laughter deafened all. A sense of desolation gripped Luis and if he could have slipped away surreptitiously, he would have done so.

"Now, your mercies, allow me to recognize a very necessary member of our voyage." With arm raised, he motioned towards Surgeon Cicilio de Ribera. "Here is someone we must all favor, as he has powders, tools and experience. He acknowledges familiarity with humors and knows how to bleed as well as any barber. Having spent time in Valencia, he received his doctor's diploma at our well-known medical university there. Let us make him welcome."

Cheers and applause followed, and Ribera responded with several nods. "One last thing, gentlemen…"

As he began, Luis noticed the Captain's voice growing louder.

"The Atocha sails as an honorable vessel. We will not tolerate desertions, stealing, falling asleep at the wheel, smuggling, or unnatural crimes. Punishments will be severe, from flogging, to imprisonment, even death. I expect each of you to assist in enforcement."

The Captain then turned the floor over to the Vice-Admiral for closing.

"Men, as Vice-Admiral of eight ships, sailing on the Atocha represents a high honor. We serve as Almiranta, the rear ship of the line and major protector. The Admiral will be in our lead galleon, our Capitana vessel. His appointment as Commander of the merchant fleet comes from the king, thus our link to the monarchy. Let us make him proud. The Marquis, our Captain–General of our protective Armada ships, will wait and sail in about a month. His four guard galleons will join us in Porto Bello, and then our protection force for returning should be complete. His 15 smaller cargo ships will split up in the Indies and join us later."

He dismissed all with handshakes as did the Captain. Luis experienced a real sense of belonging and hoped they would dismiss his sea monsters question. He knew his friend Alférez Sologuren would have his fun later.

Mariners had told him that a ship can feel like a jail without bars, as no escape comes till landing. Some men become taut. He realized it could come to that, but at the moment he fancied as a man about to be whisked away as on a magic carpet. It reminded him of his dream of soaring above the treetops. Scary at first, then invigorating, like a sense of Heaven. He knew the Atocha would have a rhythm of its own, springing from its doldrums and infusing everyone with its eager spirit. It reminded Luis, too, of a presentation at the theatre, where many would play a part, including him. The curtain was drawing on the biggest event in his life.

I am a cannonball ready to be fired, only waiting for the fuse to be lit.

***

"Good morning, Alférez."

Luis turned to see the ship's Steward on the top deck.

"Have you had your morning chocolate?"

"Now, don't banter with me, amigo. I know that precious cup of liquid gold resides aboard for our senior officers only."

With a big smile emanating from behind his Nazarene-type beard, joviality became him. Luis knew him as a man of depth, but soft-hearted, allowing galley pilferage, and probably pilfering on his own, owing to his enormous belly. He had taken a liking to Luis.

"Alas, correct, Alférez, but should you develop the retching malady from too many waves, come to see me, and I will slip you some for medicinal purposes."

"Thank you, kind sir, I hope to return the favor."

Moving to the rail in early light, he looked down at the murky Guadalquivir River.

Flowing a good 400 miles from the mountains and soon to meet the sea. The lifeblood of Seville. Spain's only true inland port. The same waters that took Jose.

Luis had never again entered it, but he knew its value for the family shipwright business. He gazed at varied scenes bankside, from simple orphans that slept along its docks to grand agent offices nearby. To him, it was a grand watery pathway leading to the future.

***

After reaching the coast, the fleet consumed time at ports Sanlúcar and Cádiz, loading more goods. Embarkation day came on March 23 with a blanket of fog lifting. Seamen loaded last-minute barrels, baskets of meat, sacks of oranges, limes, lemons and an assortment of animals. Luis watched in amazement as well-attired wealthy merchants boarded and headed for the sterncastle. With rent paid to Captain Nodal, they would enjoy spacious and well-appointed quarters. Lesser passengers scrambled to find their corner, above or below deck. All eight vessels pulled away at late morning to the timbers' usual creaks and groans, as well as the sailors' hearty songs. A splendid scene unfolded, with sails flapping and well-wishers waving. The coastline receded and the winds increased offshore, making the start favorable. The Atocha assumed the last place in the lineup.

"Pleasant day to you, Alférez. I trust all has been a comfort so far."
Surgeon Cicilio de Ribera approached with his studious and bespectacled
persona, nursing his morning coffee.

"Your first float, no doubt?"

"Yes, I do believe my whole life, short enough, prepared me for this vast
encounter. Please tell me what to expect."

"Expect to enjoy the experience, my friend, and God willing, your
military services won't be needed against corsairs or pirates. The Indies
introduce some amazing sights."

"What of the squalor of the tropics?"

"Ah, we try not to focus on that, but instead on the beauty it brings to
us. Porto Bello, Panama, is the paradox of our journey. It is lush, green,
with a deep harbor to greet us. And the annual feria is enlivening. But its
wretchedness contains the source of many illnesses. Therein falls my
duties."

"Is there anything I should fear?

The surgeon, lost in thought for a few moments, responded.

"No. Adaptation, adaptation. I once treated a solder from the
battlefield whose legs had been shattered by cannon fire. After removing
one leg, I cauterized the stump and stopped the bleeding. Reeling from so
much pain, he would not allow the other to be amputated. He deemed his
body whittled away, much as a wood carving. He even held a weapon to
me. He developed gangrene in the remaining leg and it took his life.
Enduring the pain for a short while longer did not interest him. He made a
choice and died. Adaptation, adaptation......adaptation."

***

ATLANTIC OCEAN

"It is not time!"

The indignant booming voice of seaman Tomás sounded when
Boatswain Martín ordered free time curtailed for the evening. Many
seamen, lounging on deck, heard the order directed towards a boisterous
gaming group. Though it was dusk and time to retire below, they persisted.
Not rum, but the headiness of the embarkation had vitalized them.

"I said, all make ready for the evening or prepare to accept the
consequences!" yelled the Boatswain, his countenance irritated.

A roar issued from the crowd, enough to make most officers call for
help. Not so Martín. In two motions, he drew his sword and brought it
down on the vocal Tomás' head. Blood flowed copiously as he hit the

deck, shrieking. The others scattered below like rats jumping from an ill-fated vessel.

Martín turned to Luis and the nearby helmsman with a bold look of confidence that said–*sometimes a man must show himself.* Luis, impressed enough to consider vacating also, stood speechless, witness to severe necessary action. Thus the vagaries of ocean travel presented itself early and he wondered at more to come. Martín called the Surgeon to treat the man, but to offer no consolation.

***

Uhhhh! Ohhhh! Owwww! Ooooo!

Inhumane sounds came from all over the weather deck. Almost a week into sailing and the wind increased, which led to heavings of the galleon. Many lost their meals, and for some, walking became challenging, above or below deck. The seamen enjoyed the stumbling and seasickness of soldiers and began to jeer. They looked with scorn on the infantrymen, who enjoyed gaming and card playing out of pure boredom. No fault of theirs, as their only tasks were light guard duty and the afternoon firing of the harquebuses.

Many hung over the rail, vomiting. The illness didn't discriminate, affecting men, women, children, poor emigrants and wealthy merchants alike. Even the shipboard animals suffered, especially the pigs. The Surgeon could do little. Some believed an evil spirit passed through the vessel and transformed it into a hospital ship. Passengers would project their stomach contents outward, shed tears, and wail. Many sprawled upon the deck, hoping that the wind would abate or that abdominal urgings be completed.

After witnessing the sickly, though not ill himself, Luis went to the Steward to plead that he make good on his promise.

"Alférez, I've been expecting you," he said, with a big smile glowing. "Instead of chocolate, try this ginger. It helped me, maybe you too."

Luis consumed all given to him and prayed for no distasteful emissions from his stomach. It worked. But he was troubled by the seamen's tauntings of his men and trusted it did not portend ill. After a day and night, the wind tapered and the nausea passed, so that the affected could return to their normal victuals.

***

Alférezes Armador and Sologuren once again received an invitation to the Captain's cabin for supper and joined the Sailing Master as well as Master of Silver Jacove de Vreder. The other three senior officers were on deck conferring. Sologuren admonished Luis to be thoughtful before asking questions.

"A man learns by asking."

"True, but just make certain it is on a mature level, *Mr. Sea Monster*," he voiced with a cackle, while gesturing grotesquely with his hands and face.

Luis allowed him to jest, as he liked his fun-loving counterpart.

The table conversation that evening took a turn to the Dutch.

"Reports continue that more than anyone, our longtime enemy is becoming more ambitious for the Indies," said the Sailing Master. He pushed back his chair and lit an after-meal pipe.

Luis watched the smoke rise to the ceiling. He observed a man well-groomed and well-spoken. With cartography as his passion, he required the Pilot to report the ship's position to him on a regular basis. Captain Nodal left charge of the sailing vessel and seamen in his hands.

Young Alférez Solguren, wanting to contribute, cleared his throat and opened his mouth to speak. Luis couldn't wait to hear.

"The Dutch West India Company, what gives them the right to come to the Indies, when the Pope forbade it?"

Acceptable, thought Luis.

"Well, as Protestants, they have their own thoughts about the Pope and his decree that only Spain and Portugal have sole rights to the New World," said the Sailing Master. "They want part of the prosperous trade in the North Sea, and their king has allowed West India to incorporate and use corsairs. You know, the world is like a giant cave's echo. Whatever you send out comes back to you."

"With respect to Spain's dominance, some would say it borders on treason to believe our monopoly is not divinely inspired," said de Vreder.

"My allegiance is to the Pope and to King Felipe IV, but my thoughts reflect that the rest of Europe does not like it, and I fear future consequences. We are the military and naval giant, but remember what happened to Goliath," he responded.

"But we allow them to participate in the exports and imports in Seville."

"Yes, as long as they pay the tax," he further responded.

"And they should," said de Vreder, his face reddening. "Our silver trickles throughout Europe, and they benefit as much as we."

Luis seemed to recall hearing all this before, so in an attempt to settle the conversation down, he plied a question on another subject.

"What happens to the merchants and to the King's bankers if our ships face a hurricane and sink while returning with the silver?"

A pervasive quiet ensued, and each stared at him, as they knew of the possibility, but did not want to discuss it. He knew though of the sad affair of the King's treasury. The Genoese bank loans, collateralized by the treasure due from the Indies, always loomed. Merchants borrowed for shipping and the King did for wars. Luis enjoyed this adventure, in fact, he loved it, but certain thoughts had begun to invade his mind.

Who enlivens the spirit and the culture of Spain? The King, his Senior Minister Olivares, or the Pope? The Protestants are heretics, but should we fight them? It's so costly.

His musings would be kept to himself.

Captain Nodal re-entered his quarters, a sign that the four seated needed to depart, as the meal was ended. *Buenos noches* and *gracias* came from all the diners.

Luis stood in awe of Captain Nodal as he thought of his accomplishments.

The first navigation of Drake's Passage at the bottom of the world…south of Cape Horn…discovered the Ramírez Islands…the most southerly known land on earth…no wonder the Admiral appointed him…more than a gentlemanly court captain.

"My young friend," said Silvermaster de Vreder as they left to retire, "I'm remembering your question about what happens in Spain should our ship sink in a storm. That's never happened to me, but should it become imminent, stay close to me."

Luis wondered what he meant. Vreder at times puzzled him. He was opinionated, intelligent, a little short on humor, but adventuresome. Luis figured that the essence of this travel for him must be the silver. He complained of his income, a percentage of the treasure shipped, but he exhibited loyalty, ardent Catholicism, and trust, all needed for one that handles precious metals.

***

APRIL, 1622

"We'll find him!" spouted the Captain at daybreak roll call.

Luis had first sighted the Canary Islands looming as distant boulders dropped into the ocean. The vessels docked in Las Palmas harbor for an overnight stay, with several from the Atocha going into town, on orders to return by ten. Muster would be at first light in the morning, with Luis thinking it tardy accounting for those intent on junketing.

Seaman Tomás failed to show in the morn, with each longboat thinking he had returned on the other. Nightime staggering in their cups had not helped the reconciling. The same defiant sailor that received a mob-squelching blow to the head from Boatswain Martín became the first deserter.

"It doesn't surprise me," said Martín to Luis, as they gazed toward the shore, the sun just breaking the horizon. "He fits the *picaro*. Such a shortage in Seville of good sailors requires that we have to take his sort- ruffians, miscreants, lawbreakers, gamblers, even secret emigrants who plan to desert us."

Martín had just spoken the words when the Captain motioned for Luis to come forward.

"Alférez, take two of your infantrymen with arms into Las Palmas and bring back the deserter. We must make an example."

"It will be my honor, sir."

Without hesitation, he picked two soldiers and promptly had seamen row them ashore. Luis knew that apprehension can creep in as a thief in the night, so he encouraged the men in his charge, as much to bolster his own feelings as theirs. They walked the streets at daylight, going from tavern to cantina, finding none with doors locked and many with the owner not yet present. Peering around in the half-light of a nameless dirt floor cantina, Luis spied him. Amidst the litter and stench of spilled ale, he slept with his head on a table.

"Arise, you picaro!" said Luis.

Opening his reddened eyes, Tomás tried to comprehend his straits. Uncoiling and standing, he presented a visage both unkempt and explosive.

Drawing his sword, he boomed aloud. "I shan't be taken alive!"

Thoughts raced thru Luis' mind. *Is this a lawbreaker, with a bounty on his head, or a simple bankrupt merchant who became irrational? Why did he leave Spain? Where did he acquire the sword?*

Tomás began a series of lunges, swearing all the while. Luis dodged easily as his opponent was charged with emotion and off-balance. The previous evening's activities had also left their mark. He began swinging with murderous intent, but Luis met each with strong deft defenses. The Alférez pointed and slit the deserter's shirt, drawing blood on his chest. That didn't slow him. With fire in his eyes and a cold rage pounding his pulse, the rogue swung his blade, which Luis parried. He then drove Tomás back with a two-handed swing. Moving fast, Luis swung and boxed the sword from the grasp of his opponent, who now faced a blade at his throat. With his own heart still pounding, Luis forced him down and the soldiers subdued and bound him.

A splendid mid-morning sun shone as they met the Captain at the landing. All suspected the prisoner would feel the lash upon his back before they sailed, but not so. This desertion, added to his earlier antics at Seville's embarkation, caused the Captain to want him gone from the vessel altogether. While awaiting the arrangements for Tomás' incarceration, Luis poured out his heart as he penned a letter to Isabela. That day it left on a vessel headed to Seville. He was thankful that she lived far from the violence he experienced with Tomás. As they sailed away that afternoon, he thought of the seaman in Las Palmas' jail, awaiting trial for desertion. He hoped to never again cross paths with the pitiful soul.

The Captain gave all the crew a few rounds of rum that evening, so they could see his munificence as well as his punishment. The Atocha's fleet next would sail west to garner the tradewinds across the Atlantic, following Admiral Colón's trail. Luis continued to think over the possibility of more desertions at the upcoming ports of Cartagena and Porto Bello. He speculated that his duty in that respect would increase, much as winds in a storm.

***

Las Palmas

April, 1622

My beloved Isabela,

Today, April 1, the Atocha is leaving the Canaries, and I am happy to be on our way. Early this morning it was my duty to lead soldiers in capturing a contentious soul who had tried to desert his service. All is now settled, and we sail forthwith.

Three weeks departed, and it seems an eternity away from you. The day's sunlight dances on the water as it has danced on your hair. My thoughts are daily with you, and that is what sustains me. I want forever to be your cavalier, as I believe it is the will of Heaven for us to be together. I pray that soon I will be worthy to hold you to me so that we shall be as one.

Your sparkling eyes and smile have enraptured me

and placed me under your spell, from which I hope never to be cast away. Your fragrance lingers with me even now and oft bids my senses to seek escape back to you at any moment.

  Be aware my love, I would give my life for you. Your love gives me perpetual strength, and I count the days till we are together.

Affectionately, and with earnest love and devotion,
Luis

***

SEVILLE

Isabela read his letter over and over on the day received. He wrote it in the Spanish florid style, expected of a gallant. Thereafter, she read it daily, sometimes in the moonlit garden or maybe there just after sunset, when the orange blossoms emitted fragrances. She read it in her room by candlelight, and her heart fluttered. Then she would place it under her pillow for safekeeping.

At a time with many men gone to war or to the New World, she clung to the hope of her returning caballero. Unlike most girls of an hidalgo family, she loved a suitor she had known and admired since childhood. Their families stayed close, so the mutual arrangement satisfied everyone. She realized that absent Luis, there would be a bridal arrangement of which she would have little knowledge. These primary facts existed for a señorita as Isabela.

She spent time helping her madre, participated in *closet plays* with other young women, attended daily Mass, and read when her padre wasn't watching. An exception was allowed for madre's Manual de Mujeres, which provided recipes and instructions for concocting perfumes, cosmetics, and medicines.

4
Porto Bello

1622

*Oh what a set of Vagabundos, sons of Neptune, Sons
of Mars, Raked from todos, ostros, mundo, Lascars,
Gascons, Portsmouth tars. Prison mate and dock-
yard fellow, Blades to Meg and Molly dear, Off to
capture Porto Bello, sailed with Morgan the buccaneer.*
E.C. Stedman

ATLANTIC OCEAN

Boom! Boom! Boom!
The harquebuses' volleys reverberated around the galleon as
thunderclaps across the water. White smoke engulfed the deck like clouds
descended from the sky. An acrid aroma stung the nostrils of anyone
nearby.
"At ease!" called Sgt. Valazco.
"Fire again! "commanded Alférez Armador.
"Positions. Fire!" yelled the Sergeant.
It was a daily afternoon ritual for all infantrymen aboard. The Captain
wanted assurance that all guns were in working order in case of attack. The
firing, though noisy and noxious, gave the seamen and passengers an added
sense of confidence in their military. All dispersed in short order.
Clop, clomp, clomp, clop…
Luis' heavy boots pounded the planking, echoing down the hall. His
daily mission completed, he went to join three other junior officers for a
meal in a private cabin, all provided courtesy of the Captain. He
straightened his doublet and rapped twice before entering.
"Greetings Armador," said Surgeon Ribera.
"And to you, sir, and Alférez Sologuren, and our esteemed Assistant
Pilot."
Evening approached, so with two lanterns shining, enough light glowed
for the meal's enjoyment in comfort. Two steward apprentices came
forward to pour wine into crystal glasses.
"To the health and good fortune of King Felipe IV and to our good
Captain," posed Sologuren.
"Hear, hear," said all.

Decorum dictated the manners and dining style which all enjoyed. There existed expectations of each to contribute to the conversation and to limit his wine. The apprentices brought pipes and tobacco for the men to enjoy after eating.

"As much as I admire the silver trade, it concerns me about its surplus effect on Spain's prices, which now rise like skyrockets," said Ribera. All in the room knew this oft-discussed topic could bring forth varied opinions.

"Would you prefer we imported no silver?" asked the Assistant Pilot. "And that Spain become poor as Africa? We could fight no wars against the infidels, and we could build few ships to sail the world. Armador's family would not like that."

Luis smiled and nodded.

"I know," replied Ribera, "but what a delicate balance, like trephining. When I open up a man's head, I must take a cautious approach, or he loses all his senses. The amount of silver provides much, but we know that an excess of anything breeds trouble."

"Ribera, as an honorable man, it may suit best that you attend to medicine and not to items of trade," said the Assistant Pilot, with an expression of condescension.

At that, Luis exchanged a glance with Sologuren, but neither entered the fray.

"I pose as your servant, sir, and retreat to medicine, even hastening to amputate your leg, should the need arise," Ribera said with a grin.

Following that, the table roared and another toast proposed, this time to a fair and comfortable voyage.

"Gentlemen, clear up the talk I hear of the Governor of Santo Domingo, our next stop," said Luis, making an effort to change the subject.

"What? That avaricious man, one that would sell his own mother for a real?" said Ribera.

"I too have heard less than favorable reports," said Sologuren.

"We plan just one night in port there, so maybe we shan't encounter him," added Ribera. "Say, Armador, curiosity strikes me. Why did you seek a commission? I know your family has a fine business."

"Well, let's just say that I desired adventure. Reading about da Vaca, Colón, and even Don Quixote inspired me. Spending time at my family's shipyards allowed me to see many sights that too gave me the desire."

"Enough from Mr. Quixote here. I'd like to hear about Porto Bello, where we shall spend a month or so. Who can tell me?" asked Alférez Sologuren.

"I'll try," said Surgeon Ribera. "It's mixed. A beautiful harbor surrounded by lush greenery, but the town reflects a pigsty. A village facing the water, it fosters disease, worsened when the *feria* starts. Thousands of ill-refined people milling about the fair stalls breed illnesses. Various temptations abound, which lure the sordid types from around the North Sea. Many maravedis change hands. And I can barely treat the many that succumb to *flux*. You know… the bowels' malady."

The evening concluded with another toast and then all retired.

***

"Black dogs, black dogs! You lazy *French* cannot even be called seadogs, you black dogs!" yelled a seaman on high. A chorus of oaths up top backed him, all directed toward the soldiers on deck. The day brought intense emotions to the surface, as the soldiers' lounging and cards continued to ingratiate the sailors. The soldiers retorted with an invitation to the seamen to - *come down and face us* - which they did.

Pushing, shoving and taunting from both crowds ensued when Luis came on deck. He knew of the tension that festered like a powder keg, waiting for a fuse match. Climbing atop the quarterdeck, he called for *at ease*.

"Give me your meanest seaman…and soldier likewise!"

Without hesitation, soldier Sgt. Valazco stepped forward. Shorter than most, but muscular, swarthy and bold with a large black mustache. Luis knew that he loved to fight, and for the most part, fairly.

From the crowd of seamen came a tall burly fellow with huge forearms and a barrel chest, many teeth missing and multiple scars, obvious tokens of previous fights. The two removed their shirts as a large circle formed. Gaming commenced at once.

"Come on, you toothless creature, let's see if we can rid you of the few you have left," said the Sergeant.

"Your head will be wrenched off and fed to the sharks," said the big man, a snarl on his face.

They moved around, eyeing each other amid shouts from all assembled. With lightning speed, the Sergeant circled low around the seaman, driving two punches to the kidney area. He winced but didn't go down. Turning, he brought a huge fist down onto the Sergeant's head, dropping him to the floor. The seaman lifted a huge foot to squash the Sergeant who rolled as his fellows lifted him up.

Valazco charged the sailor, tackling him and taking both to the floor. The Sergeant arose, fists at the ready, as the winded large man picked himself up. At once Valazco attacked him, delivering blow after blow to his head. The seaman staggered, but then grabbed the Sergeant in a bear hug, lifting him off the floor. By now the din had brought all on deck.

Bam!

From behind the crowd, a pistol shot rang out. All turned to see the Captain. Luis stepped up as the fighting stopped.

"I declare the fight a draw! The spirit of Spain lives among us!"

All cheered, then slowly moved away, the strain subsiding.

Luis feared of what might come next from his superior.

"Alférez, I've been watching," said the Captain. "You handled it well. But no need for it to continue till someone dies."

"Thank you, sir. I hope this relieves some of their frustrations."

Luis returned to his quarters to compose and allow his own emotions to subside. He lay awhile on his cot, trying to conjure up thoughts of a peaceful time. He dozed off and the image of Isabela came to him......

He'd just finished a term at the Universidad and on a certain Sunday walked up the Cathedral steps to join his padre and mamaceita inside for Mass. A bright spring day, blue skies, flowers in bloom, and birds singing. As the bell tolled, he glanced to see a carriage stop and a family exit. Mother, father, boy, and what he saw as a vision of an angel with white lace mantilla.

Her dark hair glistened, and her brown eyes cast a spell upon him. With senses overpowered, his focus became interrupted by two ambitious swains each offering her an arm of escort. He overheard the name Isabela, and something clicked in the back of his mind, but he could not recollect.

The young woman entreated her parents to allow her to tarry on the steps, with a promise to join them. Luis' shaky legs, with a mind of their own, moved in her direction.

"Luis? Luis Armador, is that you?"

He stared speechless, as her enchanting voice captivated him even more. So familiar, but…

"Luis, have you forgotten me, Isabela?" she said as she flashed a smile. With the two escorts taken aback, Luis reached for a hand to bestow a kiss of greeting.

"Weren't you the little brat who threw rocks at me and my friend from behind your garden gate?"

"Ah, yes, that was some years ago, before we moved away and now returned after six years. I gave up that habit. I don't recall striking anyone anyway.

"Ah, but you did. On one day, blood dripped onto my shirt from a rock to the head. I was scolded at home, but I didn't dare tell madre that a girl had done it."

Laughter ensued, with even the escorts' faces lighting up. But they implored Isabela to go inside, as the bell tolled again. Before entering, she glanced backward with a smile for Luis.

Eyes open, Luis stared at the low ceiling, a reminder he lay in his shipboard cubicle. With mind and muscles now at peace, he wanted to soon pen a letter to her.

***

SANTO DOMINGO, HISPANIOLA
April, 1622

Luis watched as Captain Nodal reboarded the galleon at midmorning. Grim-faced, he ordered the Boatswain to summon all officers for a briefing in his cabin.

Some problem? thought Luis. *And today we cast off for Cartagena?*

With all vessels secured the day before, at arrival, the Vice-Admiral had joined the Admiral on shore. They paid respects to the Governor and made arrangements for additional provisions. The fleet planned for one night at the port of Spain's oldest settlement in the Indies. That evening a few from the Atocha had made a brief foray into town to find a tavern. Most had stayed aboard, including Luis.

"Gentlemen, we face a predicament," said the Captain. He spoke in a serious tone to all gathered in his quarters.

Along with the senior officers and the Vice-Admiral, Luis stood with Alférez Sologuren. He noticed Pilot Ximenéz missing, an odd circumstance.

"Last evening our Pilot went into town to watchcare a few of our men that desired a tankard of ale. A fight broke out in a cantina, a man knifed to death. In the confusion, someone grappled with Ximenéz and pulled him into it. Next arrested by the Governor's soldiers, a murder charge fell on his head. I met with the Governor this morning and produced witnesses to the Pilot's innocence. Being a contemptible idiot, he wants to hold Ximenéz for trial several weeks hence. We have neither two weeks nor a Pilot to spare."

"What's his argument, sir?" asked the Sailing Master.

"His comment to me was, 'Captain, some things I cannot do. For example, I cannot restore my palace, as I lack the necessary 100 reales de a ocho.' So, do you see where that devil is trying to take this?"

Now red-faced, the Captain stood and slammed a book on his desk. Some in attendance jerked in response.

"We must have our Pilot, and not so much as a maravedi goes to the Governor! I'd like suggestions, as time is of the essence!"

"The prison's location, sir?" asked Boatswain Martin.

"A small jail, next to the fort. Suggestions, men, suggestions!"

"Opiate pills."

"What?" said the Captain.

"Opiate pills, sir," said Surgeon Ribera. "This evening, send a plate of food to our Pilot Ximenéz. As a courtesy, also provide the jailer with one. But in that one, I'll crumble sufficient pills to sedate him. When he passes out, our men can rescue the Pilot tonight."

"Brilliant, young man," said the Vice-Admiral.

"What of the exterior guards?" asked Luis.

"Ah, yes, the exterior guards," said the Captain. "A special plate for them too? Both of them?"

"Yes," said Ribera, "tell them compliments of our Captain. Ask them to treat our Pilot well. Maybe that will serve as a ploy. And tell the jailer inside the same."

"How long for the opiates to do their job, Surgeon?" asked the Vice–Admiral.

"Considering the dose I'm planning for each, not long. Once they consume the plate of food, they should be slumped in a deep sleep in no more than an hour. Without the food, it would be quicker."

"All right, gentlemen, this I propose," said Captain Nodal. "First, two of our men take in a longboat just after sunset. In plain dress, they enter the city gates as our steward apprentices. No weapons. They approach the guards and the jailer as my representatives bearing special victuals. Afterwards, they hide in the shadows and wait 45 minutes. Then they return to lift the keys after the opiates take effect."

"Excellent Captain, I assume responsibility with you. But who goes on the mission?" asked the Vice-Admiral, glancing around the cabin.

"I, sir," said Luis, surprising all.

"And I, sir," said Alférez Sologuren. "It's a good plan. And we know the officers back us."

"Very good, gentlemen, plan to leave at eight tonight. Master, please have the Steward prepare the food and deliver to our Surgeon for preparation."

As Luis descended below to his quarters to prepare for the evening's foray, his mind turned backward. He recalled the family story of his birth, when Grandfather Juan came to his room. Holding him aloft, he vowed to ensure a commission for Luis in the military, using his influence as a shipwright, often for the monarchy. Thus, to Luis, volunteering for the mission came naturally.

My family may not be the de Leóns or the Guzmáns, but they still remain proud hidalgo.

***

"Well, Armador, feeling a kinship with Cortés?" asked Sologuren, as he manned the oars and smiled.

"I have noticed it since the ship pulled away from Seville," said Luis. "But I don't think Hernán would be attired in these peasant clothes."

"What if the guards ask us to taste the food first, Luis, as a test?"

"No, their desire to devour it all will prevent that."

At the small jail, next to the Tower of Homage fort, the men presented the plates, which all accepted. They kept the unadulterated one for Ximenéz and whispered to him of the plan, which he accepted with glee. As they left, the jailer ignored them, gorging on his gift of food, which included sugar treats to make it even more palatable. Walking into the now dimly-lit yard, the belching of the two guards greeted them as they passed.

"So far, so good," said Luis, as they hid in the silent darkened town.

"If other military discover us leaving with Ximenéz, do you foresee combat?" asked Sologuren.

"Yes, if odds favor us. We have a mission. Otherwise, no."

After timing their wait as best as possible, they eased into the shadows outside the jail. Both guards sat with backs to the outside wall, muskets in their laps. Sound asleep. Snoring.

"Unsnap the leather key ring from that one's belt," whispered Luis. "I'll place their guns out of sight, just in case."

"Unlocking the outer door, the men crept into the darkened office, feeling their way, trying to recall the layout. From over in the corner, the jailer thrashed and snorted in a fitful but deep sleep. Sologuren passed his hand along the wall, hoping he'd find the keys he remembered hanging on a peg.

"Not there," he whispered.

Luis joined him, moving along the walls trying to grasp the keys.

Crash!

"What was that?" said Luis.

"The unlit lantern," said Sologuren.

The men stopped, waiting for another sound. None came. Only snoring.

"Luis, Cristóbal!" They heard a whispered cry from Ximenéz's cell. "He put the keys in his desk. Try there."

Fumbling around, finding a small desk, Luis began opening drawers.

"Here, I found them," he said.

Luis unlocked the cell door in the dark and Ximenéz walked out. He relocked it and placed the keys back in the drawer. The men stole out the front, gathering the three plates as they left. They relocked the outside door and placed the keys back on the guard.

"The prisoner now manifests as vanished." said Luis.

Glancing at the sleeping guards, Pilot Ximenéz said, "I trust their sleep remains deep."

"Yes, no awakening for them till morning, about the time of our embarkation with you aboard."

The men walked the Calle de las Palmas, enroute to the ship, passing the Governor's stately home. In the moonlight, Luis noticed the contrast between its opulence and the narrow, sandy streets holding stagnant water and garbage. They passed the city gates' guard with Ximenéz posing as a tottering drunk seaman that they escorted back to the Atocha. The shipyard building came into view and led them to the boat. As they paddled toward the Atocha's lights, Ximenéz expressed gratefulness.

"Thank you, thank you, gentlemen. Never have I experienced such treatment. Arrested for something I didn't commit. I didn't even have a weapon. Thanks to the Captain and I presume the Surgeon for his opiates. How can I thank you?"

"Treat us to a slab of steak in Cartagena," said Luis.

"My delight," said the Pilot.

At daylight the fleet heard the fort's bells ringing in alarm as the last ship sailed away. The launching of chase vessels never commenced.

***

CARTAGENA, COLUMBIA
May 2, 1622

One by one, each of the eight ships slipped through the narrow Boca Chica passage to deep harbor. A walled city, one of Spain's wealthiest in the Indies, it flourished as a major port. The Admiral planned a short stay.

Luis, on his first visit into town, witnessed a mulatto sale taking place in the plaza. Having never before seen a spectacle as this, he accepted it, but it disconsoled him.

"Do they all come from Africa?" he asked Boatswain Martín, with whom he toured."Yes, they do. The ones that don't survive the passage go to a watery grave, buried in the deep. The Portuguese operate it, allowed by our monarchy. Some 4,000 a year, I believe."

Luis gazed at the forlorn, barely-clad souls, bunched together on the square like animals. Guards stood nearby, one holding a lash. A sadness pervaded his countenance, the first in a long time, perhaps since José drowned. He even concealed a trace of guilt when he thought of his own privileged life.

Time passed at a clip in port. The seamen unloaded silks, linens, flour, oil, wine, and spices for the local merchants. Then they loaded gold, silver, and Bolivian emeralds onto the galleons. Two weeks passed and the Terre Firme fleet departed, headed to Porto Bello to acquire the major delivery of silver.

***

PORTO BELLO
May, 1622

Boom! Boom! Boom! Boom!

Gun salutes roared from Fort San Felipe as the fleet sailed into the harbor, which held water deep and wide enough for 300 galleons. Admiral Colón had delighted in its discovery. Raucous cheers sounded on the shipdecks in reply to the cannons, as dreams of fanciful nights danced in the crews' eyes.

"Behold Porto Bello, Spain's jewel of the Indies, at least for a few months of the year," said Pilot Ximenéz to Luis. "Time to gird up your fortitude," he voiced with a hint of resignation. "All the revels of the Spanish Main await our men, and we must attempt to dissuade them. A monastery it is not."

"You echo our Surgeon. Please continue."

"Feria elicits all manner of merrymaking and allures. The rum and victuals entice, as do the women in the dark places. The pestilences lurk in every hovel, shanty and tavern. Each year at this time, 300 to 400 die."

Porto Bello rose imposingly with its forts and hillside gun emplacements overlooking the harbor. It reigned as the port of embarkation for all the Peruvian silver brought across the narrow Panamá isthmus from the Pacific. Once a year it became the most important port in the New World. That evening brought all the crew onto the top deck for the Captain to speak.

"Men, the unloading of merchant goods takes a month. No one sleep in town. Miss curfew and face the lash. Then feria and the silver loading onto the galleons begin. I would like everyone alive and well when we sail in about two months, so be cautious what goes into your bellies and try to avoid the French Pox. Mercury cannot be considered a cure of certainty."

He paused a few moments, gathering his thoughts for a final

volley of words.

"Here, they acquire our pesos but not our souls!" his voice rising as if a horn had been lifted to his lips and blared. "The safest time in town? Daylight, when the gentility of the Spanish Main trade with our merchants."

Perspiration filled his brow with his white shirt soaked at the armpits. He impressed Luis, who wanted to keep his own
humors in balance and his health intact. He would mind what entered his mouth and would forego tempting pleasures. He knew many others would not do the same and would suffer.

***

Armador and Sologuren talked at their meal one evening after several weeks in Porto Bello.

"What do you make of the port, Luis?"

"The harbor and vegetation provide beauty. But it stops there. A village set in a half-moon design, homes of wood, but only a few for hidalgos. Without feria, one has no life. As a career soldier, after marriage I want to take Isabela to Habana to live. She will like a city of its size. I hope someday to be a galleon captain."

"What does she think of those plans?" asked Sologuren.

Facing Sologuren and appearing sheepish, he responded.

"Well….I haven't really discussed it with her yet."

Sologuren gazed with perplexity at Luis, but did not comment.

"Garrison duty here would not be my top choice," said Sologuren. "One might live almost as a cimmarón. You know, it's been said the monarchy thought years ago of building a canal to the Pacific, to accommodate the silver shipment across this narrow country. What if….."

Boom! Boom! Boom! Boom!

Cannon fire from the fort broke their conversation and they hurried to the top deck.

"The Marquis de Cadereita and four Armada galleons sail in, to complete our fleet," said Luis.

"Ahh, our Captain–General. But no silver yet from across Panamá to greet him," said Sologuren. "He won't arrive pleased. Look for him to take action."

Luis penned another letter to Isabela and planned to place it on a merchant vessel headed to Seville.

***

Porto Bello
June 11, 1622
My dearest,
How long the days and nights are without you. Your presence is always on my mind.

I trust all is well there and that your hours are filled with activities. I will try to provide high points of our recent sailings which cover quite a period.

Prior to achieving port at Santo Domingo, I was able to quell a near-brawl, for which, happily, the Captain commended me. Then in Santo Domingo we had to bring about the escape of our Pilot from the local guardhouse. He had been falsely accused by the unworthy governor.

We've been in Porto Bello one month now, where there is a beautiful harbor but a dirty town, which may be the worst of the Indies. In your your honor, I would be naught to bring you here. Habana would be much more preferred. I have made many friends on this journey, but with no doubt, the best is Alférez Cristóbal Sologuren, a fellow young officer also on his first voyage.

As I send the letter, much of my heart goes with it to you. The love of my soul and the desires of my life are yours. Please pass my love to mamaceita.
Two months to see you my love,

Luis

5
SILVER TRAIN
July, 1622

There lies Peru with its riches;
Here, Panamá with its poverty,
Choose, each man, what bes becomes
A brave Castilian.

Francisco Pizzaro

PORTO BELLO

Whump!

The Marquis' fist slammed onto the Governor's table.

"Whence comes the Silver Train?! Two days ago I sent a rider to that imbecile President in Panamá City!"

The Governor did his best to conceal it, but he trembled.

They sat to converse at El Cabildo, the government house on the town's smaller square. Clean-shaven, prematurely gray, and a determined visage, the Marquis commanded respect. Attired in pale green with silver braiding and a striped doublet, he wore black boots, polished to perfection. The previous night they enjoyed a vast repast. With all the fleet's senior officers, they drank deep and exalted one another. This day dawned to a different mood.

"We need the galleons loaded and be on our way so to avoid the hurricane season! The king demands his silver!"

"Marquis, they walk El Camino Real, which takes at least three days from Panamá City. It is thick jungle, mountains and receives daily rains. I'm certain of their arrival late this afternoon or in the morning," said the Governor, timidly. "Otherwise, a cadre of our soldiers stands ready to hasten up the trail to find them. Please, go enjoy the feria."

The Marquis departed, satisfied for the moment but unsmiling. His guards followed, as he walked through town, impressive with a feathered hat, gleaming sword with black scabbard and belt. With a dignified stride, to many he conveyed a posture only one rung below the monarchy.

Walking to the waterfront, he stopped to observe the Rosario and the Candelaria, careened for caulking and shipworms removal. With due payment, he had acquired the Rosario galleon in port to augment his guardian fleet. This gave him a sense of accomplishment for the time being.

***

Panamá City
Pacific Coast

Jasper hoisted the heavy bags of silver atop his pack mule. Taken across the mountains from Potosí, Peru, shipped from Lima on the Pacific coast, a fortune sat in Panamá City. It awaited the overland trek. Jasper and the mulattos looked forward to the walk to Porto Bello, as the ship stifled and confined them. Three days through the thick jungle loomed along the stone-lined path. The Congo, now a mere wisp in his memory, would never again be Jasper's home. He long ago made peace with that. But he didn't care for the word Jasper, some silly English name the Portuguese slavers bestowed on him. He was Lunga.

Soon a hundred black muleteers would stretch three and a half leagues in single file as the famous Silver Train. When the mounted trailmaster made the call, mules, mulattos and guards would begin. With staggered starts, it could take almost a week of continuous arrivals on the North Sea coast to the east. The Spanish dreamed of silver, but Jasper dreamed of escape. Someday, somehow. He thought of it daily. Walking, he reached up and stroked his nosebone, a lone, tangible reminder of his status as a warrior. He wondered, too, of how life would be as a cimarón...*they who lived in the woods as runaways slaves and sometimes stalked town womenfolk drawing water from the river.*

The first day's heat grew oppressive. The second, cooler, as they ascended the mountains. Afternoons brought drenching tropical rains. The Africans, by some good fortune, did not contract malaria and other tropical diseases, as did the natives and Europeans.

"Never have I passed on a trail as this," said Jasper to a friend. "The jungle is above us as well as to the sides. No stars at night."

"True," said his friend. "It is thick and contains us like a mine. But after another day and night, we come to the ocean and unload the silver. What will happen next? Back to the mines or sold at auction?"

***

PORTO BELLO

Silver!
The call went up from town as the first of the muleteers arrived. Twenty to begin, then another twenty daily, all over five days, untill 100 had come. Silver upon silver-bars, coins, and an assortment-filled the Royal Treasure House. It spilled over into the street, sidling next to the building, with guards doubled, then tripled, and some thinking that inadequate. For those

close enough to watch, it bedazzled, but most stayed a distance, fearing a harquebus ball.

"Let not your fingers be tempted," said Silvermaster Jacove de Vreder to his clerks. "At this point, our charge is to register and affix seals. Then, see that our load of precious metals make transfer to the Atocha and that our Manifest is accurate."

He sounded an order repeated by each vessel's silvermaster. Above all, their central focus led to making certain the king acquired his quinto, or 20% tax, on all silver.

"No one likes the tax," said the Assistant Pilot. "In fact, smuggling is commonplace and overlooked. How many pesos have you stowed away, Luis?"

Luis recoiled from the question, proposed from a man he thought honorable.

"Nada. Is it expected of me?"

"No, not by the crown or by our Captain. But don't be surprised should the abundance tempt you."

Now Luis wondered not only about his own cross currents, but about his enforcement duties.

Did Captain Nodal's warnings come only as a perfunctory ritual or did he give it in sincerity? And from whence did this all-consuming desire for silver arise?

***

The coming of silver and the annual feria provided for Luis scenes both amazing and appalling.

Daytime activity drew wealthy citizens from towns like Lima and Panamá City for their yearly purchases. Great sailcloths were spread over booths that sheltered spices, silks, stockings and exquisite European wares for sale. Merchants and agents filled their money bags. Nighttime drew the vessels' workmen as well as renegades of the North Sea to torch-lit booths. Though debilitated from the days' labors, seamen sought to refortify with rum.

To Luis, the evening scene produced a crowd direct from some netherland. Fights and stabbings were common, with even known pirates permitted to mingle. He stared wide-eyed at the bucaneros, the most sordid. Island cattle hunters, many French, who bothered not to clean their shirts, smeared with dried blood from butchering. Leather caps, hogskin boots, and huge knives on their belts signaled their presence.

"Flux, bloody flux!"

Luis watched an early evening scene on the Atocha's deck as a seaman wailed, staggered on deck, and pleaded with the Surgeon to treat his emaciated form. Given nutmeg, he downed it and proceeded to sit at the head of the ship, lining up with many others. Some would be alive in a few weeks, some would not. In town he saw men's pants bloody from the knees down. Some squatted over heated bricks for a cure, and some lay lifeless from opium taken as another flux remedy.

A slave auction struck the strongest chord. Alférez Sologuren and Luis observed one taking place at the Plaza
de la Mar. *Their forms seem ghost-like,* thought Luis, as a wave of emptiness washed over him.

"What keeps them all from swallowing dirt?"

"I don't know, but notice the one about a foot taller than the rest," said Sologuren.

"The one with a bone through his nose and with his head held high?"

"Yes. If a revolt came about, I believe he would lead it. Yet his buyer can fetch twice by re-selling him in Santo Domingo for a sugar plantation."

As they passed through town to the quay, Luis saw black flies swarming, putrid food discarded, standing water from almost daily rains, and the lack of sanitation.

Given this mass of humanity, no wonder this place produces fevers, flux, and even gangrene on untreated wounds. Admiral Colón would be saddened at his puerto de belleza, mused Luis.

***

Overseeing his soldiers on duty presented an unusual episode in town.

"Your mercy, may I aid you?" said Luis.

The well-dressed gentlemen on the pier watched every movement of silver bars being loaded for sailing. His eyes darted from the bars to his papers and back, as if he expected Drake, the famed privateer, to appear. Luis knew most treasure from Potosí mines found ownership in individuals but handled by shippers or agents. He was curious. The man eyed Luis for a few moments, then replied with a polite *no, but thank you.*

"Alférez, I am Lorenzo de Arriola, fresh from Potosí and Lima. I came with the Silver Train from Panamá City to
accompany my 60 silver ingots. Since the Silvermaster finished the registration, I wanted to watchcare the loading. I have been in Perú for ten years and am now sailing to Seville to visit my patron."

Luis wished him well and left him alone, as he continued to focus on his bars in the manner of a miser. He suspected Arriola profited from either slave trading or mining. A few bars exposed from the wooden cases displayed Arriola's silver mark, an A and an L overlapping, with a light square at the top. It looked to Luis like *a man walking.* Soon the gentleman and his stevedores departed on a loaded barge for the Atocha.

***

"A scant three weeks of feria and it claims 200 creatures to malaria and flux! Fortunately for the Atocha, we've only lost one page and two soldiers. No one knows the number affected by French pox. I don't want to know."

Captain Nodal, disgusted and dejected, waved away with his left hand, as if to say *good riddance*. He stood briefing the Vice-Admiral as they waited for all hands to assemble on deck. Two months in port and now two days prior to departure, he wanted to address the crew.

"Felipe IV and his Minister Olivares will be pleased," said the Vice-Admiral, "as we have much aboard that will produce royal revenues. But I imagine there is also much that has not passed the Silvermaster's table. We also have 48 new passengers to transport. That includes some nobility, whom I will do my best to comfort."

"Yes, I counted 14 on the passenger list that have Don or Doña added to their name. We're even hauling 21,000 reales de a ocho due to a descendant of Admiral Colón. 100 years later and his family still profits," said the Captain, shaking his head.

***

"Quiet! Now hear the Captain!" shouted Boatswain Martín, as Nodal stood atop the forecastle to address the gathering.

"All seamen and soldiers must be aboard early tomorrow night. Unless already on the ship, you must be at the quay for longboats' embarkation at 9 P.M. The following morning we cast off. Any man not at tomorrow evening's 10 P.M. muster will be sought, captured and brought aboard. His back will receive 25 lashes. The Atocha's success depends on you. Were anything to go awry, I alone would be held accountable to the crown. We look forward to a successful voyage home after we stop at Cartagena and Habana."

Luis sensed that success rose as a high point of honor for the Captain, as if the fate of Spain itself resided in his hands. He also knew that if there were deserters, he and the soldiers would be needed.

At next sunrise, as a sliver of orange appeared on the horizon, the men paddled to the dock for final labors. After all cargo had been transferred to the ship during the day, the penned animals in Porto Bello were brought aboard. As the day waned, excitement spread among the boarding passengers, eager now for home. About the time the sun flamed in the west, all merchants that would sail closed their feria booths. As expected, a final night in town enticed many crew members.

"Two men not accounted for!"

Luis was lounging on deck about 9:30 that evening, while lanterns glowed for boarding. One of the longboats bellowed the news that two missed the planned ferry. Desertions loomed as probabilities. Luis' stomach knotted into a dull ache.

It's like the Canaries, he thought.

"Alférez Armador!"

Luis made haste.

"My Captain, I am here."

With balled fists and reddened cheeks, he faced Luis ready to spew fire.

"Take a Corporal and four soldiers and find the pigs! I want them alive! For the lash, they will *kiss the cannon*, perhaps the *mast* and maybe the *ocean floor*! Don't return without them!"

"Yes, sir, thank you for the honor to serve. We hasten to the task!"

At the same time, the mixed twinges of fortitude and anxiety passed through Luis. After his briefing on the missing, all six men, well-armed, set out in a longboat. They all shared the same angst.

Soon as the soldiers pulled away, gaming began on deck. Along with a host of others, the Assistant Pilot and Alférez Sologuren wagered 10 maravedis each on the capture of both deserters. Sologuren favored Luis and his men. Upon witnessing the display, Chaplain Val was stricken. Gaming surfaced often enough, but when it involved their own men's lives, he stood dumbfounded. He considered calling for Mass and a sermon.

Approaching the quay, they could hear the rousing noise, see the street torches and smell pots of food on barbacoas. With clanking swords and harquebuses, they scrambled from the boat. Somewhere above the din of town could be heard the lilting voice of a woman singing.

A siren song, thought Luis, as he grouped them together.

"Now hear me. The soldier's name is Yglesia. He's of average height and bears a scar over the left eyebrow. The seaman is called Gobeo, a Basque. Blond hair, with one hand missing a finger. They both enjoy rum and fighting, so they will not lay down for us. We will have to overpower them."

Plowing through the rabble, spilled rum, and the fights, the soldiers inquired at booths and cantinas. Responses of scowled-faced *no's* and inebriated laughter greeted them. With arms at the ready they persisted, until, in a low-ceilinged, pitiful ale hut, they came upon Yglesia. He shared a table with a loud and ragged bunch. The word went out and Luis' squad converged.

Yglesia snarled at Luis, his long matted black hair shining in the lantern light. Forsaking all military bearing, he wore a red bandana on his forehead.

A freshly bloodied ear, a victim of the evening, now joined his scarred eyebrow.

"Stop, Alférez!" he shouted. "I am not returning to that dungeon of a galleon and that heretic of a Captain! He shan't pull any more work from me!" He followed the tirade with a quaff of ale that spilled from his mouth, dousing his shirt.

Drawing his sword, Luis unleashed a swath across the table, scattering all but Yglesia. While his men leveled their harquebuses on the dungy crowd, Luis made his case.

"Come with us, you runaway, and take your lashes, or prepare to spill your red blood on the dirt floor."

Yglesia rose with a growl and drew his sword. Blades clanged as the two combatants fought, moving onlookers right, and then left. With the crowd noise escalating and bets hastily made, cold steel swished and swirled. Three minutes into it and Luis took a cut to his left arm. He then twisted his torso and slashed his adversary's right calf muscle, sending him to the floor. A sword handle hard to the back of his head and he became their prisoner. Two men bound, then dragged him through the streets to the longboat, his cries being heard long after midnight aboard ship. This left Luis with three men to now search for Gobeo.

Word came down that he left walking west on El Camino Real in the company of several deviant cimaróns. All knew that an ambuscade possibility existed anytime from a group such as that. Luis cautioned the men to be ever ready as they proceeded on the stone road in pursuit. They alternated leading with the torch, with the others walking single file to the rear. Should the group they sought leave the path, it would be impossible to find them at night. Luis admonished the men to speed along, as their eyes balanced more and more with the dark. Eerie night sounds arose from the jungle in the form of big cat screeches and monkey howlings, more cause to keep the soldiers on edge.

After an hour, ahead they saw a dim glow and heard murmurings. The night soon became brighter and the voices louder. Here was the knot of cimmaróns, some white, some dark-skinned. Nearing the group, Luis observed eight of the scraggliest-looking men to be found in Panamá. Gobeo, blond and absent the one index on his left hand, sprawled on the ground. His unkempt beard and four missing teeth accentuated his eye of depravity. He looked easy for the taking, but Luis knew better.

As the torch cast its light on the group, Luis' eyes went from one man to another, appraising the circumstances. Ripples of light reflected from dirty pools of water along the trail, and the adjacent thick jungle growth stood as a palisade. Though the group looked somber and listless, Luis knew he had to act.

"Get up, you blackheart! Be taken back to the ship or plan to die!"

Springing to his feet, Gobeo lunged in Luis' direction but fell, tripping on the road stones.

"Fire to the Heavens!" ordered Luis.

All three soldiers fired, and the cimmaróns scattered like hogs chased to the slaughter. Some ran down the trail, and some disappeared into the almost impenetrable jungle. Reeking of rum and emboldened, Gobeo drew his sword, yelling at Luis.

"Arg! You won't take me, you pig of an alférez!"

He thrust toward Luis, moving with hostility thick as smoke. Luis sidestepped, hit him aside the head with the butt of his sword, and he went down. No swordfight and Gobeo lay subdued, bound, and set to march back to town. All defiance now gone, he pleaded to stay in the jungle, as should he return to Spain, the constabularies would seek him. Luis instead took time to rebuke him.

"A masterless man has no allegiance, and you, my captive, shall soon have your countenance reversed."

Nearer town, songs of the dissolute bawled in the night, as feria neared an inglorious end. Luis' sense of accomplishment heightened as he thought of the morrow and sailing. He looked forward to departing from the sordidness of Porto Bello and arriving again at Cartegena. Somewhere in Flanders, cannon smoke swirled, blood flowed, and Castile's standard stood high. Tonight, however, on the edge of the Spanish Main, Alférez Armador felt proud to serve King Felipe IV, regardless of how small the task.

***

Morning and Gobeo received his lashes, Luis shuddering at each. All cargo loaded and new provisions secured. The fleet would leave many new gravesites and the surviving sick would become patients in Cartagena's hospital. Embarkation shone as a grander scene than the arrivals, as a new total of 13 craft now sailed away, saluted by the Fort's guns.

They made harbor again in Cartagena in late July, so more treasure and goods could be loaded. A few passengers gained passage while the post-feria fatigued crew garnered some rest time. By now, the remaining 15 smaller ships of Terre Firme sailed in after taking on cargo from the islands, having separated earlier from the Marquis' guardian ships that had gone on to Porto Bello. Now, 28 vessels strong composed the fleet, poised for sailing to Habana in August, enroute to Spai

6

LA FLORIDA

September, 1 6 2 2

It was a melancholy spectacle we were
Compelled to witness.
Atocha galleon survivor

OFF FLORIDA'S SW COAST

As Luis continued tossing about on mammoth waves in the Gulf,
recalling recent months' events, another scene unfolded on the Atocha.
First light on September 6, 1622, and ashen clouds allowed only make-
believe day. But a few seamen ventured onto the Atocha's top deck.
Waves continued pounding as the vessel lumbered along, out of control.
The foremast long gone, and plankings, railings, sails, and riggings missing
or in disarray.

"Put down the stream anchors, men!" yelled Boatswain Martín, as he
attempted a slowdown in momentum.

"They sounded at two hundred feet!" yelled a sailor. "Maybe it will
hold!"

"Try the bow anchors!" came the next order.

Loud snaps, like pistols firing, rang out as all three anchor lines snapped
in succession, their ends whipping back like lashes. With tiller and rudder
of no use, the high sterncastle caught the wind and spun the galleon
backwards into a one-hundred eighty degree turn.

"It's useless!" yelled the Boatswain, his anguish rising.

Dismayed, spent seamen staggered below, their vessel now headed
straight for the deadly reefs. Downstairs, passengers and crew waited,
prayed, moaned, and accepted their probable fate. Chaplain Val and the
three Agustínian friars aboard continued hearing confessions. Several
passengers in the forecastle, beset by terror, forced open the hatch to the
outside. As they spilled onto the top deck, waves swept them overboard.

With a heavy load of ballast, cannon, and treasure, the Atocha continued
to wallow, and with an eighteen-foot draft, it ran susceptible to shallow
coral. With no one in its path, the top of the mizzen mast crunched and fell

to the deck with a resounding crash. Flailing overboard, it left the bottom half and five lashed seamen in shock.

The Atocha crossed the outer reef. Riding a fifteen-foot crescendo, it ploughed into a hole and struck the inner reef. Amidst cracking and snapping, a gaping hole opened in the ship's lower bow, pouring in water. Above, the main mast shuddered, cracked, and fell into pieces. The crash loosened two cannons from their cradles and caromed them around the gun deck below, battering helpless passengers and crew.

At 7 A.M., with hatch covers firmly in place, the magnificent galleon Nuestra Señora de Atocha, with 260 souls, less any that washed overboard, sank in 55 feet of ocean, about four leagues west of a nameless group of islands. The only survivors were the five hardy men tied to the above-water mizzen mast, protruding like a woeful towering tombstone.

***

I am but a cork, floating about at the whims of the universe.

Luis' thoughts again returned to the present.

He knew not whence nature would take him, but he perceived possibly north. That meant somewhere toward the coast of La Florida. Time and space lost all concept, and he muddled as to what had taken place, his mental grasp elusive. He flashbacked to some of the prior shipwreck stories told to him. So many allowed few survivors. The ones that did survive, unless fortunate enough to be rescued, often met with further horrific travails.

To his joy, the sun shone at mid-afternoon, the wind and waves lessened, and the rain stopped. Luis became aware that the melee had ripped away his trousers, but that his shirt remained intact due to his cross-chest leather strap. As the day began to unwind, the sun dropped from behind dissipating clouds at the horizon, which he noted was at his back. Thoughts began to rise.

What of the Atocha? Did it sink? Did all survive? What of the other twenty-seven ships in the fleet? Would there be boats looking for survivors? Am I presumed dead? Can I escape bites from sharks and jellyfish, and the plucking of my eyes by albatross? What fate awaits on shore, if I make it to shore?

Dusk approached as strong breezes continued to push Luis northeastward. Between waves, he imagined seeing specks of land in the distance. His muscles relaxed now, but apprehension lingered. Fighting to stay awake, he held onto the plank. Reality posed that he might not survive should it slip away.

Night came, and he drifted, seeing a thousand stars above, but absent that fateful new moon. The conjunction theory still bewildered him, but he acknowledged some validity. Brief dreams came to him, or, he thought, pure manifestations of his terror-filled mind. *Monsters, dog-faced men, one-breasted Amazon women, cannibals, lagartos, and large snakes.* Though waves would revive him, he still lapsed into some unknown place where….*leeches, guinea worms, heathen sacrifices, slavery, and maladies with no cures* were thrust upon him. He heard gentle rolls of the sea, and, with a parched mouth, he longed for the morn.

When dawn's first light broke, his spirits lifted. Now he could see plain and clear a grouping of islands within swimming distance. But he was scant strong enough to swim. In time, he washed up on the tiny beach of a low-lying vegetated isle, crawled on shore, and closed his eyes. Through grogginess, he felt his body warming. It had been stiff and drawn, like a doused shirt that had shrunk. To his gratification, his organs still functioned, even after the coldness he experienced.

Bites like the pricking of pins, along with a whining in the ears, told him he had met La Florida's mosquitoes. He crawled back into the water to avoid them. Desperate, he rose from the sea and did his best to cover his body with sand, hoping to deter the little creatures.

Remembering his sword as well as the leather satchel gift around his waist, he sat to open it. It was a boon, holding 25 silver reales de a ocho, bound in cords, plus an assortment of survival gear. Flint, stone, metal fishhook, cord-line, tiny knife, small bottle of purgative secured in padding, and a shirt, covered in oilskin. To Luis, it all appeared as *manna from Heaven.* Silvermaster Jacove de Vreder must have cared for his welfare and somehow sensed impending doom. Thankful beyond belief, he knew with this kit and his sword, he mustered a chance. The coins would be of no value in the wilderness, but would when he reached a Spanish settlement.

Time to seek sustenance. The island consisted of scrub vegetation, palmettos, palms, weeds, and mangroves. From time spent in Porto Bello he knew it held little fruit. If food could be found, it must come from the water. With trembling hands, he speared a small crab onto the hook and attached it to the cord line.

A small fish bit in the shallow water, and with little labor he hauled it in. Using the knife to sever the head and empty it of entrails, he cut it into small pieces. Savored, these bits of flesh produced life-giving fresh water. Preparing a fire challenged him, as finding dry tender took searching, but with persistence he succeeded. He used his flint, and soon small fish bits roasted over embers. He caught more fish, and with each cooked morsel, his strength returned.

Meandering, he discovered a low tide bar on the island's back side, which revealed all the oysters he could eat. Bare feet soon bloodied, but he deemed it necessary if he wanted food. Forcing open the shells required the aid of his sword, which never left his side. The afternoon he spent enjoying rest, nourishment, and warm sunshine, and that evening he gathered branches and leaves for a pallet. Stoking his fire produced smoke that he allowed to cover his body. It burned his eyes and made him cough, but he hoped it would deter the mosquitoes. That night he passed in sound sleep.

Peace. Awakening refreshed and with a restored sense of confidence, he recalled his grandfather's words.....*first, relax the body, control emotions, then you can think...and take action. All alone? True, but I also contain within me all the encouragements and moldings of my family, along with my military training.*

He determined to grasp hope and recalled that courage is action in the face of fear. Luis estimated his time drifting in the water some fifteen hours. With the varying wind speeds, he figured the drift took him at least thirty leagues to reach shore. Somewhere out there Castile beckoned to him, and he resolved to return.

Habana must lie to the south or southwest. Would a raft take me there? Could I paddle that far? Would the ocean river take me away? Privateers? Should I strike for San Agustín, far to the northeast? How? Is my memory of the Pilot's map sufficient? Should I attempt to join the natives so to survive and to await rescue? Is that safe?

Perplexed. But he soon realized his hunger upon spying a pigeon–type bird perched above his head. He reached for a stone and sent it straight to the mark. Roasted over the fire, it satisfied like beefsteak. Walking down the small beach area, Luis noticed large white shells discarded in piles, either by humans or animals. One area disclosed what looked like a canal from the ocean into the island's interior. It stretched about 15' wide and 50' long. If manmade, he presumed it served some purpose.

On the north end of the island a current flowed from east to west through an apparent inlet, as does a river. Walking out, he found all the water shallow until closer to the ocean, west of the inlet. With morning fog still hanging, he observed movement out in the inlet.

Vague forms, maybe Indios, he thought.

Back on the bank, an enormous creature waddled onto shore. Three feet long and almost as wide. A huge turtle of which Luis needed to partake meat and juice. Rolling it onto its back, he severed the head with one hack of the sword. Kneeling, he struggled with the blade to remove the enormous shell. All of a sudden he became aware of pain on his left forearm. Looking down, to his horror, the severed head had clamped on with its jaws. Excruciating discomfort almost dulled his ability to react. He switched the sword blade from the shell to the detached head and with much strength pried it open. The bite marks sank a quarter-inch deep and blood oozed. Tearing an old cloth from his satchel, he wrapped the arm to stop the bleeding.

Alférez Sologuren would have chuckled at this scene.

The pain endured, but he retrieved the meat, savored some juice, and prepared a roast. Recovering from the head's attack gave cause for the meal to taste even more succulent. He smiled. As usual, he let smoke cover his body to alleviate the stinging insects that evening.

No more nightmares? Even on land?

Arising the next morning to the singing of birds and dolphins blowing, he realized newfound freedom from night terrors that had stalked him. He welcomed the cleansing. With a foggy morning again, in the distance he caught a glimpse of men in canoes, or so he thought. Once again, the scene passed veiled, with no noise. He sipped dew droplets from large leaves nearby to quench his thirst, then bent down to stoke the still warm banked coals from the evening's cookfire. Time came to pursue breakfast from the shallow warm waters at his feet. No solution of deliverance came to him overnight, but he knew with a certainty it would.

Without warning, from out of the mist, three dugouts came forward, each carrying two men. They spoke not, but peered at him with steely-brown eyes. One occupant in each craft stood and held his lance aloft, at the ready. Luis thought to draw his sword, but knew before it cleared the scabbard he would be speared. He tried an alternative, to convey a sense of welcome, but no one moved or spoke. Taller than him, with red-tinted skin and black hair pulled together on top, their bodies showed lean and muscular. They wore loincloths of animal skin as their only apparel, except for small earrings and beaded necklaces.

Luis grasped that this posed not as a tavern encounter, nor even an emerging military engagement. Much quieter. As he tried to gauge their next move, they stood like statues in a town plaza.

I will not die without a fight.

Uttering no sound, the natives eased out of the dugouts. Aware of his status as interloper, if necessary, he would engage them. As he backed up, ready to fight, another native unheard and unseen approached from behind and applied a large club to the back of his head. Time once again escaped him. An aching head, tightly bound limbs, and now a prisoner, he lay in the bottom of a canoa. He could only see sky and hear paddles dipping into water. No plans came now for effecting a rescue scheme, his current fate decided.

His worst fears realized, he moaned, knowing he'd become captive to the Calusa, southwest La Florida's fiercest tribe. He knew that Spanish castaways often suffered torture, slavery, and sometimes death. Even cannibalism was rumored. That he still could breathe became his one redeeming thought.

After setting woven fishnets at the canal entrance of his island, they paddled to the island's north end, then turned east. He supposed they would return after the tide ebbed so to gather the fish. After about thirty minutes of paddling, they arrived at a larger island. It teemed with activity at a settlement just off the mainland. In an apparent act to show dominance, one of the natives heaved Luis' sword and satchel high into the limbs of a large tree. They would serve as marked reminders of his captivity. With a rope binding his neck and weariness in his heart, he was led into the village and his tether tied to a tree. He lay in stark wonder and fear. Like the men, the women wore little, except for moss draped below the waist. Each gleamed with oil, spread to combat mosquitoes and small bugs. Luis could only watch in silence.

About mid-day they squatted around a fire and enjoyed meals of smoked oysters or fish, consumed with no utensils. Glancing in Luis' direction, a native with a menacing look tossed something in his direction. Luis hungered, but the sight of entrails in the dirt did not look appealing. He decided to wait and see how long he could go hungry. Later they did provide boiled pumpkin leaves to munch and a cup of garfish oil to coat his body. That night as he lay under the tree in his bed of dirt, he decided to do whatever it took to survive.

He would adapt and keep his mouth shut. He would comply, but plan an escape, though he knew not when an opportunity would arise. Along the Main many knew that the Calusa often did not kill their captives for fear of retaliation. They did make slaves, some of whom spent years living among the Indios. He did not plan to do that.

Daylight, and a group looked his way, he supposed deciding either his fate or duties. After much discussion, one came over, took the rope around his neck and led him to the water's edge, close by several dugouts. From the motions, he determined they wanted him as one of the day's dugout canoa makers. That included going inland with them to gather cypress logs to float back for the tedious toil.

The crude nature of their shell saws made felling a tree an enormous task. A full day's work did produce one and they dragged and floated it

back to their island. In the days to come, Luis scraped and burned out one
side of a seasoned log that would become a canoa. Often, instructions
came by handsigns and grunts. If he didn't comprehend, he could expect
slapping. In time, his compliance and ability gave them confidence, and
they removed the neck rope so he could wander about the village. He
acquired his own fish, oysters, and crabs. Sometimes a Calusa would
tender a morsel of deer meat. The vast improvement over entrails amused
him. He observed their jewelry, bowls, knives and trinkets, all made from
shells, which abounded in piles of discards. Their shelters, cone-shaped
huts, utilized palm fronds as roof thatch. After a while, they allowed him
to sleep inside one with some of the younger men. He learned that the
Indios called the village *Casitoa, and that the islands further south at
Florida's tip were called the Matecumbes. The Spanish had named them
the Mártires.

***

One morning while working on a dugout, he noticed several Calusa
leading a bedraggled captive with a man slung over his shoulder. They
came from the other side of the island. His joy at seeing what looked to
be another Christian halted as he witnessed the sight of no less than the
troublesome seaman Tomás, whom he'd left in the Canaries. With hair
snarled, face bloodied, and 20 pounds less weight, he needed pity. As the
Indios pushed him onto the ground, he turned to face Luis.

"Hola, mi amigo del diablo."

Not a cordial greeting, but pure Spanish words gave Luis comfort,
albeit in an odd way. An unreliable soul, but Luis wanted to hear the
rogue's story.

"Tomás? Did not we leave you in jail in the Canaries?"

"Ah, yes you did, but they never built a jail that could hold me. After
you left for the New World, I escaped and tagged up with pirates. After
sailing and spending time in Port Royal, we headed to the shipping lanes
to seek a Spanish galleon. Running aground on a reef wrecked the ship.
I survived, but the Calusa captured me. Thus my lament. Each day I think
of escape, and each day I become more weary. I'm not meant to be a
slave."

Luis related to Tomás his own plight and the storm out of Habana and
how he too thought every day of escape. He pondered whether to align
with someone of Tomas' caliber.

"What happened to your dead friend?"

"Last night he became deranged from the excess of toil. Swallowing
*Chokoloskee, near Everglades City

dirt was his only means of ending life. Perhaps he now fares better than we."

Have you been assigned to a family yet, as their slave?"

"No," responded Luis.

"You will be."

***

Luis heard them call it *cassina*, a concoction brewed from holly leaves. One evening, many of the Calusa men consumed this black drink in their lodge. It began a ceremony, which required their shaman to consume it in excess, then expound on a vision that he claimed to have seen. Dancing and chanting then ensued all night, making it difficult for Luis to sleep. The rites continued on into morning when Luis witnessed a sight more discomforting than the shipboard amputation. An Indio captive from another tribe hung lifeless in the middle of the village after being sacrificed overnight. A pool of blood sotted his body and the ground beneath him. Luis lost all food eaten the previous evening. In pure desperation, he sought out the ill-refined Tomás, his only semblance of a contact with civilization.

"Alférez, they're not going to eat him. It's a ceremonial sacrifice. Besides, we Spanish grow too tough and stringy for a native victual." He then roared with laughter.

Luis knew that fear hovered over Tomás, just as it did him. *He just handles it in a different manner,* he reflected.

"Yes, but what if their food becomes in short supply?"

"It'll never happen here. Food from the sea abounds."

Somehow, in accepting Tomás' amazingly wise answer to his own odd question, Luis let it drop. He then had a brief flashback to his misspoken sea monsters question on the galleon.

"What's your latest plan of escape?"

Tomás shot him a dismissive glance, much as a senior officer would do. "Opportunity, mi amigo, opportunity. We must wait, watch, and use our cunning."

Luis appreciated the conversation, but just as a man may enjoy watching a colorful but poisonous snake, he does not want to handle it. He couldn't collaborate with the scoundrel, so he began to plot and plan alone. Paddling to the Gulf's shipping lanes presented too many hazards, so he would plan to wend northeast to San Agustín when the time came, by canoa and by foot. The sword and satchel would be necessary, but only a bird or a monkey could reach them high in the tree. That solution needed to come also. At times, he would lie down and gaze upward at his valuables, worth more to him now than the thousands of pesos that may have sunk with his galleon. At the moment, they may as well be on the moon. Somehow, he would retrieve them.

The survival kit and silver were important to an escape journey, but more so the sword, which served as an extension of his self. Issued at enlistment, he learned its use and its danger. It boasted a sharp-pointed three-foot long blade, made of forged iron in Toledo. Upon removing it from the leather scabbard, Luis could always read the inscription –

DO NOT DRAW ME WITHOUT REASON,
DO NOT SHEATH ME WITHOUT HONOR.

Luis knew he could not leave without his prizes.

***

Over a few weeks, he learned many native ways. He could acquire sea life, pluck certain fruits and plants, and keep his body blackened from smoldered corn cobs. Now and then, he caught a garfish, whose oil sufficed in place of cobs. He knew it doubtful that friends would recognize him, with a sooty body and untrimmed beard of almost one month. The area waterways became familiar, as they took him along to help with fish traps and the felling of mainland trees. He could envision the best escape as by water, as savannas covered the interior, where lagartos and snakes thrived.

Like mariners, the Calusas lived under superstitions, and anything unusual created volatile emotions. About one month after his arrival, an abrupt change in the weather came about. Birds flew inland east in droves, the sky blackened at midday, and the wind increased. The bay ebbed more than normal, leaving large open sandy areas, with dying fish flopping. The Indios took to wailing and gathered around the chief and shaman for guidance. Luis suffered an inner wailing of his own, as it reminded him of the hours preceding the hurricane aboard the Atocha. The Calusa decided to desert their island and move further inland. In the confusion, Luis took the advantage and stayed behind hiding in the bush. If he could survive another possible hurricane, it might give him the moment for which he longed. Escape.

As winds strengthened, he remembered the monster waves around the Atocha. He decided to climb high in a tree in case they came inland. It took about an hour to reach the upper parts of a tall oak. Once again lashing himself down, this time with a Calusa–made rope, he braced for the storm, as the winds whistled and roared. The big tree swayed and groaned, and he prayed it would not crack and fall. Other trees did fall around him. He maintained a greater sense of peace in this storm than the last, though the rains came just as violent.

A little more in control this time, he allowed, though in a strange kind of way.

In the distance, through rain-clouded vision, he could see *his* tree. The one that held sword and satchel. He focused on it for hours, and to his elation, eventually it trembled, cracked, and fell. He couldn't hear it fall due to the roar of the storm, but he could see it, and he acknowledged the gift. His gear recovery loomed. He let out a shout of exuberance, which not even he heard. In the midst of the fury, he exuded a warm glow.

All day he suffered the wind and rain's pounding, but this time he lashed his body tight. No giant waves, meaning they crashed outside of the bay. Water did cover parts of the island, but it drained away. By the next morning, quiet descended, and the sun broke through the clouds. Wet and weary, Luis took an hour to climb down. Debris littered the island. Limbs, branches and trees of all sizes covered the ground. He fixed his course toward his tree and spotted the gear. Buried under branches, but intact. With deftness, he extracted it, as a barber pulls a tooth.

His way now set, excepting a means of water transportation. Then he saw it—a one-man dugout, sound, but blown onto a small tree. Left behind when the Indios vacated, to Luis it beamed as a ship of gold. Pulling it down, he inspected and found it unscathed. Soon the Calusa would return, so he hauled everything to the water, found a wide split limb for a paddle and slid into the bay. He paddled west into the ocean, then north. Watching the makeshift paddle slice the water, he thought of the *makeshift* life of Tomás. He wondered how he'd fared during the storm and if he would encounter him again.

This area of La Florida contained a myriad of islands, inhabited by birds, raccoons, manatees, and lagartos. Tomás mentioned that the native village of *Muspa lay about ten leagues north, and that **Calos, the senior chief's village, rose at least ten leagues beyond that. In trying to remember the mappings, Luis figured that ***Bay Espíritu Santo was a good forty leagues further north of Calos. He considered the Bay his immediate goal, as there lived the Tocobaga, beyond Calusa territory. He hoped there to find assistance in plotting a route to San Agustín. It could take a full week's paddling in and out of the coastline, and most of it by moonlight so to avoid recapture. His heart leaped to the challenge.

The next six days he spent resting and sleeping, concealed as best he could, while at night he paddled with the moon above. Food came from raw fish, coco plums, and oysters.

Water came from the glistening dew on leaves and spring runs discovered flowing from the mainland to the salt water. Either Muspa or another village's fires he passed about midnight on the third night, so his confidence increased. At times he slipped into a dreamlike state, with movements composed of instincts, like an animal. Paddling provided contentment.

*Muspa-Marco Isl. area   **Calos-on Mound Key in Estero Bay   ***Tampa Bay

After six nights of stealth paddling, his mind and body revolted. Weary, with thoughts clouded, he knew diet and odd hours affected him. He wondered too of the closeness of the big chieftain's Calos village. As he eased into a large bay in the first light of dawn, a huge island came into view but with no sign of life. He trembled from fatigue, so he pulled onto the bank, placed his gear in thick bushes and lay to sleep nearby. As he dozed, low sounds of an unintelligible dialect entered somewhere in the recesses of his mind. It augured ill.

7

CALOS' STARK SLAVERY

1622

None of us understand the words they speak.
COLUMBUS

FLORIDA PENNINSULA SW COAST

Luis lay in deep slumber, a dream also slipping into the crevices of his brain. *Ponce de León, semi-conscious and lying on a bed… cautioning… using words like Punta, Calos, Muspa…enduring pain, all the while pointing with a bloodied arrow towards me…almost as a warning…*

His body tingled as though he'd stumbled into a bee's hive, while he floated somewhere between waking and sleeping. The unrecognizable dialect grew louder, and his eyes blinked open to a startling sight. He now stared up at a group of Indios, poking and prodding him with spears. Blood trickled and ran down his body and limbs.

Is this how it will end?

They lifted him up and placed a tethered vine on his neck. With glaring eyes, they uttered the word *Calos* over and over, thumping their chests. They then spoke the word **Escampaba* and pointed to the large shallow bay. Sunrise, and they led him up to the top of the island, which looked to him like a huge mound. His bare feet suffered cuts from loose shells, but if he faltered, he could expect a blow from a lance.

Slavery again, he thought. *It turns like a drama in Seville. I stepped outside the theatre at intermission, and on returning, the scene continued.*

The Indios spoke not, but Luis could sense a purpose in taking him up. He deliberated breaking free and running back to the dugout, but five Indios with spears would hit their mark before he made ten steps. Two or three he could handle with the sword, but the odds did not now lean in his favor. Thinking of his gear, he hoped it could stay hidden. They stopped at the highest point, which captured a 360 degree view of the island, which he estimated at one and a half miles in circumference. Everyone waited outside a large thatched-roof house for the chief.

Soon Luis beheld a commanding figure emerging from the enclosure, a group of females and children following behind. Gold earrings hung from his ears, and a large gold necklace adorned his neck. A pantherskin

*Estero Bay

covering with head intact surmounted his black hair, with multiple hawk and eagle feathers attached. A large carved belt almost covered his breechcloth. Only the chief's face and arms bore tattoos, none others. Armador now faced him, who also spoke the two words, *Calos and Escampaba.* The moment found him besot with dread, and he imagined being strung up and sacrificed like the captive at Casitoa.

No such event came about however, as the crowd dissipated, and one of the Indios led him to a tree and attached the tether. This time a woman gave him dried fish to eat and blackened wood to repel bugs. He took these as signs, though small ones, of his value as a slave. Sitting in the dirt, facing an unknown fate, he knew it would take something other than a hurricane to free him this time.

After some days passed, he began to feel safe, though he knew not of his future. This village exceeded the previous one in size and it did boast of the major Calusa chief. Luis estimated it held around 1,000 inhabitants. Circumstances unfolded much as they did at Casitoa, except Luis was turned over to a family as their personal slave. The tribe's women decided whose prize he became. The sea and its bounty supported life here also, and they did little farming. They used shells for everything - cups, hammers, chisels, and fishhooks to catch large fish. Bows and arrows came into play for the larger sea creatures. Luis noted the Spanish origin of some knives and utensils, no doubt from shipwrecks.

As before, he found it necessary to catch and prepare his own food from the sea. An abundant supply of sea grapes, coco plums and other wild plants augmented his diet. He received a hammock, woven from cotton, and though most of the men wore deerskin breech-cloths, Luis wove his from palm fronds. He began to tie up his lengthening hair like the Indios, as an act of compliance. There were times when he could see slaves not only from other tribes, but those of Spanish origin. Some looked pitiful from months or years of arduous labor. He kept cautious about approaching them, but decided to seek one out soon, as he so longed for communication in his native tongue.

***

"Mi amigo, I have been here for two years, I think."

Luis reveled in the sound of his voice. He went by the name Ronimo, came from Aragon in Spain, and shipped out on a merchant ship, from which he deserted. He wound up with pirates who cast him away in the *Matecumbe Islands, deeming him not unsavory enough.

"I know what's south of here, but what lies east?"

*Keys

"Some call it *Cautio, a vast savanna, a wide shallow slow-moving water, and a great lake. Then more Indio villages lay further east."

"And to the north?"

With a questioning look at Luis, Ronimo answered. " **Tanpa, their most sizable village,which is on an island. Many other villages lie scattered along the coast and they would find you if you tried to escape."

"Where do you arrive at friendly Indios ?"

 "The Tocobaga may be less hostile, if the soldiers have not attacked them of recent. They differ from the Calusa. Their main villlage stands at the head of a large bay, much further north."

Luis knew that the path to escape lay offshore, by paddle or sail, just within sight of the coastline. Next captured by the Indios and brought to Calos, Ronimo learned the area and some Calusa dialect. His smile exposed his blackened teeth, the few still remaining. He bore a large scar on his left cheek, and his breechcloth hung ragged like his hair, which resembled a deck swab. Luis stood amazed that pirates considered him too genteel, as the man's countenance proved otherwise. Nevertheless, Luis enjoyed hearing his native tongue.

"How long do you plan on staying?" He asked, smiling.

Luis returned the smile as he spoke.

"I would like to think that tomorrow brings embarkation, but destiny deems it not so. Therefore, I enlist patience, so that I may learn how to escape," said Luis.

"Escape. Ha! That is a word no longer lodged in my brain. I have seen what they do to recaptured escapees, and it might make the Holy Office squeamish. My main goal is to stay alive and try to achieve some small measure of comradeship with the other castaways. Many toil here for years, some get traded, and a few killed. The Calusa try to instill fear in us from the beginning. Our best hope? An armed galleon will appear and provide ransom."

"Does that happen often?"

"No, but one can wish. If free, I'd seek out those pirates that mistreated me. I would string each up and carve him to pieces."

His face flushed, and Luis sensed that his desire for revenge grasped him in a stranglehold. He watched as Ronimo's mood shifted from joviality to anger and then quiet despair, effecting a
sad face. The Alférez came to the stark realization that, over time, he too could slip into such a state. He didn't want that to happen. He must find

* Cautio--Everglades   **Tanpa--Pine Island area

another captive who had a zeal for stealing away as he did, but without a tortured mind due to loss of freedom. He took a stick, cleared a circular spot on the ground and drew the points of a compass. He must head north, but not venture too far west, so to keep his bearings. Plus pirates, corsairs, and ships of foreign nations would be a hazard further west on the Gulf. He would strike for San Agustín, the only port in La Florida.

***

A nose-bone? Luis thought.

He ventured to talk to a mulatto captive, who somehow seemed familiar. Then he grasped why, recognizing the
nose-bone slave from Porto Bello. Upon approaching him, Luis received a large smile from the tall man, who waved a greeting. Communicating created difficulty, as he knew few Spanish words. With sign language, Luis elicited some accented but recognizable words--

"…Congo…Potosí…Porto Bello…boat…fight…escape…Calusa capture…Lunga…escape?" He pointed to his chest with the last two words.

Luis realized that he came from the merchant ship out of Porto Bello that underwent a slave revolt. His escape ran short as the Calusa captured him and again made him a slave. Apparently emboldened by one fleeing, he wanted to try again.

"Escape, yes," whispered Luis, while nodding his head and placing an index finger to his mouth for silence. Luis wanted to know him better before he committed to a joint plan.

***

SEVILLE
FEBRUARY 1, 1623

"Eight ships of the Terre Firme fleet have been lost! A September hurricane off La Florida sent five hundred and fifty people to the bottom! Two million ducats in treasure and cargo gone!"

The rider from Cádiz,Spain downriver rode all night with the message from a merchant ship out of Habana. He stopped and shouted the news up and down the Arénal on his way to the Casa de Contratación, the fleet's supervisory office. Next he would ride to Madrid to take the official letters from Habana to the king. That would take nine days.

The clamor caused the Armador family shipwrights to accost the rider at his next stop.

"What of the Atocha?" yelled Antonio Armador, Luis' father.

"All lost, except five. A seaman, two apprentices, and two mulattos!"

Antonio and Luis' grandfather stood stunned as they watched the rider gallop down the strand toward the town gate.

"A sad time, Antonio," said Grandfather Juan.

"Yes. We all knew the risks. He made us so proud. Our hopes that they wintered in Habana are gone. I must go home and tell his madre. News like this spreads like wildfire, so she may learn of it before I arrive."

"Yes, *silver has wings*," replied Juan, "I'm just going to sit here for a time before going home." His face and body slackened, tears forming in the corners of his eyes.

***

"Gentlemen, we may face bankruptcy."

Following the rider's report, the Senior Factor at the Casa de Contratación had convened his officers. This included the Avería Committee, which had borrowed heavily to handle preparations for the Armada galleons, protectors of the merchants' cargo ships. It included a massive undertaking to assemble 2500 seamen and soldiers plus foodstuffs. The Factor groped for words, as he still reeled in a state of shock.

"The Atocha galleon, with seven other vessels, all containing 40 tons of silver, sank in a hurricane off La Florida September last. There is no profit for those ships' merchants. So, we cannot tax to satisfy our Genoese banker's loan of 200,000 ducats, much less acquire our fee. I'm open suggestions, even if it means selling some of our own prized galleons."

***

The door swung open into Carlo Dorio's office, and a sputtering page announced that the Atocha and seven ships sank in the Florida straits. The young Genoese banker, in the midst of enjoying his morning chocolate, jolted and spilled the drink on his desk, ruining the day's paperwork. Well-groomed and always composed, he gasped, unable to speak at first.

"Ahh! This devastates! Not only did my family lend 200,000 ducats to the Avería agents for equipping the fleet, we advanced much more to the crown for its wars!"

His junior officer, now standing at the office door, added a reminder.

"Mr. Doria, don't forget the numerous merchants who also borrowed to ship their cargo."

"I know about them!" he screamed, like a man drowning. "Do you think I'm an idiot? My family will suffer a huge loss! They will recall me to

Genoa!"

He slumped in his chair, his face in his hands.

Carlo's Counting House office enjoyed recognition in Seville and maintained direct contact with the king in Madrid. As a Spanish protectorate, Genoa enjoyed status throughout Europe, and Doria's firm held sway as *the King's banker*.

"These loans ventured to make me *rich as Potosí*. Now I will face shame when going home."

"It's not your fault, Carlo."

"Doesn't matter," said Carlo, now speaking softly, with eyes closed. "I wallow like a man in a nightmare."

***

Near the Cathedral, inside the Hall of Merchants, the growing crowd murmured. Wine sellers, silversmiths, goldsmiths, wheat producers, silk merchants, cord producers, soapmakers, and many kinds of artisans gathered. As members of the guild, or *Consulado,* who shipped cargo to the Indies, they feared the news.

After all became seated, the Senior Officer stood up front and motioned, palms down. The room enveloped in a tenuous state of silence. He took a deep breath and poured out the report of the fleet's losses. What they always feared now came to pass. Muttered oaths filled the room, and a din arose with each one calculating and bemoaning his losses.

One by one, many rose to vent their anger.

"Why did the fleet leave Habana so late and in the midst of hurricane season!?"

"What delayed them, Spanish tardiness, or junketing!?"

"Is there salvage ongoing!?"

"They didn't tender to any of us a *by your leave* to sail in the late fall!"

"Gentlemen, gentlemen, please arrest your wrath for a time! Please!" said the Senior Officer, waving his arms. "I too am exasperated, but we must focus on our next step. I will write his Majesty King Felipe IV to request a meeting. We will beg forbearance of any Avería tax claims on us, until a future date. Each of you must, of course, talk to any financiers to whom you owe for cargos shipped."

***

Isabela de Aragón relaxed in her room, reading a smuggled copy of The Trickster of Seville, the first book about the notorious Don Juan. Little occupied her time in the last four months since she set aside wedding plans. Luis planned a return in six months, but now ten months had passed. She presumed from his last letter that they spent the winter in Habana and would be home in the spring, so she lived with hope.

On this day, Francisco de Aragón came home early from his goldsmith's shop. After the meeting at the Consulado, he retained no stomach for work, so he closed the business for the day. He dreaded the walk home, and his feet trod like two huge metal anchors. He dragged himself into the courtyard and called upstairs.

"Isabela, Isabela, please come down!"

Hearing her father's voice, she bounded downstairs, flashing her usual smile.

"My, Padre, you're home early, do we have a holiday of which I'm not aware?"

A downcast face greeted her and conveyed a sad message she was daunt to hear.

"What is it?"

"I'm sorry, my dear, but we have just been told the Atocha sank in a hurricane off Florida, September last."

"Any survivors?" she asked, horror-stricken.

"Of 265, only five–a seamen, two pages, and two slaves. The rest, along with a treasure in silver, lies at the bottom of the ocean."

Isabela's face wrenched, and her hands pressed against her chest, as if to keep her heart from bursting.

"My poor Luis. My brave caballero. What happened to him? Did he sink with the ship? Have they found any bodies? Oh, that he did not suffer, that he did not languish. Why did he go? Why did he go? I so feared..."

She staggered on the point of swooning, her father rushing to lead her to a nearby bench. Her mother, hearing the news from a doorway, began to cry.

"What's to become of me?" cried Isabela. "The worst day of my life. Silver did this. I hate it! I hate it!"

"Rest, my dear, and tomorrow let us attend Mass."

As expected, the news spread like wildfire in Seville, and Mass at the Cathedral's chapels included prayers for the grieving families.

Isabela spent several weeks in mourning. Grief-stricken, she cared naught for food, company, counseling, or even Mass. She envisioned her future now as did every señorita, a marriage arranged by her father based on what he thought best. She stayed alone in her room, clutching the only three letters from

Luis. No more to see her brave soldier, her handsome Alférez, the Universidad student, the shipwright. She could not allow Luis to escape from her thoughts–waking, sleeping or attempting to sleep.

His dash, his passion, his polish, his charming countenance–they can never be replaced. Of what use are my memories or desires–they are but a hollow sound echoing from nothingness.

***

MADRID

Nine days of riding, and nights at the usual unkempt Spanish taverns took the appointed messenger to the city gates of Madrid. As he told his mission, entrance to both the city and the palace by guards accommodated him. Seventeen year-old King Felipe IV, the first minister Condé-Duque de Olivares, and multiple advisers and military men all received the message.

"Your Majesty, I bring December letters from the Marquis de Caderieta and Admiral Cordoba from Habana. I'm sad to inform you of the loss of eight of the Plata Fleet's vessels, including the Almiranta galleon Atocha."

Imagining now to be shot, he did his best to shrink into the background as Olivares read the letters aloud.

Salutations and compliments to the king somehow became lost to the ears of all assembled, but they did hear some specific words –

Hurricane…Atocha…Consolación…Rosario…Margarita…de Reyes…a patache... González…Ayala…all lost…550 souls…forty tons of silver and fifteen tons of copper on Atocha alone…two million ducats…total.….

Deafening silence followed gasps and moans throughout the palatial room.

"What to do?" said the youthful king, looking toward his Minister.

Olivares' mind had started turning during the reading. He did his best to address the question.

"Your Highness, our immediate concern points to the funds needed to continue our war with the Dutch and to support our armies in Germany. Far less new silver quinto tax shall flow to our coffers, so we must ask the Genoese again for advances. The repayment of our current debts must wait.

If they act too wary, then we may need to approach the Portuguese financiers.

He continued, "Apparently, any salvaged vessels, plus the other 20 surviving ships won't arrive till spring, so we must
act now to bolster the Treasury. I suggest we communicate with the Marquis to spur the salvage activity before our enemies do. We must examine the future daily, as tomorrow could bring another war. The honor of our far-ranging
empire is in the balance.

"So be it," said the youthful king.

***

SW FLORIDA COAST

Life became a series of repetitive labors for Luis with few diversions except occasional conversations with other Spanish slaves. He now understood the despair of plantation mulattos and mining Indios. The worst he'd heard on the ship was that for each peso produced at the Potosí mines, ten lives were claimed in the process. He didn't understand it all.

Some taunting and demeaning behavior did come his way. One morning, even that escalated. In spring, 1623, with the mild winter passed and the days longer and warmer, he was assigned to one mean-spirited Indio, whom he always tried to avoid. They were to gather the small fish caught in an island canal at low tide and held there by the woven net. The men set out, with no noise but the swish of paddles and the call of gulls. The Indio would grunt and point whenever he wanted the dugout turned by Luis, who enjoyed the blue sky and gentle breezes, but wished it the Guadalquivir River in Spain.

At the island's canal, the Calusa delivered an unexpected blow to Luis' head, to remind him of his bondage status. Luis thought it odd as he did his share of net-pulling and fish-collecting for the baskets. The Indio jeered often, almost as if intending provocation. While Luis strained at the net, the Calusa next swung his conch ax down on Luis' shoulder, drawing blood. His assailant just glared.

Recoiling from the water, Luis went back to work, but his nemesis continued. Alert to the next swing of the ax, he dodged and put his combat instincts into motion. Upon receiving only a glancing hit this time, he grabbed a limb from the bank and delivered his own. Luis did not know where this would lead, but he did not want to die in an Indio fish trap. As his combatant surfaced, Luis slipped behind him and grasped his neck in an armlock stranglehold. Up and down, over and over, in water and out they struggled, but his grip stayed firm.

In time, the Indio succumbed, from strangulation and drowning. Luis climbed on the bank, exhausted. Stunned from the event, his senses tried to react at what to do next. Not the time to flee, he reasoned, as he did not have his weapon and survival kit. He realized that an artful fabrication of the incident would have to suffice. Wrapping the body with vines and attaching heavy rocks, he took it two arrow lengths out to sea. There he rolled it off the dugout, hopeful that it would not resurface. Returning, he gathered more fish for the basket, then paddled back to the village, all the while preparing his story.

Luis tensed, as a multitude of eyes bore down on him easing into the Calos canal. They stared puzzled at the absence of his former companion. Straightway to the chief's abode he trudged, where he requested an audience, by hand-sign. He wove his tale with gestures and emotions, telling of how a shark in the canal grabbed the Indio with gaping, toothed jaws.

Among much thrashing, it broke the net and took him out to sea, leaving a wake of blood. He hoped his lamentations and animations conveyed enough, as he squatted, face in hands. Soon cries of anguish arose from the family of the departed. The chief said nothing.

Did they believe me? How can I tell? Should I attempt escape tonight?

Luis' mind raced as he awaited the chief's reaction, but it never came. He went back down the hill, cleaned all the fish and presented them to the day's cook. Half-satisfied and half-fearful, his thoughts ran as in a familiar gamut.

***

"Hola, mi amigo. I'm not certain they believe you."

Stepping out of the late afternoon sun and into the shade, his demeanor and grooming made Luis think that the man just left his palatial estate in Seville. He wore no breechcloth, but instead short-length pants and a sleeveless vest, fully buttoned, all of Spanish origin. Feet enclosed by deerskin moccasins, clean-shaven and hair cropped and combed, he gave introduction as Alaniz Estaban. Luis abided speechless.

"I heard of your report to the chief, and I thought it might be helpful to give you my thoughts. Like you, I have been a slave here, but for a number of years longer, following a shipwreck in the Mártires. I have learned the Calusa dialect and others, so they preserve me *to be their tongue*, as they say, for interpretations."

They swapped stories, and Esteban, educated and successful in Seville, elaborated.

"I left as a black pearl merchant to Habana for purchases to be resold at home. Soon as we set sail home, our vessel grounded in a storm and broke up. It happened fast. Some drowned, some fortunates saved by rescue boats....and some of us captured. And so, here I reside. My trunk survived also." He turned away, as if musing, and then looked at Luis, smiling.

As they talked, it became evident to Luis that here stood a man whose heart missed Spain, but who accepted his plight and adapted without resistance. He remained hopeful of a rescue someday by his countrymen and would even consider sailing away with the French or English.

"As I stated, they may not believe you. They often don't respond when perplexed, and they'll just walk away, saying nothing after an encounter. I'd be on my guard."

Having just met him, Luis did not divulge the actual circumstances of the Indio's death, deciding to relate it at a later day. He did admit to Alaniz his constant thoughts of escape, hoping to make his way back home.

"It would need to be a clever plan, different from the previous, which a hurricane made possible," Luis said.

"Escape." Alaniz spoke and then paused before continuing. "Yes, many have tried and thus brought back, sadly for slaughter. A rare man escapes for good. They have a vast network that enlists sub-tribes when necessary."

"What precipitates recapture?"

"Well, almost all Spaniards run away on the inland trails, so finding them comes easy. An Indio slave will often go into the marshes or plains, but be outnumbered by his pursuers. If an escapee steals a canoa, many strong paddlers in large war canoas seek him."

"Alaniz, my life plods along as a picaresque tale," said Luis, "with none of the pleasure, but all of the pain. If you can help me plan, I would be forever in your debt."

Esteban smiled, reminded again of their slavery and to stay guarded, then took his leave.

A slave. An hidalgo, an officer, a shipwright. But a slave. Alive, but a slave. I will change that.

As the days passed into summer, Luis likened his life to that of a toiling animal, as he did the constant bidding of his Calusa family, moving from one labor to another. Conversations with Alaniz, when available, worked like a tonic on him and enriched his spirit. The only time that discussion of escape surfaced in conversation came when Luis broached it. The mulatto, Lunga, would cross his path in the village and mouth the word escape to him. Once he pointed to his muscles and then motioned to let Luis know he could paddle and swim. Another time he gestured as if throwing a lance, then pointed to his chest. He smiled, as if to say—*I'm waiting on you.*

Ronimo, the deserter and pirate, caused him to be cautious in discussing the subject. Friendly enough, but Luis thought his background unstable, like many that came to the New World. Luis needed another, someone judicious, but not hesitant to act when necessary. Too, he must be skilled in combat.

Luis had read of other cultures but was now thrust into one. He wondered how a civilization as this existed so long without changing, as Europe changed, due to Gutenberg, the cultural awakening, the theatre, and city-states joining into nations. In spite of that, he admired the serene aspect of their life. The seacoast effected their Garden of Eden, providing an endless supply of food, and the interior produced red meat from hunting. They grew few crops, but trading supplied vegetables. They interacted more easily with one another than Europeans did and lived life in simple splendor. Luis also knew they could be violent if provoked, lived as polygamists and were described on a map as *canoa maneaters.* The village of Calos oversaw numerous sub-villages, each expected to pay homage to the senior chief.

Summer fused into autumn, with the natural signs of shorter days and longer nights. Humid and bug-ridden work hours filled Luis' time during the day, but evenings plied his mind with scheming. Sometimes, with stealth, he would check his cache of gear and wonder how long it could stay hidden. Early mornings he liked the best. Lying in his hammock, as a slight touch of coolness greeted first light, he could look up and enjoy the sights and sounds of birds with their chatter. Many sunrises now greeted thousands of black and orange butterflies, hanging from bushes and trees, on some type of migration.

The Calusa mastered everything that came from nature. Luis watched as they used sharks' teeth, cane shafts, and crow feathers to fashion arrows. A large conch shell served as an alert horn by blowing on the small end. Carvers used woodto make masks and totem statues, then colored them using herbs and water. He could see they wasted little and savored all available, appreciating the world as the source of their existence.

He feared that if he stayed too long he would lose his identity. He knew that Fontaneda, rescued after seventeen years, wrote of captives that declined an opportunity for ransom and rescue. They became *white Indios* and changed much as a snake sheds its skin and acquires a new one. Their craving for precious metals dissipated. Luis thought of silver, which underscored the reason he sailed on the Atocha, but which also fostered his captivity. His coin satchel lay hidden in the bushes, but no escape assistance could come from it, for at Calos it lost all its power. It could help him later, but here it provided less value and usefulness than a conch shell.

***

"You must welcome me to the headquarters of La Florida, amigo. My name is Pedro Martins. Remember that we conquerors all band together, so we should have few problems," he said. A large grin rose on his face.

Portuguese, he related. Sent up from the Muspa village, he came as barter in a trade. Luis could tell from comments that humor cast as his equalizer. Pedro and a rival tribe captive each carried water in deerskin bags for the Indios. Returning as a trading party, the group headed to report to the chief. That evening, Luis happened upon Pedro again.

"As a child, I lived in a small village in Portugal, but the love of the ocean proved too strong. When of age, I shipped out on a slaver, and after one of our successful runs to Africa and then Cartagena, we faced a storm in the straits below here about a year ago. Many died from the shipwreck. A few of us survived but were picked up by the Calusa, who made us slaves. I've tried to adapt and learn from them how to fish, find oysters and pick coco plums. I've found their diet acceptable and hope one day to use it to my advantage."

"Do you mean to escape?"

"Ha! Possibly. That is a word with many meanings. Escape means freedom, but freedom in the Florida wilds to what? Escape means a potential recapture, and that could bring death. So for the time being I stay, shall we say, observant."

Luis took a liking to Pedro and considered him a prospect in a fleeing venture.

***

Many times Luis could rest at the end of a day's labor and feel a serenity unlike any he'd ever known. It became a delight to lie at water's edge, feel the ocean breeze on his face and watch clouds drifting across the blue. If the breeze stiffened, it deterred the insects, even better. Dolphins and manatees would play in the bay and often come close enough to touch. If he never knew the joys of Spain, he reflected that maybe he could live among the Indios—if a free man.

But he did not enjoy freedom, and the lure of his old country called to him. He pictured Isabela, standing at her front door, arms outstretched, her eyes glowing as they met his, sailing with his Abuelito Juan, feasting on madre's meals, and even toiling in the shipyards. It reached out to him and created a longing in his heart. And so he determined again to conceive a plan and decide who should go along.

Luis, Ronimo and Lunga often were assigned by their families to build dugouts from logs. He realized that, if necessary, he could construct one on his own, given enough time. From the one-sided burn-out using resin to the packing on of clay to spots that were not to burn, he could fashion a watercraft, however crude it might be. The most arduous part was the scraping out of charred wood, using simple conch shell scrapers. He observed that sometimes two dugouts were tied together several feet apart. They added small logs as a deck to allow items to be transported.

Four men, four paddles, two dugouts bound together. A mast and sail in the middle. Dried fish, tubers, plums and deerskin bags of water. It all began to form in Luis' mind.

***

"Amigo, time for more of your education on the Calusa and their ways." Alaniz Esteban stopped by at nightfall for a chat.

"Have you noticed the pox and its effect?"

"I see some with black marks and sores on their bodies, and then I never see those Calusas again."

"Yes, our arrivals bring the malady. Each time one dies, they blame the Spaniards, and their anger grows. They seethe like a powder keg, waiting to be lit."

"Do our people know this?"

"Maybe. Maybe not. They observe but often ignore, as they believe it a destiny to missionize them, especially further north."

"Why do the Calusa resist missions?"

"It's uncertain, but they move proud, and when necessary, fierce, perhaps more like those south in the Indies, rather than those to the north. Pagan, and often savage-acting, but yet they maintain rulers and classes, just as we. The chief here controls many other villages, all of whom bow down to him. As I've said before, Calos owns a vast communication and trade bond with these villages. That means if someone escaped, news would travel fast, by foot, canoa, conch horns, and smoke signals."

"Escape? That's the first time you've mentioned it in a while. Tell me the best time and means to do so," he asked, ignoring Alaniz's cautions.

Alaniz gazed at him askance, but proceeded to answer.

"You would need a special opportunity, and you would need to move fast, perhaps far offshore."

"Will you come with me? Your knowledge of dialects could serve us well."

"No. I've witnessed too many escapees recaptured and put to death. I await the arrival of a rescue galleon that will pay a handsome ransom for me. Maybe you could find another Spaniard to go."

"Possibly, but I prefer you."

Esteban did not respond but looked out toward the bay.

"How far to the mission San Juan de Guacara to the north? The Atocha's Chaplain said it lies near the river of the same name."

"That's the big black *Guacara River flowing into the Gulf. You probably drifted around 100 miles from the Mártires to the La Florida coastline where you landed. I think it's another 100 miles from here to Tocobaga, on the **Bay of Pohoy, the one de Soto named Bahía Espíritu Santo.   *Guacara River--Suwannee River   **Bay of Pohoy--Tampa Bay
I would guess another 100 miles up the coast would take you to the Guacara's mouth. I think the Spanish now call it the San Martin. You would then need to paddle upstream to the mission. I'm not certain how far that it, perhaps another 100."

"How long?"

"If you are unimpeded, at least a month. Many Calusa towns lie along the coast, where otherwise marshes and mangroves cover. Or, as the Calusa call the latter, *trees that walk,* as they reproduce in great numbers. Parts of the trip you may elect to go on foot. So all of it would be a challenge for you. Fate smiled on you to bring you this far." He then drew in a deep breath. "Most captives would not attempt it, but I understand your longing for home."

Alaniz inquired why he did not strike for Habana, a closer target.

"I've thought of that often. To head south, I would go across the Gulf, a large body of water, subject to storms and high waves, which I've experienced. I have no charts, no instruments, no compass, and I fear pirates. Plus I would have to negotiate the ocean river flowing through the straits. Along the coastline here I would at least have a point of reference and can stay in sight of it. I realize that constant alertness for Calusa would be necessary. If I can get to the Bay of Pohoy, I believe that I can make it all the way to San Agustín."

He paused, then looked at Esteban.

"Come with me," Luis implored.

"Well, mi amigo, I prefer the quote-*Whereas, patience favors my life.* But I wish you good fortune."

"Thank you. A Spanish proverb that prods me says–*Delay always breeds danger, and to protract a great design is often to ruin it.* "

***

A plot. All along, it formed in Luis' mind. He would take Lunga and Pedro but not Ronimo. He could not determine a fourth member. The group would compose of one to garner palm-fiber cord, small logs for a deck and a mast, and one to bring rig lines, deerskins of water, foodstuffs, and lances. Two small dugouts and sail material would be his quest. Upon a prearranged signal, they would leave at night, paddle beyond the bay, the inlet, then turn north and set sail. They would need a suitable time, an ebbing tide, a good south wind, weapons, and a moonless night. A sail would let them move faster than with paddles on the open water.

He conveyed his plans, as privacy permitted, and each man fained eager but composed. They knew the risks and accepted them. He promised freedom papers that he would sign for Lunga at San Agustín. Knowing the Congolese's strength and learning of Pedro's fighting skills gave Luis comfort. He knew the Navidad season must be soon, as nights became longer and much cooler, and tree leaves turned and fell.

How wonderful to gain freedom for this time of year, he thought.

***

One evening, Luis retired to his hammock amidst a million stars shining above. The moon, the king of the night, shone with brilliance. A special stillness pervaded, and the thatched roof of his open hut could not block all the light from above. Dozing away, he began to hear a clamor in the distance. It grew louder and louder, as if heading in his direction. Opening his eyes, he could see torches and a large procession of Calusa heading up the trail. His first clear picture came of masked faces like hideous creatures of the wild. Chanting women next, all in unison and with rhythm. The entire scene vexed him, like a terrifying dream.

They accosted and then escorted him up the trail toward their plaza area at the top of the big mound. With some type of ceremony taking place, fear struck in Luis' heart. Atop a high wooden platform sat the chief, resplendent in feathers and face paint. At his side sat the shaman, their spiritualist, whose white painted face shone as a beast in the firelight. On the other side, Luis saw a creature bound and hanging from vines in a tree, like a pig waiting for slaughter. A captive from another tribe would soon meet his fate.

Luis watched the shaman take a pot of the black liquid cassina. He poured part into a bowl and then swallowed the brew in large gulps. Falling upon the ground, then writhing, to Luis he seemed to be in either agony or ecstasy. As the loud chanting continued, the shaman moved alone into the council house, the largest structure on the island. His shouts and wailings from within echoed from every board of the building.

They positioned Luis by the large fire surrounded by many Indios. Soon the shaman reemerged and, by tradition, conferred with several women. He next pointed toward the pitiful captive. Two men proceeded to slit his throat. The group then turned towards Luis, shouting *soc! soc! soc! soc!* Alaniz yelled to him that they shouted about the shark thatLuis claimed took the life of the Calusa.

"They do not believe you! The story about the shark! They want to extract what they consider the truth from you!"

"Please tell them *no! no! no!*" exclaimed Luis, fearful of his survival. "Tell them-*I could have escaped, but I came back!*"

The din continued, and they prodded him with lances.
As his blood trickled, he continued to express-*no! no!* Alaniz repeated the same to the chief and the shaman. Luis thought of the matador's bull and of the spears dangling from his flesh and wondered if it knew what awaited him. Now he held compassion for the bull.

In time, he noticed the noise lessening, though he trembled. Alaniz spoke that the Calusa still doubted his shark story, and they wanted to put fear into him.

"Your trial has passed for now," he said. "A useful slave you must be."

As the Indios moved away from him, he stood and made his way back to his hut down the trail. Consumed with anxiety, but at the same time strengthening his resolve. Deep within, the honor and fortitude of his forbears rose to the surface, like an anchor drawn from the depths. His mind filled with many thoughts that night.

Would the next time be a gauntlet, with many striking out with clubs and axes? Yelling and screaming? Would it be a chase? Just for their amusement? Combat with their tallest and fiercest warrior? Leaving now is of utmost importance.

As he walked the path, all the while refining his plan, he noticed in the bushes a brown crumpled sheet, reflecting the full moon shining. Close observance indicated an old sail.

Did the Calusa acquire this along with trinkets of gold from a wrecked ship ? His heart began to race.

Florida

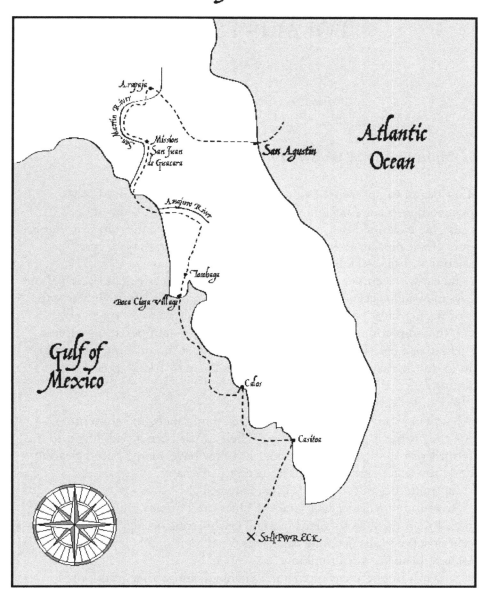

Atlantic Ocean

Gulf of Mexico

Arapaja

Martín River

Mission San Juan de Guacara

Amajuro River

Tocobaga

Boca Ciega Village

San Agustín

Calos

Casitoa

✕ SHIPWRECK

8
POLARIS ESCAPE

1623

Fortune favors the brave.
Cortés

FLORIDA PENINSULA SW COAST

Luis began to observe the tides. Discovering the remnant of a sail quickened his plans for flight. A distant goal yesterday, today it drew closer. He examined the sailcloth, but did not remove it, from fear that it would create an alarm. He'd heard that Florida Indios sailed, even sometimes as far as Habana, but he never witnessed it.

The early December outgoing tide of the bay waters began ebbing about dusk, and each succeeding day it did so about an hour later. He knew the act of fleeing must be done at night and he preferred to go on an ebb. Even the bugs cooperated, with fewer annoying as temperatures cooled.

"Have you heard about the big council soon at the meeting ground in Cautio, to the east?" Alaniz Esteban, Luis' Spanish friend, posed the question.

"No, but please tell me."

"Knowing their language lets me understand much, and sometimes I think they forget that I overhear. Their canals permit paddling into the interior from all of south La Florida, and they have a large raised clearing among the watery grasses, so to accommodate many."

Luis' mind began to turn. "How many will go?"

"Surrounding villages will send the chiefs and nobles, but Calos sends most of their men, so to guard our chief, who controls all."

He observed Luis listening intensely.
"Alférez, I can see your thinking."

Esteban's bright, pleasing manner changed, and with a grim look, he focused at Luis.

"They'll leave a small but capable guard to watch over the women, children, and slaves. Remember, they can be pleasant enough, but they would also take great delight in slitting your throat."

Luis swallowed hard. He heard Alaniz but ignored the comments.

"When do they depart?"

"They leave one day before the new moon. It's traditional. I believe that happens again in three weeks, by our calendar."

"So, the nighttime sky will shine less then. But the Polaris star will still locate north."

"An ambitious slave. Admirable. Do you have accomplices? No, don't tell me, I'd best know little, since I'll accompany them for interpreting." A faint smile creased Alaniz's lips.

"Thank you, Alaniz Esteban. I am grateful." He smiled and stretched out his hand to clasp.

***

Luis continued plotting, with San Agustín the goal. In hushed tones and gestures he conveyed the final plan to Pedro and Lunga whenever circumstances permitted. An outgoing tide appealed to him, but a new moon moreso. They must gather and hide everything in preparation to escape after the Calusas leave for the Cautio interior. He made certain to remind them of the risks also.

He would bring the sail, locate two small canoes and three paddles, plus one extra as a backup. Reclaiming his sword and kit remained paramount. Pedro would bring two deerskins of fresh water, dried fish, leftover tuber cakes, and vine ropes for rigging. Lunga would somehow secure three lances, a pole for a mast, and ten more poles for a makeshift deck atop the canoes. Attaching the mast pole would require some skill, but they were determined.

Luis would hand-signal each man of the specific departure day, time and embarkation point. Secrecy took on utmost importance. He considered starting a fire as a distraction, as was the hurricane when he escaped Casitoa, but dismissed it. All slaves would be aroused to fight the fire, and their own absence noticed. Luis hoped the Calusas would think that his group headed for Habana, the closest port, after noticing the missing canoas.

***

The appointed evening came in late 1623, after the Indios left for council the previous day. Luis had signaled *midnight* to his partners and did so by pointing straight up into the sky, for when the slight moon rose to its height that night. Though the tide would be incoming, the time to strike came into view. Dark, and Luis arrived first, then Lunga, bearing his assignment of poles plus three pointed spears. Muscular and in his mid-twenties, he could be the best fighter of the three, to Luis' reckoning. Pedro followed soon thereafter, bringing sustenance and woven ropes.

They moved with silence to attach the canoes and pole planking, with the mast and sail to be affixed later.

No sound emanated as they loaded all gear and prepared to launch. Just before climbing aboard, Pedro motioned towards someone moving down to the water's edge. Luis knew they would have to take him down, as one Calusa yell would awaken the village. He made no sound but walked right up among the group. With sword ready to run him through, Luis held back in amazement.

Ronimo! Sleepless and stumbling onto them, or did he know of the plan?

With no time to waste, Luis waved him back, but Ronimo answered by signaling that he too wanted to go. Pedro and Lunga gave the thumbs-down sign and shook their heads, but Ronimo persisted. He motioned that he should go or, cupping both hands to his mouth, he would alert the village. Luis wanted to skewer him on the spot, but here stood a fellow Spaniard, though hapless. He motioned him aboard. A finger to his mouth signalled for quiet. They left the south side of the island and moved west, toward the inlet that led to the open sea and freedom. Four paddlers would serve better than three, but Luis could sense the tension that Ronimo brought aboard. He also brought nothing else, certain to create more resentment.

A slight breeze blew from the south as they continued west paddling out of the inlet. Luis delayed setting the mast and sail so the crew could first adapt to the double-craft and to paddling together. The dugouts each stretched to about thirteen feet with two and one-half feet of width. Running stable, made more so by the poles lashed across the middle, helped the foodstuffs lay secure on top. He knew they must go west about fifteen miles to move beyond a large island to the northwest. Then they could turn due north. Luis sighted Polaris, comforted that they could turn toward it when ready, believing that would come just prior to first light. They moved along at about two and a half knots.

The sea obliged them, as it only produced a slight ripple and provided a chance to make needed speed. The cool night air posed no match for the body warmth generated by their paddling as they powered together in rhythm. Each man sensed control and freedom with each movement of his arms. Fleeing with an unspoken spirit of camaraderie evoked special feelings. Perhaps akin to a grounded galleon finally being tide-swept from a sand bar. All golden moments in time. But Luis noticed that Ronimo found it difficult to match the others' strokes. As a dim line of light eased out of the east behind them, they could see no land, so Luis ordered a turn to the north. Along with Polaris beckoning, he judged it safe to talk.

"We have moved out of sight of smoke signals, but rest assured, Calos will alert other villages along the coast. We must stay at ready."

"It's time for Ronimo to match our efforts," said Pedro, his discomfort rising, along with an indignant glance towards Luis.

"I do my part the best I can," scowled Ronimo. "Becoming accustomed to paddling takes time."

"Amigo, you should be accustomed by now, so pick up the pace or go overboard," said Luis. "We agreed to let you come because of your threat, but on the open sea no obligation remains."

Luis hoped that the scoundrel's combat skills, if needed, showed better than his strokes. He did improve his pace but sulked and communicated with scornful looks.

About mid-morning, the men sighted land to the northeast, the anticipated large island that curved out to the west. Since a fresh and favorable wind blew from the south, all agreed to set the mast and sail. Speed would increase as they leaned to the northwest, away from the island. Before they began rigging the sail, Lunga pointed north and uttered *Calusas*. They could see a dot on the horizon, becoming larger by the moment.

"Turn west again!" yelled Luis. "Put your backs into it!"

An occasional glance told them that a war canoa closed in their direction. Bigger than their craft, it held six Indios, who stroked fresher at their paddles.

"They paddle from *Tanpa," said Luis. "The Calusa took me there once with a trading party. Either from smoke or runners, their communications work."

As the enemy approached within range, three put down their paddles and placed arrows in their bows. They prepared to shoot as necessary.

"Lay down your paddles and raise your arms in surrender," said Luis. "On my signal, Lunga will use the three lances," said as he gestured. Then Pedro must topple their canoa. We must move fast, before the remaining paddlers unquiver their arrows."

"Looks like a good day to drown an opponent," said Pedro, epitomizing bravery, as he would use only his hands for weapons.

They came alongside, bows drawn, and an apparent leader motioned for Luis' group to paddle northeast toward the large island.

Instead of killing us on the spot, they plan to take us back for torture, thought Luis. *Not so.*

*Pine Island area

Lunga and Pedro watched him.

"Now!"

With lightning speed, Lunga dispatched three lances in quick succession. Each hit a vital spot and the bowmen went down and over the side. A couple of arrows their shot waywardly.

The remaining three, now too close to put their bows to use, raised axes and issued blood-curdling yells. In one movement, Pedro stood on deck and leaped onto the war canoa, taking a Calusa into the water, both submerging. The impact flipped the Indio craft, sending the other two into the sea. One surfaced and grabbed to come aboard the double-craft, but Luis reacted. One slash of the sword to the neck, and hence a shark's meal. The other Calusa surfaced next, reached up and struck Lunga in the side with his shell ax and pulled him into the ocean. Luis waited for someone to resurface, his sword in hand. Pedro, who had been grappling underwater for about a minute, rose up, gasping for air.

"One less Indio," he sputtered. "But it's cold down there. Where's Lunga?"

"Down below," said Luis. "I'm waiting."

In an instant, the last remaining Calusa raised his head above the water and yelled in victory. But Lunga resurfaced and put a lockhold on the Calusa's neck. They thrashed about on the surface, with the Congolese's blood spotting the water. Lunga rammed his opponent's head into the deck's side, which gave Luis an opportunity to dispatch him with the sword. Pedro and Luis dragged Lunga onto the dugout's deck and applied pressure to his wound using a deerskin bag that once held water. The men lay on the planks, regaining their energy. Now able to relax and concentrate on their next move, they noticed Ronimo slumped in his seat, one of the wayward arrows protruding from his chest.

"A sad end for a sad man," said Pedro. "Perhaps if he had lived, we could have helped him"

Luis heaved him over the side, but not before offering Christian prayers for his soul.

"At least he possesses a better chance of entering Heaven than the Calusas. Now let's tend to Lunga."

An errant arrow had also punctured the deerskin bag Lunga held against his wound. Just enough water remained in the other bag to clean the wound, but they carried no balm or salve to apply. Lunga lay on the deck to rest and help balance the weight for the double-rigged canoas, now with one paddler each.

"Time to rig the mast and sail," said Luis. "The wind is up and steady, and we need to increase from about two and half knots to around four, if we can."

Pedro added, "when the six natives don't return, some of their tribe may follow. I hope their sunken canoa and the sharks' work will leave no trace, granting us a favor."

"Yes, I agree. At any rate, we need to move north up the coast and try to spot a beach around nightfall." .

Lunga's wound needed attention, and all needed fresh water. But Luis' attention now focused on the sail. He'd sailed small boats before, but on a river in shipwright-constructed vessels. On this day he and Pedro would need to improvise. The tree pole mast stood three inches in diameter and eight feet tall, and if they could secure it upright, it would suffice.

With one end pushed down perpendicular between two deck poles, the men next attached four lines independent of each other, half-way up the pole mast. Each loose end went to a deck corner where they secured it. Next came the sail. With much effort they removed two smaller deck poles and bound them crossways to the mast as separate yard arms. They affixed the old sail and off they went. It strained and creaked and looked as though it could collapse at anytime, but they sped faster. Luis wielded a strong arm on his paddle, rudder-like, to control the direction.

About fifteen minutes later, two more large canoas headed in their direction, from due east. This time, paddling-wielding Calusas could not close on them as the now sailing craft sped faster.

"I think we left them out of sight," said Pedro, after about thirty anxious minutes.

"Nevertheless partner, let's keep moving till dusk, then move in and look for a deserted beach."

"Luis, so far, freedom feels better and better, but my baked skin and raw throat would relish some cool fresh water."

Luis didn't respond as he strained his eyes on something in the distance.

"Pedro, see that odd, smooth area of water ahead?"

The appearance of a near placid lake in the middle of the ocean grew larger. As they passed over the clear, glass-like surface and dipped their hands, the colder temperature startled them.

"Strike the sail!" said Luis.

After doing so, each man cupped a taste into his mouth.

"A *spring in the middle of the ocean!" said Pedro.

            * Aquifer surfaces in ocean

Even Lunga leaned over and drank it in. It refreshed and re-energized the three and they refilled the one good deerskin bag. Pedro nor Luis could resist, both plunging into the spring.

"Brrrrr, its cold," said Luis, upon resurfacing.

Climbing back onto the deck and purposely splashing Lunga, he remarked of hearing tales of galleons straying off the coast and finding ocean springs.

"I thought it too ridiculous to even repeat. Too much of a myth for me."

"Now you can tell the tale too, upon our return," said a smiling Pedro.

"Thank you for your fighting skills and your vote of confidence! I look forward to regaling some señorita, even if it's not Isabela."

"Do you think she's waiting for you?"

"Doubtful. I've been gone for almost two years, and she's heard the Atocha story by now. I also told her not to wait after a year. Though I'm saddened to think on it, I've accepted it."

The men sailed on, well away from the coastline, with it remaining a small line on the horizon. As long as they came near the land of the Calusa, danger lurked. The sail continued to provide a swift means of travel and with the sun now in the west, they kept their bearings.

"Luis, what can we do for Lunga's wound?"

"If we can find an island with a beach where we can stay tonight, perhaps we can make a poultice with comfrey leaves. Then strap it with woven fronds. Let's hope for no sepsis."

The late afternoon wind increased, causing the double-crafted vessel to rock up and down with the chop. They knew it caused Lunga pain, but he did not wince. He responded with a thankful smile if the men inquired of him.

"Ah, I look forward to a bountiful feast of dried fish and tubers when we stop," said Pedro. "And perhaps I may sleep on the deck tonight to avoid mosquitoes, as we don't want to build a fire that would alert the Calusa."

"Yes, very true, amigo."

After sunset, Luis held his paddle firm in the water on the right side, so the blade would turn the craft east. As they came closer to the coast, the men scanned the horizon.

"I believe I see a beach. It summons," said Luis.

"Perhaps an island," said Pedro, "and so far no sign of life."

The surf broke about an arrow's flight offshore at a shoal area. It tumbled the vessel up and down, it creaking all the while.

"Don't break up, don't break up!" yelled Pedro, as if the deck-boat could hear him.

A few minutes later they reached the beachhead's surf, which also pounded their craft. It crashed onto shore, Lunga fell overboard, and the other men jumped into the water, attempting to push and pull the vessel onto the beach. Waves continued to crash against it. They struggled, dragging and heaving it onto shore, waves lapping the back.

Lunga crawled onto the beach, his wound bleeding again.

"First the wound, then the food," said Luis, as they helped him up.

"I'll look in the woods for comfrey leaves and palmetto fronds that we can weave," said Pedro.

"Good. I'll try to make him comfortable. Be on your alert, although I imagine any villages lie on the island's back side."

Luis placed Lunga further up onto the beach and tried to make him comfortable. He gave him a dried fish on which to chew and helped him take a couple of swigs from the deerskin water bag.

"Once we treat and bind your wound, and you have a good night's rest, we'll have a new man."

Luis spoke not knowing if the Congolese understood but hoped that his helpful manner conveyed encouragement. He was concerned, due to much blood loss, but relied on Lunga's strength and good health to allow him to recover. For the moment, there existed one less fighter should the need arise. Pedro returned and made a poultice for Lunga's wound, which they bound with woven fronds. It would be sufficient. He also brought a few palmetto hearts dug with effort using Luis' sword. The men devoured them.

Covered by the sail, the trio lay not far off the beach, enjoying the evening's breeze. It allowed no insects. They had struggled to find a clear spot, as bushes thickened further inland, and crashing waves made sleeping on deck not an option. The night passed, and the men enjoyed the rest, much needed after a night and day of heavy exertion.

Creeping first light. Like a glimmer of hope. Early sky colored like a real de a ocho lying in the shadows. Awakening, Luis decided to stroll the beach, to gather his thoughts before the others awoke. Islands dotted the coastline, and to Luis this one looked five to seven miles long. They camped near its northern tip. He could just see Polaris to the north, and it bestowed its usual comfort, from the end of Ursa Minor. His thoughts went back to Seville's Universidad, to astronomy, one of his favorite subjects. Then, he couldn't get enough of studying the stars, the planets, the moon, the mythological figures dotting the sky. The study of the ancient art of celestial navigation-all taught within the guidelines of church doctrine. He continued walking the beach, though the multitude of shells aggravated his bare feet.

Truly an *island of shells, he thought, *holding more than I've ever seen.*
      *Little Captiva Island

He knew they'd need to find fresh water, as Pedro found no streams or springs in the near interior. Fish may need to be caught so to suckle fluids. Still, in these quiet moments, Luis became aware that his life once again bore meaning. Not as a prisoner with no rights, no respect, only toil. Slavery lay behind him, and he reveled in the thought, determined to stay free. To strive like his hero, Don Quixote, but with different dragons to fell. Wind, water, Calusa, the wounded and the unknown. But in spite of it, he relished the challenge. It played out in the theatre of freedom, and that made all the difference.

"Arise, men, it's time. Allow me to apprise you of *Nochebuena,* our celebration the night before Navidad! Today may or may not be the exact day, but the season for sure. What a joy living free at this time of year."

Pedro arose, but Lunga still slept. They could see that he'd lost more blood during the night, with red staining the sand.

"Should we leave him?"

Luis was taken aback by the question.

"Leave him?! No! He helped to save our lives. He trusts me."

"But he cannot help us now should we have to fight, and he adds more weight to the canoas."

With a look of incredulity, Luis' eyes met his fellow escapee's.

"Pedro. Have I misjudged you? ...I hope not. Would you leave me if I were lying there, instead of him?

Would you care if I left you in a similar state?"

"All right, but we have no more lances and only one sword. We would be hard pressed to protect him."

"Let me remind you, Pedro, that your hands became weapons, and how well they served you."

That seemed to end the subject at the moment, but Luis knew it could rear its head again.

Pedro harbors great survival skills. They come naturally to him, but he thinks naught of others right now, thought Luis.

Pedro announced a foray into the woods to look for food. After a spell he returned, bearing a more relaxed manner.

"Would you hang the sail and check the rigging while I help him aboard?" asked Luis. "We need to move out before full sun-up, and we need to cover many miles again today. Perhaps we can find another deserted isle at dusk, so we can catch some fish. We also need fresh water, and finding that poses our biggest challenge, as sailing too close in continues dangerous."

He did his best to redress the seeping wound with comfrey and palmetto frond straps, then helped Lunga aboard. Along with the pack food, the men ate Indio figs that Pedro gathered in the woods. They loaded for sailing and eased the double craft into the gentle ocean, paddling out, hoping for wind. Traveling began much slower than the previous day with only two paddlers.

Lunga rolled over toward Luis, his face conveying a sense of sadness rather than his usual smile.

"Lunga...die...," he struggled to say. He then made the sign of the Cross.

"No, Lunga," Luis responded in earnest. "Today you live as a free man again." He spoke and gestured as if breaking bonds that tightened around him.

"When we arrive at San Agustín, we'll make it official," he said, pointing east, and gesturing again.

Lunga did not speak but stared motionless. Luis asked a question.

"Lunga," as Luis made the sign of the Cross and questioned him with gestures, "where did you learn?"

"Potosi...mines...friar...God..." He struggled to speak, but his answer rang clear before he passed out.

The men moved out beyond the shoal line, daylight lighting up the beach. They paddled until glimpsing land as only a speck to the east. The vessel then turned northward. Pedro sat now at the rear of his canoa, ready to till with his paddle. Luis sat in front of his, to keep balance. The wind increased, and they began to sail again, heading north.

"Pedro, a dream came to me last night. I know it arose from my fatigue yesterday, but it was stirring."

"Tell me."

"I flew like a gull above the beach, following the coastline. At first it scared me, but then it became exhilarating, as I continued to soar. I would swoop up and down, in complete control of my movements. I could see east of the islands the waterways, and beyond to the mainland. I know only birds can fly, but the feeling was invigorating. What do you think, divinely-inspired or devil-inspired?"

"Tell me what else you ate last night, besides the tuber cakes and fish, so I can have that dream." Pedro wore a big smile and joined Luis in laughter.

"Amigo, it either means you may turn into a bird or that you feel free as a bird. Like I said, tell me what special victuals you kept hidden and of which you partook."

Both men enjoyed the dream review, and it lifted their spirits. Sailing continued with the craft traveling at about four knots an hour.

"At this rate, we should cover 35 to 40 miles today," said Luis, "and be closer to the Tocobagas."

"How will we know when we reach their tribe?"

"When we reach the second large bay, I believe, and no one attacks us," Luis said, adding a chuckle.

During the morning, dolphins encircled the craft, putting on a show. Surfacing, diving, flipping, and blowing out their breath holes, they entranced the men. About mid-day both stood on the deck so to reset the sail which had blown loose. Time-consuming and requiring much concentration, but they had success. Returning to their sitting positions in the canoes, they saw to their horror that Lunga no longer lay aboard.

9
TOCOBAGA VILLAGE

1624

Those Indios that did not know me
Desired and endeavored to
See me because of my renown.

Cabeza de Vaca
1542

FLORIDA PENINSULA WEST COAST

"Lunga! Lunga!" shouted Luis. "I didn't hear or see anything."

Each man strained his eyes in all directions for a sight of him but to no avail.

"When did it happen?" said Pedro. "He must have slid off the deck when we hit a wave, but I didn't hear him cry for help."

"He didn't slide off accidentally," said Luis. "I tied his arm to a pole before we cast off. He knew death approached and didn't want to be a burden. His wound caused too much blood loss."

"Luis, I'm sorry…for what I said…"

"I know Pedro. Rejoice in the consolation that today a good man dwells in Paradise. He confirmed that for me. We owe our lives to him."

Each man held back tearful emotions and set his sights ahead. Luis knew it happened from Lunga's choice, but it didn't erase the pain in his heart. They didn't speak for awhile, until at last Pedro broke the silence.

"The west wind increases and gray clouds head our way. I pray it's a downpour coming so I can open my mouth and the deerskin wide. My lips parch and my mouth dries up."

Within thirty minutes the afternoon rain drenched them. They unfurled the sail so to stabilize the craft, and each
man lay on his back, mouth gaping wide. The air temperature dropped ten degrees, noticeable, but they minded not, grateful instead. After about an hour, the rain slackened and the sun began to peep in and out of the clouds. When it set, the men turned the vessel east and reset the sail, proceeding closer to land. A *barren white strand presented itself behind the surf, with no visible sign of humans anywhere. It stretched as far as could be seen in both directions.

*Nokomis, Fl area

"Get ready to beach it, Luis!"

Swells rolled from the rainstorm, so it required an effort to keep the craft straight for landing. Luis sprang into the surf alongside and muscled it onto the beach amidst breaking waves. Pedro did likewise. To secure it, they tied one end of a rope to a large driftwood log. With the sail laid on bushes behind the beach, they hoped it would dry before nightfall, as it made good cover.

"If you'll give me the metal hook and fishline from your kit, I'll find some tiny crabs in the sand and catch supper."

Luis never removed his sword or his satchel, not even to sleep. He reached in the bag and found the gear, alongside the silver reales de a ocho of which he made no mention.

"Here, fisherman. Just remember, we have only one hook. It must last us. I'll use my flint and steel to start a small fire after I've gathered some tinder. We have come far enough north that the Calusa shouldn't see our smoke."

Survival skills served them well that evening as they enjoyed roasting and devouring three small fish of unknown origin. They also finished the rest of their packed food. As a pall of smoke died around the fire, they sat on the sand, resting from the day's rigors.

"Luis, have you noticed that the Indios never seem to have flux, and as captives we have not suffered from it?" "I have noticed. I also believe that their food cleansed my body of foul humors and rendered me healthier and stronger."

"Perhaps you can determine how to eat Calusa food when you return home," said Pedro, with the usual brightness in his eyes, along with a soft laugh.

He sat pensive for a few moments, as a strange mood overtook him. With a faraway look in his eyes, he spoke. "Not certain, but I don't think I will go back into the slave trade. After seeing Lunga fight along with us, then give up the ghost so he wouldn't be a burden, my thoughts on mulattos have changed."

He looked over at Luis as if to say-*do you understand?*

"What about you Luis, what will you do? Stay in the military?"

"Well….I appreciate the military, as the skills it taught have helped me to survive. But the military also brought me to this deserted beach. Felipe IV may have to get along without me. Anyway, this discussion is odd. Here we sit, on a lonely shore, talking of our return to Europe. We could be the first Europeans back on this spot in 100 years. Think on that."

He lay back on the sail upon the beach. Gazing out to sea, the scene intrigued him. Pink clouds from the sunset mirrored in the water and cast their glow above and below the horizon. It put a settling into his mind and body. Pulling the damp sail over him, sleepy-eyed, he thought of home.

Isabela, smiling as he shoved a small boat into the river for a lazy day paddle, her madre on the bank, of course…afternoon debates under the columns of the Universidad…swordfight practices with his abuelito…and…

Pedro shook him, frantic at early morning light.

"Get up, Luis! Noises coming from the woods. We need to move."

Untying the line from the driftwood, Luis threw it and thesail on board, and he and Pedro pushed their vessel into the water. Yells and whoops rang louder from the dense forest.

As they paddled out, reaching the sand bar, a pleading voice rang out.

"Amigos, wait…take me!"

The men stopped stroking and turned toward the sight of a naked, bearded, thin Spanish captive, running for his life. Behind him ran three Calusas, each carrying bow and arrow in hand. Seabirds scattered on the beach, screeching and flapping. The double-hulled craft floated now about an arrow's flight from the land, which meant going back would make them easy targets. As they sat dumbfounded, the decision happened for them, as arrows filled the would-be escapee's back. He fell face down in the surf. Still groggy from his quick awakening and departing, Luis saw the scene as from a bad dream.

"Paddle hard!" yelled Pedro.

The Calusas began to scalp, whoop, and then turn in the men's direction. The multitude of arrows fell just short as the men pushed with all their strength on the paddles.

"Soon we can sail and hope they will forget us and not tell others. Today I want to speed north without brandishing my sword."

"I agree, and I prefer not to brandish my hands," said Pedro, causing them both to laugh.

He added, "I regret that fellow didn't make it. We'll never know his name or how he knew of us. Maybe they saw last night's campfire, and he came to warn us."

Winds increased at mid-morning, and they moved faster, as land to the east showed as a small black line. No more Indios made an appearance on the water.

"If we can continue to run around four knots, as yesterday, maybe by day's end we can reach the big Bay of Pohoy."

"And out of Calusa land, Luis?"

"If Providence continues to favor us that should be true."

"Luis, do you believe in fate?"

"What do you call fate?"

"The Portuguese influence their lives with a sense of fate. Though an enthused people, we think some things meant to be. It helps us accept the unexpected that happens."

"Like being captured by the Calusa?"

"Yes."

"I don't know, Pedro. I do believe we have choices. And the right choice can make all the difference."

"Like you chose me to escape with you?"

"Could be."

"Well, anyway, listen to an old Portuguese folk song."

> *Quando?*
> *I was a small boy,*
> *Having just been born,*
> *Barely had I opened my eyes,*
> *And already all I could see was you.*
> *Someday when I'm very old,*
> *Having just died,*
> *Look deep into my eyes,*
> *Though lifeless they'll still see only you.*

"Arg, Pedro. Who sang, you or a scratchy-voiced lagarto?"

"Ahh, amigo, my voice still develops. But, do you get the message? Can you see? As long as you live, fate may someday place you back with Isabela."

"No, Pedro. She would not want me. I've sunk to such a vermin. Anyway, too long has passed and she's married for sure. Such a choice for a wealthy merchant."

With no food or water, they were sustained only by the will to survive and to flee the Calusa. They pushed hard all day, never striking the sail or stopping. As the giant, golden ball set in the west, a paddle was set hard right to make for another island. Coming into sight, it looked to be the last of the chain. To the north, they saw no more islands, portending a large bay of open water.

"Could that be it?" asked Pedro.

Luis strained, peering out.

"Hard to tell with nighttime approaching. Perhaps we can see better in the morning. See any sign of life?"

"No, but you never know what lurks or even watches us from the bush."

"I believe we've made 30 miles today, sailing from early morning to dusk, and I hunger. So, Pedro, I wouldn't be displeased if you prepared our feast tonight."

"All my pleasure, Armador. Would you prefer crab or deer meat?" he answered, smiling.

Both men jumped into the surf and drove the vessel against the shore, once again pushing with all their might to lodge it on the *beach. In the waning hours of daylight,Pedro scooped up a small round sand crab from the wet beach. Attaching it to the hook and tossing the rock-weighted hand line into the water produced a silvery fish which he propelled onto the beach.

Luis sliced it into slivers so they could suck the fresh fluid they needed. They welcomed raw fish for supper, needing to avoid a fire after the captive's chase incident. They untied the sail and covered their tired bodies for a night of rest.

"Perhaps tomorrow, Pedro, the Tocobagas will welcome us with a feast of…", Luis whispered, as he drifted off.

***

"Say, Amigo, for what use do you plan the reales de a ocho?" Pedro asked, while gazing seaward and casting into the surf. Semi-awake at morning and startled by the question, Luis sat up and wondered how his partner could know, since the
leather satchel never left his side.

"What reales?"

"While you slept I spied them while taking out the fishing gear. I have no use for them, just curious as to what you will buy on the coast here," he said, with a slight smirk.

"From the Atocha. We may need them when we arrive at a
mission or at San Agustín," he said, not desiring to discuss it further.

They spoke no more of the silver coins, worth a goodly sum in circulation. But Luis felt exposed, as does a deer when smelling man in the wind, alerting him to danger. Pedro, he knew as a valuable friend, but still he decided to remain cautious.

"Pedro, can you see far north? The mouth of the big **Pohoy Bay is supposed to be five to seven miles wide and have scattered islands in the mouth. But so does the ***Bay of Tanpa, south of Pohoy."

"I see a speck across the way. I pray its Tocobaga land so I may cease

* Anna Maria Island   **Tampa Bay   *** Pine Island area

this meager fishing."

"We best depart north now, as dark clouds approach from the west," said Luis.

The morning began chilled, so they decided to paddle in addition to sailing so to warm their bodies. The lack of food sapped their energy, but their spirits stayed high as the sail billowed. Thunder rumbled, and the wind and waves picked up as they neared halfway across.

"Should we go back, señor Captain Armador?"

"Let's press on, as we've come so far. Plus I'd like to believe we will enhance our safety on the other side."

"Luis, big waves bring no safety! You know that!"

"Trust me, Pedro. I survived a 100 mile float in a hurricane."

"But, Luis…," his words trailed off.

The storm moved in fast, and large rollers pounded the craft with a southern wind blowing. Luis' mind flashed back to the Atocha's deck, and it made him shiver. Keeping the vessel straight became a challenge for the men.

"Should we …?"

Pedro never finished his sentence, as a huge gust flung the canvas sail from its deck straps and sent it flying through the sky. Hopes went with it. The rain now came in torrents and the bay boiled and foamed in a tempest, as if in the middle of the ocean. The double-craft tossed and turned out of control.

It happened about a mile from a large island south of the mainland. A huge wave engulfed the men and craft, sending all end-over-end. The water, though warmer than the air, still shocked with its coolness. Each man surfaced, gasping for breath and disoriented by the spill. The noise of wind, waves and rain surrounded them with no sign of their double-canoa craft.

"Swim, we can do it!" Luis yelled.

They could see land and made for it as best they could, with waves breaking all around.

Luis thought-*I've done this once and I can do it again, and this time I see the shore.* Though immersed for only a short period, he felt muscles stiffening and wondered how long they would enable him. Unlike his castoff from the Atocha, this was four months later in the year with cooler water. He made progress, first swimming forward in troughs, then rising above the crest of waves. With teeth now chattering, he swam on and hoped too for Pedro's survival, though he did not see him.

Ignore the cold, my body adapts, I will handle it, I will make it.

From out of nowhere, he received a bump on his leg but ignored it, thinking it debris. Next, something rammed his left shoulder and the blow stunned like a cannonball shot. Painful, though he received no cut. He realized only one creature attacks in that manner. Turning as much as possible to look behind him, he saw a fin headed his way. He knew its jaws veered off target on the first attack, and that the next could be fatal. Luis made ready to defend himself.

The shark closed, but just before a deadly bite could be executed, Luis raised as much of his body as possible out of
the water and came down hard with both fists on the shark's head.

"Whooiiii!!" he grunted.

It worked, but for how long?

His shoulder ached, but he pushed on through it towards land, with his spirit surging as much as ever. Wave after wave shattered the white sand ahead and wind carried the foam further onto the beach. When he tried to stand, waves took him down. He would surface and start again. A stone's throw from the beach he touched bottom. Knee-high in churning water he could see off to his right his old nemesis, or a new one. This time he came fast, but Luis readied. A millisecond before the impact, Luis flung his body upward out of the water and again brought down his fists, striking hard. Stunned, the shark disappeared and did not return.

Luis made haste to shore, walking, swimming, riding the waves, and to his notion, flying. He did not wish another encounter.

As the last few breakers pushed him to the beach, he fought back a heavy sense of weakness. He went limp as the ebb and flow rolled him out, then back, flinging him around in the shallows. Salt water filled his nostrils and throat, causing a deep choking. His body exhausted and mind numb, he wanted so much to crawl onto the beach.

I am as a dead fish, eyes protruded, body bloated, smelly, seen by no one.

As he flung about, for the first time he began to have doubts of his survival, and a paleness of despair, deep within, gripped him. With consciousness failing, strong tugs at his arms realerted his senses.

The shark again? He may get me this time.

Two strong natives braved the water and pulled him out. His shoulder, rammed by the shark, cried out in pain, but Luis made no sound. Grateful for whomever hauled him, he was taken to a makeshift lean-to. It sat just off the beach, in a grove of palm trees where the wind broke. They spoke, but he couldn't comprehend. The Indios laid him down beside a fire and gave him sips of water and a koonti cake. To him, the finest tavern in

Seville could not have served finer fare. Soon, his body stopped trembling, and he could feel warmth freeing his muscles.

He gazed at the men, who now said nothing but stared with a look of incredulity. Not Calusa, their hospitality told Luis that. Tall like the Calusa, but both men bore many tattoos. At Calos, only the chief did, plus a Calusa chief would not be staying in a temporary hut. He concluded them Tocobagas and did his best to convey a sense of gratitude, after which they gave him a deerskin for cover. He lay on the ground and almost cried as feelings of thankfulness and relief swept over him.

When he awoke, three faces looked his way, and one smiled. Pedro.

"Amigo, glad to see you alive," he said, stopping between koonti cake bites.

"How long have you been here, Pedro?" asked Luis, still groggy.

"Maybe half an hour-glass, so you have napped at least that long."

"What, how did you…?" Luis fumbled with words.

"I didn't think I'd make it, but I decided I would press till my last breath. Afterwards, I rested a long time in a grove of palms."

"How did you find us?" asked Luis.

"After the rain stopped, I searched the *beach for you and could see the smoke drifting upward, so here I am."

"I think these kind souls are Tocobagas."

"Yes. I extracted that from them using signs. Their dialect is different from the Calusa. They think we come as big medicine or something like that since we escaped. They know most Calusa escapees face recapture and wind up with a slit throat. I don't think the two groups assemble with each other much."

"Let's hope not. We must be at the Tocobagas' southern border."

The Indios signed and conveyed that they came on a fishing trip and, like the men, were caught in the storm, but on land. Luis and Pedro surrendered to sleep that night, as if on an aimless journey, but warm and dry under deerskins. They awoke rested, with a stream of light pouring around the lean-to's edge. To his comfort, Luis' satchel and sword stayed in place, never touched. For an interval, he lost sense of time and place.

"Was yesterday a nightmare, or did it happen?"

"Luis, it's murky, but I think it took place. So glad to be alive, but so sorry we lost the double-canoes and deck. It served us well."

As one of the Indios gave each a koonti cake, Luis pointed northeast, asking, "Pohoy?" A brief nod came in reply. With palms up and arms spread wide, Pedro inquired of Tocobaga. He indicated that's where they

*Mullet Key-SW Tampa Bay

wanted to go. The Indio pointed north. Pedro responded with signs showing thankfulness and inquired if they would take Luis and him to Tocobaga. He received no response.

Sometime that afternoon, the Indios provided an answer. They motioned for the men to follow, as they began walking north on a trail. Each native carried a pack of dried fish on his back. They arrived at the island's north side, where each Indio loaded his pack into a canoe and waved to the men to climb aboard. For the rest of the day, they paddled an inner passage among small islands and sea grasses. About sunset they veered to the east side of a small bay by the mainland. Here sat a small village with huts of timber and palm-leaf roofs dotting the shoreline, with each home sited atop a shell and clay midden. Further back, a large hut belonging to the chief perched on a high treeless mound. An earthen ramp led down from it to the plaza.

Luis and Pedro received welcomes along with the returning Indios. In the middle of the plaza they beheld a barbacoa with a large pot boiling and several women and children active in food preparation. The peacefulness and genial atmosphere overwhelmed the survivors. One of their rescuing Indios motioned that on the morrow, guides would lead them to Tocobaga.

"Luis, is this happening?" Pedro asked, as he was provided a bowl of boiled fish and warm koonti cake.

"Well, if they plan to kill us, at least we won't die hungry." Gazing around, Luis tried to recall from Cabeza de Vaca's memoir of the Narváez expedition 100 years earlier, searching for Pohoy Bay. *Something about entering an almost blind pass from the Gulf into a small bay. * Bahia de la Cruz? Then landing at a village on the mainland. Is this it ?*

***

Morning came, and Luis and Pedro followed several Indios north along a trail from the village. Allowed to keep their deerskin jackets, it evidenced the Tocobagas way of honoring them for escaping the Calusa. They walked about thirteen miles the first day, from Luis' estimate. Several smaller villages appeared along the way.

*Boca Ciega Bay

Early on the second day they received tanned moccasins as the group turned northeast on a rougher trail through a thick forest. Along the way the Indios fed them and continued to convey homage to the Europeans. Another estimated thirteen mile trek brought them at sunset to the large *Tocobaga village on the northwest side of the Bay of Pohoy. As dusk coincided with their arrival, they received a grand welcome with a sumptuous meal placed before them.

"Either this represents fattening for the slaughter or somebody likes us," said Pedro.

"Yes, it's certainly different treatment than by the Calusa. Roasting us? It would've already happened."

"Gentlemen, welcome. I am Owahee."

Startled to hear the Spanish language, they looked into the face of another friendly Tocobaga. In a broken form of Spanish, he explained that he was the son of a Spanish castaway and his Indio wife.

"My father was captured following a shipwreck, but he learned to love the Tocobaga. He became a trusted member, not wanting to return to Spain. He taught me your language and educated me as best he could before he died. Please know that no harm will come to you. Our chief wants to honor you tomorrow for your bravery and skill in escaping the Calusa. Tonight you can stay in my hut to sleep."

The men could tell by all appearances that Owahee related to the Tocobaga culture, down to the tattoos on his legs. But his height likened more to the Europeans, shorter than the natives. His complexion resembled the Indios, but his mannerisms likened to Spaniards. He wore a smile and conveyed genuine interest in them.

Dawn brought much activity to the village. Luis and Pedro could observe the comings and goings of the Indios, whose huts made a semi-circle around a central plaza. Several mounds lay adjacent to the water, the largest supporting the chief's dwelling. Fishing nets and piles of shells attested to their main source of food. Pottery and rough furs too lay about in abundance. Luis figured the town had about 1,000 people.

Owahee brought newly-woven frond breechcloths for the men and told them of the upcoming ceremony. He led them to the long council house, presided over by the chief. Many men were in attendance, and Owahee interpreted for their guests.

"Our chief wants to recognize you for your daring and successful escape. Many have tried and many have failed. He respects bravery and has communicated of your feat all along our

*Safety Harbor, Fl

coast. You may stay here for a time or pass unharmed throughout our territory. You honor us by your presence."

The chief motioned for a feast to begin while Luis and Pedro made their thanks known through Owahee. They did not show emotion but became bewildered by one noticeable feature of the chief's face. Later they inquired.

"Owahee, why does your chief have no nose?" asked Luis.

"Gentlemen, I can understand your shock. Thirteen years ago, Spanish soldiers came down the coast from the Guacara River. They came with guns, armor, and savage dogs. They shot some of our people, then bound our chief and slit his throat in front of everyone. They tied his honored nephew to a tree and sliced off his nose. The solders said the action came as punishment for some of our people's raid on the lower Guacara that killed seventeen Christian natives. After the soldiers left, the nephew became our new chief."

They noticed that he spoke without anger and no seeming desire for revenge. At any rate, Luis and Pedro decided to accept their offer and stay for a couple of months, until early springtime. Then they would continue their journey northward. They experienced freedom to come and go at will, with no work required. They observed tattooing, preparations for small cornfields, and the varied uses of gourds. The Tocoboga owned slaves from other tribes, but no Europeans, and the men did not broach that subject. They soon slept in the council house as visitors always did, and food was provided whenever they desired. Owahee spent much time with them, teaching his skills in net casting, bow and arrow fishing, and spear fishing, all mostly for mullet in the bay, where they swarmed in the thousands.

***

"You must leave," said Owahee. He spoke in a harried manner.

"Why?" asked Pedro.

One morning after about two months had passed, the admired guests observed a large contingent of warriors entering the town and making their way to the chief's house. Soon after, several Tocobaga warriors assembled with them in the council house. At times, the sound of loud discussions and anger rose from the building.

"The Calusa, from whom you escaped, have come, asking to take you back." The alarm in his voice continued.

"But you have more Tocobaga than Calusa here. Can't you protect us?" asked Luis.

"Yes, but with the purpose of their mission removed from sight, no disagreement will grow. At any point, I've been told you must leave."

His firm and resolute manner made it clear.

"Fair enough," said Pedro. "But will you come with us, as a guide, to the north? We'd like to walk trails for a while through your territory."

"Besides, the Calusa will think we left by water, should they try to find us," added Luis.

"Very well, meet me at the north end of the village. Try to slip out without causing notice. I will pack food and weapons.

Luis and Pedro realized that they must gird up from their current relaxed state and prepare once again to be on their guard. With moccasins, deerskins and Luis's satchel and sword,
 they moved to the appointed area. Knowing that soon the
Calusas would discover their absence and try to find them, they hoped that no harm would come to Tocobaga.

The sandy path ahead looked clear, though treachery could lie in wait later. However reluctantly, they heeded its beckoning as a single shining lamplight in a darkened town.

10
GUACARA RIVER

1624

*Only in solitude do we find ourselves;
and in finding ourselves, we find
all our brothers in solitude.*

Miguel de Unamuno

FLORIDA PENSINSULA WEST CENTRAL

Owahee led them on a brisk pace north on the trail from the village.

It ran narrow and canopied and plainly well-trod. Luis figured that if the Calusa didn't know about it, they could find it and begin tracking them. But with their determination rekindled, they readied for the challenge, refreshed and renewed after two months of Tocobaga hospitality.

"How long do we have, Owahee, before the Calusa discover our absence?" posed Pedro.

"When the sun crosses the sky's mid-point, we need to run, as by then they will know. I don't know if they will try to pick up our trail here, or cross back over west to their dugouts and paddle north on the sea, thinking you've gone there. They could do both, or nothing."

Owahee will move us fast and safe. But how far will he take us before sending us on alone? Luis wondered.

The path, packed hard, made walking comfortable. Palmettos spread along it on each side, and giant moss-draped oaks kept it shady. After mid-day, the men broke into a trot, with Owahee's superb physical condition evident. After two hours, he called for a walk, but no stopping. The men consumed koonti cakes, fruit, and swigs of water while on the march. Several times rattlesnakes slithered across the trail with their Tocoboga guide deftly skirting and imploring the men to do likewise. Sunset brought a small clearing where they would spend the night, they hoped in safety.

"Will the path continue smooth? And how far to the next big river that flows to the ocean?" asked Pedro.

"It stays smooth and dry," said Owahee. "If we traveled closer to the big seawater it would become low, wet, and filled with lagartos. Over the next six days the trail stays clear. Then we arrive at an area just upstream of a big bend in a large river. There we will find a small village of our people, one of the last on this side of the river. Above that lies the Ocale land, which is dry north of the river, but swampy on the south side, going downstream."

He continued. "At the village, we will acquire a canoa for you, and you can wend your way down to the sea. After that, you paddle north to the *Guacara River's mouth and ascend it to the Guacara mission. There you may inquire for further directions if your goal is San Agustín."

"Will we have problems with the Ocale?" asked Luis.

At that, Owahee drew from his bag a small carving. He handed it to Luis.

"Carry this with you, and should we become separated, present it to the Tocoboga village at the end of this trail, at river's edge. They will honor any request of yours, including your need for a canoa. Upon floating down the river, you will pass Ocale, so show it to them also. You should pass unharmed."

The next five days and nights passed pleasant and uneventful. Days they spent in slow runs and fast walks and evenings in eating and sleeping. Wrapped in their deerskins with leaves piled on for insulation, they kept comfortable. The travelers acquired more provisions passing at a tiny village of six Tocobaga huts near the trail. They detected no word or sound of the Calusa, but the men stayed alert. Owahee expressed that once they reached the river, he thought it unlikely the Calusa would appear. On the evening of the fifth day, as they sat around the fire warming tuber cakes in fronds among the coals, he briefed them on the final leg of their journey.

"Tomorrow evening we should arrive at our people's village, after which you can depart downstream, and I will return. We should..." he stopped at mid-sentence, and raised his hand signaling quiet. Motionless, he listened with intent, as if trying to detect some unusual sound.

"What is it?" whispered Luis.

Frozen, responding only with his eyes, Owahee waited a full minute before speaking.

"I sensed a strange noise, not of the forest, but of some other source. It passed, but we must watch and listen."

"I agree," said Pedro.

That evening Owahee peppered them with many questions about Europe, as though he considered a future there. But he spoke also of the Tocobagas and made it evident he loved his life there. Then he adopted a serious look, half obscured by the campfire's smoke, and talked in a sad tone of his people.

"Ours once stood a large and proud nation, with our chief having sway over many villages. But Spanish diseases have wiped out many of us and

* San Martin River (Spanish) or Suwannee River (Seminole)

we could not fight the Calusa with strength now. I do fear the future of our people and whether or not we can stay here."

He continued to talk, but Luis became sleepy. He lay down by the glowing embers of their fire, took a final evening's swig from the deerskin bag and began to doze. His last image saw him floating downstream, happy and relaxed, as the current sent them along.

Stirring in the coolness at first daylight, he arose, adjusted his ever-present strap, satchel and sword, and stepped into the woods to relieve himself. He spied a huge oak with base limbs so low it cried out to be climbed. Remembering the hurricane at Casitoa and his time in a tree, he decided it would be fun to climb again, dry this time. Warming up his muscles, then climbing, he went up as high as possible. A good stone's throw above the ground he stretched out on an enormous limb with his back to the trunk and felt immersed with the forest. Too thick to see beyond the tree tops, but he could watch quiet movements of morning squirrels.

It happened fast down below. No visible movement preceded the sounds that rose through the air. Like the crescendo vibrations of cicadas at mid-morning on a summer's day, the whoops became louder and louder. A group of Calusas poured into the meager camp, taking hold of Pedro and Owahee. Luis now realized that Owahee had sensed their presence the previous evening. The intruders jostled and slapped and made a point of bloodying Pedro's nose. The cries of the Indios sent chills up Luis' spine. It tensed his muscles almost to cramping.

"Lu-ees! Lu-ees!" they shouted first into Pedro's face, and next into Owahee's.

All ten intruders began yelling together like a pack of vicious dogs, hungry and bloodthirsty—"Lu-ees! Lu-ees!"

Gripped by a combination of fear and guilt, Luis froze in stages of survival and perplexity. He could not match ten hostile Calusas. If he went below, he would either die or suffer as a slave again at Calos. He wanted neither. His heart raced. Below, in a pitiful state, Pedro pointed west toward the ocean, though he knew not of Luis' whereabouts. A whack to the head with a conch ax reflected the unsatisfactory reply he gave.

Nevertheless, they headed south on the trail, with a line tethered to Pedro's neck. They set Owahee free and pointed north, in the opposite direction. Without a word, he complied. For a long time Luis lay prone, not flinching a muscle.

Is this a ploy, will they double-back and try to find me later? Will they leave several hidden to the south, or north, on the trail, or will they go west to try to find me at the

Gulf? Remember, Luis, in times of trouble, it's best to first relax, control the emotions. Then you can act.

As his Grandfather's words rang true, he took several deep breaths and pretended to meld into the magnificent oak. As often happened in the wilderness, Luis lost all account of time. Soon his heart's pace abated, and he noticed the forest once again quiet, broken only by bird calls. The Calusas' outcry had silenced, as did the repetitive echo of it in his mind. He could now think clearly.

Waiting till mid-morning, Luis crept down, as a panther stalking his prey. He mustered great effort to prevent the sword and satchel contents from clanking. Moving on the trail with stealth, he headed north, eyes moving in all directions, instincts heightened. Once again, an invisible force prodded him to run north. And run he did. He dared the Calusa to catch him. Hoping they continued south motivated him to put even more distance between them.

Late afternoon brought him to the Tocobaga village on the banks of the large river, as Owahee predicted. He speculated that it was the *Amajuro River, so denoted in the area on one of the Atocha Pilot's maps. As he walked among the huts, he held the wooden carving high for all to see. They welcomed and fed him, then provided a covered place to sleep. Somehow, his admired escapee status preceded him, or either they acknowledged the carving's presentation. He inquired of Owahee but received no response. Happy to still be alive, he next looked to float downstream alongside Ocale land, toward the ocean.

In the morning, they awarded him a canoe and two carved paddles, each about a man's height in length, with blades six inches across. They packed dried deer meat, koonti cakes and raw maize for his satchel, and two deerskins of fresh water. Many stood and watched as he paddled away, turning to wave a goodbye salute. He considered the gifts special, so it left no doubt in his mind that they disliked the Calusa.

The float went smooth, with no fallen trees or floating logs to impede. Banks high on the right side of the river offered campsites, with the other side too low. Sometimes the river would traverse through lakes, and Luis would have to search for downstream outlets. He took pleasure in paddling again and became eager to reach the sea and venture north. His mind still wracked with guilt over leaving Pedro, and a vision of him dying from torture persisted.

Stopping mid-afternoon, he made camp on a spot well above the water in a small clearing. The food provided by the last village filled him as good

*Withlacoochee River, South

as he could want. He'd been told that the more he moved north, the more he'd find Indios hospitable. As the sun dropped below the horizon, Luis sat and gazed at the water flowing by him. He thought of it as dark liquid glass, the only force on earth that never stopped moving. He lay down, wrapped in his deerskin and let his thoughts drift free and easy.

How long to the sea? Is this really the Amajuro River? Will the Ocale let me pass? Will I encounter hostile Indios? Am I still a Spaniard, proud soldier of Felipe IV, if he still reigns? Or have I become a lone wandering Indio, who has no home and no people? And sometime this year, I think, I'll turn twenty-four, and then...

Morning fog enshrouded the river when Luis awoke. The previous night brought sounds of crickets and frogs, but daylight elicited a cacophony of birds singing. He noticed his two paddles on the ground, lying handle-end to handle-end. Somehow, the thought struck him to lash them together, into one single paddle, a blade on each end. He set out early, paddling at a steady pace, achieving, he estimated, 15 miles from dawn to mid-afternoon using the attached blades. Encountered were braided currents, swamps, islands, and the distant sight of an enormous lake to the south.

The third day he heard Ocale before he saw it. As the huge village came into view on the north bank, he looked up to see hundreds wailing and crying in a grand spectacle. In the middle, on an elevated structure, sat the chief. He was resplendent in pantherskin cape, shawl of large white feathers, and a band around his forehead holding plumes. A large shell ornament hung from his neck, with his body covered in red ochre and tattoos. Luis realized he witnessed some type of honor ceremony and felt as the intruder. To the Indios at water's edge, he held his carving aloft. No acknowledgment, so he presumed to float on down with no resistance.

The end of the fourth day brought a large, clear, spring-fed *stream into his river's north side. He refilled his deerskin water bags and drank his fill. Over what he counted to be eight uneventful days, he floated some seventy-five miles as best he could determine from his paddling speed. The current moved slowly, with the width a decent arrow's flight across.

Further down, marshy grass at riverside signaled that salt water loomed, as oak and palm hammocks sprouted among the tidal lowlands. Riverside campsites became non-existent and would've given Luis cause for concern were he not to soon reach the Gulf. There he would turn north and look for a beach or island. In the entire time on the beautiful green river, he did not encounter another craft. He counted this as good fortune, though he longed for human interaction. Stopping at a low tide oyster bar

* Rainbow River

near the mouth and utilizing his sword, he partook of a plentiful supply. Next, turning north into the shallow bay, the winds increased, so Luis kept paddling close to the sides. Small islands protruded nearby and broke the plain of the westerly horizon, with sea cows and dolphins now making an appearance. Another sight, a longboat, came into view, about a musket shot distance south, just off the coast. Straining to see, Luis spotted a small flag of three golden fleurs-de-lis on a white background.

French corsairs! The dogs themselves that mock us, calling the moss Spanish.

Luis thought that either their large ship had grounded offshore, sailed off course, or they came seeking slaves. In any event, he wanted no part of a crew that delighted in attacking Spain's vessels and slaughtering their military. He continued with a wary eye while paddling north, close on the bay's right side.

"Arrêter! Arrêter!" Came the cry from the boat, which had seven seamen aboard.

Luis didn't understand what it meant, but judging from the tone, it didn't convey an invitation to a meal. He doubled his paddle strokes, utilizing all the muscles developed from days of paddling. He pushed not from fear, but a pure sense of survival.

"Arrêter! Arrêter! " He heard repeated several more times from the boat but did not look back.

Boom!

It whizzed past his left and landed in the water 20 feet in front of his canoa. He continued dipping frenzied strokes. A brief glance over his left shoulder now produced a scene that struck with alarm. The French were stroking the oars of the longboat. Either they were short on amusement or desperate for a Spanish slave. He hoped it impossible for them to match speed with his light-weight craft, but they had six men rowing in his direction. With verbal inducement from their tiller, whose bellowing Luis couldn't comprehend, they rowed as if to attack. They began closing, and Luis knew that a sharpshooter could take him with one volley. If no way to out-paddle them, he must out-maneuver. A small tidal creek came in view on the right, thick with marsh grass on each side. He took it. The tide was ebbing, as the wet bottoms of exposed grass roots showed on the creek's sides. His canoa floated more shallow than the longboat, which would ground should it follow in too far.

He kept paddling, turning here and there, moving into smaller flowing sections. At a point, even his small boat couldn't ascend, and it stopped on the bottom's mud. Luis lay back, spent, sweating, and hoping they became discouraged enough to head back to their ship. He knew that the incoming tide would come much later and in the dark, so he sat and waited as dusk descended. With the moonrise, he wanted to move, but the canoa lay mired in the muck. He needed to float in navigable water before the moon's bright light, so he decided to at least try dragging the boat.

With the first steps out he sank all the way to his knees. Straining with all his might, he pulled and crawled back onto the dugout. Walking in the muck would not work. In desperation, he began to push with his paddle against the mud. It moved ever so little at first, but he struggled on. The marsh stench of *spoiled eggs* plus array of mosquitoes helped to motivate him. Soon the moonlight's rays cast on a small amount of water downstream and it gave him hope.

After thirty minutes of prodding, he slid into just enough water. Though disoriented in the dark, he continued in what he perceived a westerly direction to the ocean. The night's clouds covered some of the stars, including Polaris, on which he relied so much. In time, the water widened, and he turned right to paddle along the coast. Far to the west could be seen a ship's lamps, but no sight or sound of a longboat nearby.

He breathed easier and kept moving north all night. With the marshland to his right and the North Star now visible, he confirmed his course. Stars twinkled, and Luis imagined that he could be one too, moving across the sky. He paddled until light spread across the east and visibility improved enough that a dry spot to stop could be found. Seeing a few tiny beaches with no surf, and after paddling all night, he decided to take advantage of one. Too tired to fish, he pulled the canoa onto the sand and lay down to rest. Wrapped in the deerskin, feeling content, with a breeze deterring bugs, he closed his eyes and soon reached deep sleep.

Isabela emerged wondrously at the Universidad graduation ball, which I asked her to attend. As we danced, her dark eyes, beautiful long black hair, and hint of lavender water all dazzled. An angel descended from
Heaven to become my partner. I knew I could never leave her. So why did she now move to the other side of the room and begin staring at me, not smiling? I can't reach her…an inconsolable anguish…uncertainty…

Mid-day and he arose, body rested, but mind mentally drained. He sensed a vague recollection of a bitter-sweet dream of Isabela. Hesitant to recall too much, fearing it would lead to lamenting, he strived to collect his wits and focus on survival. Having finished all his water during the previous evening, his mouth begged for moisture. He must fish. Small crabs on his hand line produced nothing, which seemed to increase his need even more. An hour of wade-fishing the cool water in the warming sun comforted, but did nothing to whet his longing for food and water. Luis pulled his boat from the beach, eased into the shallows, climbed aboard and took up his paddle again. Heading due north, he did not know if the Guacara was ten or fifty miles hence, but he knew a wide river mouth would open up for him to ascend. Perhaps friendly Indios would assist.

Late afternoon brought him to the mouth of a *blackwater river, which he considered taking. In the distance he could see two Indios paddling south along the coast. Trusting his instincts, he called out to them. They spoke little, as he expected, but did respond to signs and brief questions as he approached.

"Guacara?"

They pointed north.

"Spaniard," said Luis, pointing to himself, and then to them.

"Potano," came the reply.

Signs for food and water produced a corn cake and a draft from a deerskin pouch. After twenty-four hours of novictuals, he welcomed it. Luis thanked them as best he could. Saying Guacara again and signing to ask how many moons, he received a reply of two fingers. Thinking he did well, he waved and paddled ahead, but kept an eye at his back. A small island sandy beach presented itself, and Luis pulled up for an overnight camp.

He estimated covering a distance of about fifteen miles from pushing hard since leaving the Amajuro River mouth. Now he gathered wood and kindling for a fire, as he needed something charred to ward off bugs. Fishing again could come in the morning.

Off to the west he could see continuous lightening flashes, much like large fusillades from a distant battlefield. The rumble of thunder made him wonder of the storm making landfall. Fatigued from his hours of paddling, he tossed and turned, adjusted his gear, and tried to become comfortable.

Maybe tomorrow I'll reach the Guacara, and I can ascend. Maybe the Indios will…

He awoke in the wee morning hours. Dampness on his face told him of a light rain falling. Not enough to fill a deerskin bag, but it did provide moisture for his lips. Lightning and thunder still made their presence known from far across the sea. Luis did his best to wrap in the deerskin to stay dry. Fruitless, so he just rested till dawn, wide awake. With the rain abating, daylight produced a nice-sized fish pulling hard at his hand line in the shallows. It provided a challenging fight, blood staining his hands as the line bit in. Finding dry leaves and kindling took some work, but he did and soon began a fire. After suckling cut strips for fluids, he

*Waccasassa River

cooked part for breakfast and some for later. He wondered of his fate should he lose his sole metal hook.

Could I fashion one from a stout branch or fishbones as the Indios?

After gorging on the tasty flesh, he wrapped the remainder in palm fronds and stuffed it in his satchel. Mid-morning and the sky cleared with a mild offshore breeze, so Luis slid out and headed northwest, following the shoreline. Winds soon blew stronger from the west and made it difficult to keep his vessel straight, but he worked and again made fifteen miles before stopping at an *island.

Moving due north again the next morning, he scanned the coast, observed activity on several islands and noticed canoes moving in and out of marshy areas on the east. He hoped to sight a village or two nearby as an overwhelming desire for corn cakes possessed him. He turned eastward. Passing among small islands, he saw in the distance a large **mound that went up from the water's edge. It reminded him of Calos, though smaller. The triggering of Calos memories almost made him turn and paddle out to sea. The mound gleamed in the sun, from piles of shells and clay. Here and there, groves of evergreen trees emitted an aroma new to Luis, though not unpleasant. He beached the canoe and climbed out.

Off to the side, but yet to look at him, sat several Indios women, clad in moss-draped skirts, cleaning the morning's catch. Their naked small children ran about nearby. He approached and tried to offer peaceful signs. After they acknowledged him, he begged with signs for corn cakes and water. Two dispatched children soon returned with enough for three men, most of which he consumed forthwith. To his utter amazement, it fell true that the farther he went north, the more accommodating the Indios. It pleased Luis that no apparent European raids had descended on this part of La Florida in recent times. That aided his plight. Saluting them and taking his leave, he paddled out and again turned north. Most of the coastline persisted marshy, so he picked a large island on which to stop for the night. His first task came in building a fire for char to smear his body for the evening. He mused that in Seville he would appear as a mulatto. He still carried some corn cake and a replenished water bag, so for the evening he enjoyed a meal.

Inlets continued to appear on the coast the next morning, but none produced a noticeable current. After paddling all day for about fifteen miles, he came upon a large river opening with a discernible flow. Moving downstream it carried logs, bushes,and various kinds of debris. Thinking

*Atsena Otie Key   **Shell Mound, SW of Chiefland, Fl

this might be the one, he turned northeast and ascended. The more he moved up, the darker the water became, with marsh grass and low areas on each side. Late afternoon and it merged with another large arm of the river, also flowing westerly. He could now see the large single flow from upstream splitting here into two parts, and he'd gone up the lower arm on the south side of an island. The upper arm spread much wider across.

Birds abounded, and along with gulls, Luis saw the great hawk that dives to the water for fish and the web-footed bird that submerges to feed. As he turned east into the broader current, he could see the silhouette of two men in a canoe, far downstream, floating towards the sea. He thought of the lives of birds and of the natives, of how they both spoke their own language. They knew what their friends said, and he longed for that kind of company. He lived free as a bird, but yet somehow *imprisoned* by the wilderness. He longed to arrive at the upriver mission and hear his native tongue from the friar.

The river extended a thousand feet across, to Luis as wide as the Guadalquivir. Perhaps a long arrow's flight from one side to the other. The area behind the marsh grass sustained tall trees, with bell-shaped bottoms and hanging moss. Thousands of them postured as soldiers guarding outside city walls. Now he needed to find a dry spot before nightfall. At last he sighted a tiny high bank, but on it lay two large lagartos. The beasts moved not an inch as he floated by. Harmless, he'd been told, unless they kept young ones nearby, but he didn't stop, regardless.

Just before dark, he strained to see, and a low bank came into view on the right, so he turned his boat straight into it. As best as he could tell in the dim light, no vermin perched nearby, but the ground stood wet and covered with dead limbs and brush. Not a good spot to sleep, but he did eye an oak tree with limbs that would support him. That would satisfy as his bed. Devouring the last of the corn cakes, he rubbed the leftover char on his body and stretched out, resting about ten feet above the water. The moon rose and shone on the water.

The same moon above Isabela. Doing what at this moment? Just finished the evening repast with her husband of one year, he who owns several galleons, a tavern, and a large orchard. She may even have a baby, with servants to assist. I cannot dwell on it…it may even be sunrise in Spain…

Sometime in the night's deep slumber, another scene came, not of Isabela, but of Pedro.

Hanging upside down, from Calusa woven fiber, above a fire, between two trees. Singed hair and upper body red from the heat. A hundred pairs of eyes watched him. I can almost hear the crowd chanting "Lu-ees, Lu-ees, Lu-ess!" I wanted to rush in and release him, but couldn't. Blood trickled down Pedro's body, from the cuts the Calusas inflicted. I felt drops on my own face. Pedro's blood? But I'm not there! At the chief's signal, a Calusa handied his spear to Pedro's throat, readying it to slit.

"*Ahhhhhh!*"

His own scream awakened him, and he rubbed his face for Pedro's blood. Only drops from a light rain. He rose up shaking and climbed down to the riverside and squatted, splashing water on his face, as if trying to cleanse of remorse. No sound in the dark but the current swishing over a small protruding limb. He sat awhile before stumbling back to the deerskin and wrapping it around him in the tree.

I'm sorry Pedro, I'm sorry…

Morning, and fog covered the river, as he experienced weird feelings from his dream and a sense of eerieness fell upon him. Looking toward the water, Luis imagined he saw canoas passing and the sound of paddles.

Calusa? Or just a memory of my first encounter with them?

He now observed a more immediate concern. A large lagarto lay between him and the canoa. The black river stained its hide, with a covering like hardened corrugated leather. Looking to be ten feet long, it moved not an inch, the steely eyes producing a menacing glare. Enormous jaws hid huge razor–sharp teeth. Not something Luis wanted to incite.

Is there a nest nearby? Little ones? Eggs? Will it charge me? Could my sword penetrate that leathery hide? Should I walk upstream in the marsh grass, float down to my vessel and pull it off the bank?

Luis pondered what to do. Here he beheld a creature that conveyed no notion of his next move, like a skilled player at cards. Or, as a Calusa, that can smile one minute and kill the next. A loud staccato call echoed frrom the faraway woods behind him, breaking his concentration. It sounded like the big bird with the black and white body and red head, whose beak tapped, hammer-like, into rotten trees for bugs. For a long time he waited and stared, the beast staring back.

With the fog lifting, and Luis' stomach growling, thoughts of food reminded him of something. Wrapped and pressed down into his satchel he'd kept the two day-old remnant of his roasted fish-catch, now too smelly to eat.

He pulled out this one remaining foodstuff, unwrapped it from the fronds, and threw it as far as he could into the river. The large lizard went for it, submerged, and did not resurface, evidently appeased.

Satisfied that the incident passed, Luis paddled on upstream, helped by the tide coming up the river.

In time, the riverside marsh grasses gave way to *higher banks, lined with palmettos plus hardwood trees, filled with moss. Some banks stood ten to fifteen feet high and then dropped off at the rear, creating a levee, observable only when he climbed up to rest.

*Wide and beautiful, what else but the ** Guacara ?*

Far upriver, he could see two men in a dugout approaching, paddling with speed. With stomach aching and his trust restored in Indios, he decided to ask for food. Paddling over to their side of the river, he hailed

* Fowler's Bluff   ** Suwanee River

them with as much gentility as possible. They didn't return his greeting. Muscles stood out on their arms as each pulled against the water, and their minimal garb exposed many tattoos.

"Guarcara?" Luis yelled.

The men nodded, without skipping a stroke.

"Food?" he said, patting his stomach and mimicking the process of eating.

Once again, they did not answer but continued moving. Luis accepted their behavior since they brought him no harm and confirmed the right river. Following an afternoon of moving against the current, along with tidal influence at ebb, he settled the canoa along a small strip of sandy riverside, below a high bank. After two days of achieving maybe 15 miles, he judged that surely the mission could be reached in ten days. Going all day with little break and no food or water, fatigue set in. He climbed the bank, wrapped in his deerskin and lay down with a thick mantle of trees above.

All in all, a good day, and on course …I can almost hear the friar chatting with me…at sunup I'll fish, and…

Luis slept till the morning sun shone warm on his face, with most of the early morning fog dissipated and little dew on the ground. Well-rested but famished, he decided to wade in the shallows and fish. Overturned logs produced some white worms about the size of his little finger tip. Attaching one to his hook, and attaching his line to a five-foot reed, he dropped it into the silky black water. An immediate response produced a hand-sized dark fish with a red underbelly. The roasted flesh tasted tender, and Luis learned that the scales should first be removed by scraping with his sword or small knife. With his fire still going, he caught another and cooked it for later. After casting off, he discovered a small bubbling spring not far upstream from his campsite, allowing him to fill the water bags.

*Fowler's Bluff-16 miles from Gulf **Suwannee River

Paddling up, he continued to be amazed at the huge river, which carried limbs, reeds, and groups of ducks along its flow. Long-necked white birds would often fly overhead, and groups of huge black birds with long beaks could be seen perched together in tree tops. Something of a sameness pervaded, but beauty was always there to behold. Afternoon and he turned into a large *spring run on the right, which led to a wide opening where water bubbled up from a cavern below. Two sea cows rose up from the boil and startled Luis as he passed over them.

He beached the dugout in the enchanting glade and bent down to sample the clear fresh water. To him it tasted sublime. For a meal Luis ate the fish caught earlier, then smeared char on his body and congratulated himself on his fortune thus far. He said prayers and gave thanks for his deliverance. Somehow Providence guided his way, which he estimated at 25 miles upriver. Before complete dark, he removed the coins and gazed at them one by one.

Worthwhile to continue carrying them? Someday put to good use? Or just holding on to civilization?

As twilight descended and the stars lit up, comfort came to him from the familiar sound of crickets. From somewhere upstream he heard the gurgling of water.

Peaceful…but it does seems so distant from everything…maybe I should have struck for Habana…but the English and…

Luis awoke at daylight and decided to look for worms and again try his luck at fishing. The spring displayed many inviting spots, but none more than a large area of weeds about twenty feet in circumference adjacent to the north bank. The vegetation grew three feet high and thick.
He waded along the swampy edge and tossed bait on hooked line into the water next to the weeds. After one minute, he pulled it up and plopped it into another weedy spot.

The only warning came as an ear-splitting bellow, as a six foot lagarto sprang from the weeds in his direction. With jaws open, it moved like lightning and snapped within inches of Luis' foot. Without retaliation, Luis eased back up the bank. The big creature slid under the water. Panicked, but relieved, he realized there must be eggs or little ones nearby. He wanted none of that. After taking in and letting out a deep breath, he turned and walked along the bank toward his canoa. *Time to depart*, he concluded.

He moved about ten steps when a foreign sound filled the air. Luis turned to see the beast coming out of the water, hissing. Its jaws clamped down on one foot, and no amount of tugging could pry it loose. Losing his
*Manatee Springs

balance and falling backwards onto the ground, Luis sat up and beat on its head as the reptile began dragging him toward the water. A great fear seized him.

With a primordial yell from deep inside, he reacted with an impulse and instinct honed from months of living in a wilderness environment. He thrust himself towards the animal's head, the only part now showing above the waterline. With deftness and ferocity he poked his thumbs into the only soft spots available–the eyes!

Issuing a loud howl, it released its vise-like hold on Luis' leg and slipped beneath the water. He lay bitten and bleeding, but the panic coursing through his body offset any pain. He clambered up the bank, breathing hard, leaving a splattered trail of blood. Grabbing his meager gear, he launched the dugout. Not to afford a third attack. Shaking, but in control, he knew he must stop soon and attend the leg. A short ways upstream he came to a small spring rise near the bank. He plunged in, as much to revive himself as to treat the wound. Wrapping his foot in the deerskin, he applied pressure to curb the bleeding. He laid there, half in the water and half out, until no more red flowed. The numbing effect of ice cold water helped alleviate the now throbbing pain.

Not till the sun shone at mid-morning did he remove from the water. As a rush of pain stabbed him, he unwrapped the deerskin to examine his wound. Teeth marks and lacerations almost encircled his leg above the ankle, and they ran deep. To his amazement, no bones showed. Luis knew they needed sewing to aid healing and to prevent becoming septic and scarred. He garnered no choice but to use his fishing line and metal hook. It must be done, pain or no pain, skill or no skill. He tried to remember the surgeon's demonstration to him on the Atocha, when in Habana.

Perhaps it also compares to madre's stitching of torn clothes. She made it look simple.

Wasting no time for fear of the hurt discouraging him, he proceeded. Each of his punctures of the skin stung when he pushed the tiny hook through. After three or four times his confidence rose, though the discomfort intensified. He did not stop, cutting the line with his small knife and tying ends as he pulled opposite skin pieces together. Altogether, he did it ten times and still retained line for fishing. When finished, he again plunged his leg into the cool spring for the numbing effect. He decided to rest awhile and savor his survival.

The sun's rays eased beyond the trees on the east bank and cast brightly at mid-day, making the slight ripples of water sparkle like diamonds. Soon he decided that it was time to paddle again, thinking somehow to distract from the ailing leg. He dug the paddle deep against the current.

Allowing the baited line to dangle in the water as he paddled, he hoped another red-bottomed fish would bite. About mid-afternoon the line went taut. Pulling the pole up, he met strong resistance so he pulled harder. The line snapped. To his dismay his hook had hung somewhere below set into a log. Losing his main link to sustenance, he would have to try to create a hook from wood as some Indios, though fishbones worked best. That would come at evening, though he wished now for something to eat.

Late afternoon, feeling fatigued, Luis could see two dugouts heading downstream. He resolved to stop them. Placing his craft broadside in the stream, he tried to convey a posture of peace and need, and held his lacerated leg high for all to see. It worked as both boats stopped with no words from the occupants. Luis labored to look haggard and helpless. One Indio produced several leaves of tobacco, still green, from his bag. He mimicked chewing and then placed them upon his leg. Luis accepted with gratefulness. He thought one of the men said the word *annoc*, but he didn't question it. Luis then pretended chewing and pointed to his stomach. Another Indio produced an acorn cake.

"Guacara?"

They nodded yes.

With hands first clasped in prayer form and then using his right hand to make the sign of the Cross, he conveyed the mission question. An Indio pointed upstream. Pointing to himself, he announced his Spanish status. Pointing to them, he again made a questioning gesture.

One of the men spoke in a low guttural sound, "Yustaga."

Luis gave them thankful signs and sat and watched as they went on downstream. He paddled to the bank and slashed off several palmetto fronds with his sword. After chewing the tobacco, he placed it on the cuts and bound it with fronds tied together. He breathed a sigh of gratification and relief. After enjoying the acorn cake, he too set about paddling, but upstream. Due to the morning's event, he could only travel for a half-day before dark, though he made a good eight to nine miles. He stopped to camp at a *large spring on the right bank, his leg aching as he dragged the craft onto the low bank. He anticipated swelling by morning, so he planned to attempt fashioning a new hook before dark.

Finding a stout branch of an aromatic green-needled tree, he slashed off about one foot, its circumference a small finger size. The bark he stripped by sword and by hand. Towards the tapered end Luis made a diagonal

*Fanning Spring

slice, then sharpened the end. The sharp-pointed branch now needed bending into a *j,* or hook, so he used a small vine and bound the curved shank. The hook point would now stay in placeand hold a fish that bit.

Severing the branch again at the top made the hook and remaining shank portion only two inches long, so he notched the non-hook end for a means on which to tie a fishing line. Wielding his knife, he whittled down the hook tip more so it would fit even easier in a fish's mouth.

By now exhaustion from the day overcame him, so after partaking of fresh spring water, he lay down to sleep at dusk. Leg pain plagued him during the night, but he realized it meant life. In the wee hours it developed a spasm, which didn't cease till dawn.

But no law. No constabulary. No Captain. No Calusa. Not even a hurricane.

Thoughts surged through Luis' mind, and though he suffered no manmade constraints, he knew it all a test of survival.

Not easy. Like the life of a wild animal, who spends each day searching for food and a place to sleep. But ultimate freedom.

For now he relished it and knew he would live to tell about it. Smiling inwardly, he professed richness in life. He fantasized that the silver coins in his satchel made him a man of wealth, though he knew they could not buy his life.

***

Rain sparse, the river gentle, trees beginning to bud, and the days became warmer. The crude hook produced enough fish to eat, and springs frequented the river, each giving solace to throat and body. Sometimes he bathed in the clear waters and sometimes in the river's edge, always avoiding weedy areas. At the end of his fifth day on the river, he stopped *springside to establish camp. A strong aroma of rotten eggs greeted him and motivated his pressing onward. Another spring further up soon presented itself, suitable for camping.

Morning and his wound continued sore but did not deter his paddling. A few shoals hindered his advance and often required exiting his canoa to pull it through the rocks. At the end of his eighth day on the Guacara, a large dark-colored **stream entered from the right. A sandy beach beckoned, and Luis stopped for the night. He estimated having paddled some sixty-five miles upstream.

The river now showed white clay or rock banks, which contrasted with the black water. Lustrous in the mornings and evenings, and sparkling at

*Little Copper Springs   **Santa Fe River

mid-day, with the sun high. It harbored many largatos, snakes, and turtles, all of which had backs the color of soot. They each submerged upon Luis' approach. Along the way he sighted bankside at separate times a very large cat and a black bear, neither of which noticed him on the water. Indios in dugouts appeared on occasion and gave him tobacco for dressing and corn cakes or gruel. He may have perished without them. They also continued to point upstream when he inquired of the mission. Many Spaniards would consider the solitude he spent as maddening, and Luis suffered his moments, but he realized he was not alone. Life endured here, just a different kind, and he adapted to it. On his twelfth day, he saw several Indios conversing at a beach on the right, their crafts lodged on shore. All sounds ceased when he arrived.

"Mission?" he asked, while making the sign of the Cross. This time he received no finger pointing upriver. Instead, they pointed to a path through the woods. Luis disembarked and saluted. Quivering from anticipation and from legs bereft of walking, he headed up the trail. After propelling almost 100 miles up the Guacara, his current goal loomed at hand. The only occasion to surpass it would be sighting Seville from a foredeck. He was ecstatic.

The sand footpath lay packed under his feet, and the tracks evidenced its use. Canopied and bordered by stands of oak, holly, pines, and plum trees, it allowed much cooler air in the shade than on the river. He passed low areas where it was obvious water flowed to the river after heavy rains. He also observed several sink-type holes in the ground and one large *spring area. The water bubbled up from a cavern and then reentered underground.

After about fifteen minutes of plodding, he could smell the pleasant aroma of meat cooking, but he also could hear the sound of whacking, followed each time by a wail. An unmistakable combination, which he'd heard and witnessed on the Atocha. The further he walked, the louder became the cries. He placed a hand on his sword handle, for a measure of reassurance.

Upon entering the mission grounds, he halted, taken aback by the dreadful scene.

*Peacock Springs area

11
RIO de SAN MARTIN

A quien no tiene nada,
Nada espanta.
(He who has nothing,
has nothing to fear)

FLORIDA PENINSULA NORTH CENTRAL

Whack! Whack! Whack!

Lined up alongside the mission church stood five young male Indios, each receiving whippings in turn from the friar's large switches. None were bloody, but whelps rose on those he strapped. A small crowd of adult Indios stood nearby, but no one moved to stop the thrashings. The scene repulsed Luis.

Is this the Spanish man of God whom I have been longing to meet, to converse with?

He went straightforward, grabbed the switches and shouted in a loud voice.

"Enough!"

As he came face to face with a gaunt, bedraggled sword-carrier from out of nowhere, the friar retreated a few steps. Fully cloaked, balding, short and at that moment, he glowered with a face turned beet-red. Luis envisioned a red pumpkin sitting atop a stack of hay. He thought to laugh but maintained his composure.

"Who are you?! By what right do you have to stop this punishment, señor?!"

"I am an alférez in the military of Felipe IV, and I will not witness the whipping of young boys."

"These are my students, and they face reproachment for not studying their catechisms. Besides, you do not appear as a soldier to me. Give me the switches, it is my duty."

"No," retorted Luis, "I will not stand for this."

Deciding to acquiesce to Luis' military demeanor, in spite of his appearance, the friar waved away the boys and the crowd.

"Come with me," he said, while motioning toward a small friary of clay walls and thatch roof.

Luis followed, bending his head to walk through the low doorway. Inside he could see one room, plain and simple, with a few pieces of crude furniture. Each wall covered about seven paces in length across the dirt floor. Window shutters opened out, and high pitched rafters spanned above. A central hearth opened to a clay chimney that went through the roof. It all made the smallest mission friary in Spain look like a palace.

He sat in the only chair and stared at Luis. As he spoke, Luis eyed him with an odd combination of resentment and admiration.

"I am Fray Gaspar Mobila, from the Aragón region of Spain, via San Agustín. This mission of San Juan de Guacara is my charge. I came to convert these poor souls to Christianity, and it is both gratifying and challenging. For what purpose did you arrive today?"

Louis thought, *here sits an educated man, who speaks my tongue.* He could feel his anger and tension subsiding, gratefulness replacing them.

"Fray, I come as Alférez Luis Armador, originally of Seville. Late of his majesty's service aboard the Atocha galleon of the Terre Firme fleet. I fear it sank in a storm, which first washed me overboard. I lived as a captive of the Calusa Indios for a year but escaped and made my way up the coast. I seek San Agustín and passage back to Castile."

"My son, having you here could prove a blessing. I will do my utmost to accommodate you, but I must insist that you not interfere."

Luis wore the sword, but he began to gain respect for the Friar.

"Forgive me, Fray, but I was trained to protect and defend, and it pains me to see young ones thrashed, unless for a criminal deed. I have survived many incidents, and all I have in addition to my honor is my sword, my satchel, its contents, and my meager coverings."

Reflecting a life committed to servitude and humility, the Friar arose and took leftovers of the day's meal from a cupboard. He bid Luis to sit. Roasted deer meat, acorn cakes, and heart of palmetto tasted like a captain's meal to Luis. A wooden fork almost brought tears to his eyes, as he recalled meals with the officers on the Atocha.

"I am most thankful, Fray, for both the food and the conversation. It's the first time I've experienced a sense of civilization in over a year's time."

Noticing the bindings on Luis' leg caused Fray Gaspar to inquire, and so Luis told the tale of his attack.

"You are fortunate, my friend, for most do not survive such an attack. I will redress it for you."

The Friar snipped the sewn-in lines and removed them, but not without some discomfort to Luis. He did not flinch, recalling the more painful sewing-up procedure. With wounds cleaned, the Friar applied salve of aloe,

brought from Spain. He then tied one strip of white cloth around the leg.
In the process, he also removed several ticks from Luis' leg.

"You may sleep here tonight, and tomorrow we can talk."
Luis noted that the Friar's face no longer glowed red as he exited.

***

He continued to lie on his pallet even as the first glimmer of light eased
through an open window. Dozing on and off, he soaked in the respite he
needed. As full sun shone through the window and lit up the room, he
witnessed the most beautiful dawn in two years. A sense of relief settled
over him like the calm after a rainstorm. He recalled friend Alaniz
Estaban's words at Calos, his slavery sojurn for one year. *One month's travel
from Calos to Guacara, if unimpeded. It did take a month, plus two month's sojourn at
Tocobaga. Some impediments yes, but success.*

The Friar, an early riser, entered and invited Luis to a tour of the mission.

"Next door is my church," he spoke proudly. "It's similar to the friary,
but larger and has a bell. The Utinas worked hard to construct it. We pray
the Rosary daily." He smiled, as one pleased to have familiar company.

Inside, Luis noticed long crude wooden benches, which sat on
roughhewn wooden floorboards. A wooden Cross hung at the church's
rear, and a wooden box served as the tabernacle.

"Fray Gaspar, what an outstanding mission. Surely your work here
creates fulfillment."

"Yes, it does. I'm proud to be part of my Franciscan Order's great
purpose. We have 27 friars serving 32 missions, plus some 200 villages in
which we minister."

With a dismissive gesture he spoke. "No gold exists in La
Florida, and there flows no river of youth, as some Spaniards believed.
Even Indios sought it at one time, bathing in all the streams hereabout.
The treasure lies in the converts," he said, beaming. "Now let me show
you the village. We have 30 huts, a central plaza, a council house, a burial
mound, and the chief's hut, much larger than the rest. Several deep pool
springs rise here, none of which run to the river, but all contain clear water
and they reflect as mirrors, as you will see. When here, the soldiers encamp
in the woods to the east. That works best."

After the tour, Luis advised that he wished to stay for a month or two
for his leg to heal, and then he'd strike out to San Agustín on the mission
trail. He'd understood that it lay nearby.

"Fortune shines on you, my son, as *El Camino Real is close to us. With
slow riding or steady walking, it takes me ten days to cover the one hundred
* Spanish Mission Trail

miles to the Atlantic coast. Other missions dwell on the route, too. This mission is a *doctrina*, a permanent site where I reside, but I do have area villages to visit also. We have no constant military, as they visit just twice a year to bring our laborers back and to take fresh ones to San Agustín. The troop comes again soon, and I must say they enter as a rabble, especially their Sergeant. They also expect foodstuffs to transport back to town – like corn, dried venison, and honey."

***

The days passed in peace for Luis, with the Friar and the Indios being hospitable. One evening, the military-led group arrived from San Agustín, 30 fatigued Utinas walking and six soldiers on horseback, all led by a sullen-looking sergeant. Luis knew the soldiers would stay for several weeks, then take new workers back to the coastal town to help with the spring planting.

Introductions came in due time, and Luis could sense a brooding presence in Sergeant Manuel Torres. Cracking a wry smile from his dark face, he posed to the Friar, "another Spaniard here?", while motioning toward Alférez Armador. After explanations, he provided a brief comment.

"I maintain jurisdiction here, Alférez, so I submit we'll do well if you remember that."

"I will remember and will not interfere unless I should see someone mistreated."

"That will be up to me," the Sergeant answered sourly, as he turned and walked away.

Soon thereafter the Friar confided in Luis. "Our Sergeant has a troubled past, as do many that serve in the La Florida interior. His conduct is often misguided, having suffered through a demotion from alférez to sergeant. He never seems happy about his duty. Here he exercises high-handed control over the Utina, and he and I have differed often."

"I'll consider that a caution, Fray. Thank you."

"It's not you, but your rank that offends him. Envy seems to be a pox that appears often in the human race. It saddens me."

***

Luis avoided the soldiers and spent his time helping the Utina or the Friar. As in the other villages he visited, there abided constant activity. The aromas of the village pleased him—animals, tanning of hides, food cooking, and herbs in abundance. They reminded of a world that he'd missed over the past several weeks. He moved around more easily at the Guacara mission than at Tocoboga, where, though well-treated, he perceived his presence as an interloper. Without a doubt he relaxed more than as a slave at the Calusa villages, where fear compelled him to stay on guard. Here the Friar's presence and influence made the difference.

The sturdy Indio men had olive-colored skin and long black hair, which they tied. Christian converts cut their hair, and all wore trinkets on pierced ears. Most wore tattoos. The men wore only deerskin loincloths, except the chief, who often draped his body with skins and feathers. When carried on a litter, he sat adorned with necklaces and bracelets. The women had lighter skin, due to the constant application of bear grease, either for appearance reasons or to deter insects. They allowed their hair to hang loose and wore woven moss as coverings.

They built round living huts, stabilized by wooden posts in the ground. Bark or clay covered the sides, and palm thatch covered the roofs. In keeping with convention, Luis moved into the large council house and received daily meals from the Utina. Although the village kept only about 200 people, it controlled several smaller area villages. Parties from them would visit, bring gifts to the chief and fill their water bags from the springs. Provided with old clothes by the Friar, Luis reveled in their evening conversations at the end of workdays.

"They have taught me natural ways of living, and I have taught them the Ten Commandments. They showed me how to blacken my face with charred corn cobs to prevent evening insects, and I have taught them from Fray Pareja's Confessionario, using pointed questions to eradicate pagan ways."

"Fray, what superstitions have you seen?"

"Difficult to believe, but some still remain, even though the mission is fifteen years old. For example, they consider the sighting of an owl bad luck. They believe that praying to maize and to fish will bring them abundance. There are many more, all folly."

"They act so docile, agreeable, and receptive to you. Has anyone been aggravating?"

"Oh yes, their shaman, or sorcerer, as we might call him. He purports to cast spells, or withhold favors, unless given something of value. All sorts of nonsense, which I have sought to dispel with the gospel. I pose a threat to him, and so I try to change habits slowly, with the chief's help."

"Does the chief like you?"

"Ah, yes, even more after our Florida Governor's hospitality when I took him for baptism at San Agustín. He likes the gifts of tools, clothes, pigs and chickens. Everyone desires notoriety, especially chiefs. But, Luis, one of my biggest goals is to change some of their physical activities. Not the favored stickball games, but the behavior that precedes them. Writhing dances and the resulting ill behavior causes me many sleepless nights."

Armador awed at the selfless and hard-working Friar as he conducted Mass, taught catechisms and Spanish, and sought to erase pagan practices that lingered. But witnessing repetitive deaths from the pox or fever saddened the Friar. He told Luis that it escalated each time a group of workers returned from San Agustín.

***

Luis continued bothered by the thought of leaving Pedro with the Calusas. The image of himself frozen in the tree would not go away. Nor would the thought of Pedro having his throat cut or roasted over a fire. He had led Pedro all the way, and now his friend suffered recapture, possibly death. Luis anguished like a fish caught in a long-unattended net. Still alive, moving around, but with no escape. In Luis' case, from the ruminations of his mind.

"Fray, I need your counsel, and I need confession," he said, after a restless night.

"Very well, after morning's Mass, we will sit together."

Daily Mass brought a number of Indios in attendance, and on this day even a few of the soldiers attended. The Friar looked pleased and offered blessings for them. Later, he and Luis retired to a corner of the church.

"Fray, I have faced many perils and physical obstacles and with help have overcome them. But torments of the mind resist dismissal. I believe that I need penance and absolution"

He then related circumstances on the trail from Tocoboga, Pedro's recapture, his own escape, his resulting grief and self-incrimination spilling out. Fray Mobila sat pensive for a few moments before speaking.

"Alférez, in this land of a different culture, many things happen of which we're not accustomed. Pedro made a choice to go with you, to freedom. The Calusa made an aggressive, though improper choice to come after you. You made a choice by hiding so as not to confront them, and it saved your life. Pedro would've done the same. You have done nothing wrong. In fact, you may be here at this mission to serve a purpose. Go in peace."

Luis stared in quiet repose for a few moments, soaking in all that the Friar said. He could sense a weight lifting from his shoulders, replaced by relief and thankfulness. He realized the power of words that could only have come from a noble man of the cloth.

"Thank you, Fray. I stand indebted to you in many ways. May I contribute a silver real de a ocho to you for the mission?"

"Oh no, we cannot touch coins, or any form of specie or treasure. When you arrive in San Agustín, give it to the senior Franciscan friar at their offices on our behalf."

***

A few days before the soldiers planned to leave for San Agustín with their new workers, Luis witnessed a disheartening scene. In a senseless act of aggression, Sgt. Torres struck a Utina with the butt of his sword, and wrestled a large shank of cooked deer meat from him. Luis confronted Torres.

"Alférez, I must remind you of my command here. Do not interfere."

Angry Indios stood nearby, afraid to intervene. Not Luis, though he recognized the Sergeant's anger and resentment rising.

"Give him back his meat," Luis said, as if giving an order.

For about ten seconds, nothing happened.

The Sergeant then threw the meat toward the Utina where it landed in the dirt. With a scowl, he turned to Luis, speaking in a harsh tone.

"You, Alferéz, must leave here by the morn. Otherwise, at mid-day tomorrow, we will duel with swords."

Luis stayed silent, turned, and walked away. That night he counseled with Fray Mobila.

"Please go, Luis. I want no bloodshed at my mission. This is a place of peace."

"Fray, I sense that this type of ill-tempered behavior happens often. It must stop."

"But he might kill you."

"As Cabeza de Vaca said—*I would rather risk my life than give up my honor.*"

"Son, I will pray for you tonight."

That night Luis slept, but not with ease. He reckoned it inevitable that he and Torres would clash. Though harboring no fear, he didn't want to bring misfortune to the Friar and his mission. If he could subdue the Sergeant, he would leave posthaste, not allowing the other soldiers a chance to confront him. A two months stay was long enough anyway. He conjured the plan, but as came about at Tocoboga's swift departure, he knew that well-laid designs often become altered. He envisioned a matador who fought and killed four bulls all on the same day. Then was confronted with another, even bigger.

The Sergeant received word that Luis did not leave and so became eager for the duel. A crowd gathered at late morning in the plaza, assuring many onlookers, with some gaming on the duel, to the Friar's discomfort. Luis ate well, knowing he would need energy for combat. From the open door of the council house, with the sun streaking in, he could see Torres swagger into the plaza well before noon. He proceeded to pace in a restless manner. Luis thought him too impatient and he hoped it would work to his own advantage. He reasoned that he could hamper Torres' wits even further by tarrying inside the house a while longer. The Alférez waited a good thirty minutes more, took a long draft of water and then strode out.

Crowd noise filled the plaza, but he heard none, his sole focus on dueling.

He recalled his skirmishes in Las Palmas and Porto Bello, handling those opponents with moderate effort. He knew this fight came more challenging, but he assented to it with confidence.

"Prepare to die!"

With sword in hand and eyes blazing, the Sergeant roared at Luis. In an inexorable manner, he wanted to heighten the drama.

Luis said nothing, drew his sword, saluted and assumed the position, aware that success comes from anticipation of the adversary's strikes. He let Torres make the first move, with him slashing down from overhead. Luis deflected it and then used his blade to encircle Torres' sword so to dislodge it onto the ground. A cheer went up, but Luis did not hear it. The Sergeant stood stunned. Since Luis did not move, Torres grabbed his sword. He then charged with a forward thrust, at the same time emitting a yell of ferocity.

Armador stepped aside in time, clanking down hard on Torres' sword, the noise reverberating throughout the forest. Thrusts and parries continued for another three minutes, as Luis respected Torres' skill, sharpened from other fights. He also was aware of his disturbed countenance, borne of a desire to inflict deadly pain. He thwarted a misguided thrust by Torres, slipped to his side and brought his sword handle down hard to the head. The Sergeant fell face down in the dirt, breaking a tooth and bloodying his face. As he raised his head, spewing dirt and coughing, Luis kicked away his sword. A murmur of awe went up from the crowd of Utinas.

Standing over Torres, he made deep slashing cuts in each hamstring muscle, his pants' legs sotting with blood. The pitiful creature cried out in pain with each slash. He would not die but would be hobbled for some time. Luis placed his sword back into its scabbard and leaned over the Sergeant.

"Torres, I spared your life. I pray that henceforth you will spare discomfort to the Indios."

With the Utinas cheering and the soldiers glaring, Armador turned toward the small friary to gather sustenance for leaving. Inside, he and Fray Mobila entered into an intense final discussion. In grim spirits, the Friar spoke.

"You have pleased the Indios, as they do not like the military. But you must leave, as I cannot predict what Torres' squad may do. They outnumber you, and the natives fear their guns."

"Fray, I plan to leave now, as I agree with your assessment. I'll strike the trail east."

"No, no, no, Luis, that's what they expect you to do. They have horses, now rested, and they would chase you, even delaying taking the workers to San Agustín. You must take to the canoa again. One possibility is to float south on the Guacara River, which many Spanish now call the San Martín. The Santa Fe River flows into it and there you could ascend up to the El Camino Real mission trail. It will lead you east to San Agustín. Or, you can paddle north from here, taking the long flowing curve of the San Martín River turning east. A walking path south will present itself so to find the same mission trail to San Agustín going east."

"Which do you suggest, Fray?"

"The latter, as they will least expect you to go upstream. Be mindful of the burnings for spring plantings, and be certain to convey what happened to any priests or officers you may encounter. Vaya con Dios, my son. Perhaps someday I can repay your efforts here."

Having agreed, Luis slipped out and made haste south on the short walk to the river. Pushing his canoa out, he began paddling upstream. His first paddle in two months and on his own again, he soared like the fledgling eagle leaving the nest. He bent to the task, his new plan in place. This time a lower flowing river greeted him, and banks exposed more of the white pock-marked rock, contrasting it with the black water. No rain had fallen for weeks prior, and as the river dropped, cypress trees remained wet at their base riverside. He wanted to make at least seven miles a day, so this first day he pushed hard, owing to the late start. He knew that, barring mishaps, it would take days to complete the river's big curve going north and east so to then strike south walking to El Camino Real. Having enough food packed for four to five days, he would then fish and forage, unless Indios offered assistance.

Day one produced light rapids about a mile upstream of the launch. Luis secured his food pack, climbed out and pulled hard in knee-deep water, trying not to fall. A healed leg helped support him, but he didn't want another injury from jagged rock. One more mile up he repeated the process with no problems.

At day's end he spotted a beautiful *spring run from the left bank. Entranced and tired after going five to six miles upstream, he paddled into clear blue water that flowed into the main stream. He camped at the source.

Mid-day next he passed a clearing on the right bank that contained a single hut. A spring run emptied into the river and a dugout lay on the bank. Curious, Luis eased in and sighted ** twin springs flowing out. An Indio greeted him, so using his best signing, he inquired if the man lived alone. Replying in broken Spanish, he said yes and that he operated the ferry on El Camino Real, which crossed the river at this point.

"Gracias, amigo," said Luis. He smiled, waved, and headed on upriver to seek a campsite.

Alférez Armador spent the next day paddling, pulling above light rapids, and camping with the sound of shoals lulling him to sleep. Based on the sun's location, he no longer moved northwest, but north. The weather continued dry, as blue skies and puffy clouds prevailed, with the quiet river comforting. At times the screech of a hawk, eagle or heron would pierce the sky. Bankside trees and bushes now unfolded in full spring foliage and daytime temperatures stayed warm.

About two miles into the fourth day Luis again faced a run of light rapids that stretched across the river. Stepping out into the water, he moved slowly on slippery rocks. His luck gave out. Slipping, he fell hard, tipping the canoa which swiftly moved downstream, partly submerged. After falling on the rocks, he lay for a time, bruised, trying to regain his wits. His remaining morsels of food left outside his satchel went downstream with the watercraft. Sword, satchel and waterbag remained strapped onto him. Gazing downriver now produced no sign of the boat. Luis floated down, swept with his feet, swam underwater, and grabbed rocks, logs, and sand, but found no craft. His heart sank, with his main link to the water trail now gone.

He swam and then walked in shallows to the east bank, the nearest to him. Easing along, he viewed a spot clear enough to climb. Scampering up the high bank, Luis lay there pondering his next move. By dead reckoning, he estimated having covered around 20 miles, not even half the distance planned. Only one solution surfaced. He must walk, even with no trail. He considered walking east to attempt to pick up a trail but feared becoming lost in the woods. He struck upriver, amidst the thick bushes, trees, palmettos, and, he figured, denizens of snakes.

*Lafayette Blue Springs   **Charles Spring

Traipsing along the high bank at river's edge in the woods, he moved slowly. By evening, he calculated having covered five miles. When a large *spring boil of clear water stood out below, he decided to camp for the night. Before going down, he walked back a short distance into the woods and stumbled into a clearing covered with ripe blackberries, on which he gorged. With nightfall upon him and stars breaking out, he eased off to sleep bankside. No food, so he didn't have fear of animals bothering him during the night. He had also lost his deerskin wrap with the canoa, but with summer, nights passed warm.

Morning of day five came with a smoky aroma in the air. Thinking it came from a village nearby that could provide food, he stirred with anticipation. After taking his fill of the spring, he returned through the woods to find the open field again. He once more enjoyed blackberries, along with nearby ripening wild plums, while filling his satchel. The smell intensified and overhead in the distance he could see clouds of smoke billowing above the trees. Being further away from the river, he became apprehensive and conscious of losing his point of reference. But the lure of a possible nearby village still enticed him. In the corner of the field, through the haze, a north-south trail opened, and Luis sped north.

The smoke thickened, and the hazy clouds began descending on the trail. Sunlight beams lit up the smoke and projected an eerie scene. From off in the distance he heard shouts and he now remembered the Friar's caution of Indios' pre-planting brush fires. The area endured a dry period anyway, making it risky for burnings. Luis wondered if it burned out of control.

The sky darkened, and the fearsome sound of fire crackling could be heard. Flames were visible in the woods off to his right. The hot air fatigued him and after two miles up the trail h, he became dismayed at not finding a village. Someone shouted nearby, and he heard more yelling off in the distance. Then a more immediate concern presented itself. Larger flames gathered strength from the east. His eyes began to water and he coughed to clear the fumes. The fire roared like a great dragon trying to consume all in its path.

Time to head west back to the river?

Suddenly the fire leaped across the path at treetop level about an arrow shot in front of him. At this, Luis turned west into the woods and ran for the river. Some spots allowed passage but some grew thick, and hastiness led to cuts and scratches.

The begrimed matter obscured his vision, and the fumes filled his eyes

* Anderson Springs

and nostrils. Crashing through the forest, he prayed that it did indeed lead west so he could plunge into the beautiful black water. There he would find safety. Brush was beginning to burn all around him, and the tops of trees lit up like huge night torches. The heat blasts from the conflagration fanned his face as if he stared into an open cauldron. Particles of ash swirled everywhere. Still, he advanced, running, coughing, eyes burning. Up ahead the land sunk down into a low area, then rose back up. He recognized the land rise along the river. Luis dashed over logs, through branches, up the embankment, then scrambled down the bank and fell into the water, submerging for as long as his breath would hold.

Rising up in the stream, he could still see smoke everywhere, and the morning sun now appeared as an orange ball through the opalescence. At some point, the fire would burn out at riverside, but Luis decided to pursue the opposite west bank. Swimming across refreshed him, and it mattered not that the current swept him downstream. Reaching the other side, he climbed up the bank and sat to rest. The smoke hung just as thick on the west bank, but he would not risk becoming burned.

He ate some plums picked earlier and then resumed his northward journey. Same as the east bank, it grew thick with bushes. Many times he went back into the water to swim and wade when the smoke and heat overwhelmed. The only real relief came from submersion, over and over.

After fording a *smaller stream flowing into the **San Martín, he trudged several miles east on its now northern bank, moving upstream. Less smoke filled the air upriver, still he felt like a human chimney. Springs on the river kept him in water, and he always filled the deerskin bag at his waist before continuing. His stomach ached for food, but he lay too tired at evening to forage or fish. The next day he would make good use of his new line and metal fishhook given to him by Fray Mobila.

At dawn's light, Luis found a few white worms within the rotting stump of a tree atop the high bank. They made perfect bait, and within sixty minutes he cooked two fish over a fire.
He relished the soft white flesh of one, saving the other, along with the last of the plums. The smoke from across the river had dissipated a considerable amount, but the sooty aroma still permeated the air. Luis perched at the top of the river's supposed big curve, but not far enough to see a north-south trail crossing. From his breakfast site high on the bank, he spied a canoa with two Indios, paddling up. Then another, and another.
Solitary feelings dogged him for the first time in a while. Losing his
* Withlacoochee River, North ** Suwannee River

dugout, his lifeline to the river, had consigned him to loneliness. Nonetheless, he again plodded east, following the river upstream. The woods continued dense, and the riverside trails elusive. Luis walked most of the day, satisfied of moving in the right direction. He speculated having covered five miles, stopping only to fish or to seek wild fruit.

The next day found him continuing his relentless march east. After an hour he found a point where a tributary normally empties into the river. Now a *dry river bed, due to the parched season, it merged from the north. Sand the color of bleached cattle bones lined it, and the path beckoned as a luring siren call. A *door opened*, and without comprehending, he could not deny entering, as much to escape thick banks riverside.

He ascended the dry bed, which he knew must carry dark water when it flowed. Trees overhung, and logs lay scattered, with the sand punctuated by myriad animal tracks. The banks rose 25 feet with the white rock extending along both sides. He traipsed all day to see if it brought any more surprises. Only fascination. His clouded mind cleared enough for him to remember he'd left the river, where fish, his main food source, abounded.

Perhaps, he thought, it'd be best to return in the morning. Desperate for food, he whacked a palmetto to harvest its heart. As shadows deepened in the arbored trail, he stopped to camp,and that night, lying on the high bank, he gazed at a million stars above. Instincts led him to believe this new course could lead to a friendly settlement, even if it varied from the Friar's directions.

At daybreak, he awoke to familiar cries. Peering down the bank from behind the bushes, a ghastly sight unfolded. Two Indios led, sometimes dragged, a third, by thick vines. As he looked at the tormented and bloodied torso, he wondered how the captive even had the strength to cry out. Each time he did, one of his captors struck him. They moved toward the San Martín River's black water, where a dugout must lay hidden.

A law-breaker, a slave, a new captive of a neighboring tribe?

With heartfelt sympathy, Luis garnered all his fortitude to plan and effect a release. The captors strode tall, muscular, and determined, their bodies showing tattoos. Abandoning thoughts of safety, Luis slipped down the bank behind them as soon as they passed. With an ambuscade to advantage, and a flourish of his sword, he sliced the vines holding the poor soul.

Though startled upon turning around, the captors prepared to fight. A rock blow to the head dispatched one to the ground, but Luis's elation

*Alapaha River

lived short. The other fell upon him, attacking with a vengeance. As they plummeted to the ground, his knife slashed Armador's arm, with blood on sand producing a stark contrast. With sword still in hand, he blocked the next slash with the leather satchel. Luis wrestled and rolled the Indio over, sliting his throat, all in one fluid movement.

He sat for a few moments to catch his breath. It didn't last. The other Indio, revived, now charged whooping, blood streaming from his temple wound. He lunged like a mad wounded panther and toppled the rising Alférez onto the sand. Luis grabbed a handful of sand and sprayed his eyes. A second later he thrust his sword twice into the ribs and finished the deed.

Trembling, he lay down to regain his energy. And reflect. He believed that dispatching another soul came neither triumphant nor debase, when one must defend his life. However, he took a sober look at his actions, so to satisfy a sense of right and wrong. Vindication came, knowing the two creatures chose to face death than their own sense of dishonor.

Garnering a time-honored victor's spoil, he sliced into the top layers of one of the dead Indio's abdominal skin. Reaching in, he drew out smooth, wet body fat, to use as a salve. After applying to his wound, he bound it with cloth and knot, and deemed it fortunate the cut needed no sewing. Next he looked to the now-freed Indio, battered and tired. After sips of water, he whispered a few words, taken to be appreciation. Using his deerskin bag, meager bandages, and just-extracted salve, Luis did his best to aid him. Though weak, his youthful body reflected a rigorous life.

With signs, Luis implored him to rest, as little else could be done. He deliberated if this would unfold as a blessing or a curse, but realized the man's need of aid prompted his own self from a sense of loneliness. Luis rifled the scant belongings of the two deceased and acquired some dried meat and parched corn. He also kept their steel knives, configured of Spanish origin. Burying the men, he gauged them as Tocobagas, who intruded from the south to acquire a slave for trading. Though misplaced, their boldness impressed him. For the rest of the day, he and the Indio ate and rested.

The next dawn found Luis reinvigorated, but undecided about pressing up the newfound trail. Upon awakening, his new companion produced a slight smile, and, with signs, implored Luis to go up the dry bed with him. This augured as a good omen to Luis. So they proceeded and then plodded along throughout the day, as the trek resembled walking on loose beach sand. They made stops to drink and fill the deerskin from small springs flowing from the banks. The tiny freshets flowed a short ways, then dissipated into gleaming sand. Just before stopping for the evening, a buzzing, rattling sound caught their ears.

With lightning speed, the Indio grabbed a fallen limb and dispatched a huge rattlesnake in the path. They tasted roasted snake meat with much pleasure that evening. Afterwards, using a specific plant, the Indio taught the art of leaf-crushing and smearing it on the skin, as a bug repellant. At twilight, the new partner did his best to communicate with Luis that his village lay four moons north. He also indicated that the river would flow again soon.

The journeying continued the next day at first light's cooler air. Luis estimated now that the distance covered since leaving the river to be about 15 miles. He wondered if his companion feared that Luis might do him harm. Luis pondered the same of him. One fact gleaned from recent sojourns with the Indios was their unpredictability. Maybe not to one another, but to Christians. Luis kept his guard on, even if not apparent to his companion.

That morning brought marks of fresh moccasin footprints, belonging to a party walking from the opposite direction. The Indio, who apprised Luis of his name, Chukka, stopped to study. He upheld four fingers to indicate four sets of prints. He showed no alarm. Luis, though, hoped they represented members of his friend's people. The tracks vanished up the bank into the woods, but his fellow trekker continued to walk the sand, providing no explanation. Luis tensed, with eyes now darting from tree to bush on the high banks. Hawk-like screeches from the woods startled him, like confronting an eerie presence.

Whish!

From out of nowhere a vine encircled Luis' right foot and launched his body upwards, upside-down. Disoriented and panic-stricken, he realized that a hidden well-set trap dangled him from the over-hanging limb of a large oak tree. Three feet above the sand, blood rushed to his head, and his body flailed. With his right hand pulling out his sword to cut the strands, he received a hard ax blow to the head. Now not only bottoms up and desperate, his head reeled from pain, and he struggled not to faint. His thoughts churned.

Overpowered. Have I become the hare in the snare, to be roasted over the barbacoa before nightfall?

Chukka rushed over, waved away the on-rushing Indios, and proceeded to cut Luis's trap vines, easing him down. He spoke to them in a dialect Luis could not recognize. Even in his light-headed state, he gathered that Chukka made explanations. The atmosphere changed from night to day.

Several men assisted Luis up the bank into the shade. One gave him water, and another gave him a corn cake. Each in turn smiled and spoke obvious words of appreciation. Too dulled to talk, he delighted in the attention from members of Chukka's village, who had sought to rescue him from afar. They all rested till Luis recovered enough to walk, with the pace being moderate.

No blood loss, but a large bump formed on the back of his head. That evening Luis again received kind treatment. One of the four men gathered weeds and brush and made him a soft pallet for the night. He dozed off to the comforting hum of crickets.

Sunrise and Chukka held up three fingers and pointed to the moon. Then he pointed northeast up the riverbed. Luis's head ached, but he understood three fingers meant days or moons to their village. They quickened the pace, and he now could handle it. That day they seldom stopped, eating from the Indio's packs and refreshing from small springs flowing down the bank. White rock continued lining the bank above the sand as did moss and bushes above the rocks. Canopies still hung over much of the river bed.

Afternoon and Luis could see * water ahead beyond the dry trail. Dark, like the San Martín River, with the shallow areas colored clear light orange, reflecting sunlight. He heard a roar, like a swift rapid, coming from the left bank area. Soon, he gazed in astonishment to see the entire river avert the dry bed and flow swerving to the west into an opening. It created a narrow descending rocky ** run, which they hiked beside upstream for a short distance. At the end, water pooled at the base of a high rounded circular bank, draining into a cavern, or swallow hole.

"It's a *sumidero!*" he exclaimed. "How can a river flow underground? Where does it go? Does it re-arise?"

*Alapaha River ** Dead River

SEVILLE

She expected the knock on her door. Her madre opened it just enough to peer inside.

"José is here, Isabela, and we should go down, otherwise they'll talk business for the rest of the evening. And…one year constitutes long enough to mourn."

"I know, Madreceita, I must go on."

Luis shall not return, and I gave up wearing black after a few months. So colorless. Besides, she remembered*, I never really married him. Betrothed, but not married.*

Padre arranged well, and on this night he would announce nuptials to come three months hence in the Cathedral. She settled her mind, if not her heart. He had told her of José Allycon and his family and how they couldn't have asked for a better match. He was a 35 year-old silk merchant widower to whom she could give children that his deceased wife could not.

Remembering her padre's words helped to soothe her feelings, and she knew him well-meaning. So, she applied orange blossom water to her neck and considered her face in he mirror one last time. Her hair in place, the gold and crimson brocade dress impressive, and the gold earrings hung perfectly.

José receives the prize—me. No dowry necessary. But I know custom dictates rings, goblets, silk, and silver coins to reflect good taste.

All waited as she descended the stairs, smile aglow. José looked splendid with his satin sleeves, velvet shoes, gold-colored doublet, and amethyst ring. She took his arm while they listened to padre's announcement to the crowd. Next came the priest's prayer over the betrothed, after which they served wine, cheese, nuts, and fruit. It passed as a convivial evening.

In June, 1624, the wedding took place and Isabela moved to José's house a few lanes from her parents'. She followed the plan expected of her, now the wife of an hidalgo, same as her mother. She knew proper conduct. José never endeavored as an overly ardent husband, but proved to be a good provider. Isabela attended their home and filled her time by reading poetry, attending Mass and keeping the company of other women. And of course, she enjoyed all the silk she desired.

But some women, they say, hang themselves with silk...

12
ARAPAJA FORTUNE

1624

Spain is a nation of armed theologians.
M.M. Pelayo

FLORIDA PENINSULA NORTH CENTRAL

Luis gaped at the unbelievable feat of nature, the likes of which he had never before witnessed. He watched the flowing water, first pooling and then sucked down at the rounded high bank's back rim, as into some unquenchable nether region. Like seawater pouring into a vessel's open side, water rushed into the swallow hole, seeking a route into the earth.

Can a man enter it and return…or would it carry him beyond the point of return…does it contain caves where a man may walk…does it lead to the abode of the devil?

His head was spinning as he tried to make sense of it. The only thing obvious to him was that the river would again flow also in the main bed after sufficient rains.

Chukka called, breaking Luis from his fixation, and motioned toward the woods. From there, his brothers hauled several dugouts from their hiding place. The Indios slid them down the bank and into the main river with all gear loaded. The placid, slow-moving waters made paddling easy as they began ascending the stream. Luis inquired by signs how far they planned to go, and Chukka responded with two fingers.

The river wound a serpentine course between high banks. Trees provided shade, periodic springs continued to trickle down into the water and a smaller darkwater tributary flowed from the west side.

Their progress became impeded a few times by rapids, which required pulling the crafts over the rocks or up the banks and through the woods. Occasional low walls of rocks in shallow areas stretched across the stream, above and below the water's surface. Openings in the middle allowed everyone to either paddle or climb out and pull through. Chukka did his best to convey to Luis that baskets placed in the openings of these man-made dams trapped fish moving downstream.

Luis realized, that with every stroke of his paddle northward, he moved deeper into the primordial world, away from his goal of civilization. But at this juncture, he didn't mind. His spirit sought a transitional time away from his quest, for a period of repose, though he couldn't explain why. At any rate, contentment prevailed.

After two days and one night, they reached the village, which the Indios called Arapaja. Luis estimated they had traveled about twenty miles by water, following a similar distance walking on the dry riverbed. The village sat in a clearing near the east bank of the river and spread out two arrow flights in all directions. No low land and it lay on the highest ground in the area. He counted sixty wood and clay huts, all topped by palmetto thatch. A council house, a dead house, and another large building, presumably the chief's home, occupied the center. No mounds, but a central plaza stood like the Calusa and Tocoboga villages. He thought it peaceful as he walked through the village, estimating that about three hundred Indios resided there.

"Lu-ees," said Chukka, as he motioned him to the food spread out for them.

Pointing to the fish, he said *cuyu*, to the corn, *uqua*, and to the fruit, *ituhunulege*.

For the first time, Luis sensed a developing bond with an Indio who accepted him and took the time to communicate. As he enjoyed the food, he vowed to make a conscious effort to learn their language, instead of relying on signing. After the meal, they led Luis to the round council house, where visitors lodged. Entering, he observed unlit torches, racks around the inside walls for sleeping, and logs for sitting around the fire area. The high cone-shaped structure was vented at the apex. In various places hung carved masks and wooden cups for cassina, or black drink. Happiness prevailed as he again had a roof over his head.

"Lu-ees, our chief Sana-gestin," said Chukka, who held up ten fingers and then repeated the signing twice.

Luis understood, but was interested as to why their chief went to San Agustín, and why for so long. There was no mission at Arapaja.

Over the next week Luis met their warrior chief and became friends with many of the men of the village. As did the Tocobagas, they treated him with honor and deference, owing to his rescue of Chukka. He formed a real affection and thought them more genteel and hospitable than others he'd met. Many attractive young females lived in the village which made him understand why some Spaniards took Indio women as wives, but he had no desire to pursue a pagan wife. Chukka and his villagers implored him to stay and live with them, as he came to them as a fierce warrior. After almost two years in slavery or arduous travel, he wearied. So he graciously accepted their invitation, though he knew not for how long.

He studied the language, watched the corn planting, and, with help from the villagers, built his own hut. Luis roamed for wild fruit, helped with the fish traps, and made a bow and arrow. The warrior chief allowed him to sit in on council, and, for the first time, he smoked their pipe. Several weeks in the village brought a steady sense of peace and he even ceased to wear his sword and satchel. But at the waist, he wore one of the long steel knives taken off the slain Tocobogas. The other he gave to the warrior chief, as a token of honor. Grooming as the Indios, he shaved daily, using the long razor given to him by the Friar at the Guacara mission.

***

Familiar musical notes came from the wilderness, surprisingly out of place. Though two years passed since Luis' ears heard such sounds, they were unmistakable. Drums, bugles, flutes, and tambourines grew louder and louder, and soon he witnessed the source. The returning chief, dressed in finery and carried on a litter, came accompanied by all the pomp and circumstance the Spanish could muster. Joining the musicians in the parade walked a friar carrying a hand-held, gold-embossed Cross. Following him rode a group of ten mounted cavalrymen, led by a helmeted and silk-adorned alférez, astride a splendid speckled-grey steed. Pigs, cows, goats and chickens followed, either on tethers or in cages on donkeys. Indios attended them.

It dawned on Luis that he stood witness to the establishment of a new mission. Though awed and scared, the Arapajas found comfort in the sight of their chief and began wailing as a greeting to him. He climbed down from the litter and waved a benevolent hand to all.

"My people, these are our friends who have come to our land from across the big water. They are here to start a mission, a church and a school, and they will protect us from our enemies. Hear their fire sticks."

With ten arquebuses firing in succession, the booming noise scattered many into their huts. As the chief continued to speak, the frightened carefully re-emerged.

"In San Agustín I learned about their God, and the priest baptized me. They want the same for all of you. We will help to build a church and a lodge for the friar, and he will instruct us. The soldiers will build their quarters."

He then passed around his gifts for all to see and hold—steel knives, mirrors, blankets, beads, and trinkets. The friar then spoke, though it was doubtful many of the villagers understood. They did take notice when their chief bowed and kissed the friar's hand.

"I, Fray Rodrigo Díaz, am pleased to be here at Arapaja. Our Pope wishes the fruits of Heaven bestowed on you, and
my goal is to help. We will call our mission Santa María de los Angeles de Arapaja."

Luis recognized a man more confident and educated than the typical Spaniard. Congenial, cracking a wry smile as he spoke, he wore the usual garb of sandals and cloak. He longed to know Fray Díaz, but for the present, he decided to keep his background a secret. Soon all newcomers dispersed and set up camp, with food brought forth at the chief's instructions. Meanwhile, the Arapajas gathered in small groups, talking, motioning, and moving about with a look of puzzlement on their faces.

"Lu-ees, this scares me, I don't understand. Will we become a different kind of people?" asked Chukka, with an expression of astonishment.

"Yes, and no, as your chief remains your chief, and his sway over your people will stay the same. But the priest wants to do away with your old gods, and instruct you in Christianity, to worship one true God, through faith in his son Jesus. They do expect obedience. In turn, they will provide protection and teach you new helpful ways to live."

As he lay in his hut that night, Luis empathized for the Arapajas, as he thought of his own Spanish forbears. *How threatened they too must have been when the Moors came and conquered. How should one act when his ways are to be changed ?.....resistant.... hostile…servile? Will they cling to old ways while adopting new? How can thousands of years be changed within just a few? If it worked at Guacara perhaps it will work here too.* He found himself confronting a paradox of thankfulness for the mission, but with apprehension for these hospitable people.

***

"Do I see a Spaniard, my son?" Luis turned to face Fray Díaz, speaking in Spanish.

Content to remain unobserved and blend in with village life, he grappled with the question. He could not lie to the Friar,
though he preferred silence.

"Yes, Fray. How can you tell?" Luis presented a somber
and questioning look on his face.

"Ah, I have a gift of observing men and their bearings.
Though attired as an Indio, you have many features that distinguish you from others in the village, notably your beard stubble. And the way you move about, almost as a noble soldier. Of course, your Spanish verbage is clear."

"I have been a weary soldier, shipwrecked and seeking solace from my travels. I beg, Fray, that you will not press me too much at this time."

The Friar eyed him with unease but could sense his earnest request for cover.

"As you wish, but in time our Alférez may observe you and desire to communicate." He spoke with a look of deference but also disappointment.

"I am long from Seville, Fray. I would be in your debt for news of my homeland, if it pleases you." Luis asked, though doubtful of a response, since he himself was not forthcoming.

With a comforting smile, the Friar warmed to the request and stared briefly aside, gathering his thoughts.

"Very well, let me see. We have a new Pope at the Vatican, Urban VIII, as Pope Gregory XV has passed. You may know that we have been at war again with the Dutch, and earlier this year England declared war on us."

Luis listened, savoring each bit, as a hungry man enjoying a huge banquet.

"King Felipe IV, reeling from criticism of the crown's extravagance, outlawed the wearing of the popular fine ruff collar. Also prohibited are clothes embroidered with gold plus silver threads and silk in men's apparel. Oddly," he chuckled, "he suspends these laws on grand occasions, especially at court. He also offers rewards for large families, to increase our population. Its success is in doubt, as so many men departed for war or have come to the New World, the reason our birth rates remain low."

"What of the Atocha?"

"The shrine in Madrid?"

"No, a silver galleon, of the Terre Firme fleet, caught in a storm two years past."

"Priests can't concern themselves with matters of silver or gold, but I remember a number of ships of that fleet sinking in a hurricane off Habana that year. I know nothing else."

The news dejected Luis, who still did not know the fate of his shipmates.

"Oh yes," said Díaz, "this is interesting. The Pope banned the new habit of taking snuff and has threatened excommunication if one is caught. As do many, he thinks it's from the devil." Cracking his lopsided smile, he added, "how can we judge if someone uses it, since the nose or mouth contain it?" He spoke with palms outstretched, then waved it off.

As they concluded the conversation, Chukka greeted him.

"Our chief wants to speak with you."

"Any special purpose?"

"He heard of your bravery on my behalf and wants to thank and honor you. Come with me to see him."

As they entered the largest village hut, Luis tensed, remembering the chiefs at Calusa villages, where he feared torture or losing his life. Even though Arapaja posed different, it still challenged him to release old feelings. The chief still wore his Spanish clothes, as if they represented some newfound sense of rank. He greeted but did not arise.

"Nickaleer?" he said to Luis.

"Nickaleer?"

"What does he mean, Chukka?"

"He wants to know if you are English."

"Why?"

"Because our people despise them, as do the Spanish."

"No. I am a Spaniard, a shipwrecked soldier in my king's service."

The chief nodded and questioned him no further, but instead thanked him for his bravery. He bid him stay at Arapaha as long as he wished. He then smiled, arose and embraced him, then motioned to servants to bring food for the men. Luis' tension subsided.

***

Over time, Fray Díaz taught the Indios from the Bible and the catechisms, and led many into baptism. The Arapajas made willing students, especially the young, and embraced the Rosary and regular Mass. The chief supported and encouraged. Still, Fray Díaz often accosted pagan beliefs, superstitious ways, and customs steeped in thousands of years of culture. Armed with Father Francisco Pareja's 1613 <u>Confessario</u> questions, he dealt with sorcery, polygamy, wife-beating, prayers to inanimate objects, owls as omens, and all sorts of bizarre beliefs. One day he sought out Luis for help.

"Pitiful and disgusting!" he said, with the appearance of a man having nausea.

"What?" asked Luis.

"The Indios. And their continued reliance on their herbalist, or whatever he's deemed. They can handle small wounds with clay and herbs, but stronger maladies they cannot. He dances over them, chants, blows tobacco smoke and sucks on a reed next to their heads. It doesn't work, but they persist in these useless practices."

He stopped conversing, ruminated for a few moments, then looked despondently at Luis.

"The warrior chief's son suffers an apparent toothache, and my suggestions have not been heeded, for I am neither herbalist nor physician.

They admire you. Please see what you can do." The Friar looked desperate. "And they and the soldiers want nothing to do with each other."

Luis agreed to observe the boy to see if he could help. As he walked into the hut, the small group separated to allow him to approach the ailing native. The herbalist eyed him intensely, as if to make it known that Luis entered his domain. The warrior chief stood and greeted him, which gratified. The suffering lad looked to be about sixteen, healthy enough except for his face. It paled, and his right jaw swelled, closing one eye. He moaned, prompting the herbalist to issue a chant or unintelligible saying. Luis knew he faced a choice. He could feign ignorance and walk away unscathed or try to help and risk retribution if unsuccessful. He did want to provide some type of aid. An examination inside the mouth revealed swollen and red gums surrounding a lower tooth. He knew that if it got worse, sepsis would set in, unless it already had.

It must come out, but how? Blacksmith tongs?

He went through explanations with the boy's father and asked that all leave but the two of them to attend the boy. After the father's heated discussion with the herbalist, he left, giving Luis a scowl. Luis then stepped outside to retrieve the soldiers' blacksmith tongs. Slender enough, so he thought hey just might work. He sat astride the boy's chest as his father held his head. He proceeded to pull and work on the tooth with all his might. The young man did not cry out. Blood began to ooze from around the gums, and when the tooth finally popped out, blood and pus flowed copiously.

Luis was relieved, but also repulsed. The father pressed a cloth into the opening and held it. He looked at Luis and nodded.

A poultice placed in his mouth would assist recovery. Luis arose, sweating, and walked outside, holding the blood-streaked tooth aloft. Seeing the results, Fray Díaz spoke to the group assembled outside the hut and gave prayers of thankgiving for Luis' help. The herbalist sulked in the background as the cleric proclaimed that Luis was sent from their one true God.

The Friar confided to Luis, "I think we made progress today, thanks to your help. The herbalist provides comfort in some illnesses, but his incantations ring meaningless. However, my biggest challenge remains the shaman, their spiritual leader. He does not even acknowledge my presence."

***

Luis wiped his moistened brow with his hand, trying to keep perspiration from running into his eyes. Even at mid-morning the autumn's sun eked through the trees, sending streaks of light to every corner of the village. He ignored it as he moved the slender ax head again and again, scraping across the char of the newly-forming dugout. With a constant rhythm, he pretended to be a sculptor preparing a work of art for display in Seville's plaza. *An incongruous thought*, he reminded himself, *but approval of the chief and his Indio brothers did matter.* He knew this preparation would take less time than his slave labors at Calos, where the canoes ran two and three times longer, enhancing travel on the bays and Gulf.

"Water?"

He looked up to see Chukka's sister and several other young women bearing pots.

"Fresh from the spring," she said, displaying a shy smile.

"Yes!" he replied.

Luis and the other men dropped their tools and reached for the water-laden pots. Pouring it into his mouth and over his head served well, and it brought a sense of reward as well as refreshment. Striving to offer conversation to show his thankfulness, he inquired if Reyeeta ever traveled outside the village.

"Only once. I went with my father and uncles on a many days journey to the ocean, where they caught fish for our village. But some villages along the way did not act friendly to us, and so I like it better here."

Luis returned her shy smile with an awkward one of his own, then motioned that he must return to his work. His comfort level came more with the men and the scrapings. He didn't know why, but believed it could have something to do with Spanish madres always in the background. But he couldn't deny the beauty of her dark brown eyes.

***

On the eve of the departure of Sergeant Valdés and most of the soldiers to San Agustín, Luis strolled over to listen to their campfire conversation. It became plain that several had been shipwrecked near the coastal town and conscripted into military service after rescue. He disliked the deluge of coarse talk but relished hearing his own language.

"The question I ask is - am I better off as a toiling soldier in his majesty's service, or as a white Indio, with an Indio wife in a faraway village?" asked a soldier, in a humorous but cynical tone.

"You would be better off to be the owner of a sugar plantation at Santo Domingo, but don't plan for it to happen," responded another soldier.

The entire group bellowed in laughter.

"You, Señor Luis, have you become a white Indio?" asked Sergeant Valdés.

Believing he was unnoticed in the half-dark, Luis' head jerked around to face the visage of the large, gruff soldier. The firelight glinted on his questioner's face, outlined by a thick black beard that only allowed a few of his pockmarks to be seen.

"Why, Sergeant, do you ask?"

"Because we have all noticed you. Even with your loincloth, charred skin, and tied-up hair, you pose as no Arapaja or slave or other Indio. Your clear Spanish response confirms that. What's your purpose here?"

Luis did not want to share his story—yet. But he must give some explanation.

"I was shipwrecked in the Florida Straits. I have remained alive these last two years by the strength of will and the help
of others. With my spirit weakened, I abide here to console, before returning to Spain."

Done, he thought. *If pressed, I will say no more.*

His insides grated like corn, ground in a pot soon for the oven. The cadre quieted for the moment, yielding to the crackle of the fire and crickets and tree frog sounds from the woods.

"Well, you're a lad of spirit."

Alférez Manuel, the group's leader, slipped up unnoticed as Luis finished talking. Looking over, he spied the prominently-nosed, beady-eyed soldier, nodded to him and smiled, as the comment seemed to bring the questioning to a close. Partially unburdening his secret gave Luis a surprising sense of relief. It was akin to confession. The soldiers left before first light the next morning, taking fifteen young males to work as servants or farmers in San Agustín. Because of disease, no one could predict how many would return. And the ones who did could bring pox or fever with them.

***

Days became shorter and nights cooler. Leaves began turning, and soon it would be harvest time. Luis learned to gut and skin the deer and slice it into various parts. Though women's work, he wanted to learn. He continued in the making of dugouts and enjoyed fishing in the river. Tribesmen took him on a trading trip south and he learned of the major trail that led to El Camino Real and San Agustín. With one exception, his heart and soul was satisfied and he even thought of taking a wife, with most of the villagers now having been baptized.

"Fray, I'd like to spend some time talking. I think I'm ready."

Fray Díaz had just returned from the *visitas*, the small village missions in the surrounding areas. He would not go again for a month. It pleased him to converse with Luis, so he bid him to come into the church.

"For almost two years now, I have been able to listen to the voice of nature. It may not exist in Seville or Habana, but it does here. It gives clarity to my thinking and helps me to survive. I have developed thoughts and feelings that did not exist in the Old World."

"Luis, the mouth is the funnel of our spirit's musings. Continue."

"I favor it here in Arapaja with these warm and generous people, so gentle, so helpful to each other. Their lives improve little, true, but they hold happiness. Bringing Catholicism to them is paramount, but do we also upset a delicate balance of life?"

"Civilizations change, Luis…"

"Let me go on. I have been among the Indios now for two years. Some fierce ones, who goaded me into surviving. And many friendly ones who helped me to survive. They fed me. They took me in. We have brought control, disease, and labor needs in San Agustín, not of their choice. Did this not create a plight for the Spanish when the Moors came? I profess amazement that the Arapajas offer no resistance. Perhaps it will yet come, who knows?"

The Friar listened and spoke not. It wasn't confession, but it was similar.

"I served as a military alférez on the Terre Firme galleon Atocha. A wave washed me overboard during a storm in September, 1622, and it may have sunk the ship with all aboard plus all its silver." His mind raced back to the horrific scene on the Atocha just before being cast off. "Why do we need silver? For the King? For honor? For war? To save Catholicism? Why must so many die? Why must Indios and mulattos toil and perish in the silver mines of Potosí? Why did so many of my friends perish?"

He paused, staring at the Friar. His voice rose.

"I realize in Seville I could face execution for my comments, but here they can't reach me. I have 25 reales de a ocho given to me on the Atocha. They burden like Judas' thirty pieces of silver. Their weight increases daily, not on my body, but on my spirit. I must shed them. Tomorrow I will bury most of them in a secret place where they can bring no harm. Silver is a curse.

"Silver can also do good, Luis,"

"Does it say that in the Holy Bible, Fray?"

The Friar stepped to his cabinet, pulled down his Latin Bible, returned to his place on the bench, and opened to a familiar page.

"Ut quisnam multus capio, multus praefer. From St. Luke, chapter 12, verse 48."

"What does that mean?"

"*To whom much is given, much is expected.* The silver is yours, but it could help the Franciscans."

Luis' hardened mind could not envision silver, cursed silver, helping. Only hurting.

"Does it not also say, the love of money is the root of all evil?"

"Yes, but…"

"Then I will bury it!" interjected Luis, his voice rising higher and his face flushing.

The Friar could see Luis' steadfastness and held back making further points.

Agitated, Luis jumped up and began to walk back and forth, as if trying to shake off the effects of their conversation, which seemed to vex him.

"Fray, there is one thing more."

Now, once again sitting and more composed, he gathered his thoughts and softened his tone.

"At the Guacara mission, I received a duel challenge by an unruly Sergeant Torres, as I intervened when he mistreated an Indio. I became the victor with the sword, but I did not kill him. Instead I gashed the muscles on the back of his thighs, hoping it would teach him a lesson. On the Friar's advice, I left posthaste, for we feared retribution from his men. I think they would kill me or have me falsely arrested if they could. That is all."

Fray Díaz looked upwards, pondered, looked down at the ground, and collected his own thoughts.

"My son, the actions of the Pope and the King in seeking silver all contrive as honorable. There stands far bigger plans at work than we can conceive. We must trust. I don't doubt that you have been through troubled times. But you're alive. Look to being thankful. In time, your scars of all kinds will heal. Don't forget, you are a son of Spain."

He then stood, placed his hands on Luis' head, closed his eyes, and said a prayer for him.

***

The next morning in the early pale light, Luis, along with friend Chukka, walked through the village toward the Arapaja River. On this day, he had strapped on his satchel, whose load he looked forward to lightening of silver. Villagers began to arise and move out of their huts, snuffing inside smudge pots, used to deter mosquitoes. They stoked the banked fires under their outside cooking pots, and the pungent aroma of stew soon wafted. Pigs and goats scattered here and there, greeting the morn with grunts and bleats. Luis thought that at least the Spanish added to native diets, bringing new animals to La Florida.

Amidst the cool, early fog just above the water, the two men pushed out and headed downstream. From off in the woods came a long hoot of an owl, still awake from nocturnal pursuits.

"Now, don't tell me an owl omen story," said Luis. "He's just winding down from the night."

"I know," said Chukka. "Luis, I want to help you, but I don't want to go again into the river that enters a hole. I don't want to become bones in the cave, like those I felt after entering it in my youth. Why not bury your silver in the ground?"

"Someday I may change my mind. This way I'll know where it is for certain."

Chukka said nothing. He did not understand his friend's thinking. He knew of Luis' ability and confidence and also of his disdain for some of the ways of his homeland. He could tell that Luis was determined to rid himself of the silver.

It took a day and a half to go downstream on the Arapaja to reach their goal. Several rapids running on the lower part of the float added a sense of excitement, as the canoe splashed up and down. Approaching the swallow hole differed from the last time, as the main river also now flowed again in its stream bed. With close observation the men found where the side flow averted to an opening in the west bank, like a reverse spring run. They turned into it and let the current carry them the short distance. It contained high banks on each side, so they pulled into a lone crevice in the bank close by the cavern.

"I'd like to walk around the area before I go into the water," said Luis.

"What do you hope to see?"

"I'm not certain."

Walking along the short stream, he discovered a small overflow around the edge of the high-banked cavern where the stream went underground and followed it. It continued through the woods, gaining speed, and it too became a fast-moving stream. It took a sharp turn to the east, which Luis followed for a short distance, traversing a light growth forest. Doubling back across the woods instead of back up the stream, he walked north, back toward the swallow hole. Almost stumbling into an opening in the ground, he stopped and peered down.

"Chukka-a-a!" he yelled, "Over here!"

When Chukka arrived, they peered into a unique sight. The underground stream from the cavern flowed exposed, moving beneath the earth's surface.

"It could be your escape route, should you not be able to swim back to the cavern entrance," Chukka said, beaming.

"That's true, but you told me moving back out the way I entered would be fine."

"Yes, I did, many moons ago."

Luis removed the rudiments of his survival kit from the satchel, pulled out three silver pesos, placed them on the bank, and secured the bag. A future trip to San Agustín, even if just for a visit, would allow him to convey two to the senior Franciscan for help at the Guacara and Arapaja missions. The third he would keep as his memento. He removed his sandals and clinched tight around him the strap holding the satchel with the remaining twenty-two coins. He tied a braided rope under his arms and gave the loose end to Chukka.

"Think 50 feet is long enough?"

"More than enough."

"Go straight down, close to the back bank. Be mindful of submerged logs that have wedged below. When you reach the bottom, swim straight ahead and enter the underwater cave's opening. You should reach a ledge soon. Feel to your right and draw yourself onto it. Deposit the satchel, then pull hard on the rope and I will haul you out as you swim."

With ease he slid down the bank and entered the dark water pool next to where it flowed into the underwater cavern. Cool but not cold. The noise reminded him of a flowing well filling a large pot, resonating.

Turning his head, he smiled and spoke. "Thanks, Chukka."

Luis took a long look at the blue sky above, with scattered clouds, all framed by overhanging trees above the huge circular bank.

"I should be pulling on the rope soon," he said, slipping below and allowing the current to take him down

Little light penetrated from above, so Luis felt his way along, entered and found the ledge above his head to the right. Grasping in the darkness, he pulled up onto it, out of the water.

The stream continued flowing by, with the gurgling echoing off the walls. Feeling around for a crevice, he found one high on the back wall, and placed the satchel there. He believed that even current from high water would not remove it.

Easing back into the water, he gave two tugs so that Chukka would tighten the rope and bring him back as he swam against the current. Flowing stronger than he anticipated, the water's strength or either a weakness in the rope caused it to snap as Chukka pulled. Panicking and in the dark, released from his safety line, Luis sensed falling, as in a bad dream. He couldn't tell up from down.

Feeling around furiously, he found the ledge, and again pulled onto it, scraping and cutting a finger in the process. Gasping, he reeled bewildered. He had checked the rope, found it satisfactory, but realized it could have rubbed against a sharp rock.

The tiny cave contained little air and Luis labored to move or breathe.

Control the emotions....relax....think....then take action.....

Luis brought himself to a state of calm, breathing from the top of his lungs.

Only one way.

He slipped back into the water, exerting all his strength, swimming against the current. He made progress as the light ahead brightened.

Just a few more strokes to the surface.

But the current pressed against him. Doggedly he swam, but with energy ebbing and lung air strained. Exhaustion took over, and he shot back with the current. Unable to grasp the ledge again, he sucked scant air at the ceiling of the enclosure, dark as night.

Amidst a wave of hopelessness, he breathed as light as possible, moving along on his back, the current taking him deeper and deeper through the cavernous route. The water turned colder the further it carried him into the earth. With stark realization now, he prayed to God to accept him and to forgive him for being overzealous to rid himself of mere metal.

Taking one last breath, he went below the surface as the water met the ceiling. He pictured Isabela for what he perceived as the last time and sought peace within. Going limp, he allowed the current to carry him, with no resistance. Only a small amount of air remained in his lungs.

With eyes open, in the distance he again could see light.

Am I back at the entrance of the cavern, or have I arrived at Heaven?

13
WHITE INDIO

16 24

There is pleasure in being mad
Which none but madmen know.
<u>The Spanish Friar</u>
Act II

FLORIDA PENINSULA NORTH CENTRAL

The light became brighter as he floated. He swam upwards toward it and reached the surface. In an instant he recognized the opening in the ground where he'd seen the underground stream from above. He grabbed a ledge, held on and again breathed fresh air, gasping. He could even see the sky through tree branches, and his heart leaped.

From the flowing water to the top of the opening, rock covered the walls for a distance of about five feet. Not far, but slippery and with few handholds to aid him.

"*Chukkkaaaaa*!" he yelled over and over, his jaw shaking from exposure to the cold water.

Chukka ran through the woods, hearing but not seeing. He ran along the overflow stream beyond the swallow hole, but no Luis. Back in the woods, the calls became louder. He wondered if Luis had drowned and his spirit was calling forth. Scared, he wanted to depart, but then he saw it again. With his mind jolted, he rushed to the hole and peered down. To Luis, Chukka cast a visage of a man seeing a ghost.

"Help me up!"

"Let me get the rope. This time we will double it!"

Double-stranded, he lowered it to Luis. With trembling hands he wrapped it around one arm. With his heels dug in, Chukka pulled while Luis climbed his way up. When he reached the top, Chukka pulled him onto dry ground and both rolled over, exhausted.

"Lu-ees, you have the cunning of a fox, the strength of a bear, and the bravery of a panther, but today you were not wise. Next time, give the coins to me, and I will dispose of them."

Luis eyed him meekly.

"You're right. Thank you for pulling me out of the hole and piercing my countenance as needed."

The men gathered themselves up, recovered the remaining three silver coins on the bank and took time to eat their roasted fish and corn cakes before setting out on the water upstream. It served as a day of reckoning for Luis. Once again he survived, but he realized the misadventure resulted from his own making. He vowed that in the days to come he would exercise restraint when vexations sought to overpower him.

"Luis…my family will ask you to take my sister as your wife."

"What?" It caught Luis off-guard.

"You've become one of us. You're proven in combat as well as in supporting the village. At almost eighteen summers, she appeals to many but has an eye for you. A word to my family could arrange it."

Luis listened to what he said, though heretofore he thought of Reyeeta only as Chukka's sister.

"Thank you for alerting me. Let me think on it. I have no desire to return to Spain, and it could be best."

As they paddled upstream, the rains came, and drops hammered the water and popped on palmetto fronds and oak leaves. Though drenched, Luis enjoyed it much better than the dark cold water of the cavern.

"One more thing, Lu-ees."

"What?"

"Our chief wishes you to take a woman anyway if you stay with us. To do otherwise would displease him."

Luis turned the comment over and over in his mind. Though at first feeling defensive, he did not respond.

Perhaps, he thought, *it brings another way to adapt. A pleasant way.*

Just before arriving home the next day, they waved to several women in the shallows. They were taking turns filling pots with spring water from the bank, and the group included Reyeeta.

Beautiful. Smiling face, long black hair, and youthful body make more of an impression on this day than before, thought Luis.

***

They wed the following month, as Fray Díaz conducted the ceremony in the mission church. It could not contain the entire village, but all enjoyed the ensuing outside festivities. Feasting and games took place, and that night Reyeeta moved into Luis's hut.

He lived now as a true *white Indio,* and it pleased him. As a hut builder, fisherman, fledgling hunter, and a teacher that assisted the Friar, he was happy. Luis could not see beyond 1624, but it mattered not. He progressed as an avid player of their stickball game and excelled. His sword, survival kit, and three reales de a ocho stayed packed away, like tokens of a bygone era. Time and calendar lost all meaning as he blended into the rhythms and seasons of the Arapaja.

***

Fray Díaz began to change. Luis observed his growing sour disposition and sometimes scowling manner. He became short-tempered and quick to whip the Indios if they did not learn the catechisms as directed. Often he would correct Luis in the midst of his teachings, becoming easily irritated. He spoke ill of La Florida's Governor, complaining that he would not discipline the soldiers who abused the Indios they used as servants. Considerable conflict arose with the cavalrymen, who could attest to Díaz's unbridled fits of temper. In contrast, he was a learned man, who had once dutifully counseled Luis, who now didn't understand.

He remembered Fray Mobila's words at the Guacara mission–*many that serve in the Florida interior have a troubled past.* Realizing the Friar's deprivations and how that could affect him preyed on Luis. Still, he now deemed the Friar unstable.

But he wanted to contemplate more important things, as time alone with Reyeeta. Following harvest, he realized that they had not been on a journey together since being wed.

He also wanted to explore the Arapaja River upstream of the village. Reyeeta liked the idea and started planning the food to take.

***

On a pleasant late autumn morning in 1624 while dew still lay on the grass, the newlyweds set out paddling north for an undetermined distance. They moved with laughter in their hearts and joy in their souls.

"Lu-ees, as a young girl I dreamed of going off like this. I pictured a strong young warrior returning from battle, taking me away to some secret place. Now, I have my dream." She looked at him and glowed.

"Well, I must say that I never thought of living in the woods on a river, but my life with you is now like a dream."

Tree colors brightened at their peak, and sunlight made the reds and golds shine. The cypress trees' rust-red needles contrasted with the higher-banked evergreens. As they moved further up the river, high banks gave way to lowlands and sandy beaches. Large-trunked trees stood in the shallows of the dark water and provided a canopy above. Occasionally small tree-fruits would plop in the water, punctuating the float. They heard the bugs that sounded like distant rain and the birds singing their songs in the woods. Late afternoon found the couple camped on a wide, white sand bar, replete with animal tracks of all kinds. Sleeping under the stars free of insects, Luis and Reyeeta made good use of the time as husband and wife.

On the morning of the third day, Luis arose before Reyeeta. Due to increasing rapids the day before, they had decided to return home in the morning. But first, Luis wanted to explore before she awoke. Easing into the woods, he stumbled onto a trail that paralleled the river. While walking north, noisy hooves in the distance caught him by surprise. He slipped off the trail into the bush. Hiding, he watched ten Indios, all mounted, as they headed north. Each Indio wore black face-paint, but with no other identifying signs. With horses, he believed they came from afar.

As soon as they passed, he hurried back to the camp where Reyeeta still slept. He woke her with a kiss but did not mention the strangers, not wanting to scare her. After breakfast, they packed up and headed back downstream. He would soon tell the men in the village of the strange Indios. To Luis, something out of the ordinary stirred afoot.

"We have other reports of the *Black Faces* and their horses," said the chief. "We think it's possible they come from much further north where settlers may have driven them away. They could be slave raiding for the Nickaleers, or they may desire a settlement of their own."

So as not to give the appearance of an alarmist, Luis had waited until the day after their journey's return to make his observations known. He had asked for and received an audience with the chief and the warrior chief.

"They do not come in peace, as they have not asked to visit us," said the warrior chief. "And their horses. Here, only a few Spanish have horses, so they do not belong to our people. Perhaps they're angry for having to leave their homes in the north. We'll place guards now."

They thanked Luis and asked that he stay silent for now to prevent distress among the village. He agreed but also began to wonder of the soldiers, overdue in returning from San Agustín, now that they may be needed. A week later the soldiers did return. In the spring they would go back again, taking corn and a fresh supply of workers. They never selected Luis, choosing others instead.

***

One day he witnessed Sergeant Valdés in deep discussion with Fray Díaz. Each pointed to Luis' hut, and the Friar gave what appeared to be a letter to the soldier. Luis suspected
foul play, perhaps a plot, as on that day, the Friar's darkened eyes matched the Sergeant's. He felt an odd sense of dread,
as if night itself descended. He later dismissed the scene and continued to focus on the joys of a simple life.

For him, days and nights with Reyeeta stayed pleasant. They each worked at separate tasks during the day, with hers involving sustenance. Along with the other women, she picked fruit, nuts, and acorns and prepared their meals. Luis came to relish her acorn cakes, much like he did the corn cakes. They never kept far apart in the village. Just seeing her smile at day's waning could enhance Luis' mood like river fog lifting on a summer's morn. Thoughts of Spain came seldom now, unless coming forth in dreams.

Sometimes his fitful dreams returned—nightmares. Visions of friends roasting over barbacoas, dying, shipwrecks, or fights with Calusas. Night sweats and groaning alerted Reyeeta's soothing manner.

"Lu-ees, why do you have dark dreams?"

"It's from guilt of living, while many friends have died or are enslaved. The last few years have enlightened me, but I have also run a *gauntlet* that produced scars, though you can't see them."

"I see them Lu-ees."

"Just as I entered the dark river cavern, was sucked down, but popped up anew, my thoughts still flow through a tunnel."

"Time will heal you Lu-ees, and I will help it." She always placed his arm around her and her head on his shoulder.
She understood.

***

SEVILLE
1625

Isabela sat at her bureau, gazing into the mirror. She combed and brushed her hair, then applied rose water to her neck. Every few minutes she stopped and plucked a candied fruit from the bowl beside her. She partook of simple pleasures in early morning as the baby slept. Soon it would be time to nurse her again, and that too begat a simple joy over the last three months. No denying, husband José provided all that she needed, and the Allycon's silk business prospered. All the way from China, across New Spain to Seville it came, bolts and bolts. The finery stayed in demand by the town's upper class. A fabric she too relished.

I have arranged now whom you can marry. From out of nowhere, old thoughts reverberated in her brain, as she again recalled her father's words. She had forced a smile when told of José's qualifications.

Old Seville, purity of blood, faithful Catholic, established family business, respected, gentleman, late thirties, and widower.

After those comments, she remembered little else that he said. On that night she had cried herself to sleep thinking…*Luis, where are you?*

Those almost daily thoughts she wanted to dismiss, but this morning they crept in again. She wanted instead to look forward to the upcoming theater showing of <u>The Dancing Master</u>, by Lope de Vega. Although she would attend in the separate women's box, she would join friends. But reflections kept returning.

Maybe I should have run away and joined a gypsy band when Luis didn't return. Passionate romance could surely be found there. Some women find romance after marriage with another. That's not really for me.

She learned to manage her husband as well as she did the kitchen. Maturity came to her and flourished like orange blossoms in springtime's full glory. Her life was suitable.

But why do the French women have more freedom, more liberty to pursue their desires?

José, always *the counter*, had believed he could increase his profits if he alone handled the next silk shipment from the Orient, so he sailed on the New Spain flota. It had followed the child's birth in March, 1625, and Isabela could not understand.

Gone like Luis–what man leaves his firstborn when she is only a few weeks old?

He left his brother, Domingo, in charge of the Seville silk shop in the Alcaicerio, the Merchants Quarter. José arranged such that Isabela wanted for nothing while he journeyed. A knock on her door and her temporary mulatto servant entered bearing morning chocolate and freshly polished spectacles.

Life does have its comforting moments, she reflected.

***

FLORIDA PENINSULA NORTH CENTRAL
1625

A new year and spring planting time came to the village with many seeding corn, squash, beans, and pumpkins. The shaman practiced his art of field incantations each morning prior to the work. Fray Díaz did not like the pagan gibberish but held his tongue, seeking to phase in Catholic ways and phase out the old over time. The end of planting brought an annual celebration time. Within sight of the wooden cross the Friar erected, the Arapaja made preparations. It would begin with the men's cassina drink and purging ritual, followed by all-night chants and dancing. Fray Díaz planned for this to be the last. Luis and the Friar witnessed it for awhile but did not participate. To Luis, the evening's odd gyrations and movements gave the impression of emphasizing fertility.

As if to assert his remaining influence, the white-masked shaman, looking hideous, jaunted over to the two men. He began to chant unintelligibly, then suddenly stopped, his masked face staring down at Luis.

"You live as one of us, but not one of us…and like the bird that dives for fish from on high…he now does not come up at once…remaining longer in the water…when he does fly, he has no fish!"

He then screamed.

"He will seek another river…it will take time to find a flow that accepts him…the fish he catches will taste sour…he will need honey for his mouth…"

He screamed again, then hurried back to join the night dance.

Luis and Fray Díaz looked at each other with astonishment, but the Friar waved it off.

"Meaningless," exclaimed Fray Díaz. "He's pretending to predict the future, using riddles. I think mostly he's trying to let me know he still has control over his people. In time, that will change."

Luis sat speechless, then, with a perplexed shake of his head, slipped off to his hut. Sleep eluded him due to the chants and singing, but also because of the shaman. He pondered if the man knew of a troubling event in Luis' future. *If so, why did he choose to convey it with such frenzied chatter?* He recalled a recent scene, witnessed from a distance, between the Friar and the Sergeant. Each pointed toward Luis' hut, and Díaz handed Valdés a letter.

A fish hawk dives…no fish…sour fish…honey…?

***

Luis maintained a vague awareness of the year 1625. The completion of spring planting and the warming days helped to confirm it. Days of the week had no special significance anymore, except for Sundays, when the Priest held a special Mass. To him, time fused with nature, and a sense of the year passing in numbers vanished. It was only marked by seasons. The words *culture, theater, fashion,* or even *galleon* did not arise in his consciousness. He loved the simplicity of his life, almost as a monk, who taught the Indios the Spanish language, but who could also have a wife.

The soldiers left again for the spring trek to San Agustín, taking twelve males with them for labor in town. They would return in about a month, and Luis hoped they would return accompanied by the previous Indios taken. Though many became heartsick at seeing the male Arapajas leave, the soldiers' absence did provide a calming effect on the village. Only two were left as token guards. Luis could sense the peace even in his classroom as he taught Spanish. Sometimes, the Friar would stop in to listen. One day he did more than listen. And it broke the peace.

"No! I told you not to teach sentences till they have

learned the nouns and verbs and spelling!

He sputtered, almost out of control, with the outburst.

"Fray, I'm not…"

"I said nouns and verbs! Did they teach you nothing at the Universidad?!"

With that, he turned and withdrew, like a strong wind blowing into the church and out again.

"Don't be alarmed, children. He's just trying to help."

Luis knew something ran amiss, as the Friar was not prone to overly criticize him, though he did lose his temper with the soldiers and villagers. That evening, after dark, Luis went to the friary. Looking in, he could see Fray Díaz on his knees, one candle glowing beside him. After he arose, Luis stepped inside.

"Fray, what troubles you?"

"Did I yell at you today? I'm sorry, my friend. I sometimes cannot control my temperament. I do not know why. Perhaps it's due to the Holy Office. I have nightmares."

Luis did not understand, but he surmised that something haunted the Friar.

"Remember me as your friend, and I want to help, as you helped me."

But Luis couldn't help or counsel the Friar.

Just before the soldiers were expected back from San Agustín, the Friar confronted him again in the middle of a class. He came in the back, sat for a brief time and then jumped to his feet.

"Señor Armador, I told you not to teach that way! It displeases me! You disgrace this mission!"

"But what…?" Luis stammered.

"Your manner of instruction, I deem unacceptable. You are dismissed!"

"Fray Díaz, please tell me what I've done wrong, I…"

"We will not discuss this! You must leave! I will take the class."

Luis left baffled. Walking toward his hut, he recalled a situation aboard the Atocha. A seaman, known for his moodiness, sat in stocks more than once because of his confrontations and incompatibility. Surgeon Ribera stated aside to Luis that the man probably suffered from *Melancholia*, a disease of the mind. He then provided an explanation.

"He harbors an excess of the black bile humor, and there is no cure. Bleeding and medicinal powders help not. Sad. All seamen become angry sooner or later, but his disposition worsens. The malady alters the thoughts."

Ribera. I'd love to see him.

He decided that the Friar must also suffer the Melancholia, as he produced irrational behavior, not normal for a priest.

He also acts as though he wants to disassociate from me, thought Luis.

Having lost his job as teacher provided Luis with time to help the village in other ways. Motivated with a desire to become more skilled in the bow and arrow, he practiced often and wanted to provide deer meat for the families. Late spring's warmth made crossing the river tolerable, so one morning he did so in order to walk a trail north. But not before he embraced Reyeeta.

"We'll be picking the season's ripe fruits west of the woods across the stream. Brother Chukka and our uncle will go with our group of five women. So, until tonight," she said.

Going alone, he strapped on his sword as well as bow and arrows. Invigorated, he pressed upward on the trail. The goal was to make a silent stand and wait for his prey. He stopped about one and a half miles north of the village and climbed a lofty oak.

Mid-morning, with the sun streaking through the branches, he heard the familiar crunching of hooves in the woods.

Using slow movements, he took aim, held his breath, and let the arrow fly. It missed, slamming with a thud into the

ground. Downhearted, he feathered another, but the deer departed. He settled back to wait again. His ears now greeted the well-known sound of horses. He stayed close in the tree, just off the trail, and looked down. A group of the black-faced Indios rode by, this time headed south. At the rate they traveled, they could be at his village in a short time. He thought at once of Reyeeta and her group. Climbing down from the tree, he sprinted south on the trail, eyeing horse tracks as he went, his apprehension growing.

14
CHISCAS ATTACK

1625

The only cure for grief is action.
Life of Lope de Vega

FLORIDA PENINSULA NORTH CENTRAL

Pamunka slapped his horse to spur him on. As they neared the Arapaja village, his desire to fight and conquer grew with intensity. The leader of the Chiscas, driven out by white settlers further north, needed to vent his anger. A proud people, they rode horses, unlike many other tribes. As they moved south, no village showed friendliness to them. And so his torment grew each day. He decided the time came to show others their bravery. They needed an area to call their own, and this one lay far from the English and the Spanish.

They planned to attack without warning and drive away the people of Arapaja. Then they would take slaves back for sale further north. Behind him rode four mounted warriors, black paint covering their faces. Eager to fight. And they knew that most of the mission's military visited in San Agustín.

They came upon five women, with two men watching over them, along the edge of a field, plucking berries and fruits. It surprised Pamunka, as he intended to hit the village itself quickly and ride away.

"Attack! Kill! Eeee yiiii!" he screamed.

He caught one of the rising men in the head with his ax while another rider fell upon the second. The attacker's knife went to the throat and then to the scalp. The women ran on the trail back towards the river and the village, but one by one the intruders caught and dispatched them. Victory screams ensued.

They did not notice the dark-haired Spaniard as he rushed toward the blood-thirsty scalpers. He let loose an arrow to the chest of one, thrust a knife into the back of another and wielded it again with success on a third.

Shocked, Pamunka and the other Chiscas took to their horses in running leaps and sped away, the riderless horses following. Luis wiped blood from his knife and hands and looked around. Then he spied her. Rushing over, seeing the crumpled body and bloodied head and feeling no pulse, he could not contain himself.

"*Ahhhhhhhhhhhh!*" he bellowed. He gathered her in his arms, tears streaming, and headed to the village.

Reyeeta is gone, and I cannot bring her back. What kind of people war against women? She did no one any harm.

Village warriors, having heard the women's screams, rushed past him along the trail. But all came too late. They could only gather the slain and take them back to the village. However, one of the assaulted still lived. Chukka could not move, only moan. A huge knot formed on the side of his blood-streaked head. All knew he may not survive, but they made a litter on which to drag him. At the village, wailing commenced as they returned. By evening, the chief and the warrior chief called a council. They would discuss their response well into the night.

Chukka received attention from the herbalist, who applied a poultice to his head and blew pipe smoke on him, and the Friar said prayers for all. With one exception, the victims lay in the plaza in preparation for a funeral, which Fray Díaz insisted be Christian. Luis had taken Reyeeta to his hut and did not reappear. He was inconsolable. Each one that entered his hut could not coax him to bring her out. He would not talk and only sat and stared. In the morning the chief paid him a visit. Luis' eyes looked red and swollen from not sleeping.

"Lu-ees, my heart breaks as does yours. I think the Chisca people, the Black Faces, did this. We will do our best to find and punish them. You have achieved that in part. But first, we must bury Reyeeta and the others. Your God wants that, and the Friar is ready. Please come out."

He complied, placing her with the others. All stood and watched as Fray Díaz performed the funeral rites for the six fallen. But Luis could not hear, and he could not think. His mind went blank. Afterwards, he stumbled back to his hut, not to emerge again for two days

***

Chukka lay flat on his back, his head turned to Luis, who patted him on the arm.

"I'm sorry Lu-ees. They took us by surprise. My grief reflects yours for Reyeeta. We will see her again in the next world. As my elders would say, *now she walks with the stars.*"

Tears formed in Luis' eyes as he began to speak. "You will heal, my friend, and you may have consolation in the punishment that your warriors plan. They left yesterday to pursue the Chiscas."

"Why did you not go with them?"

"As you may know, I slew three of them as I came upon the attack. I have little fight left in me today. Besides, I must leave Arapaja."

"No!"

"Yes. My heart grieves too much to stay. The time I've spent here with you and the village and Reyeeta bestowed a blessing for me. But it is time for me to return to Spain and my other family. Thank you for everything. I'll never forget."

As tears formed in the weak and injured Arapaja's eyes, the men clasped hands one last time. Luis eased out, went back to his hut, and once again prepared for a journey. Sword, scabbard, strap, new deerskin bag, three silver pesos, trail survival gear, deerskin wrap–all his possessions were laid out. To that he added jerky, fruit, corn cakes, acorn cakes, nuts, a deerskin bag of water, and a small jar of garfish oil. It would suffice.

He spent the afternoon saying goodbye to the chief, the warrior chief, various friends and even the shaman and herbalist. Fray Díaz was the last to whom he bid goodbye. Mixed feelings pervaded his mind for this conflicted man of Spain. He concluded that maybe it mattered not, as the Friar said very little in the way of a parting. He did offer that the trail south went about 80 miles to the east-west El Camino Real. 70 miles more east would take him to San Agustín.

Luis expected to trek eight days south, then eight days east to reach his goal. Barring any incidents, that became his plan. He also anticipated stops at the missions enroute. That evening he planned to depart at first light the next day, but he found sleep wanting. Peering from his hut and seeing the moon halfway on its nighttime quest, he decided to go ahead and depart. With all his farewells done, there arose nothing left to hold him.

With two bags of goods and gear attached, he set out south on the trail bordering the river. The full moon shone through the shadowy trees, enough for the path to be seen. At openings, he could see the black sky, lit with thousands of stars overhead. Not a cloud in sight. Luis realized that his senses were numb. Somehow, he hoped to find cleansing and comfort while alone in the wilderness. Nature, his old friend, would give him solace. And he wanted to partake.

As dawn peaked on the trail, all forms in the forest became clear. Oaks festooned with moss, and palmettos, with their sharp-pointed fronds, stood guard along his pathway. Birds sang and squirrels moved among the trees, having emerged from their nests. The familiar sounds of morning. As smoke from the fire along the San Martín River once encircled him, smoke of another sort enveloped his mind. Hoping that traipsing the woods would clear it, he spent the day on a steady pace, stopping only to eat.

Nightfall came, and he estimated having gone perhaps fifteen miles. Not a soul did he see all day. He lay his deerskin wrap on the trail, covered his face and arms with garfish oil, and enjoyed jerky and corn cakes. Peaceful slumber came soon, but he suffered a nocturnal chase nightmare.

They were horsemen, all with black faces. Hundreds, and they all ride fast after me. I run, but they close and their whoops terrify. I can stand it no longer and turn to face them, my need for combat surging. But then they disappear and leave me all alone. An overwhelming sense of emptiness encompasses me.

Morning came as a welcomed sight. He grasped a vague recollection of warriors chasing him in a dream, but brushed it aside. No dew, as the air lay hot and dry. Luis took drafts from his water bag, swallowed some nuts and fruit and began walking. A clearing along the trail produced a clump of blackberry bushes, and he took his fill. A cloudbank in the western sky reminded him of the mountains north of Seville beyond the river. His homeland began to seep back more into his consciousness. On the deep woods path he knew his body accomplished something, and in time, so would his spirit. *A healing to come.*

Mid-day and familiar noises came down the trail. Men talking in Spanish and horses snorting. Luis crept into the brush to observe before making an appearance. It soon became apparent that it was the contingent of horseback soldiers headed back to the mission. They led a handful of sad-looking, fatigued Arapajas.

"Buenos días!" said Luis, stepping back onto the trail. He greeted Alférez Manuel riding the lead horse.

"Armador. What are you doing this far from the village? Are you lost?" he chuckled.

"Not lost, but heading to San Agustín. In your absence, the outskirts of the village suffered a raid. Indios, wearing black face paint, massacred five women and one man and injured another. I lost my wife, Reyeeta, in the attack. I came upon them and slew three, but two rode away. We needed you for protection!" Luis was indignant.

"Our Indios did not finish their allotted tasks as soon as planned. The Governor's staff made us stay, and it delayed our return. My regrets. Perhaps we can pursue them and mete out punishment."

"The warrior chief and his men now pursue them, but they have horses, so it may be difficult."

"Horses? That's interesting."

"I must continue on my journey to the coast. I wish you well."

"The mission San Agustín de Urihica lies not far south off this trail, about a day and a half march from here. You may want to stop there. By the way, Armador, watch your back with Governor Borgia. He's like the chameleon. Affable one day, strong-arming the next. I've seen him entertain a guest and then have him jailed a few days later on a weak charge."

"I thank you for the advice," said Luis as he took his leave.

Sergeant Valdés issued no greeting as they passed, staring through dark brooding eyes. Luis had an immediate recall to the time he witnessed Valdés and Fray Díaz in deep conversation. His manner made Luis think of a distant black cloud moving in with a storm. It gratified him to put distance between them. He knew it fruitless to bear animosity toward the soldiers, as they may not have prevented Reyeeta's death anyway. Putting the thoughts behind him, he continued his southward trek.

Several hours passed, and when the sun shone straight above, Luis felt pangs of hunger. An interruption arose from the sound of gurgling water nearby. The noise enticed him, as his deerskin bag held only warm liquid. Stepping east off the trail, he walked through the brush, pursuing the ever-increasing sound of the flow. After about 300 feet, he saw it. A tiny clear stream ran from deep in the woods and disappeared into a hole in the ground no bigger than Luis' fist. He kneeled down, drank his fill of the cool liquid and refilled his bag. He reveled that nature provided so much. After nibbling on jerky, he rose to rejoin the pathway. Uncertain if affected by the heat, fatigue, or his hazy thoughts, he somehow forgot the direction. Trying to recall some small landmark escaped him.

How can this be?

With the sun arching in the sky, he decided to sit and await its confirmed movement west, where the trail should be. Leaning his back against a tree, facing south and closing his eyes, he could see the future.

Aboard a ship to Seville. My own cabin and meals often with the Captain. Everything in place.

Sometime later, early afternoon, he blinked open his eyes. *Was it a true dream or just a daydream? But that it could happen now.*

Eyes cocked to the right confirmed the sun's direction west, so he stood to walk, feeling confident. After stumbling through the thick bushes and palmettos for about fifteen minutes, no trail yet appeared.

What of my skills? Have I been so long in the village that I've lost them? It's only my second day of traveling.

Luis puzzled over it, for he moved west from whence he came, or so he believed. The trail ran north to south. But now in the woods everything looked the same. He sat down to gather his thoughts.

…Remember Luis, in troubling times, it's best to first relax, then you can think, and take action…

He sat again to contemplate which direction would work best.

Back to the gurgling brook? Would it even be found again? Try a northerly direction? Walk south until I reach the San Martín River? Wait for sunrise, and re-orient then? Yell? No, that could attract the hostile Black Faces.

He decided to take a forty-five degree turn left and proceed. To his estimation, he should then head southwest. In the morning he would try to confirm direction based on the sunrise. It boded as a good plan. He had food and water and realized in the past he'd faced worse circumstances and survived. Walking through late afternoon till he found a cleared area good for a campsite, his mind settled for the moment. Luis knew that a night in the forest with no point of reference could feel like a night on the open ocean. But he'd experienced that once and lived.

Dark descended like an enormous cloak around him. Sounds came of crickets, tree frogs, and whining mosquitoes in his ears. Reminiscent of entering the Arapaja water cavern again, but this time he sprawled motionless. Sleep did not come, even after much time on the deerskin. Dark shapes loomed all around, and in the distance a wildcat screeched. He became afraid. Grief still lingered in the corners of his mind, and now he lay lost. How he longed for a flowing river nearby. His skin tingled, his heart raced and his muscles tightened. An overwhelming sense of fear seized him. If only there was a path, he would run, to try to lose the anxious feelings.

He did the next best thing. Sitting bolt upright, he let it out.

Ahhhhhhhh!

The verbal release felt good, so he did it again.

Ahhhhhhhh!

And again, and again, and again…

Minutes later, spent with trying to discharge his terrors, he slumped back onto the deerskin, sweating. No echo, just the quiet remained, with subdued night murmurs. He closed his eyes. But then he sensed something. Not from a dream because he lay awake. A movement, a loud flapping and then the sound of some jungle creature, or so he thought. It went above him and gave out a noise like a huge tree falling– *crackkkkk!* But then it left. It didn't harm.

He knew his survival senses needed sharpening, but he also experienced vague notions. He wanted to be free of them. No peace came to Luis that night. He longed for the morning. As he lay there, forms began to appear. *Lights, people, Indios, horses, spears…familiar sights of Seville…even voices*. He didn't understand it, so he prayed for relief. Sometime in the early morning hours, he drifted off. It lasted for only an hour, but gave a well-needed time of rest.

First light brought chirping birds and the hope of dawn. It arrived like a soft breeze blowing over him. The night had exhausted him emotionally, but he passed through it. Now more relaxed, he eagerly sought the day. After corn cakes and fruit, he gathered up the bags and readied for his walk. As in the past, his sword and satchel remained strapped during the night.

The brightening light from the east pointed him to the south. If not the trail this day, then perhaps the river, flowing from east to west. *Almost as good,* he thought.

He wished for leggings or breeches, as the thick bush and palmettos scraped his legs, drawing blood and raising welts. Moving slowly, he stayed on guard for snakes. No path, but the land lay flat and sandy, covered with pines and oaks. He still could not get his bearings and even wondered of injury.

What if I break a leg or am attacked by a wild boar or panther?

He began to fantasize about reaching the river. It would give him direction. It would take him to a settlement. First, he'd immerse and then let its water float him on down, like embracing an old friend. He could almost feel the cooling waters, as the early summer sun bore down. In the midst of his plodding and daydreaming, another concern struck him.

Could it be dried away, like the lower Arapaja, as when I first encountered it?

Evening returned, and he laid out his deerskin, covered himself again with garfish oil, and pulled sustenance out to devour. He knew much distance had been covered, but if no trail or river is reached on the morrow, he'd need to change direction.

The San Martín must be crossed. Even if it is dry, it would provide a path.

The next day he continued through thick bushes, akin to trying to push his way through a plaza crowd on feast day. Hard going, like some type of natural gauntlet. He plopped down at day's end under a giant oak, its massive limbs shading a small clearing. He'd found no trail, heard no human sound.

I'm in the middle of nowhere. The most remote spot in all of La Florida, maybe the world. Though bone-tired, he sat too depressed to eat. Lying on the deerskin at nightfall, he closed his eyes, not caring if he slept. Dark brought the usual sounds. The calming hum of crickets, but also the terrifying screams of wildcats. He thought of bears, knowing they resided here too.

Is it madness that causes disaster, or disaster that causes madness?

Somewhere in time he succumbed to sleep, but dark moments entered his mind.

I see Isabela, clad all in black, her head covered by a black scarf. She kneels near candles and an altar, with head bowed and eyes closed. 'I'm here, my love, I'm yet alive!' But she couldn't hear me, nor could other mourners around her. Is this scene of today or two years past? What's to become of her?

Luis awoke on day five of his journey. A half-decent sleep, yet he experienced another vague dream of Isabela. He shook, like leaves on a tree, remembering no food or drink passed his lips on the evening past. Delving into his satchels told him that only a few mouthfuls of jerky and corn cakes remained. Today he would have to forage as well as find the path, or the river. A morning's walk through the thick woods again challenged him. As the sun overhead reached its pinnacle, Luis stopped to drink his remaining water, now warm. He wanted to spit, but forced it down. Too numb to cry and too stubborn to give up, he continued to plod, having forgotten his resolve to change directions if he found no path or river.

A unique sound could be heard in the distance ahead, like the wind that increases before a storm. But the sky looked clear. The further he walked, the louder it became, almost like the roar of a flooded river. Up ahead, he could see a clearing of sorts. The land seemed to drop into a trough, then rise up again. It reminded him of approaching the river when he ran from the fire. He began to run again.

15

EL CAMINO REAL

1625

i nunca pudo resistir la llamada del camino.
(I never could resist the call of the trail.)

FLORIDA PENINSULA NORTHEAST CENTRAL

Taking the rise through tangled bushes and gnarled trees,
he saw it–the *San Martín River. He couldn't contain his elation and began
laughing and crying alternately.

"I am delivered! I am delivered!" he shouted for all nature
to hear.

The roaring sound came from a descending set of rapids, many yards
long, spreading across the river. Compared to the ones he'd encountered
downstream, these were much larger and dropped five to ten feet from top
to bottom in the run.

*Truly some ** big shoals.*

Luis eased into the water at the bottom of the cascade, working his way
up to a spot where he could sit in the middle. He lay down and let the
water massage his body with its riffles and currents, cool and soothing.
Black water flowed fast, but rocks stretching across turned it white, issuing
foamy brown suds out at the bottom. Achieving at last a point of
reference, he planned to stay by the river and move downstream
after enjoying the water. After about an hour, the river's song and his
fatigue almost lulled him to sleep. His head slipped underwater, and he
rose up with a start. Glancing at the west bank, it surprised him to see four
Indios dragging their canoas around the rapids. He hailed them and waded
over to speak.

"I am lost and need help. I once lived at Arapaja. Does the river go to a
trail? To a mission?"

Though he could not distinguish their tribe, his broken
native speech must have registered, for they pointed downstream. They
invited him to climb in, and when he asked for food and water, they
accommodated. As they floated down the river, soon paddling through
another set of shoals, albeit smaller, no one spoke. But Luis wanted to

*Suwannee River   **Big Shoals State Park

trust them, having no other choice. The afternoon passed with ease on the glossy black flow, which Luis noticed was curving to his right. The sun now shone in front of him.

The river flows west. Thinking it was already doing that, I have been disoriented.

The river began to produce springs along the sides. *One rose unusually large, emanating from the right bank. The Indios pulled the canoas over to river right and motioned north to a pathway.

"Urihica," came the word from an Indio.

Luis recognized the name for the San Agustín de Urihica mission, located near the north-south trail he'd been upon. Eager to reach the mission and village before dark, he made haste. The mission bell peeled at dusk as he arrived, seeking the friar. He ambled through the village, much larger than Arapaja. Finding the friar and apprising him of his circumstances, Luis received immediate hospitality. Thankful and secure, he slept well in the friary that night. In the morning, the friar again made him feel welcome with a round of fruit, baked bread and fish. He also supplied foodstuffs to carry as Luis struck further south.

"Fray, why did your bell peal at such a late hour last night?"

"My son, we had funerals for ten Indios yesterday and it produced the final note of the day."

"Ten at one time? From a battle?"

The Friar looked at Luis, looked away, paused, and turned back to Luis.

"Yes, but not a military battle, a battle with civilization. You see, each time a group of our men return from a work detail in San Agustín, death always follows. They contract smallpox and other diseases from the Spaniards. Some die enroute here and some after they've returned. They infect others, also. For every conversion to the faith, I seem to have a funeral. It saddens me."

"I see," said Luis.

"So, how did you fare with *el fraile loco*, my unsettled friend, Fray Díaz, at the Arapaja mission?"

"What do you mean?"

"Did you not notice his behavior?"

Of course Luis did, but he stymied at responding. Thoughts didn't rise to the surface as usual.

"I know we're all somewhat loco with life here in the wilderness," the Friar chuckled, "but he more than the rest of us."

Stumbling with words, Luis thanked him and bid goodbye.

*White Springs, Fl

"Vaya con Dios, young man. Go straight south, cross the river and you should arrive at Santa Cruz de Tarahica in two days. It lies near a *large lake."

Luis took pleasure in again walking the trail. The early morning lent coolness, and he could make good time. He pondered the words of the priest at Urihica, and why one priest called another loco. But he knew it true, as he so witnessed. Traveling south, he soon came back to the San Martín. Once again the smooth, dark water beckoned to him. Easing down the bank, walking across the cloud-white sand, he found a small log. Laying his food satchel on top, he waded into the water, pushing the log ahead of him. The water deepened, so he stretched out and kicked, propelling the log across with him. Stimulated, he loitered awhile, dousing more at the far bank. Soon it became time to continue, and Luis ascended the bank. He reflected, as he traversed the trail.

It extends certain, flat, straight, and stable. Unlike my life, which endures of late many ups and downs, curves and changes, and many different surfaces under my feet.

Two days to Tarahica. His mind still drifted, but on this day he would not have to make choices. He willed to keep one foot in front of the other, to stay on the footpath with no varying. Covering maybe ten miles, he rested at sunset. Food, garfish oil, and a bed of pine needles. An uneventful night, except for one circumstance–a nightmare intruded.

One ambled into the campsite. Then two more, much bigger. Huge heads, black fur, and saliva dripping from their gaping mouths as they roared. Then five more. I'm surrounded. No escape. A growling monster black bear bounds in, locks onto my arm with giant jaws and drags me. Blood oozes down, and big teeth cut the skin. My arm feels red-hot, as the jellyfish sting on the coast at Calos. They take me to their cave den and place me in the rear with no way out.

His scream shattered the darkness, and he jumped to his feet. Sweat covered his body. He pulled the deerskin more onto the trail proper and lay back down, longing for daylight.

Dawn crept through the trees as quiet as a shadow at sunset. He welcomed it and rubbed his arm to make certain it stayed intact. All there, but welts covered it, itching. No jellyfish, but a bed of ants that scourged him, as the arm strayed from the deerskin overnight. Applying garfish oil would have to do. And time. Walking the trail, he reflected on the dream.

Excessive thoughts of fear, or sorrow, or premonitions of scenes to come? Not possible for a Spanish soldier, clad as an Indio, to solve.

Early afternoon on a pleasant, if unchanging trail, Luis spied what at first
* NW Lake City, Fl

seemed an illusion. Ahead on the path sat the back of a head, covered by a large hat. Shoulders and arms completed the picture, all at ground level. If it belonged to a body, it lay buried underground. Arms flailed to swat away bugs. Luis halted, uncertain if he saw man, beast or demon. Unlike anything he'd ever seen, unless it could be a midget, like one he saw at a Seville fair.

"Hola," he called, "what be you?"

A head turned to look at Luis, thus eliciting a weird feeling. He considered bolting.

Could it be an enormous grotesque spider, waiting for prey?

The limbs reached up and removed the hat. Luis saw a well-worn face, with sagging eyes and a fatigued appearance, covered with huge droplets of sweat. Blobs of bear grease smeared his face, an attempt to ward off insects. With no large head covering, Luis now saw him uncovered from the armpits.

"Ah, señor, you have found me at my cure."

"Why are you buried in the sand?" said the flustered Luis.

"Ah, but you see I have the dropsys, and I must sweat it out. All the water in my body has gone to my legs and feet...swollen... painful. I must shed the liquids."

"I am Alférez Luis Armador, late of the Arapaja mission. I give my sorrow for your trouble. Do you need water?"

"I have water, but warm."

His canteen lay visible on the trail, beside his clothing and a pistol. Striving to help, Luis gave some of his cooler water to the man.

"Gracias, señor. You've come upon Fernando Ramos out of Andalucía, now a blacksmith at the mission at Tarahica. I went away to bury myself to avoid ridicule, or to die, if the cure doesn't work. The friar knows I left and why."

"How long buried ?"

"Two days."

Luis heard Atocha Surgeon Ribera speak of dropsy but never witnessed a sufferer. As with scurvy, sweating by burying to the neck purported as a treatment, but with danger.

"How can I help you?"

"Please, bury me to the neck, with more sand!" he pleaded.

"Fernando, I would rather dig you up and help you back to the mission, my own destination. I bid you to try purgatives instead, which I'm told can work also."

"I tried them all, to no avail!" he wailed. "I need burying to my neck! Should I succumb, then it will save someone most of the trouble."

Luis feared that covering him more would increase his dryness. Looking like a man in his sixties, he could die before any dropsy aid helped, he thought.

What if the swollen limbs reflected a sign of some other malady?

"Please, let me take you to the mission. You cannot last like this."

"No. If you cannot help me, you best leave," he said, almost crying.

"Farewell then. I hope for you the best."

Luis moved on, feeling helpless. He gathered that some things lay beyond his control, and he must trudge on. Thunder rolled in the distance, and soon dark clouds appeared above the forest. A fast-descending, hard summer rain fell. He welcomed it and imagined that it gave a further cleansing of his grief.

He reached Santa Cruz de Tarahica mission at day's end and soon realized it was larger than the other mission villages he'd visited. On the edge of a huge lake, it contained huts as far as he could see, with activity everywhere. As he walked through the village seeking the resident friar, he noticed an orderly group ahead. Recognizing it as a funeral procession, he was astounded at the number of dead. Twenty prostrate Indios lay on litters, each borne by villagers, single file, headed to the mission church. Many weepers and wailers followed.

Stopping at a hut, he inquired of the friar. When told, he decided the morrow would be soon enough to see him. That night he slept on his deerskin outside a hospitable family's hut. He'd completed twenty miles over the last two days, so on the next, he planned to linger.

***

Next morning, he told the priest of his plight and of his goal of St. Augustin. The friar had greeted him with a weary smile. To Luis, he looked to be in his fifties and was bearded, balding and with a good-sized paunch.

"Why so many deaths?"

"As you can see, we support a sizable mission, some four thousand. When the Spanish diseases visit, they wreak much suffering."

"I'm sorry," said Luis.

"I found your blacksmith, Fernando Ramos, about one-half day's walk north of here, buried in the sand to his armpits. He claimed curing dropsy. I'm afraid he'll die of excess perspiration. Can you send the soldiers to bring him back?"

"Fernando!" he said, while throwing his hands in the air. "Poor soul. I'm aware of his plight. Yes, we will ask the men to bring him back. More purgatives might help."

Luis thanked him, took his leave, and began a new three-day walk south, along with a new foodpack. The large number of deaths stabbed his consciousness as he went.

Walking alone, Luis began to think of his garments. A deerskin loincloth, leather moccasins, and a deerskin wrap for nighttime. All he needed. But he tried to envision wearing breeches and shirts, or even a military uniform again. He must, he knew, readapt when he reached San Agustín, after three years in the wilderness. Bearing essentials - sword, bags, deerskin, food and water bags - he'd had no thoughts of material ownership for some time. The stark realization surprised him. He also became aware that feelings of grief were subsiding. Alone, he even forced a smile, noting fond memories of Reyeeta.

Except for intermittent summer showers, the next three days passed without incident. On the evening of the third day, he reached the village and mission of San Martín de Ayacuto. It lay close to a large *spring, head-waters of a cool and clear-flowing river. He'd come about 25 miles from the previous mission and about half-way on his walk to the coast. As usual, the villagers and friar accepted him for the evening. Small in size like Arapaja, but, unlike Arapaja, it too suffered disease and funerals, all recounted to him by the friar.

The next day he attended morning Mass, then set out due east with a new packet of food. Luis now trod the grand El Camino Real, which linked missions across the northern Florida peninsula. Much wider than previous footpaths, it could accommodate tandem walkers. He planned another seven days travel, confirmed by Ayacuto's friar. Having seen more than he wanted of death and dying over the past few weeks, he decided to circumvent other missions till he needed food. He admired the friars, but he needed time away from that aspect.

After one day, he arrived at a natural land bridge across the Santa Fé River where it went underground for three miles. Tiny villages sat nearby, but he did not stop, choosing to sleep along the trail. The only evening sounds, other than crickets, were grunts and rustlings from wild hogs feeding in the woods. On the morning of his second day on the wider trail, Luis awoke refreshed, his zest for the woods still stimulating. As he moved along, sunlight filtered through the trees and cast beams as lanterns at night.

For the first time, low hills rose up to greet him. Encountering the

*Ichetucknee Springs

dropsy-affected man on the trail had made him thankful to be alive and healthy. Mournful thoughts continued vanishing and clearer thinking now allowed him to judge recent events in his life.

Did my grief cloud my reasoning such that it caused me to become lost? Did I become soft, living an Eden-like existence with Reyeeta? No doubt her death created a turning point in my life. I lived for a year in a 'lush valley,' but now I cross a 'rugged mountain,' nearing the other side. An unforgettable time. No regrets. Now looking forward. Yearning again for Spain. Trying to blend with nature, not outwit it. Enjoying the forest. This way may never be passed again.

It was a stone's throw beyond when he saw the movement. A large creature ran across the trail, its crunching sounds punctuating the ground. Shortly, a group of squealing piglets followed. Luis noticed the low swampy area, just the kind of muddy spots they like. Soon, the large one ran across the trail again, going in the opposite direction. He saw the form for an instant. A wild hog, a sow, that looked to be three feet high and four feet long. Besting him by at least fifty pounds and not something he'd want to encounter. With stealth, he maintained a steady pace.

He later remembered a strong stench filling his nostrils before he took the blow. It struck from behind, knocking him to the ground. Dazed, he rolled over to see the beast, grunting, growling, its snout baring two large front teeth. It backed up, pawing the ground, readying for another charge. Luis looked around for a tree to climb. Nothing but high-limbed oaks and palms. He sensed a vague awareness of pain in his right thigh, but allowed no time to dwell on it.

Struggling to his feet, he drew his sword just as the animal came at him. It moved so that Luis' downward blow only caught the rear flank, inflicting a small cut. She hit Luis, this time in his stomach, toppling him once more. Hovering over him, she snapped, bit and seemed to be going for the kill. Summoning all his strength, Luis rolled over and brought the butt of his sword down on the sow's snout. It squealed and retreated. Luis foresaw that as only temporary.

As his thigh, stomach and leg begged for relief, he scrambled up and prepared for the next assault. He could feel his combat senses sharpen like the edge of a newly honed blade. On this evening, he wanted wild hog for dinner. Still, the determined animal charged. With energy drained, he grasped the sword in preparation. As in a swordfight, he dodged at the last second and sunk the blade into its shoulder. As it crashed with a thud, writhing and snarling on the ground, Luis withdrew and thrust repeatedly into the tough hide. Soon it ceased to move. Aching and bleeding, he lay on his back, gasping for air. Sitting up, he could observe the hog up close. It bore thick, stringy black hair, and its front end was bigger than the rear.

What a monster.

It reeked of a smell so noxious as to dissuade Luis from slicing it for meat. He lay exhausted and knew the morrow would show bruises. At the moment, wounds on leg, arm and thigh hurt. He stopped the bleeding, but he needed more aid from a settlement.

The friar at Ayacuto had mentioned that the Santa Fé mission sited on a path north from the east-west El Camino Real. Plodding east, he came to a trail crossing to the north. It became his only hope. He made it a goal to reach by nightfall, though he stopped often to rest. Bitten leg and rammed thigh ached, but he tried to focus on reaching the mission. After an hour and a half, his heart leaped, as he could see a clearing and hear voices. Observing his plight, several Indios came to assist and took him to the friar.

"Welcome to Santa Fé de Teleco, my son. I am Fray Ãvila. You're attired as an Indio, but are you a Spaniard?"

He winced at the sight of Luis' injuries.

Stumbling afoot, he betold his troubles, while the Friar took him to lie down. Dozing off from fatigue and the attack, he could sense the Friar tending his wounds. The stitching hurt, but he didn't flinch, being thankful for the help. Luis remembered little afterwards. The next morning, he stood, re-energized, but stiff and sore, while his stomach cried out for nourishment. Though never keelhauled, he thought it couldn't be worse. Soon, an Indio brought him a bowl of fruit, deer jerky, and a jug of cool water as the Friar stepped inside.

"My young Alférez, you took a beating from that sow. They can be trouble if little ones are about. I believe it in your best interest to remain here a few days to rest and to let me redress your cuts. I have aloe, and the Indios prepare effective poultices."

"I accept, Fray Ãvila. You are kind, as the other friars I have met."

"You came from Santa María de los Angeles de Arapaja? Ah, and how is the conniving friar, my friend, Fray Díaz?" asking as he gave a closed-mouth, glum-faced smile.

The second time I've heard him spoken of so poorly. He must be a burden for his senior friar.

"Well, he's in good health and does good work, but he does have difficult moments."

"Yes, he would do well to have his demons exorcised, or do it himself, if it be possible. We'll leave it at that. Make yourself comfortable.

"Fray, I have seen much death at the missions since leaving Arapaja. I'd like to finish my journey to San Agustín without stopping at any more." Luis spoke with humility but seriousness.

"Yes, only last week we buried seven Utinas here. Sad. I can do nothing for them except perform their funerals. As far as missions east of here, I doubt you'll find one till you reach the Rio de Corrientes, our biggest flowing stream in the area. Disease wiped them all out. It terrifies." Tears moistened his eyes.

"Fray, I was born in the year 1600. I'm told that because of the Great Plague, my parents would not take me out of our house for two years. It took so many Spaniards. Because of that, plus bad crop years and starvations, many predicted the end of the world."

"Alférez, I'm afraid these diseases will be the end of the world for the Indios."

The morning after his third night at the Santa Fé mission found him fit enough to travel. Double-filling his satchels with food and thanking the Friar, he set off south to rejoin El Camino Real and turn east. From there he estimated a six-day walk to reach San Agustín. Like the last stretch of a long horse race, but a slow one.

Four days and nights spent on a well-cleared trail made it plain that Indio labor kept it cleared. Finding freshwater lakes in abundance, refills of cool water came easy. No marring episodes occurred to hinder his hike, and he only passed two Indios during the whole time.

At late morning of his fifth day out of Santa Fé de Teleco, he arrived at a large body of water which he took for the Rio de Corrientes. It looked to be at least two miles wide. Too wide to swim, too deep to wade, he hoped for a ferry. He sat to wait. In the midst of summer haze, with the sun's glare on the water, he could see a speck coming from a distance. Two paddlers stroked within view. Soon, in the shallows, they dragged a long dugout onto the bank. With fervor, he approached members of another indistinguishable tribe, no doubt positioned here by the garrison at San Agustín.

"Greetings. *Río de Corrientes?".

*"Salamototo," came an Indian's answer.

"Ferry across to San Agustín?"

A nod affirmative came the reply.

"When next?" he asked with voice and signs.

The answer came by signs indicating they would return across after the sun dropped below the horizon. He received the impression that they

* St. Johns River (San Juan)

didn't like their assignment. But he knew he must go along. He signed back to go across. They motioned for Luis to follow them, leading him into the woods to a small village. Seeing only a few huts and a small church, he presumed it a visita, and probably not a doctrina mission that would have a full-time friar.

One of the Indios pointed and said, "Pupo."

Luis took that as the village name, and inquired of a friar. One shook his head, but did say, "San Helena de Heleca."

Thinking it must be nearby, but deciding to inquire no more, Luis spread his deerskin and took advantage of the time for an afternoon nap. At sunset they handed him an acorn cake and motioned time to go. He could tell that his sword frightened them not, they likely having seen more than they cared. The river had a light breeze, not hazardous, but refreshing. Luis sat in the canoa's middle, amazed at the river's size, one that should accommodate galleons if deep enough. It was dusk when they struck the far shore, scattering blue crabs among the marsh grass and sandy bottom. Luis asked of a village or wharf name.

"Picolata," was all that one said.

"San Agustín?" asked Luis.

The other Indio pointed east. Luis barely uttered gracias when they pushed out and began to return. Thinking that he stood almost close enough to touch the coast, he lay down, thankful. He spread the deerskin, dabbed on some oil, and looked forward to restful sleep. .

Tommorow I'll see a Spanish town for the first time in three years. Almost like a returning conquering hero. Almost.

On the next day's long walk east, the path veered little, and he pressed on as his mind conjured up visions of civilization. Late afternoon, after swimming across a small brackish stream at low tide, Luis walked and crawled up the muddy bank. Standing, his gaze produced a view of town. Near the river, fields of corn stood tall and green and groups of Indios bent over weeding the rows.

Being so accustomed to seeing Indios mistreated, he garnered surprise at a scene unfolding ahead. Four of them pummeled a lone soldier, likely their supervisor, who'd probably abused them. Luis rushed to his aid, yelling and waving his sword. They scattered, and the poor fellow fell on the ground, stunned.

"Señor, thank you, thank you. I will kill those inept savages when I get my hands on them!"

"I imagine they're halfway to the other coast by now," said Luis, helping him up and then introducing himself.

"They're lazy, and they expect to be paid. My Sergeant will send a squad after them. Please come with me so that he and perhaps the Governor himself can thank you."

"That's not necessary…"

"No, I insist. Please come with me."

Luis complied and they walked a short ways to the entrance to town. Carrying grief on his shoulders, Luis had traveled for three weeks and 150 miles. Some rough, most of it agreeable. The sight put a stirring into his blood. His heart raced, and he began to tremble.

SEVILLE

It had been an eerie repeat from three years earlier. As Isabella sat at her window, staring into the courtyard, she grappled with varying emotions of sadness and anger. The black dress felt almost nauseating. The condolences rang hollow.

How can this be? I'm only twenty-one.

Having moved home for awhile to her parents after José sailed away to New Spain on business, she sought comfort. But in reality, comfort was an illusion. Only a dream. Just three days prior, her father again came home in the middle of the day. His pace was slow and his face grim. She knew the news before he spoke. She'd lived it once before.

"My dear," said Francisco de Aragón, "I have a sad report. A letter arrived from New Spain brought by a returning merchant vessel. José contracted a high fever in Vera Cruz and died in May. It took almost three months for the news to reach us. Alas, the authorities buried him there. His brother just informed me."

Isabela said nothing. She shed not a tear, nor swooned or wailed. Francisco hugged her and excused himself so to tell his wife. She went back to her room to hold her child.

"Dear, sweet Consuela, your father comes home no more. Just you and me. We will care for each other."

Holding the babe close to her breast, she shed a few tears, but held no need to unleash a flood this time. *Once again, no body is returned for burial.*

After the memorial service and Mass, she continued to live at her parents' home, delaying a decision on her and José's house. Her brother-in-law was José's Executor, and so all of the assets were placed in trust for she and the baby. Income assured, she would want not. Once again a light went out in her life, but this time she determined not to wallow. It would take time. Propriety expected it, but she would not long wear black. She wanted to look ahead, not at what might have been.

Who knows? One day I may appear at José's silk shop to participate in the business.

16
SAN AGUSTÍN

1625

In this presidio few things present
Themselves to relate to your Grace,
For there are so few of us that
We make no sound.
Juan de Salinas
San Agustín   Governor 1618-1624

Sandy lanes, wagon ruts, boot treads, barefoot imprints. Chickens and
pigs roamed at will. Not the grand cobbled avenues of Habana or
Cartagena, but to Luis they spread out as streets of gold. Aromas filled the
air –meat roasting, beans boiling, onions frying, and pungent salt air. For
Luis, it almost created intoxication.

He stopped and stared, then closed his eyes to make certain this
portended no dream. As they walked the narrow street, residents greeted
them with casual friendliness. His pitiful appearance would be deemed
unsightly in Seville, but here it mattered not. Homes of all shapes and sizes
appeared, some two-story wooden with balconies, and some of modest clay
with thatched roofs. Most presented open windows and side-entrance
doorways.

Class distinction even here, he thought.

Artisans lined the streets–blacksmith, tanner, baker, cooper and even a
cloth shop, though meager in content. Many shops located on the first
floor of homes, some white-washed, some left untouched. The young
soldier stopped at a cantina and led him in. Seated at a rustic table on an
unfinished wood-planked floor, they ordered warm ale, beef and bread,
compliments of the new acquaintance. Luis felt as a man just discovering
the New World, as he savored each swig and morsel. Private Enrique
Vega told of how he had been shipwrecked and washed up on the coast,
where a chalupa longboat from the fort plucked him up and brought him
to town.

"My happiness was fleeting, as they soon impressed me into the military
due to the shortage of soldiers here. The duty's not bad, but the diversions
for a young private remain few, so I hope my release comes soon, so I may
return to Spain. Like many soldiers, I use my former trade as a tailor
for additional income. Business is good, as my comrades stay badlyclothed,

suffering little pay. I have no shop. They bring work to my soldiers's mess group house in town."

Luis could only think forward. He recounted his three years' plight and inquired how often ships left for Spain. He also asked if it possible to see the Governor.

"What you desire resembles my wants," said Vega, "but ships to Spain seldom leave from here. That poses a problem. Given your rank, I'm certain the Governor will see you and advise on passage."

From out back on the porch and yard area of the cantina came noises of a fight taking place. Fists thudding, howls and furniture cracking made it obvious. Luis cringed. The owner ignored it.

"Just the usual afternoon brawl by two off-duty soldiers too heavy in their cups," joked Vega. "No one interferes unless it becomes intolerable. They'll be sore in the morning." He smiled and turned up his mug.

After the meal, Private Vega led him north along the harbor to the wooden fort, which constituted a two-story, strong-house type. Before entering, Luis stopped to observe. No stockade, it fronted the water with a view eastward.

Across the harbor, an ocean inlet flowed between two land masses. Various small boats sat in the water alongside the town pier, just south of the fort. Vega urged him inside.

"It's time to clean you up, amigo. We have a water barrel and soap just outside that you can use, and then we'll find a shirt and breeches. If you're to see the Governor tomorrow, you'll need to be presentable."

That evening, Luis was allowed to stay in the fort barracks area set aside for sergeants and corporals. Tiredness found him, and he lay down at sunset, long before the others. Sometime during the night, nausea woke him and drove him outside, so to cast up his entire meal. His body couldn't yet digest a rich diet. He stumbled back inside, but instead of the bunk, he chose the floor. Neither did his body yet seek civilized comfort.

***

Morning and Private Vega advised that his Alférez arranged for a meeting with Governor Luis de Rojas y Borgia, who invited the garrison's Alférez and Luis both to a noon meal at his home, so to thank Luis also.

That morning he took time to walk around inside and outside the fort, to understand the protection it afforded. Spacious, with barracks, separate spaces for offices, munitions, food storage, and a guardhouse downstairs. Upstairs it contained officers' quarters and a large city council room. Outside were walls of planked wood and roof of tabby. Waterside stood an attached open platform for harbor guns and a watchtower. A separate cannon platform on the back side gave protection against land assaults. All in all, Luis liked it, but wondered of the outcome should an enemy creep in at night and strike a match to it.

"Good morning, Alférez Armador. I am pleased to have another Spanish officer, obviously very capable, under our roof." Alférez Gregorio Mencos, who supervised all the soldiers for the Sergeant-Major and the Captain-General, greeted Luis. "I look forward to our meal today."

Noting him as courteous, well-groomed, and orderly, Luis took an immediate liking. Looking about thirty and slightly balding, he moved with a sprightly gait and conveyed a sense of stability and command.

Not one of the unruly military men for which the town is known, thought Luis.

"It is my pleasure, your mercy. Let me say I have been well-received here, for which I am grateful."

As they left the fort, Luis noticed several soldiers in the yard, one in particular. He walked with a slight limp and seemed vaguely familiar, as if in a brief dream recall. Sunken eye pockets and a sinister face bore down on him as they passed.

I'll wager he's a rogue.

They walked to the west end of the town plaza to the Governor's handsome two-story home, where a knock on the door brought forth a black servant. Upon entering, Luis met the sight of stained wood floors, whitewashed walls, and furnishings reflecting exquisite Spanish taste and design.

Soon the Governor and his wife entered and greeted the men with warmth. The Governor was smiling and ebullient, as he turned first to Mencos, then to Luis.

"Ah, so this is our new hero! Welcome! Welcome to our humble village. Thank you for the able assistance to one of our soldiers. I trust we can provide hospitality to show our gratitude."

As the Governor continued with his platitudes, Luis did his best to respond in a positive and gracious manner. He was also seized with a feeling of caution as he remembered the words of Alférez Manuel on the trail – *watch out for the Governor…a chameleon…gracious one day…overpowering the next.*

The Governor was curious of his journeys, keying in on the time that he spent at the Guacara mission. Soon they seated for the bountiful meal, prepared and served by servants. Luis promptly became satiated, as his stomach could not yet handle town fare, though he did enjoy it. At the same time, he felt like the target of bow and arrow practice from the Governor's constant questions.

"A toast to Alférez Armador, whom we are pleased to have among us. And whose apparent knowledge of native languages would make him an excellent interpreter for our presidio, should he join us."

Luis joined the toast, though it seemed strange. Mencos lifted his glass also, but kept quiet. Luis then posed a question of his own.

"Governor, I have been removed from Spain for three years. My goal is to return, resume my commission, and rejoin my family. How may I best sail?" he asked expectantly.

Borgia looked at Luis, smiled with lips closed, paused, then answered. "Well, Alférez, you know that our little settlement lies on the edge of Spain's empire. We are not completely forgotten, if we remind the Crown often. It likes the fact that we sit near the ocean river current that carries the silver galleons. That permits us to provide aid to those shipwrecked. And, of course, we foster the missions. But, being small and disease-prone, few want to serve here or even visit. As towns go, we are an infant, only 60 years old."

"But, sir, don't ships come and go on a regular basis?"

"You've heard the words *rich as Potosí*, no doubt? Well, here we say *poor as Pancho*. No surplus of reales de a ocho or even maravedis can be found on the coast, so few come here to trade." He paused again. "Let me offer you two suggestions. Early August, which is nigh, sees the annual Terre Firme silver fleet sailing up the coast from Habana. You may take a dugout pirogua down to Cabo Cañaveral and wait. That is our connection point with one of their smaller vessels, as needed. Pirates sometimes lurk in the area, but they should leave you alone. Of the Ais Indios, I can't predict."

The Governor stopped long enough to offer pipes and to light one for himself. Puffing and blowing smoke, he gazed at the fireplace and then at Luis.

"The other choice is to hire the garrison's frigate here in the harbor. For the price of twenty-two reales de a ocho, a crew will take you to Habana where you may embark on the next ship to Seville. If we send you soon, you may find a bunk on a silver galleon. If without sufficient funding, you can rent a room here in town and practice your trade till you save enough. So there you have it," he concluded, bearing a huge smile.

The garrison's frigate? Who benefits from the large fee–the Governor or the town? Luis wondered.

The men thanked the Governor for his superb meal and excused themselves to walk back to the fort.

"Tobacco and pipes? Where does he get them?"

"Ha! His sojourns in Habana allow him to arrange for shipping every year. He's about the only one here doing it, so consider yourself honored. He's been here only a short while, so I haven't yet learned all his likes and dislikes. We can tell he likes pesos. Puzzling is the note he handed asking that I return this afternoon with Sgt. Torres."

"Sgt. Torres? Sgt. Manuel Torres?"

"Yes. Do you know him?"

"Somewhat. I experienced an encounter with him at the mission San Juan de Guacara. I also wounded him in a duel."

"Perhaps my meeting pertains to that," said Mencos.

Perhaps I should have slit his throat rather than his legs, Luis bemoaned.

"Gregorio, thank you for arranging the meeting. Enlightening. Now I must decide on the best course to return to Spain. My next visit will be to your surgeon to have my stitches removed, then I want to visit the parish priest."

***

"Padre, may I impose on your time? I am Alférez Luis Armador."

"By all means, my good sir. I do believe you come as a new arrival. I am Padre Francisco Fernãndez. How may I be of service?"

Luis had entered the board and batten church on the plaza. Larger than the mission structures he had visited, it was well-finished and sawyered. In the quiet sanctuary, he'd walked past the altar to a door at the back. A knock had produced a young, smiling priest with a pleasant bearing. He invited Luis inside and listened attentively as he told of his quandary.

"Well, Luis, you have done well. It appears the Governor tendered some good options. Like everyone here, he always needs funds for his large responsibility in trying to support the presidio. He receives a *situado*, an annual stipend, from Vera Cruz, but it's never enough."

He continued. "We have some 700 who reside here, almost half as soldiers. Many are ruffians and rascals that no other command would take. Families come desperate to improve their lot over life in Spain. So, everyone must eke out a living, so to speak, and we depend on the Indios for corn and other foodstuffs. I labor to help nourish their souls, for all need hope. Maybe somehow you can help."

"Padre, I don't know about that, but you helped me to understand the Governor's situation. Anyway, would you see that one real de a ocho goes for the mission at Guacara? Fray Mobila became so helpful to me there. Would you also hold my other two for safekeeping while I reside here?"

"Certainly. Now, tell me before you take your leave. How is Fray Díaz serving at Arapaja?"

Luis could sense concern on Padre Fernãndez's face and in his voice, even though he made no comment about madness.

"Padre, I observed a troubled soul. I don't understand it. One day amiable and the next hateful. Perplexing. Perhaps he suffers the Melancholia. I understand your concern as you assist the Bishop in Cuba by advising."

"Not really. That purview belongs to the senior Franciscans at the Convento south of town. But, Díaz needs help. Once an apprentice of the Holy Office at Triana Castle prison near Seville, he suffered the duty to administer, shall we say, physical inducements to heresy suspects of the Inquisition. It took place in secret rooms. Displeased and discomforted, he sought the Franciscan Order for aid. They allowed him to join, whereupon he asked to come to Florida. They know he's troubled and hoped the mission duty would help him. They want to take care of their brothers."

Luis thanked him and left. Exiting the church, he pondered, *but isn't that brother Fray Díaz causing discomfort to others at Arapaja?*

Luis walked east after leaving the church to Matanzas Bay, named after San Agustin's founder's massacre of the French in the area, which Spain considered theirs. It looked so quiet and peaceful that he found it hard to imagine large-scale slaughter. Moving onto the pier, he gazed at an array of small boats at rest in the harbor, but only one sizable with tall masts, presumably the presidio's frigate. The water glimmered on the light chop from the warm summer breeze. Salt air revived memories as he closed his eyes.

I've come this far, and now only the ocean remains…surely my time is nigh…like a man nearing the top of a mountain, pulling up with a rope, one last pull, one last effort. …sailing up the Guadalquivir……. and seeing Toro del Oro, the golden tower in Seville…I can almost hear the sounds…how best to achieve it ?…

"Lost in reverie, Armador?"

Luis opened his eyes to the smiling face of Alférez Mencos.

"Somewhat. Dreaming of Seville. Thinking of the two choices the Governor presented. Sailing to Habana first would be comfortable. But it takes at least a week and more pesos than I have right now. A piragua to Cañaveral to meet the galleons would permit me to go now. Some peril indeed, Indios and pirates, but it's my best choice. I'm going to prepare to leave."

"Well, if you leave, you have two choices as to directions.

Go straight out and pass *Cantera Island on the right, then go south. Or, go south from the pier down the river till it meets the ocean, and continue south." Mencos pointed with each directional.

Now, come with me to my favorite tavern. I'll stake you to a mug of ale and a chop of deer meat. We might even have some cheese."

They walked west along the plaza and turned south onto the tavern's street. Seated at a wooden table, Luis began to wonder again of the Atocha's fate. He broached a subject which had baffled him for three long years.

"What happened to the Terre Firme fleet of 1622, struck by a hurricane?"

Alférez Mencos took a swig of his ale, wiped his mouth, and turned to Luis.

"I wasn't in La Florida at the time. The news came that eight ships sank along with over 500 souls and two million ducats of treasure and cargo.

"What of the Atocha?"

"It went down, with only five seamen rescued. They were lashed to a mast left protruding above the waterline. When the military went back to salvage the ship, it could not be found, washed away by another hurricane. ' Twas quite a tale three years ago."

Luis took a quaff from his own mug and swallowed hard. He always suspected the worst, but to hear it overwhelmed him.

So many shipmates lost. Yet fate spared me. What in life's events causes one to die and one to live? Wherein is my purpose in that?

"I lost a lot of friends then. Many from whom I learned much."

"Yes, a number of birth and renown went to the bottom that day, including I believe, Captain Bartolomé Nodal, the Atocha's Captain, one of Spain's best."

"Yes, that's true."

Mencos glanced at Luis.

"So…you actually sailed on the Atocha…serving in the military?" He cast a look composed of belief yet uncertainty.

Luis could sense Mencos' doubt but couldn't understand why. It made him wonder what his former duelist, Sgt. Torres, told the Governor.

By now, dark descended, and the tavern owner moved about, lighting lanterns and candle trays. Luis watched him lift the glass on each and touch each wick with the lit stick. Tantalizing aromas now filled the room as guests received meals from the kitchen at the rear.

"Gregorgio, tell me again, if you would, why large ships seldom visit

*Anastasia Island

here?"

"The Governor never mentioned to you that the sandbar at the harbor's entrance creates a barrier. Even at high tide it allows only seven to eight feet of depth. Large ships with deep drafts have come to naught trying to cross it. Out at the bar, a mile or so, many masts of those that have tried are now protruding above the water. Sometimes, crippled large vessels will wisely stop just outside Cantera Island and send in longboats for help. Our soldiers at the island watchtower will signal us by flag when that happens. There's no doubt that the shallow bar serves as a good defense at times, but we must use light and low draft vessels and our pilots must take lead soundings before embarkations."

Luis decided to ask no more. After enjoying the fare, he thanked Mencos and excused himself to the barracks. As usual, his mind churned.

So few ocean-going vessels come and go here. Can I hail one from Cabo Cañaveral? How many reales de a ocho will I need for sufficient passage fee to Spain? Will I need to offer my services?

After a long day, Luis readied for sleep and this night in a bunk. On the morrow he would take action, but now he needed rest for body and mind.

***

Someone or something shook him over and over. He opened his eyes, groggy from a deep sleep. No daylight yet entered the barracks, but a lantern glowed, presenting a gloomy multitude of faces at his bunk.

"Arise, Armador! We arrest you in the name of the King!" He heard the voice of his friend, Alférez Mencos.

Luis blinked, stared up at the sight and believed he must be dreaming. They jostled him from the bunk and threw clothes and moccasins in his direction.

"Put on your clothes! Under orders of Governor Borgia, you will be taken to the guardhouse jail."

"But, Mencos, please name my charge!"

"You will find out soon enough, Armador." Luis recognized the voice and the leering presence of Sgt. Torres, his swordfight nemesis.

A knave of the lowest order.

As the group of soldiers surrounded him and marched to the jail, Luis summoned a fleeting thought—*the bears in my dream on the trail?*

With lantern in hand, the jailer greeted them at the door. They led him down the hallway to a row of cells at the building's end. The cell door opened, Luis was pushed in, and the door clanged shut. The metallic twisting of the key ended in a loud and foreboding clink. Cold chills encompassed him as he wondered at the situation. From hospitality one day to incarceration the next, it mystified him. Somehow, he surmised a diabolical connection from Fray Díaz and Sgt. Valdés at Arapaja to San Agustín's Sgt. Torres, his Guacara mission combatant. It led to the Governor, of whom he'd been warned.

Rascals all, he reflected. *No pleasant augury in any of it.*

Saddened that his modest celebration on arriving at San Agustín was shortened, he tried to piece together his newest travail. Surmising that his new friend, Alférez Mencos, only did his duty, acting on orders, Luis wondered at Mencos' personal feelings toward him. Private Vega, his first acquaintance in town, would be powerless. His only hope would be the church's Padre Fernández, the keeper of his reales de a ocho. As dawn peered through the small barred outside window, the jailer returned. This time he bore a plate of food and a cup of water, all of which he slid under Luis' cell door.

"Buenos dias, señor." He spoke with alertness and a smile, though not in harmony with Luis' feelings. "As jailer González, let me apologize for the meager accommodations, but any improvements come from my wages, which would be detrimental."

Luis faced a graying, portly man, disposed to lively conversation. Though hungry, an impulse almost seized him to throw his breakfast through the cell door window at the jailer.

" 'Tis my humble duty to read the charges against you," he said. "I trust you will not shoot the messenger." He smiled.

Eat the breakfast, Luis reminded himself.

> By order of Governor Luis de Rojas y Borgia, in his majesty Felipe IV's service,
>
> Luis Armador is charged as follows: With malicious intent and purpose you caused injury to Sgt. Manuel Torres at San Juan de Guacara mission in May, 1624, after which you fled.

It poses as a crime against the Spanish military for which you will be tried. This knowledge has been dispatched from Fray Rodrigo Díaz at Arapaja, with information reported to him by you. It has also been attested by the victim, Sgt. Torres.. Trial date to be this month's normal court and Public Day set aside in San Agustín.

Luis' appetite no longer sought his breakfast, and he set it down.

"But I own alférez rank, in his majesty's service. The Sergeant challenged me to a duel, to which I responded," said Luis.

"They believe you an imposter, a wandering shipwrecked miscreant."

"A fraud?"

"Yes," responded the jailer. "But, if fortunate, your sentence will constitute just spending some time in the jail here."

"And if not fortunate?"

"You'd prefer not to know."

Luis turned away and moved to a darkened corner of his cell. Those *for* him now chose to impugn him. He wondered what the Friar in Arapaja would have to gain.

El fraile loco–the mad friar, no doubt, he reflected.

Increasing daylight poured through the window and lit up the room. To Luis it appeared as a dungeon. The lack of toiletry left a stench, and the bed accommodations spread out as a pallet of straw, bug-ridden. A well-worn short path in the dirt belied past occupants, as did initials scrawled on the plank walls. The presence of prisoners past hung over the cell, almost hauntingly. Luis bemoaned that the worst he thought lay behind him now still lingered.

What of the old Indio jarva and his gibberish at the Arapaja ceremony? Did he foresee the jailing? How could he know? Did he overhear Sgt. Valdés and the Friar conspiring? Did he know Spanish? I must forget it so to think of my current condition. But I have the sensation of sinking in a quagmire, with people standing and watching, none offering a line.

In the cell next to him someone shuffled upon awakening. Facing Luis through a small side window, he spoke in a husky voice that sounded familiar.

"What's the matter, Alférez, don't you know me?"

Luis looked upon the sight of a scarred, matt-haired, dissipated man, one that seemed aged before his time, bearing features pitiful and unrecognizable.

"Alférez, you see Tomás, whom you left at Casitoa three years ago."

Luis, taken aback, slowly recognized him. *A plaguey countenance, no less,* he observed. They swapped stories, with Tomás, between deep coughs, described being traded by the Calusa to pirates. The pirates enjoyed a lucrative time of it for a period, but wrecked off Cabo Cañaveral during a storm. Most from the wreck died, but San Agustín's coast-scouring soldiers picked him up.

"Here but a week, and they caught me taking food from the warehouse. I fear I will die in this hole. It's overwhelming when I think of the steps to destruction I have taken. I left the paths of righteousness and tread that of the bedeviled. How I wish I could retrieve my childhood." He spoke sorrowed, at the point of weeping.

Luis didn't know whether to express sadness for him or not, bu realized he must stay detached so to face his own path. This led him to ask the jailer to request a visit the next day by Padre Fernández of the church. The balance of the day he coiled on the pallet, fraught with despair.

***

"Good morning, Luis."

The keys rattled, the turnkey made, and the bolts drawn back by the jailer. Padre Fernández greeted him.

"Padre, thank you for coming." Luis embraced him and inquired of his health.

"It's fine, and I trust yours also. I see that you have a problem. What can I do?"

"Padre, my friend is Fray Gaspar Mobila of the Guacara mission on the San Martín River. He witnessed the duel with Sgt. Torres, who abused the Indios. When I intervened, he challenged me. Mobila can vouchsafe for me."

"Mobila. I know him. He's still at Guacara, but it requires almost 100 miles to reach it on the mission trail, and your trial will be in a few weeks. No one that I know can go for him. No doubt he would be a good witness for you."

Luis quivered as his sense of desperation rose.

"But he represents my only hope!" He spoke wild-eyed, as a man facing the gallows.

"Simmer, my son, and think of an alternative."

First of all, Luis, relax the mind. Think. Then you can take action…

Luis composed himself, sat in a pensive manner, then mumbled…..

"If only Chukka were here…"

"Do you speak of Chukka, the Arapaja Indio?"

"Yes, do you know him?"

"He arrived here from Arapaja soon after you. He asked to serve in the church, having lost a sister and wanting to reconcile his grief. I know he also seeks recovery from a head wound, but he moves as a man in good health. And he knows some Spanish."

Luis could not contain his emotions.

"He will help me. We are close. Please, Padre, send him to Guacara to fetch Fray Mobila, the one that can exonerate me. Chukka is fleet of foot and can make it there on the run in…I would say…four days and three nights."

"Luis, it could work. If they could acquire a soldier's horse there, they could ride double and return in maybe six days. I will direct him. Your trial date is August 25th, the monthly court day."

"Thank you, Padre," said Luis.

"Before you leave, Padre, one more thing. Why did Fray Díaz of the Arapaja mission conspire against me? I confided of the duel to him, and he twisted the truth in his letter to the Governor."

"I have heard of his letter and the charges. Díaz suffers some malady, as we discussed. In his mind he conceived a plan that he believed would bring the Governor's favor to his mission. We know that wouldn't work, regardless. A conflicted Friar that may suffer from the Melancholia. Sgt. Valdés' letter delivery help must have been motivated in hoping for promotion."

Dazed by Fernández's comments, he couldn't comprehend. In the silence that followed, he heard the distant call of a crow. It seemed to be the only sound in the world that he could grasp at the moment and understand. He sat quietly for an interim.

Betrayed by a priest?

"In time, Luis, you'll want to forgive him."

"What? Forgive *el fraile loco*, a Franciscan? I…." His words trailed off with little else he could say.

***

Luis scratched a mark on the wall with each passing day. Instead of utter despair, he now held hope. But the suspense of the impending trial and Chukka's flight for Fray Mobila concerned him. In addition, Sgt. Torres, his duelist, would taunt at his outside window.

"Armador, did you know that the eyes almost pop from their sockets at garroting? That at a hanging they let one's toes just barely touch the ground? Did you know the Indios barter for your clothing afterwards?"

Luis would cover his ears. He hoped someday for another chance at Torres. But first, the truth must come forth. His reliance rested on an Indio and a Friar. *They must come*, he thought.

He heard little from the other prisoners, except for Tomás, affected at times by fits of delirium. The jailer supposed that he somehow had contracted feverish Ague or another ailment, as Consumption. Having regular copious amounts of rum unavailable to him could be reason also, Luis believed. The outbursts added to Luis' hardship of confinement, along with the August sun baking the jail. He thought of escape, as he'd succeeded twice before, but concluded that would be a last resort, as he needed to clear his name. Honor always surfaced. Otherwise, he would be dogged throughout the New World and the Old.

***

While scrawling on the wall *day four* from Chukka's departure, Luis heard a commotion attending the shuffling of a new prisoner inside. Amid protests, the soldiers pushed him into the cell across from Luis. The door slammed shut, and bolts and keys clanked their toll.

"Buenos días, señor," spoke Luis in his native language. "Welcome to your new quarters."

"I should not be here, incarcerated." The reply came in English-tinged Spanish.

Not good for him, thought Luis.

"Nor should I," replied Luis. "Your charge?"

A response came with a hint of sarcasm.

"A crime of, as you say, the blackest dye," he yelled across the hallway. "Born an Englishman!"

"How did you happen to arrive here?"

Without hesitation, the new prisoner shared his story.

"I sailed as scribe with Captain John Powell and crew out of London in March of this year. With Barbados Island his goal, we arrived mid-May, and he claimed the land for James I in hopes of a future colonizing venture. On returning, we made the Bahamas Channel with comfort. But then he and I entered into a violent argument concerning the ethical method of establishing a settlement. I, implacable, due to my nature and my instruction at Cambridge, would not change my opinion. He, as the Captain and of a formidable temper, would neither."

"Did you duel?"

"No, otherwise I would not be here today. You see, as an academic, I know not of swords or pistols. Nevertheless, he cast me off alone in a longboat in sight of this town's watchtower. With no alternative but to row a boat into the harbor, the guards arrested me and brought me here. I am William Hartford of London."

Because of Hartford's limited height, Luis could only see the top of his head through the cell door window. His face appeared if he stood on his toes. Luis observed intelligent lines as well as penetrating eyes, the kind that could bore through a conversant. He left no doubt of his education and cultured manner. As the days passed, Luis shared his own story, but Hartford also drew him into pointed conversations. Sometimes annoying, but it always helped to arrest his anxiety while waiting for Fray Mobila from the Guacara mission.

"Señor Armador, you converse as an intelligent young man. Why do you suppose the Catholic Habsburg monarchs continue to try to suppress the Protestants?"

Luis responded with haste. "Because Catholicism asserts itself as the one true religion. Those who propose alternate teachings are heretics or infidels."

"Who says so?"

"The Pope, King Felipe IV, and all Christian citizens of Spain."

"Why mount such opposition if we all worship the same God, but want to do it in a different manner?"

"Do you claim Protestantism, Hartford?"

"Yes, serving as a proud member in good standing of the Anglican church… and devout."

"To change the manner of worship, to ignore the authority of the Pope and the sanctity of Catholicism postulates blasphemy!"

"But does it harm you if I behave and pray in my own personal way?"

Luis grew angry and flushed. He now desired to quit the discussion with someone he saw as moon-struck, irrational and irascible.

How can they want to change 1300 years of Catholic tradition and still expect to maintain the divine faith and Holy Scripture?

"If you will excuse me, William, I must lie down awhile." Vexed, he curtailed the discussion. He could understand why Hartford's captain cast him away.

***

EL CAMINO REAL
NORTH CENTRAL FLORIDA PENINSULA

Chukka rested and enjoyed a hot meal at the Guacara Mission. Almost four days of running and fast walking west from dawn to dusk had drained his energy. Close to 100 miles covered and he'd faced no incidents. On the morrow he and Fray Mobila would ride double bareback east to San Agustín, as a soldier favorable to the Friar had accommodated his request. If they pushed, the 100 miles back would take six to seven days. If they pushed too hard, the horse and the Friar would pale. They knew where to stop for food and knew of the impending trial date, so they did not linger.

***

SAN AGUSTIN

"Armador, why do the Spanish believe that all rights to the New World belong only to them? Why should you alone claim all the silver, gold and trade with the Indies and South America?"

Luis rolled over and sat up on his straw pallet. Barely daylight and Hartford wanted to debate. Luis concluded he now confronted a barrister out of place and time. Nonetheless, he would answer.

"Because papal decree and a treaty established our rights many years ago. It set our destiny. Besides, all of Europe benefits from the trade through Seville."

"Nonsense. In time you will see that the English, French and Dutch all have worldwide claim too. Have you become aware of the dark reputation that depicts the Spanish as greedy, intolerant and subversive of the Indios? Did you know that your own honorable Fray Bartolomé de las Casas spoke against your savagery? It tarnished the luster of Spain's supposed Golden Age."

Hartford broached a tinderbox subject and then stoked the fire. Luis did his utmost at restraint, but to no avail.

"Hartford, know that many a Spaniard would run you through for those words. If we occupied the same cell and my blade sat nearby, I would be tempted." He paused. "Our words should be used to seek harmony. Not to nettle. We both seek Heaven. Perchance we should lay by and muse on that. It may come sooner than we think."

From across the prison hall came only silence. Luis supposed it easier to accost a Barbary pirate rather than Hartford's pique. But from that time forward the Englishman leaned more to genial discussions, and they found ease in sharing and learning from one another. Hartford even gave over to humorous quips.

Still, Luis often grappled with feelings as if a lone cimmarón, one of the poor runaways that roam the woods of the islands. Beset by loneliness and grasping for hope, he often fancied the security of his parents' home and his bed – soft, warm, secure. He also faced the sheer realization that he now likely missed passage on the annual Terre Firme silver fleet up from Habana to Spain. At times as these, jailer González, would saunter down and want to converse, always buoyant.

"Hola, mi amigos," he greeted, then perched on a stool in the hallway between Luis and the Englishman's cell doors. "I consider you my prizes, you know, as the others that come here stay but a brief time. Drunken soldiers sleep off but one night, having caused a brief problem for the town. I receive pay for them, but more for you, so I must keep you happy and healthy." He laughed.

Luis could envision his blade running through González's large belly, all the way through. *Perhaps later*, he thought.

"If the Governor allows you to live, perhaps you'll want to take up residence here. That is, in town." He laughed again. "You could become a farmer, take an Indio wife and catch fish in our harbor. Many do this and live happy. I myself enjoy the life of a jailer. What do you think?" He beamed.

Hartford became indignant and responded likewise.

"González, if they release me from jail, though improbable, my throat will be slit by sunset. Everyone here detests Englishmen. You know that. My fate stirs unknown."

Luis did not answer. He continued to picture his sword tip plunging into González's stomach.

"Well, rest easy, Armador, for your trial arrives tomorrow, and then we will see your destiny."

His wall markings reminded that ten days had now elapsed since Chukka left. Since then, he'd heard no word, with little time left. The night passed in anguish, as he dreamt of a gallows, a noose, a priest, and a large crowd. All with somber faces. Once again he contemplated escape, but as a man who would wander with no destination.

Daylight of his trial date broke ominously. He groomed as best he could for court, though he figured it could matter not. He experienced little emotion when the jailer came and removed the body of the feckless Tomás, who passed during the night.

He died unknown, to lie in an unknown grave, with no one to weep. I pray that my death casts far better. If only I could face a worthy opponent…with sword in hand…

Mid-day and a squad came to escort him to the trial. As he said goodbye to Englishman Hartford and jailer González, he wondered if it would be the last time. He and the escorts passed a sawyer and a shipwright building a small boat at water's edge. Gripped by a poignant longing, he watched their happy, industrious labor.

Moving from east along the plaza they strode the street of the Governor to his office. It sat adjacent to the Counting House offices of the Treasurer and Accountant. Luis' heart leaped as he passed San Agustín's Padre Fernández, along with Arapaja Indio Chukka and Fray Mobila of Guacara. They smiled, waiting their turn to enter. Inside, the small trial room contained, in addition to the Governor's three advisors, a few soldiers. Alférez Mencos sat in attendance as did the sneering accuser, Sgt. Torres.

The Padre and Friar entered and sat at the rear, but without Chukka, as Indios could not go inside.

The proceedings began with the Governor opening the trial in the name of Spain's King Felipe IV. Without delay, he posed to Luis the purpose of the trial.

"Mr. Armador, this court charges that, as a vagabond and miscreant, you willfully attacked Sgt. Manuel Torres, in his majesty's service, causing bodily harm in May, 1624, at the Guacara mission. He suffered incapacitation for some time and could not serve. This bodes as an intolerable crime in our province. How plead you?"

Rising, Luis addressed the Governor. Though inwardly defiant, he contained it, having rehearsed his response. Bowing, he spoke in a humble but confident tone. If nothing less, he wanted to impress with his hidalgo gentility.

"Your Excellency, thank you for an opportunity to speak. I washed up on La Florida's shore, a shipwreck survivor of the galleon Nuestra Señora de Atocha, in duty to the Crown. My pleasure came as Alférez under the noble Captain Bartolomé García de Nodal, who perished in the sinking. After existing as an Indio slave for over a year, I escaped, ascended the San Martín River and enjoyed hospitality at the Guacara mission.

Soldiers there often mistreated the Christian Indios. On one occasion I reproached Sgt. Torres for the same, whereupon he told me to leave the mission or face a duel. Considering my honor, I chose the latter, sparing his life but wounding him as a lesson. The letter dispatched to you from Fray Díaz during my stay at the Arapaja mission does not speak the truth. My account is true, I beg your mercy, and I plead not guilty. I have one witness to the affair, and I ask your permission to present him."

The Governor waved an affirmation and Fray Mobila came forward to speak.

"Your Excellency, I come as Fray Gaspar Mobila of the mission San Juan de Guacara, six days ride from the west of here. I came as soon as the messenger apprised me of the trial. All of Alférez Armador's testimony speaks truth, as I witnessed it. Over the last three years he survived many travails but always maintained his faith and his honor. I believe he only wishes to return to Spain. Thank you for allowing me to speak."

The Friar bowed and returned to his seat.

"Thank you, Fray Mobila. Your work renders much recognition by the Crown." He paused and then gazed around the room, as if planning a military maneuver. "Please excuse me to an adjacent room for a brief period, as I confer with my advisors, the Accountant, Treasurer, and Sergeant-Major."

For Luis, the time lapse passed as an eternity. He weighed how his survival in the wilderness for the last three years could have brought him to this. He reconciled that civilization now constituted the *wilderness* and the latter his halcyon *refuge*. In time the four officials returned and took their seats. All eyes riveted on the Governor. He smiled, as at Luis' first meeting.

"Mr. Armador, based on your account of the incident, attested to by the esteemed Fray Mobila, we find you clear of any charges. You may leave as a free man."

Luis slumped in his chair, his mental faculties exhausted but thankful. He rose to embrace and thank the two clergymen, his joy obvious. Not forgetting Chukka, he hurried outside.

"Thank you, my brother. You have saved me from prison or even the garrote. My heart sings at your efforts."

"We've served each other, Luis, and may we always do so."

As they strolled towards the church where Padre Fernández would have a meal prepared for them, Luis noticed an imposing sight from the corner of his eye. Turning, he saw the vengeful stare of his accuser Sgt. Manuel Torres, sword in hand, standing alone in the middle of the plaza. "Armador, I call you out, you blackheart!"

17
DUEL

1625

Brave as Rodrigo on the scaffold.

SAN AGUSTIN

Luis shuddered from the sickening feeling in his stomach. Not from fear. It arose from yet another challenge presented to him by La Florida. He tired of it.

"Remember your position, Sergeant!" yelled Luis.

Those leaving the Governor's office and all those present in the plaza took notice. They stopped and focused on Luis and the Sergeant.

"Armador, you *French pig*, you've scorched me for the last time! Acquire your sword, or I will run you through here and now!"

He advanced toward Luis, eyes aflame.

"Will you allow me to retrieve it from the barracks?"

"There's no need for that." It was Alférez Mencos, walking from the Governor's, his sword removed from its scabbard and tendered to Luis.

"Thank you, Alférez," said Luis, smiling.

He turned in Torres' direction and boldly walked to the middle of the plaza. A larger crowd now gathered, and gaming proceeded.

Luis girded in a military manner, saluted Torres with his sword, and assumed the combat position. Torres did likewise. For a few moments they circled, eyes locked. Torres made the first move, a powerful swath, trying to clip Luis at ankle level. Luis leaped just in time to avert the swing, then twisted around to regain position and face a new charge. Torres then slashed his sword toward Luis' face, but met a stiff blade, the clang reverberating. He continued charging, but each time Luis' deft defensive moves and parries met his blade.

Luis knew that Sergeant Torres would soon tire and lose patience and control. He waited for an opening. With his anger welling up and temper boiling, Torres came with all his force in an overhead strike. Luis met it with a two-handed angled grasp, deterring the sword. He stepped aside and produced a quick cut to the challenger's left calf.

"Ahhgggh, my leg!" Torres screamed.

Taking advantage of the moment, Luis did the same to the right calf.

"Owww!" came another scream. He went down, wincing. Sword now lost, he lay writhing in pain on his back.

Staring down at the scoundrel, Luis breathed the words, "You should have learned to relax, Torres, before taking action."

In an instant he experienced a memory of swordplay lessons from his father and followed it by dispatching Torres with a deep cut across the throat. Luis watched him die with feelings of relief and resignation. He returned the weapon to Mencos, who nodded approvingly.

After reconciling their gains and losses, the soldiers retrieved Torres' body to make preparations for a funeral. No shouting or wailing came from onlookers, who soon dispersed, each to his former activities. At the end of the plaza, the Governor and his advisors returned to the courtroom to proceed with the next trial. Watching from the church steps, at the plaza's southeast corner, both clergymen crossed themselves. The door opened, and Luis and Chukka followed them inside. Before proceeding to their meal, Luis took time to kneel in a pew with head bowed.

At Padre Fernández's table, Luis once again said his thanks to all for their help. He took joy in addressing Fray Mobila specifically.

"Padre Fernández here holds one real de a ocho in the church's commissary for you. Let him know what items you need so he can arrange for the supply. I only have three left from the shipwreck and have intended that the Guacara mission benefit from one ever since I left."

"You are most gracious, my son. I will write him a list," he said, smiling.

***

"Up, Luis, up!" At the fort barracks, Alférez Mencos cajoled Luis at bedside. "It's mid-morning, and I know you're exhausted from yesterday, but we have news."

"Not another arrest, Gregorio?"

Mencos laughed. "No amigo, but the Governor wants us for a mid-day meal again."

"Another interrogation?"

Mencos laughed again. "Who knows? Maybe he wants to give you a command."

This time Luis laughed, which helped to stir him awake.

"Give me about an hour to prepare."

"You have about half that, then we must go." Mencos added a serious glance and nod so to denote the importance of timeliness.

As they left the fort and walked the street along the water, Luis tried to imagine an acceptable set of circumstances, thinking it due. *Perchance a sail to Habana for no fee?*

"Come in, come in, gentlemen."

The Governor answered the door, beaming, trying his best to convey a sense of humility.

A good start, but don't forget the 'chameleon'.

Governor Borgia made them most welcome and served an enjoyable meal, as they anticipated. He apologized for the *misunderstanding*, as he termed the arrest and trial. He then seasoned the table with anecdotal stories of Spain and his interactions with nobles, merchants and military officers. At the end of the noonday feast, he stood, plucked three pipes plus a pouch of tobacco from his desk and passed them around. Lighting one, his face took on a more somber expression. His chin dropped to his chest and his lips puckered, as if contemplating what to say.

Alas, here it comes, thought Luis.

"As Alférez Mencos knows, part of my duties requires keeping this presidio staffed, however possible."

He turned to face Luis.

"Alférez Armador, you have proven your military skill as well as your ability to converse as an educated man. I'm now convinced of your rank, honor and abilities. You're a caballero, a man of substance.
After yesterday the garrison now has a sergeant's slot vacant in our command. I believe that you would be perfect for it. I can't offer you an alférez's position, as we only have one local, the other traveling the missions. I'm certain Alférez Mencos would agree with the choice."

He glanced at Mencos, who nodded in agreement.

Luis sat stunned. It took him a few moments to assemble a response.

"Governor, I'm honored at your offering, but my plans have been to return to Spain to complete my commission."

"I know, and your service here would not exceed six months, time enough for us to determine a replacement. I must insist."

Luis paused again, searching for the words.

"And if I am not favored toward filling the slot?"

"Then you will be impressed, conscripted, whatever it takes to have you join us. Look at it like this. It can provide a good transition for you back to civilization before you sail for Seville." He nodded several times, as if approving his own comments, and then smiled.

I seem to have no choice. I best go along.

"Very well, Governor. I am your humble servant. It will be an honor, and I'm certain that serving under Alférez Mencos will be satisfactory."

"Good. Then it's settled. You may quarter at the fort's barracks along with the corporals and sergeants. You may also on occasion practice your trade, which I understand is that of a shipwright. Mencos will review your duties and see that you have proper clothing. This bodes as a good day for San Agustín." He inhaled and blew his smoke toward the ceiling, as in a victory toast.

"You know, I haven't been here long. But I want this to be an outpost of which we can all be proud. There may even be fortunes in the nearby wilderness. Men say that gold or silver *does* exist in La Florida, and I would love to discover it. We could all become men of wealth and increase the coffers of Felipe IV." He handled the pipe in his mouth and looked out the window, as a man in a trance.

***

Luis removed his sword and scabbard and threw them against the barracks wall. They clanked and crashed onto the wooden floorboards.

"An abomination! Garroted without cord and stick! First he tries me falsely, and now he impresses me! Three years across La Florida, and now unable to leave port!"

He sat hard onto the bed and covered his face with his hands. Mencos took a seat also, saying nothing. He knew Luis needed to voice his displeasure. And he knew he would reconcile to his fate, though at the moment he became unhinged. A full minute of silence gripped the room. Then Luis spoke in a sedate manner.

"Pardon me, Gregorgio, but the events of civilization require me to become reaccustomed. It will take me awhile. You know I'll be happy to serve with you...for you."

He lay back on the bunk and closed his eyes. *Only one hour ago I enjoyed a meal, and now I feel as if I will lose it.*

"Luis, you have not become the first conscription here, and you won't be the last. Six months it will be. We will keep you occupied so that it will pass quickly. I will use what influence I have with Governor Borgia to see that he keeps his promise. Feel free to rest this afternoon. In the morning we will discuss duties. You will do well."

He stood over Luis and gestured with his hands and face as if to say, *that's the way it is.*

"But, in six months, how will I depart?"

"The Governor didn't mention that twice a year the King dispatches *adviso* ships as couriers, to bring and acquire correspondence with the

Indies. They go to Santo Domingo, Cartagena, and Habana, then stop here. Next year's will be in the spring. We will look to that."

That encourages, thought Luis. *A man always needs a reward to which he can aspire.*

"Besides, we may all be rich by then."

Banking off the Governor's remarks of treasure in Florida, Mencos hoped to lighten Luis' mood. Glancing up, Luis received a wide smile.

"You didn't swallow that I pray."

"Luis, some still cling to the notion. I've dismissed it, but obviously Governor Borgia hasn't. He is shortly arrived and is enterprising. And we know that gold and silver always cloud a man's thinking. In many cases, it's just a clever fiction." He hesitated. "I just try to follow orders."

"As do I," said Luis.

***

Luis arrived at the morning muster, outfitted to serve with honor, if not willingly. Bearing in mind that some of the men had been friends with Luis' duelist, Sgt Torres, Alférez Mencos gave a special lecture following the day's orders. He addressed most of the command's 300 soldiers, though some served on guard duty or at missions.

"Men, today we bear honor to have in our midst a new sergeant at the garrison. Luis Armador of Seville is late of his majesty's Armada aboard the Atocha galleon as an alférez. He is accustomed to command. As many of you know, he has already demonstrated his honor and skill with the sword. I have no doubt he brings high value to us, and I ask that you give to him your support and response. Anyone not doing so will answer to me."

As the men dismissed to assemble in their smaller squadrons, Mencos asked Luis to meet with him alone.

"Sergeant, I want to tell you of the makeup of the men at our post, many of whom come from the bottom of the classes in Spain. Sergeant Torres, your combatant, provided an example. Prisoners just freed, ruffians that many other stations would not take, deserters assigned here as punishment, and debtors with nowhere else to go. We also have shipwreck survivors, good in character, but unhappy with their impressment after we rescued them. You may remember that before you left Seville how difficult it became to recruit quality troops. You and I hold military service in high esteem, but some don't, as seen in their arrogance and liberty-taking. So we get many rogues. Feel free to direct and punish as necessary, as they need a strong hand. I believe you can do that."

"That we can, Alférez."

"You can review my list of today's assignments for your troops. Then you, the other two local sergeants and I will meet each afternoon to prepare for muster on ensuing mornings. The men have watchtower duty, guard duty, clean-up duty, and the list goes on. I look forward to serving with you."

"My pleasure, Alférez."

***

The distant post of San Agustín functioned as a world of its own. Into this, Luis settled into the routine of military life, learning the duties of his 90 soldiers and supervising through his corporals. From sentry duty to fort maintenance to farming supervision, most soldiers could take time to practice their trades. That included Luis, who labored part-time as a shipwright and also set about building his own canoa. Acquiring a log from local mission Indios, he put to use the skills learned from the Calusa and Arapaja, aided now by iron tools. He enjoyed staying at the barracks and often took his meals with the sergeants and corporals.

At the plaza, he watched soldiers and townsfolk barter trinkets with Indios that brought their produce to market. Here also sat a watchtower and the guardhouse. He occasionally saw González, the jailer, when having to deliver errant soldiers for a period.

Luis handled mundane duties, spent time learning the residents and streets in the eleven-block hamlet, and fished the harbor. However, he began to long for adventure, some challenging military mission.

***

A break in routine came when church bells announced a new ship arriving, beyond the harbor. It came at the first of autumn, as trees began to yellow, days shortened, and the air turned crisper. The fall *adviso* ship arrived and anchored beyond the bar, sending in men by longboats. Luis, Alférez Mencos, plus the other sergeants and officers would come together at the Governor's for a briefing on the outside world. Luis couldn't wait. The ship would take on correspondence for Spain but would also bring news to the outpost.

"Welcome, men!" Governor Borgia greeted the select soldiers and local officials at his office. "Captain Sandovar of the king's messenger ship brings us news, after which they will take on correspondence for Castile."

"Your mercies, I am honored to be here. As far as news, I will do my utmost to recall all the latest," said the just-arrived Captain.

His appearance said early forties, and he proved cordial and spoke with ease. His dominant features stood out as thick black hair and beard. After swapping a few niceties with the group, he eased his chair back and took a puff on his pipe, a gift from the Governor.

"Marquis Ambrosio Spinola made history for the crown this year by commanding the capture of Breda, Holland, after a siege of many months. This sets a milestone in our war in Flanders. As strange as it is, the Dutch have begun to outpower us on the seas. But in spite of that, our combined Armada with Portugal retook Bahía, Brazil, from them by sending 56 vessels and over 12,000 men. Now, that is a conquest. The country considers General Toledo almost a saint."

At that the hosts clapped and shouted a few bravos.

"Let me see…Francisco Melián signed a contract with the crown to attempt another salvage of the Atocha and sister vessels off the Mártires south of here."

"Ah!" spouted Luis, without thinking.

"Pardon me, gentlemen, that news gave me a start." His face turned crimson.

"You must excuse Sgt. Armador, Captain. He is a survivor of the Atocha," said the Governor.

"I see," said the Captain, facing Luis. "I don't have much else in the way of specific news. Inflation still runs loose in our homeland, the rest of Europe still handles many pesos as it traffics through Seville...and... all of our lovely señoritas send their regards."

That lit up the room with laughter and smiles.

"I always enjoy my stopover here for a few days, and I look forward to seeing you again next spring, if I still command the adviso."

Luis took note of the comment and glanced at Mencos. Each made a point not to alter his expression. But Luis warmed at the news.

"And you please our townsfolk that your men patronize our services, scant as they are, while you're here," said Governor Borgia.

***

"Sgt. Armador, are you ready for some action ?" asked Alférez Mencos.

Late afternoon after the daily review with the sergeants and Luis could tell Mencos sought to propose something uncommon. He turned the question over in his mind, wondering if it involved some unique conjuration of the Governor.

"The Sergeant-Major has received complaints of raids on scattered Christian Indio villages up and down the *Corrientes River just west of here. We have reports of a small band of runaways, led by one of our

*St. Johns River

own deserters, a Private Valencia, who turned into a white Indio. Killing and pillaging have taken place. This must stop and the murderers captured. You are to command a capture troop."

Luis didn't flinch at the pointed white Indio description of fugitive Valencia, but it struck a chord. He harbored mixed feelings, though he knew Alférez Mencos did not think of Luis' own history at Arapaja.

"Sergeant, pick one corporal and eight infantrymen, each to take harquebus and sword. Take enough food for several days and plan on riding the *mules of St. Francis*."

"Who?"

"Sergeant, you've been away from military life too long. You'll be walking, as usual." He smiled warmly.

Luis nodded, trying to grasp it.

"Look at this hand-drawn map, provided by a previous scouting mission. You will go west 20 miles to Picolata at the river, then onto a Corrientes riverside path along the east bank. Walk five miles north to a crossing of a large creek, the **Nicoloa, which flows west into the big river.

"Are the raiders nearby?" asked Luis.

"We think they've headquartered somewhere upstream on the creek, using canoas. They'd be on an isolated creekside high ground, as it contains many wet lowlands. The water far up narrows down and won't be passable. So your search length will be somewhat shortened."

"Where shall we find canoas?" asked Luis, as he pictured needing five.

"From Utinas in small villages nearby. They'll provide you, as they want our help."

"One more thing, Sergeant," said as he reached into a small bag and brought out a polished wood and metal pistol. He handed it to Luis, handle first. "The Sergeant-Major favors you, so he asked me to lend to you his new Flintlock pistol, which he brought from Spain. It has only recently come into use and is very accurate at close range. It's supposed to be more reliable than the older pistols. Practice it before you leave, and of course, guard it well. It is valuable."

"Please express my appreciation. I am honored. We leave in the morning."

***

It took the small military group one and a half days going west to reach Picolata on the river. There a small assemblage of Indios managed the river ferry, once used by Luis. Going north and reaching Nicoloa Creek the next day, they found it easy to borrow five dugouts. Luis' interpretive skills

**Six-Mile Creek

helped. The Utinas, happy to assist, also warned that many lagartos lay about. Luis sat the soldiers down and laid out his plan.

"Men, the scoundrels, if they're camped upstream, should lie no more than a two hour paddle. We'll rest today and in the morning, and then move up in the afternoon. We need to locate them early so we can devise a plan of attack at the next daylight. Wasn't it Cortés that said, *surprise adds numbers to the attack*? Any questions?" asked Luis.

One of the soldiers voiced that he wanted to settle an old dispute with the deserter, Private Valencia.

"I imagine many do, but we need to take him back alive for trial," said Luis.

The warm sun shone at their backs as they stroked upstream east the next afternoon. What the Indios advised proved apparent in their seeing many lagartos in and near the water. The further up they went, the more the creek narrowed. It also received less effect from wind and became glass-like, without noticeable current. As the sun set, loud voices ahead, a mixture of Spanish and Indios, broke the quiet.

In the lead vessel, Luis motioned all to pull over to the right bank to avoid disclosing their presence. He dispatched one man to walk the woods upstream, with stealth, and report back. Forty-five minutes later, he returned and confirmed the renegades' camp. Luis planned to stow the canoes and all walk to about 200 yards from their camp. Then remain there quiet all night so to launch a surprise capture at dawn.

A long night ensued with the songs of crickets and frogs filling the woods. That followed an arduous walk through swampy areas where carefulness kept their powder dry. The men squatted or climbed trees for the night, after smearing their faces with bug deterrents. At daylight, though stiff and lethargic, they moved in, as Luis spread the troops in a semi-circle around the six sleeping raiders. He prayed none of his oft-disorderly group became impulsive. To their surprise, no posted guard was observed.

"Get up, you mongrels!" shouted Luis, in Indios language. He leveled his half-cocked pistol in their direction.

The awakening marauders rose slowly, each one facing a harquebus. Luis believed it too easy and could sense something amiss.

Iiii yee iii! came the cry. A form, without regard, ran from the woods and leapt on Luis' back, ax raised for a crushing blow.

Quickly reaching across his body and placing the barrel of his pistol in the attacker's stomach, he pulled the trigger. The discharge resounded throughout the woods, smoke pouring from the weapon.

Both men fell in a crumpled mass, crunching dead tree limbs as they dropped to the ground.

The soldiers moved in closer, guns at the ready to reinforce their captor status. Luis, shaken more from the fall than the encounter, took his time arising.

"It was the lookout," he said. "Must've been napping."

With six captives bound and guards set, several soldiers walked downstream to retrieve and paddle up with the soldiers' dugouts, so all could float downstream. Later, Luis presented the captives' tethered vessels to the local Indios, the original owners. After devouring a meal, courtesy of the Utinas, the men set off for San Agustín. The prisoners were secured at the neck and wrists, with a strong line from the front captive to the back.

On the morning of the last ten miles to town, a light rain fell, but not enough to impede the journey. If anything, it may have quickened their step. Not conducive for conversation, but it gave Luis time to think. He harkened back to that night in Porto Bello when he captured the two Atocha deserters. He knew a distinct pride then in his soldiery. *Another lifetime*, he thought, *three years past.* No similar sense came to him from the current accomplishment. Just a soldier following orders, doing his job, serving his time, looking forward to spring of the coming year, home. That caused him to think of the departed adviso ship. He cringed at not thinking to send a letter to his family.

Luis and his men received acclaim on their return and were granted several days off-duty. The trial commenced soon thereafter, with area chiefs attesting to the raiders' crimes. Private Valencia suffered a sentence to be garroted with two Indios sentenced to be hanged. The other three would serve in prison for two years, much to the delight of jailer González.

"Alférez Mencos, do you plan to witness the executions?" asked Luis, following the trial.

"Oh yes. In fact, all of our men not on critical duty must attend, so it serves as a deterrent. We expect the executions in the plaza tomorrow."

Stay in bed? Feign illness? Luis fancied. He did not have an appetite for observing an execution, especially in the plaza, but he knew he must go. In addition to the soldiers, he heard that residents plus Indios from Mission Nombre de Dios down the road would flock to the spectacle.

***

The appointed day arrived. Crowds swelled around the seven-foot high platform and scaffolding that held two noose-ropes. They hung down ominously, in stark contrast to a clear blue sky.

The two Indio prisoners swung from the gallows in short order. Then it was Private Valencia's turn. After spending a few moments with the Padre, he ascended the platform. Next came the garrotter, dressed all in black, scowling and looking like the *angel of death*. Just before placing a covering over Valencia's head, the executioner asked if he had any last words. Luis, already queasy, did not expect what came next, nor the length of it, nor its oratorical tone.

"You all bear witness to my plight! God's judgment came upon me for my evil ways and the despicable road I have traveled! I thought it to be all fun and frolic, but it came to naught! If any of you harbors evil lurking in your heart, I beg you, cast it out! Pray to God to cleanse you and turn to the teachings of your Catholic youth! You do not want to follow where I have trod!"

Luis listened to him sermonize at great length, as if seeking absolution in his remaining moments. *He couldn't be much older than I. He reminds me of Tomás, dying in our jail. Pitiful.*

His homily continued unabated. Finally, the Governor arose and signaled the garrotter to begin his work. With head now covered, the prisoner expounded right up to his last garbled breath, even as the stick twisted the cord around his neck. To Luis, the gasps and garbled speech gave a mawkish hue to the scene. Luis sensed *a man drowning*, with no one trying to assist. An element of his boyhood past drew forth.

Holding a sickening feeling in his stomach, he left post-haste. He knew the lump in his throat issued not from being strangled, but it conceived an odd association. On his way back to the fort, he stopped to discharge up the contents of his last meal.

***

As the days passed into late fall, Luis once again merged back into the garrison's rhythm. Posting sentries, supervising shipwrights, interpreting visiting chiefs for the Governor, and parading the men, all claimed part of his duties. He began to own a renewed sense of comfort. Temperate days permitted relaxed noonday lunches at the plaza or the town pier. Like most soldiers, he enjoyed biscuits, olive oil, raw vegetables, and salted meats, all issued to the soldiers. At one of these respites he made the acquaintance of the presidio's Accountant, Don Francisco Ramírez.

"Don Francisco, what is your pleasure in residing in San Agustín, so far from Spain?"

He puzzled at why an hidalgo, a man of good standing, wanted to stay in the far reaches of the empire. Physically well-built, he conveyed a kind face highlighted by a dark moustache, and he never ventured out unless well-attired. One of the few men in town that wore the doublet and ruffled shirt daily, his *signature* stemmed from his wide-brimmed felt hat. His two-story home, one of theselect, sited on an enlarged lot, and as the Governor's Accountant, he garnered the respect of all. He also assisted the Treasurer in handling the *situado,* the annual monetary stipend and merchant supplies shipped from Vera Cruz atthe crown's behest.

"A fine question, Sergeant. Being from a similar background, you have the capacity to understand my answer, though you may not agree. For now, my position is satisfactory. I have a tutor for my children and my wife has a few social activities plus ample servants. My children have playmates, many of them Indio and slave offspring. I am provided a horse, which you know is in short supply here. I have a sense of being here that I couldn't find in the large cities of Spain."

Prestige…recognition…deference, thought Luis.

"At the moment, everyone tenders special courtesies to me, as the supply ship is due before long."

"Has it ever failed to arrive?"

"Yes. Due to storms, shipwrecks at the entrance bar, or pure neglect by the Vera Cruz authorities. Then no funds and no food supplements. The people resort to eating cats, dogs, horses, fighting over corn, food rationing."

"Don't the Indios help?"

"Of course, but they just help supply corn. Even now, our Royal Warehouse for food supplies requires control and the guards you send there each day."

"That's true," replied Luis.

***

November made its way into San Agustín, with warm days and cool nights, a perfect balance to Luis. But his thought processes once again faced challenging circumstances. Alférez Mencos bore the news.

"Sergeant, the Governor still hears tales of silver and gold lodes, hills of diamonds, and lagoons of salt water pearls. He won't divulge his sources, but insists on sending out a search.

"To where?"

"He won't say. I'm not certain he knows. Several have reminded him that no one ever discovered riches here, de Soto or anyone else. He said even Cortés and Pizzaro faced detractors and he thinks it's nearby and overlooked. Once a treasure fastens itself to someone's mind, there's no shaking it loose."

"Does he plan to involve us?"

"Maybe. He wants us to meet with him, Accountant Ramírez and the Sergeant-Major for breakfast in the morn."

"Breakfast? Do we depart in the afternoon?"

Mencos looked as puzzled as Luis, so no answer came forth.

***

"Governor, I fear this will be like, as they say, *trying to plant a pikestaff in Flanders,*" said Accountant Ramírez, one of the few that would dare to question him.

"No," he said, shaking his head. "This could be a lifetime opportunity. A proper search has not been done for years. For generations."

Next, he served the chocolate drink, a rare liquid to be found in San Agustín.

He's greasing the axles, noted Luis.

The guests listened, and no one spoke but the Governor. He brought out maps and pointed to what he considered areas never before covered. He wanted to launch a full-fledged search party, and if necessary, another and another.

A relative of the mad priest? Luis pondered.

"Sergeant Armador, your interpretive skills could be invaluable. You would be compensated in an adequate amount."

Luis nodded with courtesy.

The men enjoyed an ample breakfast, even with now-tempered appetites. The only real surprise came when the Governor expressed that the expedition would not take place until the spring, four months hence. He wanted plenty of time to plan.

Spring? My planned embarkation? Luis foresaw yet another challenge.

"Gentlemen. Gold fever is most contagious. I ask that the four of you speak not of these plans. If news like this circulates in town, disruption could arise. I will know the source. Be most careful."

***

As the year 1625 came near to a close, Luis anticipated the Navidad season with fervor. Except for the small service at the Arapaha mission church, he had attended no full celebration in four years. Christmas Eve provided a sacred candlelight procession, led by Padre Fernández, from the fort to the church. After Mass, Governor Borgia provided a feast at his home for a select few, including Luis. The Governor's wife displayed graciousness to all, having set up several tables of food, with well-attired Indio servants on hand.

"Gentlemen, if we could be served as this at least weekly, I could be tempted to take up long-term residence," said Luis, holding his wine glass on high and bearing a sense of animation.

He beamed happy and comfortable to be able to express himself to Alférez Mencos and Accountant Ramírez standing nearby. He served the garrison as Sergeant, but all knew he'd earned a commissioned officer's rank.

"Your mercies," said Mencos, "let me offer a toast to King Felipe IV and wish for him a long life."

"Hear, hear!" said the others.

"And let me toast a safe passage for our situado vessel in the coming year. May its officers have the knowledge not to attempt the harbor bar without help, so our pesos and foodstuffs arrive safely," said Ramírez.

"Hear, hear!" all said.

"How goes the longboats, Sergeant?" asked Mencos.

Everyone knew that the presidio's longboats, built locally, must be kept in condition, being so critical in combing the coast after a storm. Their need doubled should a vessel ground while trying to cross the treacherous sandbar at harbor entrance.

"Alférez, we finished the cleaning and caulking of all of them yesterday. They can handle almost anything," said Luis.

***

1626 arrived explosively in Seville, Spain, with the massive flooding of its major navigable river, the Guadalquivir, seriously affecting all residents.

However, it was unknown to the colonists, with 1626 arriving quietly in San Agustín, and the brief winter months passing uneventfully, no ships arriving or departing. Everyone looked forward to the Indios' spring corn planting and the coming of the annual situado vessel, as supplies dwindled. The town also anticipated a fresh supply of European merchant goods. Luis continued to take informal mid-day meals at the plaza. Padre Fernández often joined him.

"Luis, did you know they designed the plaza dimensions with harmony in mind?"

"No. How so?"

"They prescribed the length at one and one-half times the width. Based on ancient thought and tradition, it's supposed to grant harmony."

"I didn't notice it on the day of my duel," he chuckled.

"No. And sometimes I don't either, though my church is across the street. The situado may come soon, and I pray the church will get her share of pesos and provisions. That doesn't always happen."

"Why?"

"I have no proof. Just a suspicion from my dealings with Treasurer Márquez and his current substitute, Alonso de Pastrana. We never benefit from the amount promised by the Bishop in Cuba. There's always an excuse. Even my letters do not help."

"Do you think the Treasurer withholds funds in the Royal Coffer?"

Padre Fernández didn't extend conversation on the subject, choosing instead to leave the words hanging. But he turned to face Luis with an expression that seemed to answer *yes* to the question. Luis knew that the Padre had the authority of excommunication, which he wouldn't hesitate to use if necessary. That and the Holy Office of the Inquisition created the most fear for Spaniards.

"Tell me, Luis, who waits for you in Spain?"

"Waits? My family, of course. Grandparents, parents, and sisters, unless fate intervened. I long to see them."
His smile of anticipation glowed.

"Anyone else?"

"No...not really...although, at one time..."

"Who?"

"A señorita. My betrothed. Our marriage would have taken place on my return three years ago. Upon leaving, I told her not to wait if one year passed. I'm certain her mourning has passed and that she went on to wed. Children maybe."

Luis paused and looked out toward the bay, sunlight shimmering on its surface. As from a cue on stage, he began to speak of Isabela, part agony and part warm memory.

"She displays the most beautiful black hair, sparkling eyes, broadest smile, especially when she laughs. She floats across the floor, whether walking towards me or dancing. She loves me...or she did. She didn't want me to go to the Indies, fearing I wouldn't return. I'm afraid I proved her right."

His eyes grew misty.

"Shipwrecks and weather were beyond your control, Luis. Only God controls that. Happiness comes in many forms. I'm certain you will find it."

Luis regained his composure and presented another subject.

"Padre, the Governor told me that my military service here would be six months, then I could return to Spain. Alférez Mencos witnessed it, but still I fear he may try to persuade me to stay beyond that time."

"Why, Luis?"

"He's ambitious, as most Spanish senior officers. He's planning a gold and silver scouting trip in the spring, as he mistakenly thinks treasures still may be found hereabouts. He wants me involved. Like confession, Padre, this compels confidentiality."

"Of course, Luis. I'll watchcare the circumstances and help if I can."

***

Much to Luis' chagrin, the Governor continued to have closed meetings to plan for the spring treasure-scouting trip. Luis sat tormented each time Borgia referred to a specific duty for a squadron to be led by him. He vacillated as to when to discuss his supposed six-month limit, but decided to wait till the adviso courier ship enroute to Spain next arrived. Then he would broach the issue. Clear-headedness prompted him not to chance riling a disposition until then. Otherwise, it could cumulate and work to his detriment.

***

Harquebuses fired from Cantera Island, beyond the harbor, followed by the church bells tolling.

"The situado frigate sinks at the bar!" came the cry from the waterfront.

Daylight brought an insufficient high tide on a mid-March morning. It also brought terror. To lose the situado ship could bring about calamity. It happened at the same time as morning muster at the fort.

"The bar traps the situado!" shouted a townsman running to the fort. The regimented muster soon turned into an uproar of concern.

"Sgt. Armador, take 34 men from your squadron and launch five chalupas. Posthaste!" ordered Alférez Mencos.

Although most ship captains knew of the danger of the bar, some wanted to prove their prowess. Underwater sand in the inlet and sandbar area shifted from storms, plus the tide changed the passages. It made traversing difficult without a local pilot. The shoals and breakers now stranded the laden frigate from Vera Cruz, with nowhere to go but down. As harbors go, Matanzas Bay portended as a small refuge. It still required about a mile passage from the pier through the inlet out to the sandbar and the Atlantic. Luis' men often practiced the drill, and they knew it would take oarsmen about 15 minutes to row out. Approaching Cantera Island on the right, they could see the vessel foundering, grounded and listing hard to port. The surf pounded as the vessel took on water.

Upon seeing the longboats, all hands began running and yelling on deck. Without regard for cool water temperatures, some went overboard to swim to the rescuers. Transferring seamen from ships to longboats in breakers became challenging enough, but with a sinking vessel, chaos could result. Men continued to leap into the water seeking rescue, increasing the turmoil.

"Captain, have your men stand off, or the chalupas will become overcrowded!" shouted Luis.

"I have a ship gone mad!" he yelled back.

Planned or not, longboat crews pulled seamen aboard. Transported to Cantera Island, they warmed at a bonfire built by watchtower guards.

"Where do you hold the coins?!" Luis yelled to the Captain.

"Far below, now filled with water! No man will retrieve, they all desire saving! The hull has a hole and water rushes in!"

More than once, a panic-stricken seaman in the water grabbed his longboat rescuer and pulled him in. The task then doubled. But as they plucked the last of the 30-odd men and the Captain, all headed to the island beach and warmth. Luis and his soldiers finished cold, wet and fatigued, but proud that no one drowned. Some of the rescued grew ill and were taken to convalesce in townsfolk homes. There, herbal remedies, as wine, sugar, biscuit, and chicken served as treatment. No conflict arose with the town's smallpox sufferers, kept at a small hospital.

The loss of supplies and foodstuffs dealt a severe blow to San Agustín, but losing over 8300 pesos devastated more.
Soldiers' wages were the the town's mainstay, and they could not be recovered. The rescued San Agustín-appointed *situador* representative had arranged all items shipped from Vera Cruz. Though aboard, he pleaded no influence with the sinking ships's Captain.

Governor Borgia faced livid soldiers and settlers who wanted to hang the situado Captain for attempting to run the sandbar. With mixed emotions of his own, he secreted the Captain away at the Franciscan friars' compound for his own protection. Though not his charge, the Governor would send a letter to the Governor of Vera Cruz recommending punishment for the Captain. He would also plead for a replacement situado. The locals' anger would eventually subside. It would be replaced by a wave of apprehension that swept over them like darkness on a stormy day.

The Governor advised all to plan for less sustenance. The twice-a-year adviso courier vessel would come in April, the following month, but it must maintain its own supplies. He knew the only solution required sailing the garrison's frigate to Habana. The now-stranded situado ship's men could be transported and new supplies acquired, but debt would occur.

***

When does a man have enough of a place in time? When does he reach the limit of his service, good or bad?

Luis pored over these notions and sensed his limit now reached. A feeling of restlessness encompassed him daily. He speculated it could have something to do with the change of seasons, so ingrained in him over the last three-plus years. Like early spring, when he sailed from Seville, the approaching winter as he departed the Calusa, and the early budding of spring when he had to leave Tocobaga. Now, spring greeted him each day. He realized other factors affected his travels, but something else, more compelling, motivated him.

In March, he rented a room in town with the family of butcher Alonso Ulúa. Leaving in the spring in some manner was his secret goal. A private upstairs room would assist. His simple quarters provided bed, table, chair, washbowl, chamber pot, linens, mosquito netting, and a brasero, a tiny stove for charcoal warmth. He often took meals with the hosts, providing from his warehouse food allotment. Luis' supposed tenure was up, and he wanted to prepare to leave, secretly if necessary. The Governor had promised six months and now he'd seen seven.

April arrived and opportunity floated in the harbor in the form of another adviso ship. Wisely, it anchored out and sent in word for a local pilot. With his knowledge, the vessel coursed the bar and inlet impressively. Luis once again sat in on the Governor's briefing with the arriving Captain, but his mind thought only of embarkation. The Governor made no mention. Luis left dejected, as a groom left standing at the altar.

Outside, he spoke to his friend.

"Alférez Mencos, sir…Gregorio. I now wish to complete my mission here, as promised. The adviso leaves in two days, and I seek a berth." He spoke with fervor in his voice.

"And you should, Luis. I will speak to the Governor."

Mencos did as promised and Governor Borgia asked to meet with Luis, which he expected. The next day found him walking the street to the Government House.

"Governor, thank you for the opportunity to converse. I'm certain Alférez Mencos told you of my wishes."

Borgia smiled, offered Luis a pipe and tobacco, and bid him take a seat. Later, Luis would have a remembrance of things brass, dark-stained, and embroidered, all bathed in bright light from open windows. Though plush, his chair rendered him uncomfortable, as tenseness rose within.

He contains a strong will, but so do I. I will maintain my sense of honor and propriety. He respects that.

"Luis, you came to us as a talented young man, one who proved his worth. Your service to the crown now needs recognizing. I penned a request to my superior to grant a captain's slot for Mencos and an alférez slot for you. It will be dispatched by the adviso now in our bay and I will grant the promotions as soon as we receive word."

Luis had anticipated persuasion.

"Thank you, Governor. You honor me. But, by your leave, please suffer me to return to Spain as planned at our initial discussion. Eight months here far exceeds our expectations."

"True, and I won't deter you. I'd rather coax you." He smiled. "Don't forget our gold scouting expedition, of which you will play a major part. You could become a wealthy man. We all could. Your future after that would be bright. You could purchase a profitable plantation in the islands, you could..."

"Pardon, Governor. Please pardon me. Your offer comes tempting, but I only wish to return to my family. It's been almost four years."

Luis did his utmost at diplomacy but also to convey his wish with firmness. Governor Borgia paused and gazed at Luis as if trying to understand but didn't. He rose, signaling their meeting's conclusion.

"Very well, Luis. Please consider overnight all I have said and return to me one more time, before the ship sails tomorrow. I always rise before daylight."

"Thank you, Governor, for everything."

Why does one man extend so much effort to impose his will on another? Is it born within, or developed in tutelage? Too much for a simple soldier to contemplate.

As he took his leave and walked down the sandy street, he dwelled on those thoughts. Even the warmth of April sunshine couldn't illuminate his mind, so he decided to seek another's.

"Padre Fernández, the adviso leaves early tomorrow. As I've told you, my agreed service time is passed, and I plan to be aboard, but I don't trust the Governor. His manner in discussing it today rang too genteel and obliging, even in the midst of his persuasions to stay. So, would you grant me one thing?"

"Of course, Luis."

"But first, Padre, permit me to contribute one of the two remaining reales de a ocho from the Atocha that you now safeguard. Please keep it to be useful for your church. Not to worry, I've saved others from my wages and shipwright labor and all my debts are paid. You can now return the other one to me."

***

In quiet and secret, Luis prepared to leave. He spent the evening in his room packing his meager belongings. He added foodstuffs, coins, and, of course, his sword. His one peso left from the Atocha was placed in a tiny bag and secured with a waist chord under his shirt. With a departure in mind, he went to bed early, but sleep came tormented.

Sailing to Spain, the ship faces attack from a monster of the deep…it rises up from the depths… breathing fire and roaring as a hurricane…coming aboard, its enormous tail thrashes about, crushing everything within reach…I draw my sword and begin delivering blows, but none penetrate…should I keep fighting or abandon ship?… the indecision increases my terror…

Suddenly, he awoke … *A sea monster? A sea monster? Why a sea monster?*

The town crier called out three A.M., so he dressed, assembled his goods and crept downstairs, trying to minimize the creaking of the steps. Three envelopes he left on a desk, the landlord's on top. The others he'd addressed to Alférez Mencos and Accountant Ramírez. On a note inside each, he thanked of friendship and aid, wishing each a healthy, long life. An outside note to his landlord requested that no envelopes be opened or even delivered until two days passed. Chukka would have had a note also, but he long ago returned to his village.

Familiar with the crier and military sentries' schedules, he could navigate the darkened, narrow streets unseen. In the distance a dog barked, breaking the stillness of the night. At the waterfront, he loaded his own dugout and cast off. Stars sparkled, and a full moon shone on the water as he paddled east across the harbor. He recalled previous paddle escapes and the sense of liberty each elicited. It rose up again. Soon he rounded the northern end of Cantera Island and moved through the inlet. Breakers could be heard on the sandbar, so he eased along the edge to the island's backside and pulled up the canoa. As he stepped in, the water's coolness stung his feet.

To Luis, time moved like a mountain stream. Still, he reckoned to have a good two hours till daybreak. He pulled the dugout behind the dunes and sat to wait. Beyond the bar he could see the anchored ship, placed there the previous day with the local pilot's guidance. It only waited now for the Captain from shore. Two lanterns shone, one on the prow, one on the stern. They gleamed as two beacons, summoning his way home. No sound came from the island's manned watchtower, but he stayed alert.

Closer to dawn, the aircooled, and Luis wrapped his extra shirt over his shoulders. Fog eased in and limited his vision.

Waiting for the Captain's arrival in a longboat, Luis again contemplated his undertaking. *A return to Florida's west coast bodes foolish. It could take years to berth a ship to Spain, plus no port from which to embark. Paddling a canoa to Habana from there would still be perilous. Hiring of the local frigate to Habana would alert the Governor, who now might not permit it.*

If the annual Terre Firme silver fleet still ran, it would be late summer or early autumn before he would have access. Today rendered his best chance. Though the Governor said he would not hold him, he knew it best to avail of the opportunity. He alone could set his destiny.

Light broke in the east, just perceptible due to the fog. The sound of oars and an approaching longboat could be heard bringing the Captain. Luis could not see but could hear the Captain climbing aboard and the greetings. He waited until the returning boat pulled out of earshot, then, pulling his craft into the water he paddled toward the ship, using its morning stirrings as a guide. From his left, he detected the sound of another small craft paddling to the ship. He heard a call...

"Arrest the ship, Captain Sandovar! The Governor seeks Sergeant Armador, not at his quarters! Only to confer!"

Recrossing the Atlantic

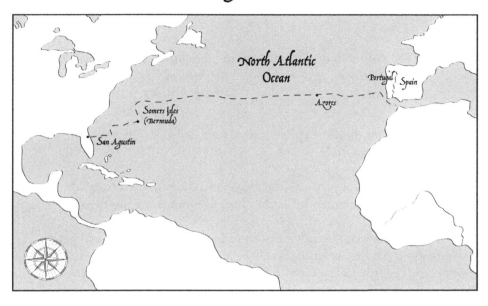

18
Barbary Coast

1626

*In the end, when all the trappings of empire are
stripped away, it is every man for himself.*
Panfilo de Narváez
1528

It startled Luis, but didn't surprise him. He paddled to the back end of
the ship as quietly as possible.

The fog is my friend today.

As the soldiers' dugout came alongside, the Captain peered over the
railing into the mist. The men looked to him as wraiths arising from the
deep.

"Gentlemen, he is not aboard. If not in his quarters, he must be about
somewhere else. You're welcome to come aboard to see for yourself.
Otherwise, my regards to the Governor, and, by your leave, we set the
sails."

Satisfied, the soldiers thanked the Captain and began paddling back
toward town. They melded back into the fog in the same manner they
approached. Luis waited until the paddle strokes could not be heard, then
moved his craft around to the side. Banging his paddle on the hull, he
called for the Captain.

"What now? Is the entire town calling on my ship this morning?"

Luis tied his canoa to the rope ladder and climbed up. He came face to
face with the Captain.

"Captain Sandovar, I am Sergeant Luis Armador. Pardon the
unannounced visit. Though my agreed service time passed at the garrison,
I'm afraid the Governor will try to keep me beyond his pledge. Please take
me to Spain with you so I can complete my commission there. I bear a
letter for you from Padre Francisco Fernández, our parish priest, attesting
to my situation."

"Sergeant, I remember you. Knowing the Governor, I have no doubt
of the circumstances. But I seek no quarrel with him."

"Captain, please, read the letter. I can also pay you the twenty reales
de a ocho that I have saved for passage," Luis pleaded.

The Captain pondered a few moments, then reached for the letter. After reading, he looked up, stared at Luis, turned away, then stared at him again, weighing a decision.

"Climb aboard, Sergeant. I'll have a seaman pull your dugout in, if it be yours."

"Yes, sir, it is."

"Now we'll proceed to sail before anyone else happens to come alongside. Boatswain, unfurl the sails, make ready all to cast off."

Relieved, Luis clambered over the rail, setting his bag down. The rake of the deck, the sounds of seamen, and the smell of the riggings called forth his memories. It came from the Atocha as a reminder of long ago. But repressed thoughts of the hurricane then seized him, like an animal trap. Shaking, he plopped onto the deck and covered his face, forcing thoughts of Atocha good times.

Amidst the unfurling of sails and shouts of orders, Luis composed himself. As light increased and the fog began to lift, he walked to the rear deck for one last look. The ship left a wake as he cast eyes toward town, the buildings now out of sight. He held a mixture of joy and sadness at leaving, as the far-flung outpost produced honorable friends who reintroduced him to civilization. At last, he sailed to Seville, to return as a current-day *Lazarus.*

"'Tis far better than a dank cell, say you, Armador?"

Turning around, Luis was taken aback with the visage of his former co-prisoner, Englishman William Hartford. The short-statued but confident man posed well-attired and effected a sly grin.

Just like him, observed Luis.

"Hartford. I thought you'd been sent to serve at mission Nombre de Dios nearby."

"Yes, and about the same as a prison cell for an Anglican. But after a while, they didn't quite know what to do with me, so they shipped me out."

"To Spain?"

"No, I'll be dropped off at *Somers Isles, a British colony enroute. Discovered by one of your countrymen, Bermúdez, I believe. I have friends there, and I hear that it's prospering. It's a good plan for now."

Luis studied him for a few moments. Remembering their background and theological differences, he didn't want to become too close, though he summoned to mind a gladness for him.

The frigate trimmed now, headed due east, soon to pick up the ocean current north. With just 70 aboard, including a contingent of soldiers, it

*Bermuda

could still pose a target for pirates or corsairs, purely for the vessel. But it carried no gold or silver, except what might be smuggled aboard, its cargo consisting of correspondence. After stowing his gear below, Luis returned up top to revel in the sailing.

"Captain, my thanks again for allowing me to board. May I present my twenty reales de a ocho for passage?"

"No, Armador. Soldiers do not have to pay a fee. Just don't mention your means of passage once you return home. I'm no big ally of the Governor, but I want no trouble."

"Of course, sir."

Luis noted Captain Sandovar as an experienced soldier *and* sailor, as he handled the Master's sailing duties also. Mild of manner and with a pleasing countenance, he garnered respect from all. Later in the day, the Captain once again engaged Luis.

"Armador, have I heard truth that you served as an alférez on the ill-fated Atocha?"

"Yes, Captain."

"I knew Captain Nodal, a grand man of the sea. I believeI have my old alférez sash stowed in my cabin. Would you like it to affix to your attire?"

Luis imaged it across his chest, the bright red across his white shirt.

"Very much, sir."

"Captain, I understand we'll make a stop at Somers Isles. How do we achieve it?"

"Well, Alférez, after encountering the ocean current by sailing compass east, we turn and set sail north to around latitude 32 degrees. Then east to the Isles. We won't seek port since it's British, but will stand off. Hartford will need to paddle in, perhaps in your dugout, if you please."

"Of course, sir. My honor to grant it."

"Upon leaving, we turn compass north again, make way to between latitudes 38-39 degrees, then turn east toward the Azores and home. If all goes well, we'll arrive at Cádiz in about six weeks. Of course, the handling of this is left to my Pilot."

"Pirates, sir?"

"You know our enemies are the Dutch, English and French. But we have no treasures aboard, at least none declared. I don't look for any encounters from their corsairs, unless they purely want our ship. Now the Turks off Africa contend another matter. They will pursue just to acquire slaves or for ransom. But man for man, we can hold our own against one of their ships. At any rate, we don't want to become slaves in Morocco, now do we? So we must stay on watch and rely on our speed," he said, glancing down at Luis' sword.

"Captain, I trust I may be of service if needed."

"By the way, we have one Portuguese below that came aboard in Cuba. He seldom comes on deck, which breeds unhealthiness. I'm told he sustains shame of facial pockmarks from smallpox, which he contracted somewhere in Florida. I would think he'd be happy to be alive. Perhaps you can look in on him."

Luis moved down the hatchway and came to a room almost devoid of light. Several sailors lay in various stages of slumber in the shadows, awaiting their time of duty.

"I seek a gentlemen that gained passage at Habana," he said, gazing about.

Raising up slightly from his bunk, a seaman pointed to a man seated on the floor in a corner. Luis walked in that direction, stumbling in the dim light.

"I say, señor, I have just come aboard also as a passenger. To what port, or inland town do you travel?" Luis spoke in earnest, trying to arrest the man's dark feelings.

"My destination matters not, as the reception I receive will come of a vile nature, of that I have certainty. You best leave me." He spoke in a low, monotone voice.

"It would please me to make your acquaintance. My name is Luis Armador."

"Armador! Midst all the troubles I have encountered, never did I think to see you again!"

"Who are you?" Luis could only see his form outlined, but he detected a familiar voice.

The stranger emerged into the low light, tears trickling down his cheeks.

"Pedro Martins, your fellow escapee from the Calusa at Calos."

Luis felt blood draining from his face as he beheld Pedro's appearance. Except for the beard, he saw a once-smooth face now punctuated with pockmarks.

Grotesque, thought Luis.

"What…happened…to you…?"

Awkwardly, he embraced Pedro, he too embarrassed to respond likewise.

"A two-year tale, Luis, and I'm certain you have one as well."

"Let's go up on deck and converse," said Luis.

"No. I can't," he said, somberly.

"Very well…here will do fine."

At Pedro's urging, Luis shared his endeavors of time lost between them, right up to the day's boarding. Pedro then recounted his story.

"When the Calusas took me from our campsite north of Tocobaga, I envisioned being sliced into pieces back at Calos. It didn't happen, as they preferred to mistreat me as a slave of the lowest order. I ran their gauntlet to prove my worth, slept on the ground for months, took some beatings and considered swallowing dirt. Something within made me want to live. Fate? I don't know. Then I took the pox. I suffered fever and awful sores, and others around me died of it. But, I recovered. Except when I see my reflection."

At this point, Pedro stopped to take a long swig from a bottle by his side. Luis wondered at the liquid and if Pedro indulged to excess.

"Afterwards, they considered me worthy, since I survived. But I was still a slave to a selected family. After a year there, I think, they sold me to another tribe in the Mártires, or Matecumbes, as they call the south Florida islands. The Tequesta were no better, and the mosquitoes worse. Almost another year passed until a Spanish fishing sloop came by from Habana, and I became trade for the Cubans' Indio captive and a few trinkets. A few trinkets! They took me back to Habana where I worked in the shipyards, saving enough for passage. I do not know what I will do in Lisbon, or Seville for that matter. I'm happy to see you, Luis."

At that, he lay down and fell asleep. Luis surmised it came from the effect of the bottle. He knew sorrow for him, as he did on the day they parted. He vowed to help him to find his joyful self again, noting Pedro's still robust appearance and decent attire. For that he became thankful. Though truly guiltless, Luis still garnered a tinge of remorse for Pedro's re-capture by the Calusa. He realized that he'd run his own gauntlet of ordeals, in spite of his feelings of guilt.

***

"Land ahead !" came the cry from on high.

"It's the Somers Isles," Pilot Valdés said to Luis, as they conversed on deck. "Soon we'll heave to and furl the sails as we're within a few miles of Hamilton. It's an English port and the Captain doesn't want to stray too close. The seamen think the whole area is cursed, due to so many wrecks. You'll notice some wearing amulets now. Superstitious."

After the Captain summoned Englishman Hartford up top, Luis watched and waited. As he expected, a slight disagreement arose.

"Mr. Hartford, are you ready?" said the Captain.

"Ready for what?" He shot the Captain a black look.

"For your departure, señor, on Alférez Armador's canoa. Your starting from here will keep us out of your countrymen's hair but give you a reasonable paddle. Seek the town of Hamilton at the island in view."

"I stand grateful for the voyage, Captain, but not for the task now presented to me," spoke Hartford.

"You can do it, William. The sun is shining, the water is calm, and the canoa is stable. It's your opportunity," offered Luis.

Seamen let the dugout down into the water, and Hartford descended the ladder with bag in tow. His nimble moves relieved Luis, who had envisioned Hartford tumbling headfirst into the sea.

"Vaya con Dios, friend," said Luis.

Speechless now, he turned and waved. He looked every bit a man tasked with circumnavigating the globe but uncertain of the direction. With mixed feelings, Luis watched until he became a mere speck in sight.

"Perhaps his countenance will settle down when among his fellow Brits," said Captain Sandovar, with a large grin.

"Unfurl sails, head compass due north," ordered the Captain, turning to the Pilot. "Let me know when we have an astrolabe reading close to latitude 38°. Then we can prepare to sail east to the Azores."

It's all pleasant, no tempest afoot, Luis considered. *Will we enjoy such for the remainder?*

***

"Mi amigo, thank you for pulling me out of my doldrums," said Pedro, nodding to Luis. "Three weeks now of recall and laughter worked as a tonic, which I needed."

"I may have succeeded too far," said Luis. "You win two of every three card games we deal. I will not wager my pesos with you." He smiled.

A few days in Angra of the Azores and Captain and crew readied to complete their journey to Spain. Luis, meanwhile, enjoyed engaging conversations with Pilot Valdés.

"It will take us about three more weeks to spy Spain's coast," Valdés said. "Then we will sail southeast toward Cádiz."

"Smooth?" asked Luis.

"Very smooth. The only danger being English corsairs or the African Turk corsos. This is the time of year when the latter roam the Mediterranean and the Atlantic coast from Africa."

Luis had heard this before, but he found confidence in the Captain and Valdés. The Pilot stood shorter than the typical Spaniard but powerfully built and hearty. He kept an ever-present gleam in his eye, reflecting his spirit of adventure and anticipation of the next day's activities.

"Have you ever encountered them?" Luis inquired.

"No, and I hope to avoid them always. I've always been told never to let the Turks take you. The worst is to become a galley slave oarsman and the easiest a household servant in Morocco. If your family maintains wealth, they love ransoms. Otherwise, you're a slave for life."

"A little frightening," voiced Luis.

"A lot, really. The Moriscos, whom Spain drove out 100 years ago, have taught their offspring to hate the Spaniards. To them it is an Islamic holy war against Catholics. The corso Muslims always seek revenge."

As he talked, Luis pictured tall, bearded, fierce soldiers that wore turbans and long flowing robes. He wondered of his skills against their scimitars.

"We do fight them if accosted, correct?"

"Yes, unless their numbers far exceed ours. You may want to join with our soldiers as our Captain drills them before the last week of sail. He always anticipates, even if an engagement doesn't happen."

***

"A toast, your mercies, to Captain Sandovar and His Highness Felipe IV," said Pilot Valdés, raising his voice and his glass.

Luis joined the Pilot and Boatswain with the Captain in his cabin for a celebratory meal anticipating one week's sail to Spain remaining.

"Thank you, gentlemen," said the Captain. "Winds and fates have been exemplary for us on this trip. And the pleasure increased with Alférez Armador aboard. We wish for him a good fortune after his four years afar, now returning in midsummer to our fair land. I trust he finds it as pleasing as when he left."

Luis' mood elevated, as though he sat in his parents' home, feasting from his madre's kitchen. Anticipation filled him as he envisioned scenes of childhood, filled with joy. The Captain interrupted Luis' fancies with a final comment of the evening. His face took on a grave look.

"This next week, of course, is the time we must be most on our guard. Corsairs have been known to attack within sight of the coast. The odds lay against, but we'll be prepared."

With that he made the final evening toast to good health and final sail.

Like a boy about to receive his first horse, my heart is gladdened.

Luis elation from the Captain's supper carried over to the next morn, so he strode onto the top deck at early light. He wanted to catch sight of the impending coast in the distance. Various shades of dawn lit the horizon as he squinted to see a lengthening speck far to the east. Having never seen Portugal's shore, he decided it came close enough to Spain's to attest arrival. The morning sun began to creep above the ever-growing coastline, which he yearned to reach out and touch. *As a man reaching for the moon, if that possible,* he mused. Unexpected warmth filled him, even in the still-lingering cool air.

"Happy, Luis?" said Pedro, who slipped up on deck.

"Ahh, Pedro, you grasp it, too?"

"Yes. My homeland in view. I could almost jump in and swim to it. But it will be far more pleasant to hire a smallboat once we make Cádiz. Unless you would like to escort me upriver to Seville and so employ me." He then cast upon Luis the biggest smile of the journey.

Luis, stunned, gazed at Pedro as if he'd just delivered a revelation.

"Amigo, my family would be honored. You could even take a room at our home for a time."

"Good," said Pedro. "Maybe there is a señorita there that likes pockmarks."

Both laughed heartily, especially Luis, seeing the joviality in his once-beleaguered friend.

Luis continued to gaze at the shoreline horizon, now well in sight. He could not hold back his glee.

"When we arrive at Cádiz, I'd like to think there will be trumpets blaring, cannons firing, flags unfurled everywhere and throngs of people to greet us. And when we step ashore, the Alcalde Mayor will give a welcoming speech."

Facing Pedro, he held both arms aloft, palms up, toward land, as if to indicate it all waited for them.

Pedro waited a few moments before speaking.

"Would you like two señoritas to take you by the arms and lead you away?"

Luis smiled, relishing Pedro's jest.

The Pilot and Captain strolled over, both with spyglasses.

"We're nearing Cabo San Vicente," said the Captain.

"The one they call the Cape of Surprises," said Pilot Valdés, turning to Luis. "Corsairs love to hide around the corners. See the high, rocky cliffs? The ancient Romans thought the sun set here, hissing into the ocean. Here lay the edge of their world."

Luis and Pedro watched as their spyglasses scanned the horizon in full circle. Captain Sandovar took his down and began muttering, his brow furrowing.

"What do you make of it, Valdés?"

"I make three ships, could be galleys, and they're flying flags with the half-circled indentations on the edges."

"Portuguese?"

"It would seem so, but why are they anchored and unfurled near the Cabo, instead of in port?"

Though nothing else of note could be seen for miles, Pilot Valdés kept the telescope to his eye.

"Sir, they're pulling anchor, but not unfurling the sails. It looks to be three galleys rowing our way."

"Still think they're Portuguese?"

The conversation made Luis and Pedro uneasy. They began to wonder if a fight loomed.

"Sir, they're within a glass and closing. They move fast. It may be three Sallee Rovers."

The apprehension in Valdés' voice became noticeable to Luis. He searched the Captain's face for an answer. Meanwhile, the Captain called for his Sergeant.

"Sergeant Pardo, I imagine each galley has 100 swordsmen, while we have 70 men, only half being soldiers. That's fighting odds of ten to one. We don't stand a chance, even using the cannons, and we can't outrun them."

"Beg pardon sir, they took my brother three years ago, and I fear he's gone for life. I say we fight! We cannot allow these infidels to rule the seas. We have cannons, arms, swords and capable troop."

"We'd never live through it," said the Captain. "Alive, we stand a chance of being ransomed."

Luis saw the fire in the Sergeant's eyes and his desire to lay on. Now realizing his own homecoming was threatened, the thought took hold of wanting to fight also. He knew that all Spanish feared the Turks from the African coast, but the ones they feared most came from Sallee and Rabat off northwest Africa. These lay in wait off Spanish and Portuguese shores and moved in fast by oars. They often could capture with no fight, relying on the terror they presented.

With reluctance, Captain Sandovar gave the order to strike the sails and for the soldiers to lay down their arms. As they approached the wallowing

frigate, the Turks lowered their Portuguese flags and raised the familiar
banners of crescents. Grappling hooks went out from the galleys as they
pulled alongside. Luis could see the Captain made a good decision
as the Spaniards gaped at their captors. Turbaned soldiers covered the
galley's decks and riggings. Large, curving scimitars in hand and colorful
robes on their shoulders added to their awesome appearance. On each
ship, a Turk sat high atop a platform, reading aloud.

"It's from the Koran," said Pedro, "their holy book and fighting
inspiration all in one."

The most menacing-looking rogues I have ever witnessed, thought Luis. *Even the
Calusa would recoil in fright. Is this the sea monster in my dream at San Agustín?*

They boarded the boat in droves and herded all the Spanish into the
middle of the deck. With Arabic language unintelligible, by example they
ordered their captors to remove everything but their breeches. Except for
coins, which were collected, everything personal went over the side, causing
Luis distress to see his sword go. He kept silent. A Turk discovered the
one remaining real de a ocho from the Atocha, strapped to Luis' waist.
With much laughter and smirking, he poked a hole in the middle with a
spike and threw it back to him. His fellow countrymen roared. Taking a
deep breath, Luis picked it up, tied a loop cord through it and placed it
around his neck. With that, the Turk sneered.

Now considered as subhumans headed for various types of slavery, the
captives were split amongst the three galleys, one third to each. There they
placed them in middle decks under guard. In the transition, Luis and Pedro
became separated again. On his new ship, he caught glimpses of the galley
slaves, numbering perhaps 200. They took no notice when he passed,
always fearful of the lash. All vessels began moving again, with only Turks
commandeering the Spanish vessel.

***

"A day and a half now, and we have seen neither sunlight nor food and
only small amounts of water bestowed," said Pilot Valdés.

He sat perplexed, with head resting on the galley's inside wall. With eyes
closed, he posed a question.

"Why don't they feed us? Aren't we now valuable as slaves to be sold or
ransomed?"

"It's because they want to control you, and they believe that no
sustenance will make you weak and dependent. They also believe you will
be too depleted to try escape. After they kidnap more along the
Mediterranean coast of Spain, they will take us to Africa. There they will
feed us. But who knows what?"

Luis and Pilot Valdés sat attentive, listening to the captive stranger converse. He could speak their tongue but with an odd accent, and he hovered a good foot over the soldiers. Blonde, blue eyes, with muscular features and a commanding presence, he impressed Luis as a warrior with a proud background, yet out of place.

"Señor, who are you?" asked Luis.

"I am Groz Guotman, from the island of Malta and the Knights of Malta."

"You're a Christian corsair, a fighting knight!" said Valdés, noting a member of the well-known order.

"Yes."

For a few moments the two Spaniards sat stupefied, puzzled that a fighter as this could be captured. Pushing their curiosity as well as forgetting their hunger, they fired questions.

"You know how quickly they took us, but how did they take you?" asked Valdés.

"Last week my ship was out cruising, seeking to encounter the Barbary corsos. We found them, we found these three vessels. We exchanged cannon fire and then engaged in deck fighting. We had the upper hand for a time, but as you've seen, there are many of them. Much slaughter took place on both sides, but afterwards, quite a few of our knights were transferred on a galley to *Sallee. I don't know what they plan for me."

"Have you considered escape?" asked Luis.

Valdés peered at him as at a lunatic.

Nodding to Luis' question, Groz answered.

"Yes, each day, but they keep us restricted and guarded. I'm looking for an opportunity."

"I know my knowledge is restricted to maps, charts and channels," said Valdés, "but even I see that escape here ranks with trying to survive 200 lashes." He shook his head, bearing an incredulous look.

The two soldiers ignored him.

"If I but had my sword," said Luis.

"I don't think confronting them will work," said Groz. "In this case, one must rely on stealth."

"I agree, of course," replied Luis.

The men concluded their conversation and lay on the rough deck inside, hoping to drift off to sleep. They lay packed as paving stones, amid constant murmurings, and suffered the air floating thick and humid. Luis did his best to sleep, with thoughts and half-dreams of escape from the

* Barbary pirates haven , NW Africa

Calusas and the Turks.

He awoke the next morning before most of his fellow captives, hunger gnawing his stomach. Sitting up, his eyes focused on light streaming in from the locked, barred door. Stiff from cramps, he rose and eased in the light's direction, careful not to step on anyone. Peering through the bars, he could see two guards down the hall playing cards. On a plate by the door was a half-loaf of bread. Driven by abject hunger and without thinking, he reached through and took it, then savored each mouthful. It didn't take him long. Satisfied, he returned to his pallet to resume sleeping. As he dozed off, he thought, *they will never know...*

Soon thereafter, someone shouting in the indistinguishable language awoke him. Realizing the Turks roared in Arabic, he sat up.

      *Barbary pirates' haven, NW coast of Africa.

Khubz! Tassaraqa! Khubz!

Khubz! Tassaraqa! Khubz!

Luis, like the others, did not understand.

The captives, all now awake, talked in soft tones.

From back in the crowd, a lone captive voiced a translation.

"They're saying that one of us stole their bread!"

Jalqkullu!

Jalqkullu!

The Spaniard that understood again spoke his interpretation.

"I think they plan to apply the lash to all of us, or at least till the one that stole it confesses!"

For Bread? Over a half-loaf of bread? Luis sat bewildered.

He knew they had strict Islamic codes-no spirits, no uncovered women's heads in public, things of that nature.

But bread?"

"What did you expect for not feeding us!?"

It was Sergeant Pardo who strode right up to the Turks, venting some long-term anger. A blow to the head from the side of a scimitar sent him tumbling.

Quite a firebrand, thought Luis.

At that point, the Turks, angered now even further, selected five men that they would take up deck for whippings. Luis wondered if they would survive. From the back of the room someone shouted.

"Turn yourself in, whoever you are, or we'll all feel the lash!"

Luis shivered. He knew he'd acted impulsively, and now many would suffer. He decided not to let that happen. As the Turks began leading the men out, Luis yelled with raised hands.

"I did it! I took it! No one else!" He swallowed hard upon releasing the words and pointing to himself.

The two Turks grabbed him by the arms and began pushing and shoving him up the stairs. He walked through a crowd of more Turks now gathered, all taunting in their tongue. Cringing, he wondered if his fate would be the lash, beheading, or some other brutal punishment. In silence, he began to pray.

The actions on deck proceeded as if patterned, as they first bound him, then pushed him to the floor. Nearby, they lit a fire under a cauldron. When it heated up, someone began to stir inside it.

Boiling me in oil, or tar, or perhaps something else?

Then, remembering the amputation tarpot on the Atocha, Luis winced. When the corsos became satisfied that the substance was ready, they brought all prisoners on deck to witness.

It's like the San Agustín gallows.

He determined in his mind to seek a sense of peace within, for he owned no control over what came next. They unbound him, and three large Turks walked him to a huge block of wood that bore pits and scars. His fellow Spaniards stood quiet, horror-stricken.

Holding Luis tightly, they encircled a leather strap around his left wrist and placed it on the block. Their closeness made Luis aware of a reeking odor, repugnant, as from some distasteful Turkish spice. The kind he could never forget. Two held Luis from behind, one held the strap extension, and another stepped forward carrying a large scimitar. Before Luis could comprehend what was coming, the Turk raised it above his head. With a loud grunt he brought it down.

Chomp!

The sound of steel on wood echoed around the ship as his hand was cleanly severed at the wrist. At first he felt no pain. Looking at the deck he could see the now-severed hand, fingers rolled up as holding a ball. Shock hit him and blood began to ooze from his arm, followed by excruciating pain.

Owwwgghh!

His scream resounded far enough to reach the other two galleys. The Turks remained indifferent, but it sent panic into the hearts of the Spaniards. The three soldiers next moved him to the boiling cauldron and held his sheared stump just above it. Another swabbed the wound with black tar, cauterizing it. The flesh around it seared and hissed, but Luis already pained so much it didn't matter.

"My hand…my hand…"

He watched helplessly as someone picked it up and tossed it overboard, into the same ocean that now held his sword. All now released Luis, precipitating for him an odd sense of falling, as if the deck rose to meet him. From dizziness and pain, hitting the deck, he fainted. Shaken, the still-hungry captives now were directed back to the galley's prison room. The Barbary corsos succeeding in conveying their message.

***

Dusk, and Luis gained an awareness of softening light and…. *pain, or is it a dream?* Then he remembered. *Left hand gone…forever…but still, the right remains… along with my life… thankful for that.*

The hurt moved his eyes down to the stump, covered with tar, now hardened.

My hand feeds the fish. How strange.

Lying on the deck, he dared not move. He must think. His immediate yearning was to be on shore, he hoped Spain or Portugal's. From the corner of his eye he could see evening lights begin to flicker from a coastal town to the east. Much to his amazement, they left him unbound.

If I can slip into the water, can I swim to the beach? Several miles? Only one hand?

He could feel himself being drawn to the town lights as an insect to a lamp. He became fixated. That became his goal, and his need for freedom consumed him. But unlike when stealing the bread, he knew to be cautious and clear-headed.

Dark came upon the boat, and lanterns lit at both ends. Though in pain, he knew it was time and slowly edged towards the railing. The rope ladder hung from it about fifteen feet distant. Inch by inch, he moved, making no sound. The moon began its rise but did not yet flood the water. Though the guards rested fore and aft, Luis stopped, imagining a shadowy form moving nearby. Perhaps an illusion, but he froze, eyes closed.

Knowing that being caught in the act of escaping could cost him his other hand, he waited. No weapon, only wits, seizing an opportunity. He must move. Being a galley slave would be worse than a Calusa slave. Especially with only one hand, the other limb strapped to an oar. Looking around, he eased to the railing, opened the gate and grabbed hold of the rope ladder.

Luis pushed his body in spite of dark water looming, stomach drawn, weak, his stump throbbing, his mind dazed. With one last glance, he eased over the rail and descended. Though difficult with only a partial limb, he went down the ladder and into the water, making no sound. Casting a look to the shore lights, he submerged and swam underwater as long as possible. After a minute, he rose up, breathed, and went under again. On each emergence, he eyed the lights for direction.

Soon the ecstasy of escaping flooded him, and he again recalled feelings from the past. It helped to stymie his pain. At what he perceived a safe distance, he began to swim on the surface, a sideways backstroke being easier with only one hand. The moon began to reflect with brightness on the water as he swam. No sound came from ship or shore, the only noise being Luis' movements. Turning to look shoreward, he imagined it still only about the same distance as when he started, so he bolstered his flight by thinking of past successes.

He even devised a method to help him focus and rest. Luis paddled for twenty-five strokes and then lay on his back, resting. But the weariness of the last two days showed on him. At times he just wanted to stop and even sink, but he knew he would not.

Somewhere in the blackness, to the west, he could see a form protruding above the water. Past experience taught him that the mind plays tricks in challenging circumstances. It looked like a large head, or bird, moving across the water. Then it stopped.

"Luis, Luis."

"What?"

"It is Groz Guotman, from the ship. I've been following you. Afraid to speak till we're far from the galley."

"What, how…?" said Luis, thinking his mind created a false notion.

"From my hiding place on deck, I watched you escape. After your punishment, they took the captives back downstairs. A brief opportunity arose in the midst, and I took advantage by hiding under a large sailcloth. I slipped over the side following you, as nothing prompts me to become a galley slave."

"Nor I," said Luis, "but I'm tiring, and I may need your help soon."

"We will make it. You are strong Luis, and I will help."

The men resumed swimming, Luis having to stop for brief periods. He began to hear breakers across the water though they still needed to cover a third of the distance. The lights shone closer now.

"Groz, I…it's becoming…" Luis grappled with the words. He coughed several times after inhaling water.

Groz went behind Luis' head and wrapped a long arm around his chest from the back, treading to get into position. He then swam, pulling him along. To Luis, Groz did it with little effort.

"Th-thank you," whispered Luis.

It took a total of several hours for them to reach shallow water, light waves breaking around them. Luis required help onto shore, but they made it. Without speaking, they headed for the closest dense growth and collapsed.

***

Luis awoke in the early morning cool and dark, hearing the surf above the crickets' hum. His breeches stuck to his skin, still wet from the night's swim, and he yearned for fresh water. But he reveled that he must be in Spain, for no other reason than that he lay on solid ground. A wondrous feeling arose as he reclaimed his homeland, never to leave again. He continued lying down, shivering and waiting for dawn. The pain in his left arm reminded him of the lost hand.

When will it cease?

Dawn came, and he stood to look around. Recalling his entry into Florida, he stooped to sip dew from bush leaves. Walking down to the beach gave him a view of high cliffs to the west and a hillside rising to his rear behind the beach. He realized with sadness the fact that he again escaped without Pedro. Not a planned situation, but still his conscience was pricked. Spying a stooped, aged man fishing alone on the beach, he went straightforward to him.

"Hola, señor."

Turning to Luis, he gauged him up and down, then replied.

"Young man, looks like you've met with misfortune."

"Escaped from a Turk's galley after they took my hand. It's possible they'll be sending longboats anytime. You may want to hurry inland."

"Ahh, the Moors. A savage, barbaric people. But not to worry, they only want young, healthy Spaniards, like you. In fear, many have abandoned their homes on this coast and moved. But I stay."

He gave Luis another once-over, as if thinking that this man really looked as a vagrant.

Where am I?" said Luis.

"You're at Barbate, a small fishing village on the coast of Spain."

"I saw the lights last night." Luis paused, and then asked humbly, "would you have some bread and fresh water?"

The fisherman rummaged in his bag and handed Luis a biscuit and a bottle of water, both of which he consumed.

"Would you have some for me too?"

Groz, now awake, had wandered down to the beach. The old man accommodated him as well, so the men expressed their thanks with fervor.

"How far to Cádiz?" asked Groz.

"About 12 leagues, or 40 miles, either by boat or wagon road."

"Northwest?" asked Luis as he pointed to the right while facing the water.

The fisherman nodded.

"We won't go by boat today," said Groz.

"Then you can take the path behind us from the beach up to the road. See the cliffs? The old Roman road winds along it toward Cabo Trafalgar. Quite a view, from which you might see the Moors' galleys. Maybe you can hail a wagon going northwest and perhaps you can stop at a farmhouse for victuals. Be mindful of the Rom."

The men thanked him again and walked the hillside path up to the road. Steep at times, the climb made more severe from their swim and lack of food. But they progressed, and the sun came up and warmed the day. The path ended in a wagon road, and they turned northwest, walking alternately through woods and fields. Soon, a small mule-drawn wagon approached from the rear, driven by another elderly man.

"Buenos dias, young men. I am a poor farmer returning from Barbate, but you are welcome to ride along."

Luis and Groz thanked him and jumped on the back. A few raw vegetables littered the wagon, left from his market sales in town. After hearing of their escape, he took pity. At his home, his wife fed them, and he supplied a few old clothes of various sizes. That night they slept in his small barn, to the men a *castle*.

"Groz, I'm pleased beyond measure to return to Spain, anywhere in Spain," he spoke, with a fatigued but contented look. "I traded my hand for freedom. Freedom from a life as a galley slave."

"A fair trade, Luis?"

"Yes. The inept act of stealing the bread and the ensuing punishment gave me the opportunity I needed. I am grateful, though it still aches."

He glanced at his pitiable tarred stump and patted it with affection.

The next day found them again headed northwest on the dirt road. They faced heavy wind along the cliff's promontory, but now well-clothed and toting a bundle of food, they made their way. Over the next few days, they passed farmlands and scattered houses. Some vacated, just as the old fisherman told them. One night, they entered an unlocked abandoned home and slept on the floor. They passed through the villages of Caños de Meca and Conil la Frontera, keeping to the coast. It took three days trekking to reach the marshes near Chiclana de la Frontera, east of Cádiz. They hailed wagons for rides and area farmers gave of their food and drink.

***

"Where is your homeland, and where are you going?"

Luis was inquisitive of the tall knight that saved his life. He saw him as aristocratic and educated but unassuming.

"I don't really like to talk of myself," said Groz.

"I know, but I'd like to know more of my lifesaver."

"I come from Germany, where my father owns many lands, lives as a noble and believes in service to the church. Along with many other young men of Europe, I went to the island of Malta, where I joined the 500 year-old Order. Support comes from many wealthy people across Europe in order to defend the island from the Turks and to fight the enemies of the church. I will return there and again don the red surcoat with the white cross. I will take up my sword and resume my duties as a soldier on land and sea. My heart lies there, and I hope to sail on a vessel from Cádiz."

The answer satisfied Luis, but he noted that Groz made no similar inquiry, accepting Luis as he was.

***

Walking along, they entered a copse of trees through which the road passed. Interspersed about were covered wagons, with horses hobbled and groups of people cooking over huge cauldrons. Not black, but dark skin, along with fine facial features, described them. The women dressed in bright colors and both men and women wore earrings.

Luis once heard of the colorful nomadic people, disdained by many in Spain.

"Is it the Rom?"

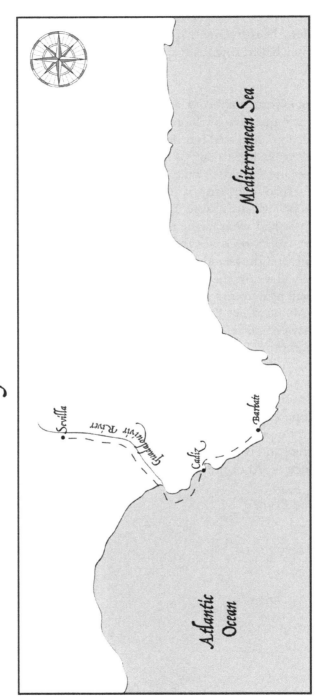

Spain Coast

Mediterranean Sea

Atlantic Ocean

Sevilla

Guadalquivir River

Cadiz

Barbatt

19
The Rom

1626

I will adorn my knighthood with true charity,
the mother and solid foundation of all virtues.
Knights of Malta

COAST OF SOUTHERN SPAIN

Who?" said Groz.

"The Rom, the *Romani, the dark-skinned people that travel from place to place."

"The ones that beg and steal and live heathen lives?" asked Groz.

I've heard that. But from here they look like harmless families, cooking a meal."

"Not that we have anything for them to take, but, I don't trust them," replied Groz.

"At any rate, Groz, my belly aches, and my nostrils smell something good that's cooking. Let's walk over."

Luis motioned for Groz to go with him, knowing that his size and bearing would help deter inhospitable behavior.

One Rom in particular peered at them with dark eyes. He bore no weapon, just a look of wariness. A small fishing cap barely covered his hair, which showed no sprinkle of gray, contrary to his middle-aged bearing. Wearing an oversized black, long sleeved shirt and tan breeches, he wore high-top leather boots. Luis approached him.

"Hola. I am Luis and my friend is Groz. Might you spare a meal for two refugees just escaped from a Turkish corso galley near Barbate?"

The man continued to stare at them, unmoving. But soon he broke into a wide smile and beckoned them to come.

"Welcome, amigos, you don't appear as the constabulary to me. Let us prepare you a plate."

"Thank you," said Luis, while trying to gauge the man's sensibilities. "Do you fear the authorities?"

"Yes, oh yes. Or they fear us. You've stumbled onto the Rom, the *proud outcasts.* They think we follow the devil and have laws restricting us, which

* gypsies

they may or may not enforce. But sometimes…," his words trailed off as he waved his hand, as if conveying disgust.

The soldiers sat and ate with Luis conversing. Groz relished the meal, but remained leery. Diego González, their host, led a group of ten wagons and fifty people, who enjoyed roaming the Andalucía region.

"If we camp too long in one area, they often chase us away," he said. "They don't want us near the cities, but we mean no harm, we are all families. At times, we have been injured."

He bid the soldiers to stay one night, to rest and fortify for the remainder of their journey. They accepted, somewhat out of pure curiosity.

"Does it hurt?" asked González, pointing to Luis' left arm but without asking how it happened.

"Yes, off and on."

"We have a healing ritual which can be performed. It may aid you."

"We have no pesos," said Luis. "Once we arrive at our destinations, our people will see to us."

"Ah, that is not a problem," he said, motioning to an older lady wearing a bright orange and red dress.

Not wanting to offend, Luis settled down on a stool while she pored over his arm. She sprinkled on an unknown substance and voiced incantations with eyes closed. Luis heard it as gibberish. *It's like the Indios.*

That evening, amidst torches, the men and women gathered to dance, clap and sing. Luis and Groz became enraptured by the colorful presentation.

"It's *our* dance," said González. "Priests that sometimes visit us do not like it, nor do they like some of our other activities."

"What other activities?" Luis asked.

He turned to Luis, a serious look covering his face, as if uncertain whether to answer.

"Palm readings, the use of tarot cards… curses."

For certain, those don't fall within Catholic teachings, considered Luis.

"But we must have a means to survive. Me, I'm just a simple horse trader." He pointed to a group of tethered horses to the rear of his wagon. "And we just want to enjoy life."

Breaking into another big smile, he gave Luis a backslap, as if to say-*come join us.*

The evening air cooled down, and though no rain clouds made an appearance, the hosts placed pallets under the wagons for the soldiers' sleeping. Groz did agree the Rom seemed harmless and in fact accommodating. But he wanted to leave in the morning.

Luis could see the flickering campfires as he dozed. In his mind he pictured home... *Would Mamaceita approve of...?"* he thought as he dozed off.

***

Thump!

A loud crashing noise, followed by a scream from the wagon, pierced the morning.

Luis awoke with a start at first light. Jumping up, he found it difficult to grasp the scene. The wagon above him had been tipped over by a horse and rider pulling a long rope. Amid shouting and gunfire from pistols shot skyward, the other wagons also faced toppling. The Rom now spilled out in various stages of confusion and terror, with women wailing and babies crying.

Before Luis could even think clearly, he saw Groz spring into action. Leaping onto a horse and pummeling the rider off, he moved to another and another with lightning speed. The attackers howled, falling one after another. Luis likened it to watching a mountain lion springing from one prey to another. He only assisted once, slamming into a would-be assailant, about to attack Groz from behind. He grasped a vague sense in the fray that some of the marauders wore uniforms.

The constabularies?

The Rom scattered in all directions, running, falling, the men yelling orders. The now-beaten attackers, eight in all, rose from the ground, dizzy and bruised, some bloodied. They moved all about, seeking their mounts. The sound of the horses' hoofbeats signaled their departures. Unintelligible oaths were flung at them by the Rom men, curses hurled by the women.

Luis surveyed the scene as the men righted the wagons and calmed their families. Surrounded by the disarray, he and Groz did their best to help.

"Groz , never have I seen a soldier of your skill. You move fast, and only once did you need my help."

"I do not like to see families treated so," said Groz. "The attackers think women and children matter not. I could have killed them, but instead I trust they've learned a lesson."

What kind of fighter would he be with a weapon in his hands? To be a Knight is to be a master at combat.

Diego and the Rom conveyed much appreciation to Groz. They promised him everything but the papacy if he would join them. He politely declined, telling them that he must return to Malta.

"You saved our possessions from complete destruction," said González. "But we must now pack and leave, as they could return with more men. We adapt, and we will survive. We thank you."

He embraced both Groz and Luis as a crowd hovered around them. As they left the departing wagons, Luis wondered of their fate.

Can a people survive if often threatened and sometimes beaten? Will their traditions continue? Will they become true Catholics? As usual, too many questions, too few answers.

"Groz, González told of two large streams flowing northwest of here that we must cross before reaching the town of The Islas, which is southeast of Cádiz."

"Did he have suggestions?"

"No. He only bade me good luck along with this pack of food and water. Ah, he did say there may be ferries, but they often require a fee."

"We may have to swim," said Groz.

"That we might."

They walked on the rest of the day and for sometime after sunset. The road stayed flat and sandy with crops sprouting here and there alongside. Soon the firm, off-road soil gave way to lowlands with marshes in spots. They spent the night in a grove of trees adjacent to a large marshy area. Their lack of sleep that evening attested to the low area, as small bugs descended at nightfall like buzzards devouring a carcass.

"Garfish oil, charred wood, or Florida bush leaves smeared on. Tonight I would give a real de a ocho for some bug deterrent," said Luis, slapping his neck.

"What of the one corded around your neck?" asked Groz, responding in the darkness.

"That is my only memento of the New World. I must keep it. Besides, it contains a hole in it," he chuckled. He handled it for a few moments, as if a charm of substance.

The next morning came welcomed. The bugs didn't disappear, but their presence lessened. The swampy spots became more abundant, with grassy beds growing along the roads and around islets in the water.

"If the constabularies came for us now, we would have to take to the marsh," said Groz.

"Join the lagartos," said Luis, smiling in his companion's direction.

"Look ahead, Luis, a big river."

As they approached, a ferryman started to row two patrons across. The soldiers implored him to return for them, which he did.

"Two maravedis each," he said, holding out his hand.

"We have just escaped a Turkish galley off Barbate. We have no money."

Without speaking, the man returned to his rowboat and climbed aboard, much to Luis and Groz's despair.

Seeing their situation, one of the patrons, a kindhearted gentleman, consented to pay their fare. The ferryman motioned them aboard.

"You are fortunate, señors, the Río Zurraque would require quite a swim."

Luis experienced a measure of displeasure with the ferryman, but let it pass.

I suppose everyone has to make his living.

At the far shore, the gentlemen's small carriage and driver waited for them. At parting, Luis and Groz made their thanks known. Their walking resumed, alongside the adjacent marshes. By sunset, they arrived at the next river, but no ferry, and no people.

"With good fortune, we'll see a ferryman here tomorrow, from the other side," said Groz.

"But will we have a sponsor, like today?" Luis replied. "At any rate, once across we can enter The Islas town and then Cádiz. Home awaits!" he shouted and threw up his arms in exultation.

At dawn a rowboat arrived from the distant shore, which Luis estimated as being 1000 yards away.

"Good morning, señors, may I row you across?" The ferryman looked poor and ragged, as one who had little means of support. They gathered the food pack and walked toward the boat.

Our only choice, thought Luis.

"Five maravedis each, if you please," he said, flashing a hungry smile with outstretched hand. "The Caño de Sancti Petri awaits our oars."

Luis and Groz stopped.

"We have no funds. The Turks took them before we escaped their ship off Barbate. Can you help us?" asked Luis.

The ferryman's smile changed to a face of dejection, followed by a frown.

"I must make a living, señors. Do you take me for a saint?"

As if fearing being overtaken, he straightway returned to his boat and rowed away, staring at them.

"Does this area have no pity, no care, no concern?" asked Groz.

"Perhaps another will arrive soon."

"I fear they're all as one, no difference," said Groz, "we may as well swim."

Sitting to contemplate, they finished the last of their food. They then stood and surveyed the river, wide and deep, even at bankside where they waded.

"The current is slow, but it will take us downstream some in the process," said Luis."We'd best swim on a diagonal to upstream so to arrive at the ferry landing."

"Several hours from the Turks' ship to the shore, we can do this in well under an hour," said Groz. "We are rested and better fed this time. Because of your stump, Luis, start ahead of me. I will enter after you swim out a good stone's throw. Then I can come to your help if needed."

"Gracias, knight sir." A broad smile creased his face.

Luis eased into the silent green water, merging into the stream with little effort. Turning on his back, he stroked with his right hand and moved his left in unison.

Groz waited with patience and pored over the circumstances. Patience, as at Malta, laboring to complete his knight training and on the galley, waiting for an escape opportunity. Patience becomes a virtue when practiced, he'd been taught, as does action, when necessary. The Rom needed his action. Now Luis needed his patience. His German father would approve.

"I'm coming now," he shouted, after a while, uncertain if Luis could hear.

Wading into the tepid but smooth water, he began the familiar overhand stroke. Long arms and legs propelled him along with ease, though breakfast still lay heavy on his stomach.Luis gazed skyward and relished white clouds against a blue Spanish sky. He rekindled the feel of strength and confidence, as in other adventures that came to mind-floating on a tumultuous Gulf, paddling on La Florida's coast, paddling up the San Martín River, even struggling in the water off Barbate.

Each water-borne passage effected a *link* to the other, in one long journey. And he conquered all. Soon he would sail up the Guadalquivir, route of the final leg of his travels. But now he must focus on his stroke. His only sense of being came from his arm moving him along, as a paddle, or perhaps a fin.

After what he guessed at about an hour of swimming and floating, he arrived. Standing up in the shallows, he gingerly walked the sandy bottom, gained the bank, and turned to look. Groz pursued as a man wedded to his mission. Luis smiled, thankful to have chanced upon a knight. For a moment, he lost sight of Groz. Then he caught a glimpse of his head.

About 400 feet out, he'd quit swimming and looked to be foundering.

"Cramps, I have the cramps!" he yelled.

Luis called back. "Relax in the water, till they go away!"

"It hurts…I cannot swim!"

"Do you need help!?"

"Yes…," he shouted, sinking again.

Without considering the fact he only controlled one hand, Luis grabbed a stout limb lying on the bank and plunged back in. The limb he kept under his left arm as he stroked with haste, backwards, again relying on his right arm. Swimming along, his mind recalled *another time, another place, a boy sinking*. This time he would succeed.

"Luis, Luis…"

Groz thrashed about, in a panic.

"Relax, Groz, relax!"

He grabbed at Luis, who sank to avoid the grasp, which he knew could be fatal to both.

Luis swam around the flailing form, surfaced and brought the limb down hard on Groz's head, dazing him just enough. Tossing the wood, he placed his stump arm around Groz's neck and swam with his right.

"We'll make it, Groz, we'll make it."

Exerting with all of his might, he headed toward land, Groz's face up just enough to breathe. He moved two men, 400 pounds total, and reminded himself over and over- *you can do it, you can do it…*

A distance of ten feet of water remained, and Luis could stand. He paused to regain his spent energy. Groz tried to stand, still dazed.

"My stomach, it still aches."

"You're safe, Groz. Walk to the bank."

Both men climbed onto the sand and collapsed, neither speaking for several minutes. Soon, recouping his strength and his thoughts, Luis sat up. Emotions came as water from a broken dam.

"Luis, why are you crying? You just saved my life."

"A time long ago. I couldn't. But today I did. This was for you too, José."

"Who?"

"A boyhood friend, who drowned when we went swimming."

"He would be proud," said Groz.

"Now, can we walk? Maybe it will help my stomach."

As time passed, Groz expressed himself, humility surfacing.

"Thank you, Luis, you proved that a man with only one hand is still capable."

"But now, I'm concerned about finding passage to Malta."

"Don't worry. Any vessel sailing the Mediterranean would be honored to take a knight. Offer your services."

Soon they entered the outskirts of The Islas, the town through which they must pass to Cádiz.

"Wet lands all around it," said Groz.

They crossed a waterway at the ancient Zuazo Bridge, conversed with the town guards, then continued west. Proceeding through town, they located a single bridge crossing more water to a narrow strip of land leading to the port of Cádiz. The men walked the rest of the day and most of the next. They begged for food and drink as opportunities arose.

***

"Look, Luis, a spire in the distance."

"And city walls and large gates," said Luis, as memory and anticipation merged together in his mind.

The gate guards questioned them, but with their plight retold, the men could pass inside. The gatemaster gave his reasons.

"You see, señors, only nine months ago our city defended and succeeded against 100 ships of English Sir Edward Creel. So now we stay on high watch, by sea and land."

Luis and Groz acknowledged them with a salute of honor.

Gulls swerved and seabirds cried as if issuing the men a welcome as they entered the city on the narrow isthmus. Dotting the bay could be seen a forest of masts, signifying Cádiz as a major port of southern Spain. Each man set out to seek passage home, with plans to meet again in the afternoon. Inquiring around, Luis found a schooner sailing to Seville the following day. He approached the Captain.

"Sir, I am Alférez Armador, of the shipwrecked galleon Atocha, four years in returning to Spain. I also escaped the Turks, losing my hand to a scimitar. Can you grant passage to a soldier who has no funds?"

"If you can prove you sailed on the Atocha as a soldier, I will grant you a sail. Go to the local office of the Casa de Contratación, our House of Trade, and bring me proof of one of your port manifests. It may not yet be sent to Seville."

Hesitant to yet ask for sustenance, Luis went to inquire at the local administrative office.

"Señor, we have a muster log of the Atocha from La Habana in 1622," said the official.

Placing it upon his counter and scanning the pages, he soon closed it, looking up at Luis.

"I'm sorry, but there is no listing of your name."

Dejected, Luis left, not understanding. Then he realized there could be only one answer.

The Marquis' scribe in Habana. Denied his own commission, he did not like young officers, and he removed my name to try to prevent payment of wages. But I can't challenge a man at the bottom on the sea.

He returned and pled again with the Captain for a position to offset his fee. Having a stump helped, as the Captain granted nominal seaman's duty as consideration.

***

"Groz, this old port once again casts a spell on me. Many ships, narrow streets, squares and plazas. But this time I'm returning home, not leaving. I will miss you."

"And I you, Luis. I have found a vessel going to Malta and will sail two days hence. They have no need of a Knight of Malta," he confided, "but I will help with loading and unloading cargo. That will do for passage. Vaya con Dios, Luis, perhaps we will meet again. The men embraced and parted.

20
Seville Dreams

1626

*My judgement is now clear and
Unfettered and that dark cloud of
ignorance has disappeared, which
the continual reading of those
detestable books of knight-errantry
had cast over my understanding.*
Don Quixote
Cervantes

Cadíz

The solace of home called to Luis like a hundred lanterns glowing in the dark, as he prepared to close a large chapter of his young life and begin anew.

Daylight, and the schooner sailed from the bay of Cádiz to ascend 60 miles on the Guadalquivir. Crossing the bar, the ship moved upstream passing Sanlúcar on the right. The rising sun shone on its white houses, castle turrets and Custom House. Vessels lined its waterfront-frigates, caravels, galleons, schooners-as it rivaled Cádiz as a major port. Moving upriver, Luis saw familiar sights of pinewoods, sandy banks, groves and orchards. Soon he settled in at a desk in the Captain's cabin, content with scribe duties now assigned to him.

As a phantom itch came from the area of his former left hand, his good hand rubbed the mis-sized shirt's sleeve. So gratified to receive it a week earlier, he now anticipated embarrassment by wearing it on arrival home. Having left Seville impressively attired and now returning with nothing and only one good hand touched a slight cord of vanity.

Will I give rise to shame when they see me? I must prepare for the shock I will present. They will need time to adjust.

He wondered what he had gleaned from his four-year experience.

To be wary of youthful expectations? To never allow fear or anger to control me? That my thirst for adventure has been quenched? Likely all.

Before the ship arrived in Seville, the last evening aboard gave over to a sense of serenity for Luis. Eager to arrive, he slumbered early in the evening and dreamed deep, the remnants recalled as he slowly awoke.

I had walked up the steps to a home. Many steps, and they went higher and higher. A señora greeted me, but I could not see her face. She minded two handsome dogs, holding one in her arms and the other by a leash. I went properly dressed, happy, and carried a small replica of a galleon. I squinted at the sun's brightness, which lit up a side garden that contained many blooming plants, their fragrance stimulating. Next I…

"Luis, Luis, wake up! We're here."

The Boatswain called to him in his tiny cubicle next to the forecastle. But he lay awhile longer, letting the dream float in his consciousness, trying to sort it out. *A peaceful occurrence, no doubt.* His first familiar sight presented Toro del Oro, the gold tower, where the Casa de Contratación stored precious metals from the Indies. Soon the sun would light up its golden roof tiles, as a beacon to all arrivals.

Luis left the boat and walked the Arénal between the river and city walls, tension and exultation together rising. His destination became the family shipwright business. He took in all the familiar scenes and sounds - ships, seamen, vendor carts, slaves laboring, and longshoremen working. Arriving at his father's office, he stepped inside. A group of men, seated at a long table poring over ship plans, looked up as he approached. No one spoke. Each one stared, as if trying to solve a puzzle but with no directions.

Luis looked at each, as if trying to remember. He settled his focus on Antonio.

"Father, it is I, Luis."

"Luis who?"

"Luis Armador."

"He is dead."

Have I changed that much? Does he think I am an impersonator?

He placed his papers down, arose and walked toward Luis. His gaze wandered from head to toe and then back to the eyes. He focused hard.

"You look like my son. But he is dead. Four years now. I don't like frauds."

"It's an apparition!" yelled an employee.

"No! Apparitions don't speak!" called another.

Time seemed to stand still, as everyone gaped, without speaking.

"It is him," said a deep voice from the end of the table.

Luis glanced toward the granite figure of his grandfather, his abuelito. *He knows.*

"Only Luis Armador stands that way, walks that way, and talks that way," said his Grandfather Juan, rising to embrace Luis.

"How did you survive?" said Juan.

Luis turned back to face his Father Antonio.

"With much effort, much help and the blessings of Providence. It weaves a long tale. But your teachings helped me to survive many perils of the body and the mind."

His father stumbled forward and embraced him also.

"Welcome home, son."

One by one, all the men in the room responded likewise.

"I declare the rest of this day a holiday!" said Luis' father, experiencing excitement and bewilderment together. "We must take him home to see his mother and grandmother. We must feed him and then hear of his travels. Do you think the women will faint?" he said, with glee.

Luis' awareness of home multiplied as they began to walk. The life of a city reflects the variety of people, permanent and transient. From the time he left the Arénal, though the wall's portal and along the streets, something special reminded him he'd returned to Seville. He heard the endless chatter of foreign languages in this busy port, serving as a celebratory background to his homecoming. He began to shake with excitement as memories flooded his mind. But warm feelings also enveloped him when he thought of friends, and of course, Isabela. He thought of the shipwright business, which had nurtured his family for generations, and which could be in his future.

"How fares the business?" asked Luis, groping for news.
Antonio turned serious.

"Well enough, but not as when you left. Arana builds six galleons for the king by underbidding us a vast sum. Word's out he doesn't plan to profit but merely seek favor at court for his family."

"But you cannot subsist on court presence," added Grandfather Juan. "Anyway, my bones age more each day, so your place in the firm comes welcomed."

Luis continued to absorb it all-the fountains, the plaza with its merchants, the Cathedral, and the familiar smells. Fish, meat, and newly-baked bread, all for sale at the market. In the distance he saw the towered Giralda, his favorite symbol of Seville.

Opening the courtyard gate to his home, Luis' heart began beating as a drum. From around the corner of the house bounded a handsome brown dog. He jumped up and kissed Luis, who stood amazed that his dog still recognized him.

"Hola, Zekatos, you remember me!"

Not able to restrain himself, he bounded up the steps, threw open the door and shouted.

"Mamaceita!"

A face peered in from the door to the courtyard. At once she knew.

"Luis.......?"

She rushed forward to hug him, tears of joy filling her eyes. Father and grandfather came in close behind, granting validity to the scene.

"I survived, to come home to you. I would often think of your prayers, and they inspired me. Soon, I will tell my tale."

Two young ladies, hearing the commotion, entered the room, at once beguiling Luis. In four years they had become beautiful señoritas. They rushed to hug him, laughing and crying all at once.

"You have come home to find gallants for us!" said one.

"You have come home to reclaim your room from me?" said the other, with a twinkle in her eye.

"All right everyone, let's feed the boy and let him rest. I'm sure he'll regale us when he's ready," said Father Antonio.

Luis soon enjoyed his mother's homecoming meal. Four years of dreaming of it now came true. After telling of the most notable occurrences, he sat back and relaxed, the security of home and family enclosing him like a cocoon.

"I must know," said Grandfather Juan. "What have you learned?"

Luis gazed around the room, searching for his thoughts.

"That...La Florida is a fascinating, though largely uncivilized place....that...Spain is my home...where I want to stay. And I learned that there seems to be a need for power everywhere, whether by man or beast. But... the goodness of man exists in the midst. That silver is a boon but also a scourge. It empowers Spain but brings about the deaths of many. And that to survive...you must have the will. I often applied the philosophy that you taught me long ago–in situations of fear or troubles, if time permits, first relax the body and mind. Think. Then take action. It served me well. Thank you."

"Good. It's well that you speak of things, good and bad, so they won't erupt unexpectedly later and cause you distress," said Grandfather Juan.

My son has become wise, thought Antonio.

"Luis," said his father, "the silver peso worn around your neck. Does it have significance?"

"Yes," Luis replied, a smile lighting up his face. "It is my only tangible reminder of the New World. It has traveled far, from Potosí, to Porto Bello, to Habana, through Florida, across the ocean and now here."

"So.......it's been on an *odyssey?*"

"Yes, that it has, that it has."
***

The days that followed found Luis reacquainting with friends and family. He would hold listeners spellbound, recounting of Indios, escapes, rivers and the way of life in colonial La Florida. The loss of his hand he spoke of as a blessing. Thoughts of Isabela naturally sprinkled his consciousness, but he dismissed them. He knew she would be married, settled and caring for children. He decided that he must live his life.

He gave a report to the Bishop of the time he spent at the missions and of San Agustín's church. A summary he provided to the Casa de Contratación at their office in the Alcazar palace. They also asked that he record his four-year trek in the Archives of the Indies. In so doing, he eulogized the Atocha's officers and crew, drawing on indelible memories. He saw his military discharge dispensed, with the military granting him a small stipend due to the lost hand. Luis told Antonio that he would soon need some time from the business, as he wanted to attempt a ransom of Pedro from the Turks, using a known charity in Cádiz. Everyhing fell into place, but one important item continued to dog him. Mamaceita eventually mentioned only that Isabela was happy and well and enjoying her baby. But he needed to hear more.

I must broach it.
***

"Can you tell me more of Isabela's life since I left?"

He'd wanted to ask about her for days but found it difficult. The words at last rose to the surface. Sitting outside with Luis in the garden, in the fading light, his mother knitted as they talked. She continued even as she spoke.

"I'm surprised you haven't inquired before now. She was very sad when you did not return. Her mourning lasted a long time. After an appropriate period, her padre arranged for a suitable marriage. As I said before, she and the child both fare well. She is sufficiently supported, though I believe some heart-filled things are missing."

"And her husband?" Luis inquired.

Mamaceita put down her needles and faced Luis. She realized he didn't know.

"She is a widow, Luis. Her husband died of a fever in the Indies on a business trip. It happened a year after their marriage. A widow for this last year, and the child never knew her father. They moved back to her parents' home."

She looked into Luis' eyes, not knowing if the news made him happy or sad. Luis said nothing for a while, trying to grasp the situation.

She is not married? Would she yet care for me?

Why has no one told me? What was I to be spared? This is news indeed.

Luis looked like a man falling into a stupor. Upon standing, he struggled, as if supporting large iron bars on his shoulders. It took effort. Kissing his mother on the cheek,he asked to be excused to retire. Time alone in his room, to think. No sleep came to Luis that night as he tossed about, thoughts churning his mind.

At breakfast, he asked his father for time from the shipyards for the morning. After consuming little, he left.

"Estella, where could Luis be going?"

"To visit Isabela."

"Did he tell you that?"

"No. But I told him last evening that she's widowed. An army could not deter him today."

Their faces glowed at one another.

Luis remembered the route to her parents' home. He'd walked it many times, in person and in his mind.

This time he wasn't certain of which he did. He focused on what he would say to her. With a racing heart, he rapped on the door. Isabela opened it, radiant as ever. Wearing a scarlet satin skirt and lace-topped blouse, her hair fell in long black tresses. He had a brief flashback to his dream the night before reaching Seville.

"Hello, Luis. Welcome home," she said, smiling.

"You…you knew I came back?"

"Of course, all of Seville knows. You've become famous now. You survived the Atocha shipwreck as well as La Florida's wilderness. Come in."

Without thinking clearly, he grasped her left hand in his right.

"I am…so happy to see you and so aggrieved to learn of your husband's death."

"Thank you. Just before he died, we birthed a beautiful girl. You'll want to meet her. First, sit down and tell me your story. So many times I have wondered."

As he talked, he could not take his eyes from her. The words seemed to spill out in rote, as he'd told and retold it so often. After having lunch, they strolled to the familiar garden, Isabela holding her child.

Luis summoned courage.

"Isabela, when in La Florida, I thought never to return. I took an Indio wife, but she died in a raid on our village. But you are the love of my life. Could you now have me as your husband?"

She sat down on the garden bench, with the child on her lap. She smiled at Luis but then turned away, her smile fading.

"When you did not return, it devastated me. After a time, my father arranged a marriage. Then, after a year, my husband went to the Indies on business and did not come back. No body to bury. I've faced tragedy twice. I cannot marry you, Luis. I cannot go through that again."

Luis sat stunned.

"Wha…what …why?"

"You may go back to sea, even with only one hand. And I can't endure that pain again."

He fumbled for the words.

"But…I won't…I'll never go again…this…this is my home now. Your memory…it sustained me through all my trials. I longed for you."

"Perhaps, you'd better go now," she spoke, with tears in her eyes.

"Isabela, do you love me?"

She looked at him, trying to suppress the emotions.

"I…I did…I…," her voice trailed off. She raised a hand to cover her eyes.

"You're right. I best go now. I'll call again."

He kissed her cheek and the child's, saying gracias to her mother on his way out.

Luis was not of a spirit to employ himself that day, though he did go to the shipwright office.

His father could sense some troubles, so he left him alone.

How can a man survive the challenges of hurricanes, slavery, combat, the wilderness, arrest and trial, the loss of a hand…and yet succumb to such a heartbreak?

***

"Your year of mourning is over ! And you won't marry Luis ?! Are you loco ?! A chance to build your own home again?! A father for your child ?! Do you need to see a priest ?!"

No hesitation existed for expressing opinions when men were absent the room. Isabela's mother had seen her daughter suffer losses, and she had suffered along with her. She also knew best. Her mother knew Isabela loved him. Isabela listened and said no more. She excused herself to attend her daughter.

***

In a few days, Luis received a note delivered to his office. Still in no mood for personal communications, he stuffed it in a pocket to read later. Business came first. He hoped commerce would assuage his heartache.

That day, he took a mid-day meal at a tavern with old friends, Lope and Andrés. They knew of his lovesickness. He found solace and laughter with them, though brief. In the middle of the meal he remembered his pocketed note. Reading it, not aloud, he swallowed hard, then pushed back his chair and stood.

"Amigos, I must excuse myself."

Out the door, his note left on the table, his baffled friends looked at each other. Lope glanced at the note, which read -

I must see you. I must speak to you.

My love awaits.

Isa.

"What does it say?" asked Andrés.

"It basically says that Luis will, as quoted in the old proverb, *marry and grow tame.*"

After arrangements, and a few months had passed, Luis and Isabela wed in a small ceremony in one of the Cathedral's 80 chapels. An enchanting bride and a handsome one-handed groom were attended by her daughter, his sisters, and friends Lope and Andrés. They moved into Isabela's inherited home, and life became happy and secure.

Following a brief trip to the foothills north of Seville, greetings came from Grandfather Juan on their return.

"Abuelito, to what do we owe this welcoming?"

"I have important news," he said, smiling.

"The Casa de Contratación has a Captain's position on next year's Armada fleet that protects silver galleons. They want you."

Without hesitation, Luis and Isabela turned to each other–and smiled.

THE END

EPILOGUE

Recorded in the Archives of the Indies in Seville is Luis' story. The closing words are as follows..........................

Veintidós reales de a ocho
Río de Arapaja
sumidero
La Florida

NOTE FROM THE AUTHOR

The idea for the novel took hold about 11 years before I began to write it, which took five years, including the research. I wanted it to be historical fiction, so Mel Fisher's discovery of the 1622 shipwrecked Atocha galleon provided that basis.

The 1620's also saw the founding of the Franciscan mission Santa María de los Angeles de Arapaja at a village near the Alapaha River, a Suwannee River tributary. Though the mission's exact spot hasn't been located, research indicates it was just north of today's Georgia-Florida line. Having canoed the Alapaha River many times over the previous 40 years, I consider it the prettiest stream in south Georgia, and I wanted to tie it to the story. So the book's hero spent a year at the village and mission in the midst of his trek east.

Over a four-year period, he traversed, with several detentions, from the southwest Florida coast beginning near today's Everglades City. He went along the coast up to Tampa Bay, then wended his way north, eventually ascending northeast on the magnificent Suwannee, which is vividly portrayed. Next came the sojurn at the Alapaha village. The early 17th century outpost of St. Augustine next covers a seven month period, followed by his return to Spain.

In 1985 explorer Mel Fisher and crew of Treasurer Salvors, Inc., found the sunken Atocha galleon off the Marquesas Keys in south Florida. It had lain there for 363 years. Many of the recovered artifacts and treasures now reside at the Mel Fisher Maritime Museum in downtown Key West, Florida. They are living testaments to those who sailed the Atocha and to those who found her.

See office@melfisher.org

ABOUT THE TYPE

In the early 1500's, French publisher Claude Garramond developed printing types that were very popular throughtout Europe. The basic Garramond font is used in the body of the novel. In 1613 Franciscan Friar Francisco Pareja published his *Confessionario,* a guide for his fellow friars in Florida to use in converting Native Americans to Christianity. He used the 1592 GLC Garamond Bold type, which is featured on the book's title page and as part of each chapter's heading.

SPANISH   GLOSSARY

except: (NA) is Native American(phonetic Spanish spelling); (Fr)-
French, (Por)-Portugese

Amajuro River	Withlacoochee River (South)- empties into Gulf
Arapaja	(Arap-ah-haw), tribe, river, bear home, Alapaha (modern)
Arrêter(Fr)	stop
Armador	surname, means shipwright
Bay Espíritu Santo	today's Tampa Bay
bucaneros	island cattle hunters
Calos	Mound Key in Estero Bay
Cantera Island	Anastasia Island @ St. Augustine
Casitoa(NA)	Everglades City/Chokoloskee, Fl
cassina(NA)	black drink using yaupon holly leaves
Cautio	Everglades
cimarón	runaway slave, stranded seaman, deserter
Corrientes River	San Juan River, St. Johns River
corsairs	pirates licensed by European nations
El Camino Real	The Royal Rd., Florida mission trail; Panamá's silver transport trail
Escampaba(NA)	modern Estero Bay
feria	annual fair
flux	dysentery
French pox	syphillis
Guacara River (NA)	(Gwah-ya-cada), San Martín River,
Little San Juan River	Suwannee River
hidalgo	lesser nobility
Holy Office	Inquisition administration
lagarto	alligator
league	appx 3 ¼ miles
Matíres	Martyrs, Matacumbes(NA), Florida Keys
Melancholia	mental illness
Nicoloa Creek	Six Mile Creek in NE Florida

Nochebuena	Christmas Eve
North Sea	Caribbean
ocean river	Gulf Stream
Pohoy(NA)	modern Tampa Bay
Potosi	(Pot-o-si) silver mines location in Peru
quando(Por)	when?
quinto	king's 20% tax on precious metals
real de a ocho	peso, Spanish silver dollar, piece of eight
Rom	Romani people, nomadic gypsies
San Martín River	Little San Juan River, Guacara River(NA), Suwannee River
Salamatoto (NA)	Corrientes River, San Juan River, St. Johns River
Situador	St. Augustine-appointed official-- oversaw annual shipment of goods & military pay
St. Elmo's fire	weather phenomenon appearing as a ball of light on a mast, from electricity in the air ; seamen once considered it an omen of bad luck and stormy weather
Tanpa(NA)	modern Pineland,Fl., near Charlotte Harbor and Caloosahatchee River
Tocobaga	Indians on NW side of today's Tampa Bay

Historic/Modern Florida Map

M - Mission

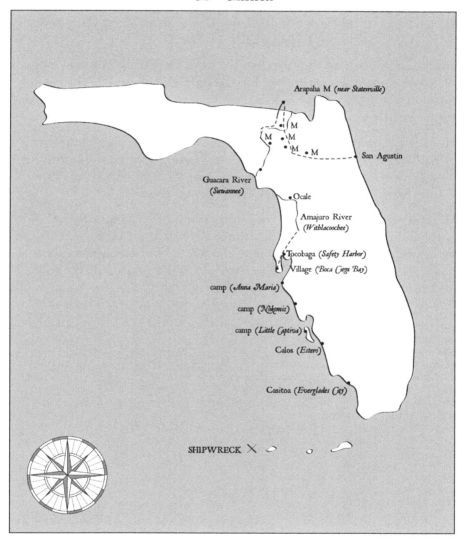

Arapaha M *(near Statenville)*

M

M   M

M   M

San Agustin

Guacara River
(Suwannee)

•Ocale

Amajuro River
(Withlacoochee)

Tocobaga *(Safety Harbor)*

Village *('Boca Ciega Bay)*

camp *(Anna Maria)*

camp *(Nokomis)*

camp *(Little Captiva)*

Calos *(Estero)*

Casitoa *(Everglades City)*

SHIPWRECK X

The Sumidero

(Swallow Hole)

CHAPTERS 11-12-13

This phenomenon on the Alapaha River can be accessed by canoeing down about three miles from the Florida Highway 150 bridge landing just east of Jennings,Fl. Swallow hole access downstream is on the west bank and appears first as a reverse spring Run from the main Alapaha.

This Run is always flowing, but in times of very low water, the main Alapaha River channel ceases flowing downstream from here. In times of very high water, all flows continue plus part of the Run circumvents the hole and creates another Run going far back into the woods.

The spot can also be reached four miles south of Jennings off U.S. 41 onto Road 25. This leads to the Suwannee River Water Management Tract (sign) on the river which is available to the public for hikes and a canoe landing. To see the hole, take a short hike along the Alapaha River going north from the canoe landing.

ACKNOWLEDGEMENTS

So many have inspired and supported me in my own odyssey in penning this novel, and I'd like to recognize a few.

I'm indebted to Dr. Jerry Milanich, the author of many books on Florida Native Americans, and Dr. John Worth, who supplied writings and advice on the same. Dr. Andrew Frank conducted an excellent historical review of my manuscript, and Dr. Amy Bushnell's books on St. Augustine were outstanding.

The books of Dr Eugene Lyon and R. Duncan Mathewson, III, relating their involvement in finding the Atocha galleon were invaluable. So was the unique historical data provided by Corey Malcolm, Archaeologist with the Mel Fisher Museum in Key West.

Dr. Roger Block's enthusiasm and interest in the Native Americans in SW Florida led him to take me to a most interesting site. Close by St. Petersburg, Fl., on Boca Ciega Bay, are the remnants of an ancient Tocobaga village visited by the Narváez expedition in 1528.

Ft. Myers, Fl.-area guide Danny Romero motored me out to Mound Key, ancient home of the most notable Calusa chieftains. Located in Estero Bay, it's only reachable by boat.

Knowledgeable Suwannee, Fl., fishing guide Larry Martin helped me gain perspective by taking me boating up and down west Florida's central Gulf coast between Cedar Key and the Suwannee River mouth.

I've had the pleasure through the years of enjoying almost all the stretches of the blackwater Suwannee River, but two recent ones stand out. Charlie Stines and the Fellow Travelers Canoe group of Moultrie,Ga., took me canoeing on a part below I-10. The ferry crossing sites of the El Camino Real mission road were very visible on each side, even after 400 years.

Lifelong friend Harold Carter took me 55 miles downstream on his hovercraft, along with his club members and their unique crafts. The magnificent riverside terrain from Bell to Suwannee, Fl., changes noticeably from an inland to a coastal stream.

The St. Augustine Historical Society and the separate St. Augustine Foundation both provided libraries and staff that were most accommodating.

Father Stephen Pontzer of Albany,Ga.'s, local St.Teresa's Catholic Church helped immensely in editing for proper 17th century Catholic vernacular.

Smooth computer guru Jim Hall of HTS promptly responded whenever I called needing help with WORD, which was often.

Successful local nautical adventure author Michael Fowler took me *under wing*, providing priceless advice and guidance.

My family's support and encouragement has been paramount, especially that of my wife, Pat, the inspiration for Isabela.

Colonial Spanish Florida history is fascinating, but may not be as well known outside of the state. My hope is that this historical fiction novel will provide insights and entertainment to all readers. A recommended *field trip* would be to St. Augustine, our oldest continuous city, which celebrated its 450th anniversary in 2015.

Henry C. Duggan,III-----Albany,Ga

henryduggan@mediacombb.net

Made in the USA
Las Vegas, NV
15 August 2021

28204653R10164